HOCKEY WIFE

A ROOKIE REBELS NOVEL

KATE MEADER

Please see my website for content warnings pertinent to this book.

1

___

January

THE ALL-STAR WEEKEND was usually a blast.

For the fans and the younger players, mostly. This was Dylan Bankowski's fourth invite and given the way his body was holding up, it would probably be his last.

Thirty-six and feeling it.

He had tried to enjoy the events. He'd gotten a kick out of yelling at the rookies, had acquitted himself well in the one-timer event in the Skills Comp, and managed to get a goal on his former Nashville tender, Jimmy McPherson.

But it had *felt* like the end. Of his career. Of the most important period in his life. Traded from Nashville to the Chicago Rebels this same weekend was about as ignominious a finish as could be expected. Heading for pasture, his body breaking down slowly.

A first world hockey player problem, to be sure. He'd had a good run. Never won the Cup but he'd come close a couple of times, including a heartbreaker of a Game 7 with the 'Ville a few years back.

The vibe at this dive a couple of blocks off the Las Vegas Strip suited his mood. *Real Housewives* junk on the TV and the crowd as miserable as he felt. A couple of old timers propped up the bar on one end while a gaggle of girls from a bachelorette party were trying to stump the bartender with tricky cocktail requests (*do you know how to make a Cosmopolitan?*).

A text came in from his mom.

Nice game, sweetheart.

BANKS

Thanks. I managed not to fall over.

The phone rang and he answered it. His mom picked up the conversation like they'd been chatting all night.

"Wasn't expecting the trade."

"Neither was I. But Chicago's a good landing place." His family lived in Apple Falls, Wisconsin, about a three-hour drive from the city. The Rebels, though? Definitely the lesser franchise in Chi-town. They'd won the Cup six years ago and hadn't come close since. Made it seem like a fluke, and the rivers of young blood running through the team confirmed it.

"Doesn't matter where you are, we'll be there for the playoffs."

It was a family tradition. They always came to visit for the first round, and as there would be fewer of those to come, this one would be special.

"Better find a house then."

"Bathrooms for everyone! You heading out with the boys later?"

"Probably. Just easing into the night for now."

She clucked. "Have a good time. Maybe find yourself a nice girl to settle down with."

A joke, but also not. He had no problem attracting women

but connecting on a meaningful level was a whole other story. That he had "the personality of a tree stump," as one ex-girlfriend had so eloquently put it, didn't help.

"I'm not exactly husband material, Mom." It was worth reminding her. His family saw the son and heir's singledom as a problem to be managed.

"Because some flighty piece couldn't see what's right in front of her? Don't you dare let any woman decide whether you're good enough."

He huffed out half a laugh. "Except the ones I'm related to."

"Damn straight. The Bankowski women determine your worth, and don't you forget it."

She always had the capacity to bring him out of himself. Around her and his family he was about 10% more cheerful, but not enough for Stacy, his ex in Nashville. Once in Chicago, he wouldn't have to worry about running into her. One positive to the trade.

Out of the corner of his eye, he noticed one of the bachelorettes had detached from the herd, like a stray gazelle in one of those nature docs, and was currently zig-zagging her way over to his side of the bar. He assumed she was heading for the restrooms until she placed a hand on his arm.

"Well, aren't you a Grizzly-beared hunk of man?" Her voice had a twang to it, Texan probably, though exaggerated by whatever she'd downed so far. "Wanna buy me a drink, sugar?"

He held up his phone and raised an eyebrow, signifying his busyness and her rudeness in one motion.

No joy. The brunette stayed where she was, all spiky-tipsy challenge.

He spoke into his phone. "Got to go. Call you tomorrow?"

"You do that. But not too early. Hopefully you'll be busy

tonight and will need your rest." On that somewhat inappropriate wish, she clicked off.

Back to the Southern Belle. "Not really looking for company."

She leaned in, giving him a clear view of nice tits that should have stirred something. Had this trade news broken his dick?

"You sure? You look so lonely down here. My friends bet I couldn't get you to buy the bride a drink."

Her T-shirt's slogan was "Last Rodeo" followed by "Kristin's Bachelorette, Vegas Baby!"

This must be Kristin, who evidently had more than cocktails on her mind. Her hand still lay on his arm but was now getting a wander on. Down to his forearm, back up to his bicep. It did nothing for him, especially with the added knowledge of her relationship status.

"Best head on back now."

Annoyance flashed over her face. This chick was used to getting her way. "You want me to look silly in front of my friends?"

Pity for her plight had him rethinking his stance. A drink wouldn't hurt, maybe a round for the entire bachelorette party. Weddings and Vegas, like PB and J.

Before he could signal to the bartender, another voice cut in.

"Hey, Big Guy, stepping out on me already?"

In rather comical unison, Banks and the bride turned to the questioner. She was petite, not more than a couple of inches above five feet, and his first thought was *Princess Peach, what are you doing here?* The dress was rose pink, the hair was cornsilk blonde, the eyes ... a stunning blue with flecks of green. But it was her mouth that really set her apart. Sin and sweetness rolled into one, it was now shaped in a wicked curve. Like she knew all his secrets, and if he was good, she might tell him, one kiss at a time.

"You're here," he said, because it seemed like the right thing, the *only* thing, to say.

A raised eyebrow, almost approving. "Now, what have I told you about talking to strange women?" She delivered a withering look to the competition that made Banks pleased to not be on her wrong side.

"Uh, don't?"

"Can't leave ya alone for a second." To the bride, she said, "Best go fishing in more available waters, honey." She curled a finger around his pinkie and gave a little tug. "I got us a booth over here."

He didn't need rescuing. He could have easily repelled the bride with his usual, unstinting rudeness, but something about this woman's command of the situation piqued his interest. Sliding off his bar stool, he grabbed his IPA and nodded at the bride. "Good luck with your wedding."

She hmphed, not liking the reminder, he guessed.

He slid into the booth, his finger still looped by his rescuer. Once seated, she let it go, and now they stared at each other, wondering where to go from here.

He went first. "Thanks, *honey.*"

There was that saucy smile again. "It's not every day I see a prince in distress. Figured you could do with the assist."

"I had it covered."

She tilted her head. "Did you? From where I was sitting, you were about to be on the hook for a round of Appletinis and a whole heap of trouble."

"Maybe I'm looking for trouble."

"Not with a woman about to get married!" She lowered her voice, which made him lean in. The bodice of her strapless dress showed cleavage and the upper swells of small tits, a very pleasant place to rest his eyes. "You're too nice a guy for that."

"Where'd you get that idea?"

"You were chatting to your mom while sitting in a Vegas bar. Only a nice guy would do that."

She'd heard that? Sitting behind him, in this booth, he supposed it was possible.

"What else did you hear about your new boyfriend?"

"Something about you not being husband material, which is good because I'm nowhere near ready for that kind of commitment. I assume Mom told you to get over yourself."

He repressed a smile. "She did. But then she's duty-bound to say nice things to me."

"Okay, I'll bite. What made you say that?"

"Just a hunch I have."

"So you don't want to go deep. I get it. I'm only your fake fiancée after all."

Graduated from girlfriend mighty quick, but damn, he enjoyed her directness.

"I've been told by previous *real* girlfriends that I'm not suited to marriage. Which is fine because I don't want to get married."

"Let me guess." She raised a finger to her chin in thought. "You're obsessed with your career or some manly hobby and any girl in your life always comes off as second best."

"Not any girl."

"Ah, your momma."

"She's the only one who understands me."

"Poor misunderstood ..." She raised her glass, something clear in a lowball.

"Banks. People call me Banks."

"Even your mom?"

"She calls me other things. All of them deserved."

Another smile, and his cock stirred. Not broken, after all.

"You sound close."

"We are. What should I call you?"

"Georgia."

Princess Peach, a Georgia peach ... the universe was trying to tell him something.

"Not *from* Georgia, I'm guessing."

"No. Chicago."

Ding ding ding, signs all over the place.

"I live in Nashville." Best to keep his upcoming living arrangements to himself. The last thing he needed was some bunny chasing him down in his new city, though a closer look told him that would be wishful thinking. No way would this girl be interested in him beyond a drink and a smile. Christ, he was old enough to be her ... older brother.

He should be moving on, or at the very least, encouraging her to. She'd evidently wandered through a portal from a world of sunshine and sweetness. This dank place was not for her, and with his dark mood, neither was he.

He took another long look, readying for it to be his last. Christ, she was a tiny thing, practically swallowed by the booth's worn leather. He would offer to walk her back to her hotel because he didn't trust this bar or the streets or anyone in this town, who would take one look at this girl and try to take a bite.

That sinful mouth curved. "You okay?"

"Not really."

"Want to talk about it?"

"Nope. You?"

A shadow crossed her face and the green in her blue eyes took on a shade of melancholy. "Oh, you don't want to go there, Big Guy."

But he did. He wanted to know why this girl was all alone

with her mouth made for sin and her eyes tinged with sadness.

He eyed her glass. "Another?"

She looked up at the bachelorette party, and back at him, wondering if a lug like him was worthy of her time. He wasn't, but man, he wanted to be. *Stay a while ...*

A quick dart of her pink tongue over her lips sent another tug of desire to his groin. "I suppose we have to keep the illusion alive."

"Otherwise, it'd look like we lied."

"Can't have that."

"No, we can't."

He should have gone with his first instinct.

2

———

Two months later
April

GEORGIA GOODWIN PEEKED out from her eye mask at her phone. It was past ten in Chicago which meant it was 5 a.m. in Hawaii, an hour past when her parents rose and shone with the morning sun. If she ignored it, they'd know she'd been sleeping, so she did her quickie AM (usually PM) routine: mask off, finger-rake through her bedhead, rush to the kitchen, bottle of juice from the fridge. Positioning her phone so the detritus from last night's party was out of frame, she answered the redial that came in twenty seconds later as she sat at the breakfast island.

"Hey there! Sorry, I was in the bathroom."

Penny Goodwin stared at her with that imperious look that said she wasn't buying it for a second.

"Darling, are you alone?"

"Of course I'm alone." *I'm always alone even when there are a million people here.*

"Not recovering from one of your parties?"

"I had a quiet night in," she lied. "Just me and Cheddar." She held her cat up for inspection, whereupon the moody orange tabby gave a puny meow and froze, his striped body stock-still until release. "How's Kauai?"

Stupid question. Kauai was always perfect. Georgia would be there now if only the island was big enough for her and her parents.

"Wonderful. So your father and I need to have a word. Marcus? Georgia's on the phone." She sipped her coffee, a small-batch artisanal Kona blend that cost more per pound than Georgia's rent. "Your father just came back from his run."

"Hey, GiGi!" Marcus Goodwin took a seat beside her mom on the white sofa and sat back, his arm over the back. His T-shirt bore a V-shaped patch of sweat and his forehead looked clammy.

"So, darling," her mother said. "We had a chat with Michael Whyte last night and he said the strangest thing."

Georgia's pulse picked up. Michael Whyte was one of her parents' lawyers.

"Oh yeah?"

"Is there something you want to tell us?"

Already? It was inevitable that they would find out, though she'd hoped she could keep it under the radar for a little longer. Yesterday afternoon, she'd heard from Mr. Lyons, the lawyer she'd hired to take care of her problem.

Her accidentally-married-in-Vegas problem.

In their standard follow-up to the filing in the Nevada court, Mr. Lyons's office had discovered that the paperwork was missing. Originally, he'd advised that they petition for an annulment instead of a divorce because the former didn't require that one of the parties be a resident in Nevada for six weeks. Intoxication was a perfectly valid ground for annulling a marriage—as it should be—and returning the couple to their non-married state. It would be as if it had never happened.

But the paperwork had to make it to its destination first.

Mr. Lyons was all apologies when he discovered the mistake. He'd immediately couriered over duplicates, which now sat on her nightstand. She would have to send them to the other party and get his signature. Again.

Only now it was complicated by the fact her parents knew.

She had used a lawyer not known to them or any one of their numerous companies or the many foundations they chaired. But they'd still found out because the Eye of Goodwin saw all. Whatever happened now, she couldn't admit that it had all been a mistake. Her parents would never let her live it down. Just another example of Georgia's propensity to make the worst choices.

"I didn't tell you because it happened rather quickly, and we wanted to spend more time together. But you'll like him. He's very focused and incredibly good at what he does." Her parents loved hard-working bootstrappers and professional athletes were some of the most driven people on the planet. "And he can't wait to meet you. It's just tricky with his schedule—he's on the road quite a lot, which I know is rough for a newly-married couple. Between that and—"

"Married?" Her father spluttered. "Did you say married?"

"Oh, Georgia," her mother murmured.

Shit. If they weren't talking about that, then what had they heard? She tried to think of something worse than secretly marrying a professional hockey player in Vegas, but nothing came to mind.

"Tell me it isn't so, darling. Were you drunk? We can get it annulled." She gripped her father's arm. "Let's conference Michael in."

"No, Mom! That's not necessary. I was perfectly sober."

Her mother pursed her lips. "Are you saying that this was ... planned?"

Georgia offered a nervy laugh. "I know you think I'm impetuous but I'm not that bad. Of course it was planned!"

"When did this happen?"

She couldn't lie. Public records and all. "Two months ago. We've been keeping quiet about it so we could try to enjoy married life without all the pressure."

Her father looked concerned. "You think we'd put pressure on you?"

"Mom's first thought was how to make it disappear."

Her mom sucked in a breath. "If you're not going to share such important news, then how do we know it's what you want? That it wasn't another one of your ..." She waved a hand to fill in the rest. "I'd like to have given *one* of my daughters away."

Another thing she'd ruined for them. Marcus took his wife's hand in his, comforting her for her loss. At least they had each other.

They would never get to see Dani on her wedding day. Was it possible Georgia had done this on purpose—snatched this precious moment from them precisely just so it could belong to her and her alone? That sounded like the kind of thing the selfish surviving twin might do.

"I'm sorry I didn't tell you sooner. I just wanted to enjoy the quiet of being a newlywed."

Her mother sent a sidelong glance toward her husband. "I remember what that was like. Your father and I ran off to Italy for a month after we married."

"Sometimes you need a little time away," her father said. "But there are issues that need to be taken care of. Such as a post-nup because I'm guessing there wasn't a pre-one."

"No need. He's a professional hockey player."

"A what?" Her mother wrinkled her nose.

"Hockey, Pen," her dad said.

"Oh, does he know Jared? Mimi St. Vincent's boy? He won silver at the Olympics in Tokyo."

"That's field hockey. Amateur, the sport of gentlemen." Her father smiled at his wife and winked at Georgia. "I'm guessing he plays ice hockey, which is not for amateurs or gentlemen. Right, GiGi?"

"Yes, Dad."

"Even so, he can't have as much money as you, darling. Or will have." Penny tilted her head. "We'll get a post-nup drawn up—unless of course, you'd rather we created a different kind of contract?"

A divorce contract. One that worked.

The papers to get this squared away, to make that night history, were mere feet away. She'd have to go see him in person this time. Not take the coward's way out like she did before.

But then her parents would know that it had been very much *un*planned. Another one of Georgia's fuck-up-first-fix-it-later mistakes.

"Why would I want a different one drawn up, Mom? Banks and I are very happy."

No thunderbolt struck her down.

"Banks?" Her mother sounded horrified. "What kind of name is that?"

"Dylan Bankowski, Mom. He plays for the Chicago Rebels."

"I think we have a box there," her father said.

Her parents had executive sky boxes everywhere, used for big-shot schmoozing and charity events.

"But you don't play any sports, Georgia." Her mother sounded so confused.

"I don't have to play to appreciate how talented and driven Dylan is. He's a very ... solid kind of person." No lie detected.

"Sounds like he's just what you need." Her father's tone was skeptical with a side of reserving judgment. He was the more indulgent parent for sure.

Her mom's smile was wan. "We've been worried about you. It's just, all these parties I'm hearing about and where you're living ... that awful place in Riverbrook. Caroline Wilkins said it's practically a transient hotel. For bachelors." Said like it rhymed with "drug addicts." "We said we'd buy you a condo—there's one for sale in our building."

Which came with strings. "I wanted to make my own way for a while."

After one too many wild escapades, they'd cut her off, but they'd promised to bring her back into the fold if she was a good girl. An impulsive marriage followed by a quickie annulment were *not* the actions of a good girl.

"But married?"

Her father cut in with a soothing pat on her mother's arm. "We'll meet him when we're back in Chicago. We're flying back tomorrow, and we'll be hosting the Humane Society gala on Saturday. Will we see you there, GiGi?"

"Sure will!"

"And we'll throw a wedding reception soon." Her mother's forehead smoothed at the prospect. A party would fix everything. "I'll have Emily draw up a list of invitees. And you'll have to tell us who to invite on Darren's side."

"It's Dylan. And sounds good." She took a calming breath. One problem at a time. "So if you weren't calling about this, then what was on your mind?"

"Right." Her father shared a quick glance with her mother. "Michael said you missed the foundation meeting."

Her parents had tapped her to head a charity foundation

dedicated to her sister, who had died from heart failure just over two years ago, a condition she'd had all her life. Philanthropy was a big deal to her family, and with this push, they hoped to kill two birds: memorialize Dani and find something for Georgia to do. All she had to do was say yes and the cash spigot would be turned back on.

"Like I said before, there must be so many more qualified people who could head something like that up."

"Darling," her mom said. "Who could be more qualified than you? You and your sister were so close, and this would be a perfect way for you to channel your energy. Dani wouldn't want to think you're moping around, missing her."

Dani would be fine with it, especially as Georgia had other plans that didn't involve being an ineffectual figurehead. If they would let her do more hands-on work, she'd be all over it. But that kind of digging deep wasn't a typical Goodwin trait.

"Let me think about it some more."

With a weary sigh, her mom moved on to an update about Cousin Bea who was about to graduate magna cum laude from Harvard. No more questions about her husband.

How did you meet?

How long have you been together?

Tell us everything!

As relieved as she felt to not have to come up with a less clichéd origin story, Georgia knew the reason for her parents' disinterest: they didn't believe this was planned. It was the ultimate game of chicken, waiting for the other side to crack. They expected she'd come to them in a couple of weeks asking for help.

Meanwhile Georgia had to figure out how to convince the man she'd married to stay that way.

3

It's just a door.

Georgia stood opposite a hunk of oak with two hockey sticks crossed like cutlasses above the entrance, telling herself this obvious thing about the barrier before her. A piece of wood. The entry to a place of business.

Just a door.

He might not be here. After all, he hadn't been here last night or the night before. Then she'd figured out that the team's schedule was public information and that the Chicago Rebels, one of the city's two pro hockey franchises, had been playing away for the last few days.

But not tonight. No game on the calendar, and a little bird had confirmed the players would be hanging at their usual haunt, the Empty Net. Not that Tara Fitzpatrick knew the value of the information she was sharing. Georgia's hair stylist also happened to be married to the team's general manager, and while Georgia hadn't gone to get her usual balayage done two weeks earlier than usual with information-seeking in mind, she was happy to encourage Tara to chat about "her boys," how psyched they were after their win in New York, and how they would be celebrating at the Net, as she called it.

Georgia had nodded abstractly, acting as if this precious intel wasn't exactly what she needed to hear.

A couple overtook her, the bar their destination. The man, built and strong, placed the hand not circling his companion's waist on the door just as the woman turned to Georgia. Almost as tall as her date, she had an athletic build and amazing cheekbones.

"You okay?" the woman asked, a compassion in her expression that felt surprisingly welcome this minute.

"Me? Oh, fine."

The woman gave Georgia a subtle once-over, taking in her pink Rebecca Vallance cocktail dress and Jimmy Choo Bee pumps (Jimmy had claimed he was inspired by her—*you are always buzzing away, Georgia!*—of course she had to wear them). It was early April and a touch chilly, so a woman in an off the shoulder sequined gown standing outside a bar typically frequented by hockey players and their fandom might understandably look a tad out of place.

"If you're sure ..."

Georgia smiled, which was usually enough to assure the world she was whatever she needed them to think.

"Just waiting on someone."

The man gave a brief tug on the woman's waist. She subtly resisted.

"Warmer inside," she said, apparently not buying what Georgia was selling.

Georgia doubted that. She had a feeling it was about to get chilly awfully quick.

"I'll be in soon. Thanks."

Not quite satisfied, the woman nodded and headed inside

with her companion. After a count of five, Georgia followed her.

The Empty Net was, as the kids would say, hopping. A quick scan told her all she needed to know. Sports people, not her demo at all, but she could spot a groupie and hanger-on at twenty paces. Plenty of those here in team gear, though she doubted trashy crop tops emblazoned with R for Rebels were official merchandise. After a quick study of the battlefield, she finally fixed her gaze on the bar and the one person she recognized. Dex O'Malley was a hockey player and her next-door neighbor and had no idea what was about to go down.

She could have asked Dex if her target was around, just knocked on his door and politely enquired where a particular teammate lived or if she could get his number, like one of these rabid fan girls. But then she'd have to explain herself, and there was no guarantee that he'd want to see her. Not after how she'd behaved.

Instead, she was here, planning an ambush because *that* was a much better idea.

Dex must have spotted her approach because he was half-smiling in surprise by the time she arrived.

"Hey, Dex."

"Georgia. What's up?"

"Oh, nothing." She cast her gaze around, seeking out a set of broad shoulders, a dark warrior, a man alone. Nothing jumped out above the heads of the crowd.

Back to her neighbor. "So this is what this bar looks like. I've always wondered."

A bit of a himbo, Dex also happened to be a complete sweetheart and was once a frequent guest at her notorious parties. Not anymore. The guy was trying to be a very good boy after his arrest following a fight with another player. (A volunteer gig at an animal shelter was his penance.) She'd been keeping an eye on him during this tricky time, but Dex was not her mission tonight.

"So most of your teammates drink here?"

"Sure, like Hudson. I think you might have met once."

The cute guy standing beside Dex nodded at her, halfway to a full blush. "Hello."

Hudson Grey, she thought his name was, and he was absolutely adorable. She was about to return a light and witty comment when something prescient had her turning to the bar's corner.

She knew those shoulders would set him apart.

He stood, stance wide, one thick, muscle-corded arm raised as he focused on the dartboard. He'd had a light stubble when she met him before, but now he was fully bearded. No matter, she would know him anywhere.

"Hi—oh, there you are!"

Dex asked, "Georgia, you okay?"

"I will be." Fisting her hips, she pondered how to play it.

March over there and tap him on one broad shoulder?

March over there and ... say "hi, Banks, remember me?"

March over there and ...

She didn't have time to think of a third option because the energy in the bar sparked electric. Banks turned. Faced her. The hand holding the dart dropped to his side with a jerk.

Then he moved toward her, plowing through the crowd, eyes blazing like supernovas.

Did the sight of her annoy him that much? It had been over two months since she last saw him. Back then, in the early dawn, she'd stolen a moment to watch as he slept, memorizing the rise and fall of his chest, the sooty eyelashes like dark half-moons feathering over his cheeks, those firm lips that had promised so much ...

Conked out and dead to the world, he hadn't awoken to see her off. She was glad. Cowards did their best work unseen.

"Georgia," Banks said on arrival, her name uttered with a disdain that didn't surprise her even if a small part of her had hoped this reunion might run smoother.

"Banks."

Then silence.

Neither of them filled it. Someone should because Georgia wouldn't want people to think she was transfixed by the man before her, rapt in her regard for his wide shoulders and broad chest, barely contained in a gray tee. (Why did it have to be gray and why was gray the best of the T-shirt colors?)

Still nothing from him, and words refused to come from her end.

Dex was forced to step in to mediate. "You guys know each other?"

Banks's cold gaze slipped to her dress, offering an even chillier disapproval. Like he thought it inappropriate for this bar or the time of year or the reunion of a hastily married couple.

"I need to talk to you," Georgia finally said.

Without taking his eyes off her, Banks said, "O'Malley, how do you know Georgia?"

"She's my neighbor at Castle Apartments."

"Come down in the world, have you?"

"Nothing you need to worry about," she managed, though that kind of snark on his lips seemed out of place. Like he knew things about her. "Could I have a moment of your time?"

"We have nothing to discuss."

"Ah, but we do."

Banks snorted. "No army of lawyers this time?"

At the mention of lawyers, she could feel his teammates' interest pique.

"This would be better done in private."

"Don't think so, princess. Have a nice life."

Princess? Where did he get off calling her that? He knew nothing about her. So perhaps that was the image she cultivated: a spoiled trust fund baby, but when they last met, it was as equals. Just a girl and a guy who hit it off. Evidently, he'd done his research since, read all the headlines, and come to the same conclusion as everyone else.

Georgia Goodwin, poor little rich girl.

Her irritation was morphing into something stormy. Dangerous. She wouldn't be typecast by him or anyone else. She opened her mouth to say so, but he had already turned away, having clearly decided this conversation was no longer worthy of his interest.

She hadn't braved this stupid bar for nothing.

"We're still married."

Oh, that got the big guy's attention.

"Fuck, no," Dex muttered.

When her husband—ha!—turned, his face was alive with anger. No more cold disdain. *This* she could work with.

"What did you say?"

"I think you heard me." She waved a hand, suspecting it would piss him off. Energy thrummed through her.

"What the hell is this?" Banks's mouth had a cruel twist to it, so unlike that last time when it had looked kissable and pliant while he slept. "It was a done deal."

"There was a paperwork error. The divorce didn't go through." She examined her nails, relishing the burst of power barreling through her veins. *His scorn. Her fuel.* "So much for the army of lawyers."

There it was, the glare that would have stopped her heart if it wasn't already dead. For a moment she thought he would turn away again. She held her breath, waiting for him to walk. It would have been what she deserved.

So when he didn't do that, when instead he turned to his teammates and said, "You heard nothing," then placed a hand on her elbow, she felt, not exactly victorious but, a part of something bigger. Impossible to ignore. Which was absurd because no one ever missed Georgia with her bubblegum pink finery and head-turning looks.

That night, two months ago, he'd worn a distinctly *un*Vegas green flannel shirt and dark denim, looking like a lumberjack whose pickup had broken down on his way to the Rockies. In his mid-thirties, he was older than her twenty-four years, and while she'd dated older men before, Banks had given off a different vibe. Not leering or pervy, but almost gentlemanly. He hadn't tried to look down her dress. He hadn't tried to move closer or even touch her. Not until later. When she'd rescued him from the overzealous bride and curled her pinkie around his, she felt closer to him than she had felt to anyone in the longest time.

But not now. Now all she felt was an aching loneliness. Had she really thought that reconnecting with him would solve her problems? *So foolish, Georgia.*

As he led her away, she turned to look at his profile. Harsh. Unyielding. Sexy?

A small shiver shuddered through her body, the answer to that question a resounding *yes*.

But then he spoke and ruined it.

"You're going to explain to me what happened, Georgia, and so help me God, if I'm not happy with the answer, you'll wish you'd never walked in here."

4

BANKS CONSIDERED HIMSELF A REASONABLE MAN.

He had three sisters after all. A man living with all that estrogen learned to be reasonable. He wasn't like his teammate Dex O'Malley, a disaster-dick on two legs, constantly getting into trouble with women, the org, and the law. So much trouble that he had to have his reputation rehabilitated with fake engagements and shelter volunteer gigs.

No, Banks wasn't like O'Malley at all.

He was worse.

And the reason was standing before him, looking like a cupcake in human form. Banks's life was one of work and ambition, but then he met Georgia Goodwin and all that fell to the wayside.

Her elbow felt soft.

It should be rough or bony. In fact, he shouldn't be able to feel bare skin at all because it was early April in Chicago, which was basically mid-fucking-winter, and this tiny Tinkerbell should be bundled up in a puffer jacket or a heavy coat or a trench. Maybe one of those sexy ones with a simple tie-off that you just unfurl to reveal—

Nope. He dropped her elbow.

The alcove on the other side of the bar should give them some privacy. Damage control would be needed after Georgia blabbed in front of O'Malley and Grey, but first he had to deal with the rubble in front of him.

"Go on."

Her raised eyebrow was like a smirk on her forehead. "Go on what?"

"Provide an explanation for why this—" He waved between them. "Is still a thing?"

"Some *t* wasn't crossed, an *i* wasn't dotted. Like I said, a paperwork flub."

The blasé attitude was really pissing him off. "So I need to talk to my lawyer because apparently yours screwed up."

"That's an option."

His Spidey senses went nuts. Or maybe he should call them Georgia senses.

"What else is there to happen here? We got drunk, tied the knot, and then you skipped out like Cinderella at midnight." Instead of a glass slipper, she had left the ring. As clear a message as any. "And when I tracked you down with a *DM on Instagram,* you refused to speak to me. Just sent the divorce papers over with a fucking courier. Which I signed, as fast as I could."

She flinched. Why the hell should that recitation of the facts bother her? Barely had he time to analyze that and she was on her tiptoes, her finger jammed into his chest.

"Poor little Banks. Were you sad because I didn't show up with the papers in person? Did you feel ignored?"

"Just seems like common decency to talk to your big mistake, but then I'm getting that's the way people like you do business. You delegate."

In searching for his runaway bride after Vegas, he had

discovered plenty about the woman he married. Most civilians had little to no Internet footprint beyond social media. Not Georgia. She was well-known in the Chicago society pages with a reputation as a wild child. Parties, premieres, nightclubs, all the hot places were her stomping grounds, and Georgia's "activities" kept the paps and Page Six busy.

Gorgeous Georgia hangs with friends at Viper Chicago opening.

Society princess Georgia Goodwin unveils new bikini at Cabo resort.

Bison guitarist Keaton Biles breaks up with narcissist Georgia. Calls her a "nightmare."

In all his research, he hadn't learned that she was his teammate's neighbor. That would have been good information to have.

This media darling version didn't square with the woman he'd met in Vegas. That girl was fun and fearless, sure, but she had also been sweet and considerate. That night, he hadn't gone too deep into his career woes, but he'd shared a little about how his life was changing. She was going through something as well—which he now suspected was related to her sister, who had died from a heart condition a couple of years ago—and while she hadn't divulged, he was there for her. They had connected in a way he hadn't with anyone before or since.

But now she was here, waltzing in like some society diva, shouting to the rooftops about the big mistake she'd made. Nothing like the Georgia he thought he knew.

"It seemed easier to let the suits take over," she said. "It's not like you wanted to ever see me again."

Mind reader, was she? She didn't have the decency to ask.

He got them back on track. "So now we fix it. Properly."

"Right."

Neither of them had a comeback for that. Something

about the finality of it, separate from words on paper, left them silent and stewing. Until he recalled something she said earlier.

"Hold up," Banks started. "You said talking to my lawyer was an option. As if there were other options. What did that mean?"

"Well ..." Before she could explain, someone pushed her from behind and she fell against his body. All soft, absurd-in-pink curves that burned through his T-shirt.

"Hey," he yelled at the asshole behind her with no sense of spatial awareness. "Watch where you're standing."

The offender turned, an insult ready on his lips that vanished at what he saw: Dylan Bankowski, center for the Chicago Rebels, rearing up like the beast you do *not* want to fuck with.

"Banksy! Man, I'm sorry." He turned to Georgia and had the nerve to put a hand on her bare shoulder. "You okay, sweetheart?"

"She's fine," Banks said, moving in between them. "Just be careful."

"Sure, Banksy. Great game last night!"

Banks turned his back on the guy, though the only way he could truly do that was to fold Georgia into the shelter of his body. They stood tightly-packed against the bar while he tried to ignore her scent—something light and floral—and make sure no one else could lay a finger on her.

Peering up at him, she smirked. "Banksy? Hate to break it to you but that's already taken."

"You were saying?" He lowered his voice. "About the options to talking to my lawyer?"

"Yes. So the option would be to *not* talk to him."

"Because *your* lawyer did such a bang-up job."

She sucked in a breath that made those pretty tits rise and brush against his rib cage.

"Because I need us to stay married, Big Guy."

"WHAT?"

That he'd be horrified at the thought shouldn't have surprised her. She considered how best to explain.

My parents think I'm a screw-up. They've bailed me out of so many little dramas. I can't let them see me neck-deep in another mess of my own making.

"So, I have a trust—"

"Money? Should've known."

She bristled. "What does that mean? You don't know a thing about me."

"I know you're already rolling in cash and spend your life getting photographed at every social event in the city. You come from wealth and now you want me to help you acquire more of it."

What a dick. He didn't know the first thing about why she needed that money.

"It's my inheritance but my parents can petition for a delay in the distribution if they think I might be liable to make risky decisions with the money."

He looked skeptical. "And you think staying married is going to make you look *more* trustworthy? News flash: marrying a stranger in Vegas and then screwing up the divorce doesn't scream stable."

But the dirty details would be so much worse. "It would just be on paper. And we're already two months in."

He scoffed. "And how much longer would we have to do this?"

Not dismissing it out of hand. Promising.

"A couple more months?" She held up her palm to stall his protest. "We wouldn't even have to do anything … couple-y."

"You mean your trust-dispensing overlords would accept it at face value and we go about our lives as normal?"

"Not completely normal. Maybe move in together for a while—"

He was already sliding past her because his previous gesture—that one of oddly-placed protectiveness from the guy who bumped her—had placed him squarely in a wraparound that kept her snugly trapped against the bar. Now he was leaving, exposing her to hell knew what.

"Banks, I'll give you whatever you want."

"I don't need money."

Said as if people who did were bloodsuckers and parasites. If only she'd drunkenly married *any* other guy instead of this judgmental jackass.

Yet she couldn't give up. Not when she was so close.

"What do you need?"

Something flashed in his eyes—something carnal. She recalled that look the night they met, the night they thought this would be a fun release, no strings, no consequences. What babies they were.

The heated expression vanished, replaced with something harder. Colder. "Nothing from you."

Her disappointment was a gut punch. Not because she cared for his opinion but because she needed the funds to be released sooner than later. She had plans for that money.

It was pointless trying to bargain with him. You shouldn't bargain with terrorists.

"Should I have my lawyer call yours, then?"

His brows crashed together in surprise. This hockey-playing lug expected her to fall to her knees because she was so desperate. *Well, think again, Big Guy.*

A desultory sniff, then, "Got a number for this lawyer?"

"Not on speed dial, no."

"Put yours in there." He dropped his phone on the bar and shoved it a few inches toward her. He couldn't even hand it to her like a normal person.

She refused to pick it up, lest her hands shook with the rage coursing through her. Like an angry jackdaw, she pecked away at the keypad and pressed the dial button. Once her phone rang, she pulled it from her Miu Miu clutch and held it aloft.

"Connected!" In her best faux cheer because that seemed to annoy him more than anything.

"Yay," he muttered. "I'll pass it on to my guy and we'll get this squared away. Properly."

"Good."

He grunted.

"What?"

"Good? You're as variable as a summer storm. One minute you want out, the next you want my ring, now you're acting like you don't care again."

She folded her arms. "You're annoyed because I'm not pleading for your cooperation? I asked. You answered. Rudely, I might add. But I didn't really expect anything more. It's not like you understand subtlety."

She expected an explosion. Craved it. Because emotional men were easier to control.

But yet again, Dylan Bankowski refused to conform to her expectations. He leaned in, bending his six-foot-three frame to bring his mouth close to hers.

"Your mind games won't work on me, princess. You think I

don't see what you're up to? In my business, we call that a deke, and no one responds to a fake-out better than me."

His breath was a hot, sultry puff of air against her lips. He didn't scare her.

He was a bully. A bearded, beast of a bully.

Was that her heart going pitter-patter? Nope. That was a very different part of her anatomy, the one that had responded to his sheer physicality that night in Vegas.

"I'm not going to beg. You want out, so we can move forward to the dissolution of the ties that unfortunately bind us. Besides, I wouldn't want to be married to a man who has to get a girl drunk to have his way with her."

That shut him up. However, the thrill of seeing him momentarily speechless was quickly evicted by the unease that came over her at his new expression.

She had offended him.

"You weren't that drunk," he finally gutted out. "And nothing happened."

"Except getting married!" As if it was a mere trifle. But what he really meant was—oh.

An accidental wedding should have been the Vegas-shaped dildo in the room, but apparently not. It was sex. The sex that neither of them had.

"Sure, you wanted to," he said. "But I was a gentleman."

Before she could get off a biting retort, he abandoned her —which seemed appropriate payback for her cowardly exit the morning after they became man and wife.

5

———

He waited a day.

It was hard to say why. He had practice and appointments with his nutritionist and his trainer, not to mention a stint on Jordan Hunt's Hockey Grrl podcast. He'd expected a bunch of stupid questions about his favorite hot sauce or the best clubs in Chicago, but Jordan knew her stuff and asked him about adjusting to the move and his hopes for the rest of the season. Being married to one of his teammates probably meant she knew which levers to pull.

Suffice to say, that day's delay fucked him good. He found out just how much when he put a call into John Delaney, his college roommate who had gone on to become a lawyer because he couldn't hack it on the ice. No way was he going to run to the Rebels legal department to fix this.

"Delaney, I need a favor."

"Lovely to hear from you too, Banks. The wife's doing great. The kids are awesome."

"And that problem you had with your dick? That worked out?"

"Baby number three is on the way."

"Congratulations, I suppose."

Delaney sniggered. "Right back at ya, B-dog! I'm touched you'd call to tell me in person. I'm guessing you need a post-nup, but given your new bride's wealth, maybe she's the one who needs—"

"Come again?"

"You and Georgia Goodwin? She must be quite the gal to have locked B-Dog down."

Delaney knew her name. He knew she *existed*.

His phone buzzed. Then again with multiple messages incoming like rapid-fire bullets, mostly from his Rebels team-mates interspersed with ones from his former cronies in Nashville.

> Congrats, man!

> Awesome news!

> You registered anywhere?

(From Hudson Grey, who was now first on Banks's shit list.)

He blinked at the phone. Delaney was still talking.

"... that time you took Mariah Jones to the Copa and she was expecting you to propose—"

"Where did you hear about this?"

"Where the world hears about everything. Twitter. Or X. Some gossip site."

Fuck. "I was calling to find out how I can get out of it."

A pause, then ... laughter. "Wait, wait, don't tell me. All Stars game in Vegas?"

"Yep."

More laughter, bordering on maniacal.

"This isn't funny."

"Oh, but it is. You were always so insistent that no one

could pin you down and now what? A few shots of tequila and some little cutie slips a ring on it?"

He wished he could blame alcohol. The real reason this happened was because he was at a particularly low point. Thinking about the end and what came next. Vulnerable to the temptation of a gorgeous smile and shapely legs and ... what else? There had to be more.

Back in college, he wasn't exactly a player, but neither was he interested in settling down. Not like Delaney who married the first woman he met at some orientation mixer in his freshman year. With New York, Denver, then Nashville, Banks had attended more weddings than he scored goals. All the guys he came up with were paired off with ankle-biters milling around. With each passing year, Banks was left squiring the youngsters on the team while the veterans headed to hotel rooms or home to get domestic with their special someones.

The Rebels were no different. More loved up idiots. He wanted to play cards at the weekly poker night, and they wanted to talk about their abundantly fertile women.

Another text came in on the group thread, and his heart, already hovering an inch above the floor, plummeted on a hell-bound hurtle toward the earth's core.

APRIL

When were you going to tell us?

SANDY

Screw that. When are we going to meet her?

APRIL

I'm guessing he doesn't want us to meet her, ergo the secrecy.

KELLY

The website said it happened in Vegas ... nuff said.

The coven, as he labeled his sisters. If they knew, it wouldn't be long before—

APRIL

She knows. And she's thrilled!

The "she" in that sentence was his grandmother, Constance Flora Bankowski.

He dragged his gaze away from the group thread, which was chirping on merrily without his input.

"John, how do I get out of this?"

The gravity in Banks's tone had Delaney switching to business mode. "You put in a petition for dissolution. Usually goes through in three months as long as both parties are in agreement and there are no complications with assets or child custody arrangements. One of you needs to be a resident in Nevada for six weeks before you file, though."

"Kind of hard for me to be in two places at once."

Delaney chuckled. "You could ask your wife to move there."

Something tickled his brain. "What about an annulment?" That's what he'd signed before. He'd been so pissed that he hadn't even looked at it closely, just dropped his John Hancock on the dotted line.

"Possible, though the bar is higher there. Bigamy, underage, fraud, want of understanding, insanity."

Insanity? That sounded about right.

He checked the family text thread again. They'd moved on to wedding reception planning.

Meanwhile, Delaney had launched into a patter about decrees and alimony implications. Banks inhaled a deep breath and seesawed back to the coven's text thread.

She knows. And she's thrilled!

Then from Kelly:

It's all she's ever wanted.

So Grandma Connie was pleased that her only grandson had finally tied the knot. That didn't mean he had to stay hitched.

He refocused on Delaney. "Tell me what I need to do."

APRIL CALLED FIRST. He was tempted not to answer but he'd have to listen to her whining for months, so it was just better all-around to get it over with.

"Make it quick. I have practice in ten."

"Hold on, I'm getting Sandy and Kel in on this, too."

Approximately twenty-three seconds later, Sandy was screeching. "I want to know everything!"

"As you can probably guess, this was not intentional."

Kelly chuckled. "How drunk do you have to be to get married in Vegas these days? I'd never have thought you capable of being so clichéd."

"That's me. A walking cliché." He cleared his throat which was the signal to his sisters to quit and be serious. Not that it ever worked but he lived in constant hope. "I can't believe you told Gran."

"Uh, *she* told *us*," April said. "She's got a Google alert on your name, dummy."

"Right, but it was months ago. I don't even know how it got out." Though he had an idea. Very soon, he'd be wrapping his fingers around the thick neck of O'Malley or Grey. Probably both. "I thought it was fixed, but apparently there was a paper-work snafu."

"A paperwork snafu?" April blurted, voicing the disbelief Banks felt right now. He was not the kind of guy who fell victim to a "paperwork snafu." He pored over the small print of his contracts. He monitored his 401(k) quarterly and made the appropriate changes if his equities allocation tipped above 60%. He didn't get married to trust fund party girls or screw up the legal documentation that severed their connection.

"Did someone forget to file something?" Kelly was being kind, trying to give him an out.

"Never mind that," Sandy cut in. "What's she like?"

Annoying, chipper, his complete opposite. "She's a socialite."

"I've seen pictures of her online." That clicking sound was April on her laptop. "She's gorgeous."

"She's like that, only ... concentrated."

"Like frozen OJ?" Kelly laughed. "What does that even mean?"

"She's a party girl." But not that night. Sure, they'd had a few drinks, but he was sober enough when he slipped that ring on her finger and said "I do."

The lead up, however? Georgia on the dance floor of some club, and it was fucking murder. Just watching her shimmy and let loose, with the eyes of every asshole on her, he'd felt positively possessive. He barely knew her, but he knew that much.

Mine.

Two months later and in the cold light of day, he couldn't believe thoughts like that had even entered his mind, never mind dug their claws in deep enough to take him to the marriage license bureau *and* the chapel. He was not an impulsive person.

What kind of witchery did this woman possess that made him go off the rails like that?

"So when do we meet her?" April's voice held a note of amusement.

"Never. I'm getting a lawyer on it."

"That's not fair," Sandy whined. "We haven't had a chance to make a determination."

Jesus.

"How did she manage to pin you down, D?" Kelly's tone was curious. "You must have seen something in her to get that far and she clearly saw something in you, though that's not hard. You're amazing. You can't ignore that kind of connection."

Kelly was a bit woo-woo when it came to this kind of thing. Fate, destiny, kismet—she believed in all that crap. He was surprised they weren't giving him a harder time. They had hated Stacy.

"The connection was fueled by a bottle of Patron." Any other explanation would be tequila on the flames. "And if the paperwork had been filed properly and someone hadn't blabbed, you wouldn't even know about it."

"Gran wants to meet her."

Those words, uttered casually by Sandy, struck a puck-hard blow to his chest.

"Dylan," April said softly when he didn't respond. "It would make her happy. Right now, all she knows is that you're married. She doesn't know the sordid details."

Just like that, his phone buzzed with an incoming call from the woman herself.

"That's her. Stay on the line."

"Time to pay the piper ..."

"Don't kill her dreams ..."

"We'll check in later ..."

They hung up. Sisters? The worst.

Drawing a deep breath, he pressed accept and said, "Hey, Gran, what's up?"

"Why did I have to hear it from TMZ?"

"It was ..." *A mistake. A catastrophe. The best night of my life.* "A surprise."

"I bet it was. The news said it was the All-Star game weekend. A Vegas wedding!"

"Right. But I hadn't just met her." Because that would be absurd. "She's a neighbor of one of my teammates."

"So it was a spur of the moment thing? I didn't even know you were dating anyone after Stacy."

His mom's voice cut in. Gran had put him on speaker. "Dylan, this seems kind of sudden."

It wasn't said to criticize. She would never, but she did worry. Plus she was right: he had spoken to her that night and hadn't given the slightest hint that he had a woman in his life.

Gran jumped back in. "Now, tell the truth ... have you knocked her up?"

"Nope."

"Any chance you might soon? I could probably hold on for another great-grandchild."

"You have four already and you're not going anywhere," his mom said. "Besides, you don't need the grandson and heir to produce."

"But I need him to be happy." Gran sounded wistful. "And having him settled with a family of his own would make him happy."

"Not sure where you get that idea, Gran."

He had a good life. A family he adored despite how much they annoyed him. A career that had treated him well. So he was bruised and battered, and hadn't reached the pinnacle in his sport, but there were other measures of success.

None of them involved marrying a flighty stranger who couldn't even file a form correctly!

For the rest of the conversation, Banks tried to steer the talk away from his new bride only to have his grandmother bring it right back to where it started. Eventually he ended the call with a promise to set up a FaceTime check-in with Georgia, who was "currently out running errands." All he had to do was say it was a mistake, but the words refused to come.

Three minutes later, his mom called. "I'm hiding in the bathroom. Want to tell me what's going on?"

"A mistake that should have been fixed by now. Maybe you can break it to her?"

"I don't know, Dylan. She's thrilled."

He closed his eyes. "But it's not … real. I'm working on making it go away."

His mom sighed. "Listen, you've never been a risk taker and it's kept you on a solid trajectory with your career and your life. But sometimes we need to shake the tree, see what falls out."

"Are you saying that getting impulsively married to a stranger in Vegas is my way of shaking things up?"

"I know you weren't too happy about your trade. You hoped to stay in Nashville, maybe win the Cup before your time is up. Things are changing—moving to a new city and team, reckoning with the final years of your career, and thinking about what comes next. Marrying and starting a family would be considered a normal move for someone in your position."

"I got close already. And that experience made me rethink whether that's for me. I decided it wasn't."

His mom hummed. "Sounds like the universe had other ideas."

"*Not* a message from the universe."

"Often it's the universe inside your head that dictates the next move."

"Sure thing, Yoda."

She laughed. "All I'm saying is that you've made your grandmother happy and given her something to look forward to. I'd never ask you to put your life on hold to please an old lady, but let's face it, divorces take time and the next couple of months will be busy with the playoffs—"

"If we make it."

"Which you will. What does your new bride think of all this?"

She wants to stay married. For money.

"We haven't really discussed it."

"Okay, maybe you should? You say it was unintentional, but you're not an unintentional person. Something led you down that aisle and made you put a ring on this woman's finger. You tried to keep it under wraps, but the news still found a way to come out. I'm seeing a lot of signs here! Don't you owe it to yourself to explore what led you to this point?"

"So I should stay married because the universe says so?"

"Maybe, and because it will make your grandmother happy."

His mom might be onto something. He hadn't been drunk, no matter how much he'd like to spin it that way. He didn't buy the because-the-universe-decreed-it argument, but he also wondered if part of his resistance to Georgia's proposal to stay married stemmed from his anger about how she'd initially handled the annulment.

Because, fool that he was, he had wanted to give this thing a go.

6

Anxious to avoid the inevitable teasing, he skipped the optional morning skate and arrived late for the game call. His teammates were too absorbed in their prep to give him more than a few funny looks and locker room jeers.

After the game was another story. They lost 4-1 to Detroit, and during the third period, one of the Motors D-men slammed Banks so hard into the boards no amount of padding could save him. It was his shoulder again. Not a complete separation, he was sure, but painful enough that it would bruise big time and take a while to heal. He'd suffered enough injuries over the years that he knew which ones warranted medical attention and which ones he could manage for himself.

A very pissed off Cal Foreman was currently pacing the locker room, looking for scapegoats. After some back and forth about whether O'Malley's tumultuous love life was to blame—hockey players were a superstitious lot—talk shifted to where these nosy fuckers wanted it to go.

"Maybe it's Banks's fault," Erik Jorgenson, the Rebels

tender, said as he pulled off his pads. "He didn't invite anyone to his wedding. That has to be unlucky."

Banks continued with taping his stick. It calmed him when each breath had him wincing in pain.

"Those All-Star games are always trouble," Reid Durand said.

Banks refused to rise. Scowling he could do, though. He sent O'Malley a pointed glare, though the kid had claimed he didn't spill. Grey had also professed his innocence as they lined up in the tunnel before the game.

"Let us know when you set up the registry," defenseman Theo Kershaw said. "Make sure you put 'sense of humor' on it along with a tuxedo for all those fancy galas you have to attend with your socialite wife."

Coach came in and began the game post-mortem, aka the listicle of who fucked up and how (spoiler: everyone). Banks tuned out, stuck to his stick-taping and breathing through the pain of his shoulder, then distracted himself with a replay of his conversation with his gran.

How happy she was for him.

How she couldn't wait to meet Georgia.

How hopeful she was for another great-grandchild.

Her health had taken a turn over the last year. She might not have much time left and this was a sliver of color in a gray world. He could do that for her.

Except it would be a lie. Pretending to be someone he was not: a good grandson, a dutiful husband.

Two months ago in Vegas, he had gone to sleep thinking this could work. So Georgia was twelve years younger than him, better suited to some young buck straight out of the draft than a has-been on the butt end of his career. But they'd connected enough to think that getting hitched was a good idea.

Then he woke up alone and realized that only one of them was stuck in that headspace. Any embers of hope were doused when he tried to contact her. The message was clear: pretend it never happened.

It was what she wanted, and after he'd calmed down, he reckoned she was right and put it out of his mind. He had a team to gel with, a city to acclimatize to, and a house to set up for the inevitable influx of relatives. And if every now and then his misbehaving fingers ran Google searches on his ex-wife, that was down to normal curiosity. Who wouldn't want to know more about the bullet he'd dodged.

Only that bullet was now firmly embedded and would require major surgery to excise.

He looked up to find that during his navel-gazing, the locker room had cleared out. Dex O'Malley remained, checking his phone for the fiftieth time because of his love life drama, and for a brief moment, Banks felt an affinity with the younger man.

He quickly swatted that away. Banks didn't have woman problems, at least not on the same level as O'Malley. He could fix his issue easily. This time he'd do it right. His family would have to slow their roll and suffer the disappointment.

"You still think I ratted you out?" O'Malley looked like one of the sad little puppies in that dog shelter where he had gone to sell his soul.

"You say you didn't. I believe you."

"Except you're looking at me like you want to use that stick in a NSFW way."

He placed the stick down on the bench. "How long has she been your neighbor?"

"Georgia?"

Banks's hand itched for the stick he'd just taped and laid to the side for everyone's safety. Who else would he be talking about?

"Since I moved in? Maybe eighteen months ago. But I don't know her all that well. It's a ships passing in the night kind of thing."

Dexter was a bit of a man whore, and Georgia ... well, he didn't know a thing about her.

A suddenly intuitive O'Malley picked up on the vibe. "Dude, Georgia and I—"

"Georgia and you?" A red mist raged before his eyes. His hand flexed again. The stick was right *there*.

"There is no Georgia and I. That's what I'm trying to say. We're neighbors, sort of friendly—" He held up a hand, that newfound intuition sensing Banks's irritation. "But that's it."

Banks released a pent-up breath. Eighteen months. Was that when her parents cut her off? Castle Apartments was where the team stashed players on short-term leases before they settled enough to find their own place. Some guys, like O'Malley, stayed longer while they waited on a multi-year contract. Basically, it was high-end corporate housing, and the fact a woman who came from the kind of money Georgia did was living there said something—he just wasn't sure what.

He hated to ask, but right now, O'Malley was his best source of information. "Is she seeing someone?"

The younger man had the decency not to betray any surprise at the obvious.

She's not seeing me.

"A lot of people come and go from her place, but to be honest, I think they're friends, or maybe just acquaintances. She entertains a lot. All night parties. I had to get my bedroom soundproofed because I had trouble sleeping when I first moved in." O'Malley took a seat on the bench beside Banks. "What happened?"

I thought we had a connection, but I was out of my fucking mind.

"Too much tequila."

O'Malley nodded sagely. "But you're still married when you thought you weren't."

"Paperwork problem."

"And now you need to get it fixed."

Correct. Letting this continue had no upside except for the fact it got Georgia out of a jam and made his grandmother happy.

Don't you owe it to yourself to explore what led you to this point?

Not now, Mom.

When he remained silent, O'Malley stood. "If you need to talk, I'm here. You've been a decent ear for me."

"I have?"

"We had dinner at the Sunny Side Up diner a few weeks ago and you listened to my whining."

"Before you stiffed me with the check."

O'Malley winced. "Sorry about that. Something came up."

It pained him to ask but the kid looked so miserable. "What's going on with you and …?"

"Ashley." Just saying her name deflated him. "We had a fight. She interfered in my business."

The details didn't interest Banks, but he'd lived long enough, and well, *sisters*, to know this much. "Relationships are about give and take, O'Malley. So she screwed up. Probably pales in comparison to your BS."

"Just not sure why she bothers."

"Who knows? She probably thinks you're not as much of an asshole as you think of yourself. Women tend to have a broader view of these things." Years surrounded by opinionated females had given him some perspective.

Yet he couldn't for the life of him work out Georgia. Was it really all about money? Or was there some other reason why she needed him?

Now you're just grasping at straws, desperate to assign her a less mercenary motive.

O'Malley looked somewhat cheered. "Hey, you coming to the Empty Net to drown our sorrows?"

"Sure. I'll follow you there." After he'd iced his shoulder and knocked back a shit-ton of pills.

Within a minute, Banks found himself alone with his thoughts, which lately was not the safest company. He checked his phone and the "wedding announcement" in the *Chicago Tattler.*

Belated congratulations to Georgia Goodwin, who was recently revealed to have married in a Las Vegas wedding ceremony in January. Ms. Goodwin is the daughter of Penny and Marcus Goodwin, owners of the AmeriTrust Corporation and noted Chicago area philanthropists. Ms. Goodwin's new husband, Dylan Bankowski, plays hockey.

The dismissive mention of his profession couldn't quite compete with the possessive clench that phrase wrapped around his balls. *Ms. Goodwin's new husband ...* why the fuck did that send a dangerous sizzle through his veins? Only on paper, yet the thought of it, of belonging to her in that way, was doing strange things to him.

He shouldn't want this. Not for any reason other than his gran's peace of mind. He certainly shouldn't want to relive the feelings from Vegas, the sense that if only they'd met here in Chicago this thing might have had legs.

She'd made it clear that the sole reason to continue this

circus was because she was running out of cash. He should accept the unvarnished truth in that.

He sure as hell should not be looking for reasons to say yes.

7

———

"Georgia, your waist is snatched and you look stunning!"

Georgia plastered on her best clown grin and ushered Skye and Paris inside her apartment.

"You guys were supposed to be here hours ago." It was already past ten and a girl needed her squad.

Skye tossed her dark waves over her shoulder. "Well, this one said she'd meet a date at Molly's, but she needed a wing-girl. Nothing good ever happens before midnight, girl."

"But it looks like you have plenty of people to keep you company." Paris waved at the room behind her, heaving with people. All the lookie-loos had crawled out of the woodwork, salivating for the gossip. Except her friends couldn't be bothered!

"Is he here?" Skye looked over her shoulder.

"Who?"

"Your husband, girl! Everyone's dying to see the two of you together. I can't believe you kept this to yourself."

A familiar panic rose within her. "It was all a big mistake. You know me, love a bit of drama!"

"I've seen pics. That guy can flood my basement anytime."

Paris fanned herself, the thirsty bitch. Georgia and Banks might mean nothing to each other, but the man was technically still her husband. Her friends should not be drooling over him like he was on the *Bridgerton* marriage mart.

"He's kind of old, though, isn't he?" Skye wrinkled her nose. "Our girl's daddy issues are showing. You gonna pull a Britney and get it annulled?"

Paris squealed. "Can't get it annulled if they did the nasty."

Not true, according to her lawyer. "Working on it now."

"So this happened when we took our girls' trip?" Paris cocked her head. "I know you disappeared there for a while—"

"Because you met that tatted DJ"—Skye pointed at Paris—"and then we went to his suite so you could lick his ink. You weren't paying attention to *anyone* after that."

Paris scowled. "Neither were you! I thought you were going to hang with our girl here and look at the trouble she got into."

Before they could get any deeper into the dirt of who was responsible for leaving Georgia alone long enough to get herself legally embroiled in the life of a professional athlete, she held up a hand.

"It was no one's fault but mine. I just wanted some alone time."

Paris smirked. "Look how far that took you. I only fucked the guy I met. *You* took it to the next level!"

Sex would have been so much simpler. As it was, she didn't even get an orgasm out of it. But there were kisses. Stubble-jawed rubs against her throat, firm lips taking control …

"Oh, G, I need a word." Skye took the moment that Paris was distracted while answering a text to pull Georgia aside. "So you're never going to guess what happened. My car broke down, just crapped out on Halsted!"

"Oh no!"

"Right? And the mechanic, who was really hot by the way, not that I'd be interested, but just an observation, he says it's going to cost me three grand to fix the transmission. Can you believe that? Fucking inflation! I have maybe thirteen hundred and I hate to ask, but it's either that or I sell myself to the hot mechanic."

Georgia squeezed her friend's arm. "Don't worry, I'll Venmo you the difference."

"You would? Oh, you're a star! Could you round up to two grand?" Her phone buzzed and she quickly scanned the screen. "That's my sister. She's such a leech!"

Georgia rolled in her lips. Skye was a good friend, but she always had money issues, which were easier to support when Georgia didn't have plans for her own funds. In the old days, she was happy to treat her girls with Sephora sprees here and trips to Santorini there. At one time, she had more money than she could possibly spend, so why not spread the wealth around?

Now her cash wasn't as fluid, but she couldn't turn down a friend in need.

Skye gave a dirty grin. "Don't think I don't want to know everything about this hockey player husband of yours. You're not getting away with keeping that to yourself."

The doorbell rang, saving her from launching into the details.

"Go get yourself a cocktail. I'll catch you up later."

Smile in place. Hand on doorknob. The game begins again.

GEORGIA COULD BARELY HEAR her voice, never mind her thoughts, above the din of the party. This was usually how she liked it. Blocking out the negative with loud music and lively chatter was her go-to. The best way to center herself and keep the boogeyman of grief away.

Only tonight, she couldn't ignore as well as usual. Part of the reason was sitting beside her, sulking.

"I'm kind of hurt, G."

She turned to Oliver, one of her closest friends, and the guy she usually relied on in times of crisis. They'd known each other since first grade, when she gave him a cucumber and cream cheese sandwich from her lunchbox, and he promptly threw it up.

"Hmm?"

"This marriage business. You could have turned to me if you needed a husband."

How thrilled her mother would be. She loved Oliver's parents. They were on all the same charity boards.

"And what would Savannah think?"

They looked toward Oliver's girlfriend, who gave them a tiny finger wave and turned back to her conversation with a baby Pritzker. Poor Sav. She really did not like Georgia.

"She'd know I was just trying to do you a favor. We had a pact. Single by thirty and we'd do the deed. Guess you don't need me anymore." *Boy band pout activated.*

She squeezed his arm. "Believe me when I say this was not part of any plan. Serves me right for wandering the streets of Vegas by myself."

"Yeah, Paris and Skye have a lot to answer for. They should have been keeping an eye on you."

A little patronizing, but that was typical Oliver. That weekend, she'd wanted to get away from everyone, commune with neon and noise where no one knew her. It had been two years since she lost Dani. Two years as the broken half, left behind, her heart aimless.

It's your time to shine, Georgia. I won't be around sucking up all the oxygen. Make me proud.

All those promises to live life to the full and figure out her place in the world had shattered in a seedy chapel, a few blocks off the Strip. She couldn't even get that right. Her parents already thought she was a disaster and Banks obviously thought so, too.

Before that fateful night, she'd had three marriage proposals in as many years and one broken engagement. A nice ratio. Everyone wanted to marry Georgia, even Oliver who should be thinking about his real girlfriend. But the one guy she'd gone all the way with, so to speak, knew instantly the mistake he'd made.

"Don't worry, it'll be fixed soon, and we can go back to our original plan."

Oliver was still hung up on the sordid details. "But a hockey player? Whatever possessed you?"

"Tequila, Oli. Tons of it. Do you really think I'd have done that if I was in my right mind?" A pang of guilt pinched her, though she didn't owe Dylan Bankowski a single kind thought, not after he'd dismissed her so rudely. Neither had she been that drunk, but alcohol was as good a scapegoat as any.

He chuckled mirthlessly. "No, I suppose not. He's not exactly your type. You prefer them with all their teeth."

Another pinned-on smile. She was pretty sure the guy had all his original teeth, not that he'd ever used them on her. All that glowering, and still she'd let him lead her down the aisle.

Oliver wasn't done. He had quite a nasty streak when he got going. "Multiple pucks to the head, too. Probably brain damaged. And don't forget he's a fists-first kind of guy."

"He is?"

"They all are. That's what hockey players are known for. Duking it out on the ice."

That sounded familiar as a concept. The reality, not so much. Dani was the sporty one in the family, a big hockey fan. She'd be laughing her head off if she could see Georgia now.

What do you think, sis? A hockey player!

Oli's right, G. So not your type.

"He was quiet." Contemplative and stoic. But when he spoke, it felt like he saw right into her. Not that she told him much about herself, so that was her overactive imagination for sure. Now he knew that she came from money, that she liked to party, and he obviously had "opinions."

She'd done some research herself.

Dylan "Banks" Bankowski. Thirty-six. Center position. Wisconsin native. Winner of several awards, including the Calder Memorial and the Frank J. Selke. (But not the Cup, which she knew was the big one.) *Played for New York, Denver, and Nashville before being acquired by the Chicago Rebels in January, the weekend of the All-Star game.*

The weekend he became her husband.

But soon not to be. Perhaps the bar ambush wasn't her best idea, but subtlety had never been her strong suit. With his refusal, she was forced to reckon with telling her parents how much she'd messed up. They'd want more control over her life, make her return to college or ... marry someone they chose. Like Oliver. Which wouldn't be terrible because he was a friend and wanted to be with her.

Not like her current husband.

∿

BANKS HATED PARTIES.

At his age, he was no longer interested in hanging at clubs or even attending gatherings at his teammates' houses, unless it involved cards and beer. A quiet cookout he could do.

Maybe a night out at a bar with the boys. He should be there now, but everyone was zeroed in on O'Malley's love life and his various schemes to stay out of prison. Banks had already said his piece and had no desire to rehash it in a group setting, especially as he needed to rest his shoulder and not let on how much pain he was in.

An ice bath would be good. A pack on his shoulder and a couple of whiskeys to help him sleep would be better.

Instead he had Georgia on his mind. He had been dismissive and rude to her the other night, annoyed at her for showing up and dangling the possibilities of a rematch in front of him. Residual anger at how things had ended between them had colored his perspective.

He was here to talk calmly about next steps.

Entry to Castle Apartments was a little too easy. The doorman recognized him immediately and told him "Ms. Georgia is on the fourth floor. Go on up, Mr. Banks."

It's Mr. Bankowski, but whatever.

Any concerns that she might be licking her wounds vanished as he stepped out of the elevator and registered the vibrating bass. Circling a couple mid-grope in the hallway, he followed the *thump-thump* to its origin.

He checked his watch. Almost eleven o'clock. He'd hoped to find her alone, maybe a little sleepy. Kind of like she'd looked as she fell into a deep slumber in his arms ...

No, not like that. Forget that.

He really should be taking care of his shoulder and not chasing down his mistake. But he'd put this off for too long already. Give it another day and the tabloids would be talking about how Georgia was pregnant with twins and which color they were picking for the nursery.

He pushed the door to her apartment open. That Miley

Cyrus song was playing, the she-anthem about flowers that seemed to be on an eternal loop when he visited his sisters and nieces. No one paid him any heed as he walked through the packed entryway, except to instantly move aside because he was a husky guy and people usually did that when he entered a room.

He scanned the space quickly, eyeing it like he'd just cleared the boards. The barriers to his progress. The defenders in his way. The goal where he would soon sink the puck.

She was currently marked. Some guy in a suit, extra douche points for the matching vest. Ignoring him, Banks took a good look at her.

His wife.

People flitted around her, butterflies to whatever sustaining nectar she dispensed into their sad little worlds. A half-smile. A flutter of her eyelashes. A low chuckle and a quiet word.

Dressed in pink—again—she laughed at something Suit Boy said, but even from here he could see it. Her eyes, usually so blue and bright, were dull. Faking it.

Time to put some life back into them.

He could come in from the side, out-flank the mark, but he figured direct was better. Just like the moment in the Empty Net when he knew bone-deep that she was there, Georgia seemed to sense his presence.

Their gazes locked. The music fell away. A weird shiver shuddered through him, some sense of déjà vu, because yeah, they'd been here before.

Christ, he wanted her.

He shouldn't, not after everything he knew about her. How she discarded him without a second thought. How the paper-work mistake and her cash flow problem were the only reasons she sought him out again. It was purely chemical attraction, nothing more.

Yet, here he was, thinking of ways to have her all to himself.

She stood as he approached, probably because she felt at a disadvantage while sitting. He had at least a foot and a half on her.

"Celebrating your impending divorce?"

"Oh, I don't need an excuse. Every day's a party around here."

Her defiant tone didn't quite match her expression. So she needed to play at tough girl for a moment. He'd give it to her, but not for long.

"Hi, I'm Oliver, Georgia's oldest friend." Suit Boy offered a hand and, after a second, Banks took it.

"Banks. Georgia's current husband."

Her little gasp was the sexiest thing he'd ever heard.

Giving himself a second to enjoy her reaction, he released Suit Boy's hand and turned back to Georgia. "Let's take a walk."

Without waiting for a response, he grasped her tiny hand and led her away.

8

If Georgia could wish for anything right now, it would be for everyone to leave. Go home. Let her be.

With Banks.

His hand wrapped in hers felt big and safe, its warmth vital and life-affirming. Vaguely she heard Oliver calling her name, asking if she was okay. Did she need his help? No, she never had despite their joking about a marriage pact. She could handle Banks, even if the last time she'd gone down that mental ditch, she'd woken up married.

He took her toward the back of the apartment, still holding her hand, as if he knew the layout. Maybe he did. Maybe he had visited her neighbor Dex at some point over the last couple of months. He might have been mere feet away from her all this time.

He found the restroom, pushed open the door, and pulled her inside. With the door closed and locked, leaving the din of the party behind, he released her.

And stared.

Likely trying to puzzle out who she was and how they got here.

If you find out, let me know.

He cast his gaze over the small space with her kooky shower curtain of a cat riding a shark, the wall of cosmetics (Amazon's "subscribe and save" was her friend), and today's mantra in lipstick on the mirror: *Choose joy.*

Banks didn't seem like a mantra kind of guy. If anything, he was probably anti-mantra.

The quiet drew taut as a wire, and as she had never been good with silences, she filled the void.

"What's on your mind?"

"Your big mouth got us in the papers."

"*My* big mouth? You're the one who pitched a fit in a crowded bar because I gave you some bad news." Embarrassed to be associated with her, she'd venture. "Your teammates probably blabbed."

"Not if they value their balls. No, the leak is from your side."

She threw up her hands. "Who cares? It's out there and now we need to fix it. I already texted you my lawyer's number, so why are you here?"

A muscle ticced in his jaw. His eyes, that deep golden-brown, dipped to her mouth, flashed, then looked over her head in the direction of the mirror. Choosing joy, perhaps?

"Circumstances have ... changed." Each word exited his mouth like precious cargo. She was supposed to savor it, apparently, because he immediately clammed up.

"Circumstances?"

"Yep."

"Okay."

Two could play at the cagey word reveal game. The silence

was becoming more familiar, almost cozy, like hygge with a side of who's-gonna-crack-first.

Finally, he broke it. "The staying married option? I can do that."

Her heart jumped so hard she had to hold a hand to her chest. *Play it cool.*

"And what makes you think *my* circumstances are the same?"

"It's what you want, isn't it? To get your money." As if her reasons for staying married were distasteful while his were what? Altruistic?

"I'm going to need more information."

He loomed over her. This bathroom was suddenly as small as her building's elevator car. "Why?"

"Because I'd like to know if your goals align with mine."

"Assume they don't, but at the base level, we need the same thing."

"Which is?"

"To make this fake marriage look real."

The answer to her prayers. All she had to do was agree, yet something in her balked at being treated like a puppet on a string. She had enough of that from her parents.

The doorknob turned and a knock sounded, bringing with it a renewed urgency. She just had to say *yes.*

"Who's going to believe it when we haven't even been together since it happened?"

"We don't need to explain shit."

"That's where you're wrong. Because I need an explanation for your complete three-sixty."

"One-eighty."

"What?"

His deep rumble reverberated against the bathroom's

subway-styled tile. "It's a one-eighty. If it was a three-sixty, we'd be back where we started. Both wanting a divorce."

He was here, agreeing to her request, but still she pushed because Georgia Goodwin never knew what was good for her. "I need to know why you changed your mind."

"Isn't it enough that I have? You get what you want. I get what I want."

What I want. The way he said that … as if he *did* want this.

He wasn't going to spill the tea. Could she live with that? Did it really matter that she didn't know his motivation?

He didn't know hers, at least, not her true one.

"But if you don't need to get back into your parents' good books, then I suppose we can just go back to the original plan. Get the lawyers on the case. Properly." Pivoting away from her, he placed a hand on the doorknob and winced.

"What happened?" She jumped forward, blocking his exit. "Are you hurt?"

"It's nothing."

"Was it a fight?" Oliver's words about the fists-first nature of hockey came back to her.

He sucked in a breath. "Just my job. Sometimes it gets physical."

"Oh my God, sit." She pushed him down, none too gently, on the closed toilet lid. Amazingly, he acquiesced.

Now what? He was staring at her, waiting for her next move. She hadn't really thought this through. Visions of wrapping bandages around his bruised, banging body floated through her brain. They would be standing close enough for her breasts to be level with his mouth and he'd be acting like a big, brave idiot while she played at sexy nurse.

There was that costume she'd worn one Halloween hanging in her closet. But this man needed real medical assistance, not the slutty nurse kind. She opened the doors below the sink and started to search.

This was a terrible idea in a playoff series of terrible ideas.

1. Coming here instead of going home to ice his shoulder;
2. Agreeing to Georgia's request to stay married, but most of all,
3. Sitting in this tiny space while temptation herself bent over and wiggled her ass in his face.

She was looking for something, a completely innocent task, but that didn't stop his imagination from running wild about that peach-perfect ass inches away from him. His cock twitched. His fingers tingled.

He sat on his hands. "Georgia—"

"Oh, here it is!" She placed a Barbie lunch box on top of the vanity and opened it. First, out came Nurse Barbie, who was placed near a tap, for moral support, he supposed. Next emerged an assortment of tiny Band-Aids, mostly of the Hello Kitty and Disney princess variety. His nieces had taught him well.

Georgia assessed the meager options and blinked a few times before meeting his gaze. "Any cuts? The smaller the better."

He repressed a smile. "It's more of an ache." And not just his shoulder.

"Well, I have hydrocortisone, a sewing kit, and, hmm, one latex glove."

"Could have ourselves a real party."

She laughed, and God, that brought it flooding back. *Georgia skipping down the Strip, her eyes bright as blue suns, reflecting the lights and energy of the city.* "We need to see the fountains!"

His heart rate soared. *This* was why it happened.

This was why he was letting it happen all over again.

Someone tried the doorknob.

"Busy in here!" Georgia called out. "Try the other bathroom!" She rummaged again and took out a single pack of aspirin. "Would this help?"

Christ, she was so sweet with her pathetic medical supplies and her nervous energy that was somehow sexy at the same time.

"Probably."

Her eyes lit up. "Oh, good!" She rinsed out a glass and handed him the pill, which he downed with a gulp.

"I feel better already."

"Banks," she murmured with a head shake, and just the soft way she said his name made him warm. "How did you get hurt?"

"Some asshole D-man from the Motors shoulder-checked me against the boards."

"I understood about one in three words there."

He shrugged, which sent a stab of pain through his shoulder. "Occupational hazard."

"Will you get to rest before the next match?"

"It's game. And yeah, a few days." He stood, anxious to get out of this small space before he did or said something truly stupid. "So have your circumstances changed, Georgia?"

"About needing to stay married?"

He nodded, while his pulse rate picked up. *Say no. Say no.*

"No, they haven't changed."

Fuck, yeah.

Tonight, he walked into this party with every intention of having an adult conversation with Georgia, one that would lay out a clear path to marriage dissolution. Offer her the courtesy she hadn't bothered giving to him.

Seeing her alone in the crowd, something tripped in his chest. She had looked so exposed, in need of someone to shelter her from this crazy world she'd built around herself.

For a few wild seconds, he thought: *I could be that someone.*

Everyone, from his family to his teammates to Georgia's parents, assumed it was the age-old equation of Vegas plus alcohol equals a sham.

That he was a fool.

Well, he wasn't a fool. He didn't make impetuous, life-changing decisions. Marry in haste, repent at leisure, was how the saying went. He might have the first part of that down, but he sure as hell wouldn't be spending long repenting.

It wouldn't hurt to give this time. Give Georgia the space to fix things with her parents and assure the world he wasn't an idiot who married a pretty young thing because she made his old, decrepit heart feel shit. Besides, his mother had the right of it: he needed to see it through. Figure out what led them down that aisle. It might be about money for Georgia now, but it wasn't then.

"So, we doing this?"

Her eyes flew wide, all that ocean-blue, and for a second he thought he saw a spark of relief. Maybe even a flash of power.

"Sure, I'll stay married to you, Big Guy." Like she was doing him a solid. Georgia Goodwin was back in the saddle, and man, he liked that look on her. "But I need a favor."

"Another one?"

There was that sinful curve to her mouth. It was going to be the death of him.

"What are you doing tomorrow night?"

"Darling! You made it!"

Georgia smiled thinly at her mother. "Of course I did. You invited me."

Penny Goodwin gave a raspy, knowing laugh. "And whenever have you paid attention to your poor old mother? Your father will be thrilled." She looked around the glitzy ballroom at the Drake in downtown Chicago, bannered and beautified for the Humane Society gala, seeking out Georgia's dad. "We were just saying that we need to meet Derek. Have the two of you over for dinner and talk about a reception for the newlyweds."

Her mom's voice lifted on that last phrase, sounding a touch hysterical.

"It's Dylan, Mom. Dylan Bankowski."

"GiGi, you're here!" Her father kissed her on the cheek.

"Why is everyone so surprised I accepted an invitation?"

"We're not surprised," her father said, as if Georgia was the one getting it all wrong. "It's lovely to see you. Your mother's been worried."

"I hear Darren's from Wisconsin. Is that last name Polish?"

"It's Dylan, and yes, my husband is Polish." She wasn't sure if the mention of the word "husband" or "Polish" made her mother's eyes twitch; either way, it was most gratifying.

Her father stepped in before her mother could say anything else. "It's nice to see you settled, GiGi. Can't wait to meet him."

"Good, because he'll be here tonight."

Penny Goodwin's eyes went as wide as the Villeroy & Boch plates they'd be serving foie gras on later. "Here? But darling, why ever would you think that was a good idea? We really should be doing this in private, don't you think?"

"Well, nothing's been private about it so far. Why start now?"

Her mom got that pinched look between her eyebrows. "Georgia, I'm thinking of Dar—Dylan. How awkward for him to meet his in-laws under such strange circumstances."

At this rate, Georgia didn't care. Her parents weren't terribly awful, just a little bit awful. No worse than most parents except they took their jobs very seriously: they disapproved of everything she did.

While her mother jabbered on about which locations might be suitable for a last-minute wedding reception (*cart before the horse, darling, but we'll manage!*), Georgia cast a nervy glance over her shoulder. She should have insisted they meet beforehand. Make an entrance together. But he'd said he'd be busy "with my job" all day so he'd see her here. She'd left his name at the door but maybe she should text him again.

She turned toward the entrance just as a male model in a suit appeared to block her view.

Only that was no male model.

That was ... Banks.

When she asked him last night for a favor—put in an appearance at this gala her parents were hosting and by the way, it's black tie—she had hoped he'd show in something decent. He hadn't spotted her yet, but he was scanning the crowd, which gave her time to appreciate the spectacular form that was the man she had accidentally married.

Holy fucking wow.

He looked like he'd walked off a Paris runway. But there was also something indefinable about how he wore the threads, like he'd happily rip them off as soon as the director of this scene said "cut!"

Director Georgia would be happy to rip them off on his behalf.

He spotted her, and she remembered why she was in this mess. The world fell away. That night in Vegas, she had needed an escape from her life, from the version of herself that was forced to exist without Dani. Banks had done that for her. He'd given her that comfort.

But it wasn't real.

As he headed toward her, she reminded herself: *Not real.*

As the crowds parted—because that's what everyone did when Banks strode through like a god among mortals—she repeated the words. *Not real.*

And when he stood before her, those deep brown eyes locking in and finding new ways to incinerate her panties, she whispered to herself. *Not real.*

"Georgia." Reality crashed through her like a soul-sucking wave.

"You came!"

There was a slight twitch of his lips at her innuendo-laden declaration.

"Sure did," he murmured before leaning close to her ear. His lips brushed the sensitive lobe, and anyone watching would think he had kissed her. A husband greeting his wife. "Your wish, my command, right?"

That was different. He sounded almost ... flirtatious. She turned to her parents who were looking on with interest.

"Mom, Dad, this is Dylan. Dylan Bankowski. Um, these are my parents, Penny and Marcus Goodwin."

"Mr. and Mrs. Goodwin. It's great to meet you."

Her mom's eyes lit up. "Likewise. Though we're a bit surprised it took so long."

"You've been out of town for months, Mom."

"We were in Chicago in early February before we went to Gstaad and then again in March before Hawaii. Not that my daughter tells me anything."

Before Georgia could defend herself, Banks jumped in.

"Yeah, that's my fault. I kind of wanted to keep it under wraps so I could spend some quality time with Georgia before the press got ahold of it. She was kind of worried it would look weird, how it all happened so fast."

This did not pass her mother's sniff test. "But to keep it from her parents?"

"To be honest ..." His hand circled Georgia's waist and pulled her into the haven of his hard body. "What we did was a touch impulsive, and I wanted to give her time to back out if she had second thoughts."

Georgia swallowed hard, shocked that the man beside her had come up with a coherent statement that plugged the holes better than anything she could have conjured.

Her mother narrowed her eyes. "That's quite ... *mature* of you, I suppose, especially given the strange start to your relationship. Vegas is rather clichéd, don't you think?"

"Well, it's not as if we met there for the first time."

Three sets of Goodwin peepers fixed on Banks, who squeezed Georgia a little tighter and gave her a wry look.

"You didn't tell them you're neighbors with my teammate?"

"No, I didn't." *Even think of it.*

Banks smiled and it was like the clouds had parted to reveal the sun after a storm.

"We met a while back when I was visiting Dex O'Malley, one of my teammates. He's kind of an idiot, but Georgia's beyond patient with him 'cause she's a saint. Anyway, we ran into each other in the elevator. She'd dropped a couple of oranges out of her grocery bag and one of them went rolling down the hallway. I chased that sucker like it was a puck heading into the blue zone."

"The blue zone?" her mother asked, enthralled by Banks's easy manner.

"Where I score goals, Penny. On the ice rink. Anyway, I scooped up that orange and returned it to Georgia and we got to talking. That was what—how long before Vegas, honey?"

Honey. She looked up into the gorgeous, lying eyes of her husband and tried to get with the program. He was helping her save face, framing their relationship as something historical, planned. Solid.

"A few months, maybe?"

"Yeah." Another little squeeze of encouragement, maybe even approval that she was finally on board the Origin Story train. The people pleaser in her morphed into a praise whore on the spot while he went on. "We didn't go there to get hitched, but when in—"

"Vegas?" her father offered.

"Yep, Marcus, it seemed like the best idea in the world. Only ..." He leaned in, like he had a secret to tell. "She got cold feet after we did the deed."

"She did?" Her mother turned accusing eyes on Georgia, the big bad of the story once more. *How could you do that to this lovely man, darling?*

Georgia spluttered, "It all happened so quickly!"

"Too quickly," Banks said with a chuckle. A chuckle! "I

kind of strong-armed her into it. Georgia wasn't completely sure, and the day after, she hotfooted it out of there. Once we got back to Chicago, I had to beg her to give it a shot. She was being the sensible one, y'know. She wanted to live apart at first so we wouldn't be overwhelmed with setting up house. Or letting that honeymoon period weigh too heavily on the facts. Too much pressure."

"That sounds very reasonable," her mother said, though it hadn't sounded reasonable at all. He had spilled the beans about her running away, but her mother wasn't focused on that. She was too busy staring at Banks as if every word out of his mouth was utter perfection. "It's nice to see you're approaching this with a modicum of common sense. I'm guessing it's because you're a little older, Dylan. A calming influence."

Good grief, had he not just told a version of events that painted *Georgia* as the sensible one? No getting out from under that misconception.

Her mother turned to her daughter. "I just wish you'd told us. We want to get to know our new son-in-law."

She smiled at Banks, a warm, generous smile that she usually reserved for the beneficiaries of her charitable largesse.

He returned it, holding her gaze until she dragged it away and blinked in confusion. Dylan Bankowski, Mother-in-Law Whisperer.

"Oh, there's Mitzy Layton. We really should talk to her, Marcus."

"Indeed," her father said. "We'll catch up later. Good to meet you, Dylan."

"Likewise, sir."

He kept his hand on her waist as her parents walked away, then inclined his head, his lips brushing her ear again.

"I think we need a drink, don't you?"

BANKS SIGNALED TO THE BARTENDER. "Gin and tonic, and an IPA."

Georgia looked up at him with those big blue eyes. "You remember my drink?"

"We shared quite a few of them in Vegas."

He looked around the ballroom, about as glitzy as you'd expect for a gathering of wealthy do-gooders. Everything was gilt-edged and shiny and a little bit phony, including Georgia's parents.

The Goodwins were rightly suspicious of him—after all, they'd never heard of him until now. Obviously not hockey fans. He'd expected to wing it once they met, but that skeptical look from Mama G had inspired some light improvisation. They had the connection in O'Malley, so why not use it to give the story more weight? Hopefully no one would delve deep enough to discover he hadn't moved to Chicago until after Vegas.

She took a quick breath. "You saved my ass back there. I know we should have discussed the backstory beforehand, but I've obviously not thought this through. And there you were, with all the answers."

"Just thought it would sound better if we said we'd known each other from before. Makes it seem less weird."

"A *little* bit less."

"A *tiny* bit less," he countered and watched her lips curve into a gorgeous smile. Jesus, he would come up with any number of lies and cheats to see that flash of sun.

"And telling them I got post-nuptial jitters? That's genius. Covers us in case they get wind of the first annulment."

His thoughts, exactly. This girl was sharp. He remembered that from Vegas.

"Do you think they bought it?"

"My mom was very taken with you, which is incredible because she's not easy to impress. I'm amazed at how quickly you came up with that story. You're a natural liar."

"I'm a natural storyteller. There's a difference."

"Well, I owe you. Big time."

I accept Visa, Mastercard, and hot, wet kisses. He looked her over. Her long, platinum blonde hair fell down her back like a wave of sun over another strapless pink dress, similar to what she wore that night. Her wedding dress. Those round, creamy shoulders were right there, awaiting his lips ...

She waved at him. "What? Do I have a stray booger?"

"Come again?"

She rubbed her nose. "You're staring at me like I have spinach in my teeth."

"No, you're perfect."

She blinked, like she'd never heard that. People—men—must tell her that all the time.

He evicted thoughts of compliments from previous boyfriends, none of whom were her husband, he might add. "What's this gala for?"

"One of my parents' many causes. This one is for the Humane Society. Fifty thousand dollars a plate."

He gave a low whistle. "How much will they raise?"

"Five million. Maybe more."

"That's a lot of cheddar."

"It is. They're very conscious of giving back, putting good into the world."

"They have a lot of money, and you can't take it with you."

She shook her head. "I'm not criticizing. Of course they're doing great work."

"But you think there's something performative about it."

She shrugged. "Maybe? They're very aware of how they look. But people are getting helped, so I shouldn't be so nitpicky about it."

She'd brought it up so there must be something to it that bothered her. Maybe she thought that money was hers by right. Maybe her parents expected her to do serious things with her life and didn't approve of how she lived it. Professional party girl wasn't exactly the noblest of professions.

"So, they cut you off?"

"What makes you say that?"

A guess, but he suspected a good one. "You're living next door to O'Malley."

"A wealthy hockey player."

His turn to shrug. "Castle Apartments is fine but isn't exactly a palace. That's temp housing for the new guys on the team. Decent, but not your style."

She finally gave up the act. "My parents haven't been all that happy with some of my choices of late. They cut off my allowance, are threatening to withhold dispensation of my trust, and are trying to blackmail me into doing what they want."

"Which is?"

"Take a job with one of their companies."

What a drag to be set for life without doing a thing.

"But you're not partied out yet?"

Those beautiful blues went wide for a millisecond. Had he hurt her feelings?

"Me? Never."

He looked around. People were staring at them, likely wondering what the hell this gorgeous young woman was doing with him. Beauty and the Goon.

"So what's the end game here?"

"I figure a couple of months should keep them off my back and get me back in clover."

A couple of months he could manage. The playoffs were just around the corner, and he'd be so busy he would barely notice her. But his family would have questions about why he was letting this drag on. As for his grandmother? She'd have a whole other set of expectations.

The notion that time together would help him figure out the why of it all was still there, simmering away.

"Be ready to move in tomorrow."

"What?"

He passed her drink to her. Looked like she needed it. "You want this to look legit? You need to move in with me."

She glowered at him. Kind of cute, to be honest. "Is this what I have to expect? Bosshole husband?"

He liked that. *Bosshole.*

Eh, *husband*, too.

"Sounds about right."

10

Georgia looked up to see Tara Fitzpatrick standing at her open door. The woman was a goddess. With her marriage to Hale Fitzpatrick, the Rebels' GM, her lovely daughter, Esme, and her thriving hair stylist business, she really had her shit together.

Georgia closed a suitcase and put it standing beside four others.

"I've been summoned by my husband."

"That's quite the turn up, I have to say. Are you okay?"

It was the first time anyone had asked her and an urge to be honest for once gripped her.

"I don't know. It wasn't exactly planned, and it really should have been resolved by now, but ... Banks asked me to stay married."

So, not completely honest.

Tara considered that. "Is that something you're open to?"

"Yes. I have my own reasons. I just wish he was a bit more forthright about his." She closed the final case and stood upright. Cheddar sniffed at the closest one before giving her the bum view and flouncing off. He wasn't good with change.

Tara's mouth curved in sympathy. "If you need a friendly ear, we could always go for coffee or something stronger. No need to wait until your next appointment."

That pleased Georgia more than it should have. "I appreciate that. So, do you know …?"

"Dylan?"

Dylan. She'd introduced him as such to her parents, but she couldn't imagine calling him that in regular conversation. It sounded so … personal.

"Not well. I've cut his hair three times and he's not the chattiest I've had in my chair." She chuckled. "But you two must have hit it off."

"Alcohol is responsible for so much nonsense."

Tara looked skeptical. "But you must have seen something in each other. And the marriage clerk isn't going to hand out licenses to people who look like they're trashed, are they?"

True. Georgia remembered far more about that night than was safe for her mental health.

I just want something, someone, who's mine.

I can do that for you, Georgia. Let me be that person.

Had he said that or was this just a figment of her foolishly romantic imagination?

"Maybe they were having an off day. The clerk, that is." It was easier to blame some anonymous bureaucrat than the actual dummies who promised to have and to hold.

"Hmm, maybe!" Tara sounded cheerful. "So, have you seen Dex by chance?"

"Not today. Is everything okay?"

"He's fallen out with Ashley."

"Oh, I thought they were having a fling."

Tara scoffed. "That's what *they* thought as well, but no.

Now they need to figure it out. I'm just here to nose my way in and guide them to the true path like their fairy godmother. Plus Dex has his court case tomorrow, and I wanted to see how he's handling it."

Dex was lucky to have Tara as a friend. Georgia had her girls, but they were only interested in the tabloid-tawdry details. Skye hadn't even thanked her for the cash she'd sent to fix her car and Oliver was still sulking.

"Could we get together soon for a coffee or an adult beverage?"

"Of course! And Georgia? Don't let Banks push you around, okay?"

"Okay."

BANKS PICKED her up dressed like an Abercrombie and Fitch catalog model complete with gray marled sweater, dark wash jeans, and sexy scowl. She had explained that her Mini Cooper didn't have the space for her luggage, so he'd stopped by and stacked them in his trunk with ease. No signs of the injury from the other night.

"What's that?" He looked down at the cat carrier.

"Cheddar."

"You never said anything about a cat."

"You never asked."

More waves of scorn, as if *this* was the straw that broke the cat's back, as it were. She placed the carrier in the back seat of the Mini.

"I'll follow you."

Another disgusted look at the cat, and then they were on their way. The man with all the charm for her parents was no longer in the building.

They took Willow Road east and turned left onto Sheridan, a familiar route for Georgia whose family lived in Lake Forest, a few miles north. A couple of minutes later, he took a right into a driveway. Georgia's research on the topic of "hockey player living arrangements" told her that newer acquisitions usually had bachelor pads for their first year in a new city because they needed time to get the lay of the land. No one was buying property or setting down roots, which suited her just fine. She didn't need to establish roots with Banks—she just had to project the perception of such.

So, color her surprised when their marital home turned out to be a gorgeous townhouse in Winnetka, just two towns over from Riverbrook, home of the Rebels. The house was Nantucket style with blue cedar shake shingles, trimmed in white. It wasn't the biggest house on the shore—Georgia knew this neighborhood well—but its setting was perfect, fronting Lake Michigan and overlooking Maple Street Beach.

Banks was already unloading her luggage when she stepped out of her car.

"Do you own this place?"

"Leased."

"Why do you need a house so big?"

"My family will be visiting, so it's easier to set up something with room."

His family. Another hurdle to overcome.

With relative ease, he picked up the two biggest suitcases —the ones with wheels, but let's not use them for their intended purpose because apparently it was necessary to prove something—and headed into the house.

Dragging two of the cases and Cheddar, she followed.

Praise be, Nancy Meyers Beachcore!

The main living room area spread out before her with a couple of gorgeous black-and-white gingham sofas and blue tufted coffee tables. The fireplace was bricked and painted white with a huge flatscreen TV over the mantel. And the view. Huge picture windows overlooked a terrace with perfect vistas that would showcase gorgeous sunrises and even more spectacular sunsets. The outdoor furniture was covered in tarps, which made sense. Her parents didn't open their Cape Cod summer house until late May.

What surprised her most was that it looked lived in. As far as she knew Banks had moved in less than two months ago, not long after Vegas. But he had already personalized it with tons of framed photos on the mantel and sideboards.

His family. Three sisters, his mom, his grandmother, and several little girls. Probably nieces. There was one of a man in a military uniform with a teenage Banks, who had clearly mastered the art of glowering at an early age. Even a dog, which was probably female because it looked like Banks was the fox in the henhouse. Could be good because he understood women or not so good because all these women would be incredibly protective of him.

What had Banks told them about her?

His sisters were dark-haired like him. They smiled a lot, though Banks didn't. Stoic with the people he loved, not just her. But she could tell he was happy. An air of contentment permeated these frames that did not exist in his real life, the one he was supposedly building with her.

Because it's not real. He can't be happy with the woman who trapped him.

Good thing it was only a business arrangement. A marriage of convenience. It might have started out as a mistake but now they would make the most of it.

She returned to the foyer and was grabbing the last case just as Banks descended the stairs and reached for the handle.

Their hands brushed, and he pulled away like the touch burned.

This was going to be a long couple of months.

"I've put you in one of the guest rooms. It has an en suite and overlooks the lake." He moved a hand over his mouth and rubbed at his beard. "You can move to one of the other rooms if you prefer."

"I'm sure it's fine." She gestured to the cat carrier. "Is it okay if I let him out?"

Another dark look. "Sure. Make yourselves at home."

She unlatched the door. One orange paw emerged, then retreated.

"Come on, baby. It's okay."

Another foray with the paw, then a second followed by a stretch. Finally, a cute little head popped out for a recce. Georgia looked at Banks, who was watching Cheddar with a mix of disgust and apprehension.

"Not a cat person, then?"

"Not an anything person."

How was it possible she felt enough of an affinity with this person to get so far as the altar? Because now, they had no chemistry at all. They had anti-chemistry.

Cheddar didn't have the decency to feel the same way, however. The little traitor beelined for Banks's boots and placed a paw on the toe. When he wasn't rebuffed, he went further with a head-rub along the man's ankle. Georgia waited for Banks to shoo him away—after all he wasn't an "anything person," whatever that meant. But he stood patiently, waiting. Maybe for Cheddar to get bored.

It could happen. But not today. Cheddar was enjoying himself far too much.

"He likes you. He doesn't usually like anyone."

"No accounting for taste."

Banks remained still. He could have walked away, but he seemed to want to test himself with Cheddar's presence.

"You should pick him up."

"Why?" Banks stared at her, then at Cheddar, as if his opinion mattered.

"Because he'd like it."

Instead, he picked up the remaining suitcase and went ahead of her up the stairs, which gave her a nice view of his ass. Was that what attracted her to him in the first place? A hockey butt? In that bar, she'd seen his strong back and broad shoulders tapering to trim hips. But mostly she'd liked his voice, that laconic way he spoke to his mom on the phone.

She'd never really been an ass-girl, but looking at Banks's very nice behind, she wondered if that was about to change. Hopefully not. This place seemed big enough that she wouldn't have to concern herself with Banks and his excellent butt musculature.

He dropped the suitcase inside the door of one of the rooms. Bright and airy, it was painted a light mauve color and had fresh flowers on the cream-colored dresser.

"Oh, this is lovely!"

Banks sniffed. "Cleaner comes in on Fridays. Food delivery twice a week, just add what you want to the list on the fridge."

"Sounds good. I'll pay for rent and groceries." She moved the cat carrier to the closet.

"No need. You're a guest."

She might be broke, but she had enough to pay her own way. One look at Banks told her making this argument wouldn't get her very far.

"How about I make lunch?"

His expression was pained. "I'd planned to head to the gym after this. And I have a five-day road trip starting tomorrow."

He'd be gone for five days? She should be glad of the space. All the benefits of married life without having to spend time with your mistake of a husband.

So it was a surprise when the next words tumbled out of her mouth. "Come back for dinner tonight. I'll cook."

And even more of a surprise when he agreed.

But he didn't sound happy about it.

11

———

"Smells good."

She turned quickly. Banks stood at the entrance to the kitchen, leaning against the door with arms threaded over that wide chest. He wore dark sweatpants and a gray tee covered with a Rebels blue zip-up.

"I know it's a bit of a mess ..." She gestured ineffectually at the flour-covered counter, the remnants of her meal prep. "I'll clean up after, I promise."

His gaze skimmed the mess and landed on the kitchen table, where she'd placed a bottle of Cab Sauvignon, place settings for two, and a candle. Not yet lit, and the more she thought about it, not likely to be, either. Far too romantic.

Another thing to which she should have devoted more brain space: offering to make dinner for the man she'd accidentally married and was now living with for "appearances."

The problem: she couldn't cook.

The solution: order in.

But that seemed like a cop-out for their first night in their marital home.

Finding the Kitchen Aid mixer and the pasta attachment

in the pantry was a sign. Dani loved to cook and had once perfected little pockets of sweetly savory pumpkin ravioli with a butter sage sauce. Georgia wouldn't be trying anything as complicated as that, but she could make linguine. How hard could it be? Flour, water, salt, an egg—the most basic of ingredients. And she'd watched a video that told her how to do it.

Banks's low rumble cut into her anxious thoughts. "What can I do?"

"Nothing!"

"I'm used to helping."

Of course he was. All those sisters, who wouldn't let him get away with a thing. Neither did she want to set up a dynamic of herself as the little woman toiling away in the kitchen, so she relented.

"Maybe open the wine? I also bought beer. Well, I ordered it using this concierge service that Tara recommended. Can Do. Have you heard of it?"

"Yeah, Reid Durand's wife owns it."

Reid was one of the players. She'd added them all to her flash cards this afternoon, along with the names of their wives, children, and playing positions. That was how she usually began a project. A new set of flash cards and bullet points to guide her.

"Wine good for you?" he asked.

"Great."

He approached, an almost predatory move like he did at the Empty Net, then again at her party. Was he going to touch her? Take her hand? *Kiss her?*

She swallowed. "Need something?"

"Uh huh."

He stepped closer. She held her breath.

"Wine opener. The drawer behind you."

"Oh!" *Stupid.* Jumping aside, she turned back to the

bubbling pot of water and added salt, then stirred the meat sauce next to it.

He sniffed. "Pasta from scratch?"

"I thought it might be nice to have something ... home-made." The more she thought about it, the more absurd it was. He came from a family that probably cooked together, ate together, and prayed together, if that was their jam. What was she trying to prove here?

She picked up a coil of linguine, shook off the flour, and dropped it into the pot. Then another.

Ten minutes later, after Banks directed her to a colander, she served their meals. He had poured a couple of glasses of wine and even had the foresight to pull a hunk of Parmesan from the fridge.

"Sorry, I forgot to get bread."

"That's fine. I can carbo-load tomorrow. This is a good start."

"Carbo-loading? Is that what you do before a game?"

"Typically."

She filed it away in the segment of her brain now devoted to hockey lore. "How was the gym?"

"Good." He picked up his fork and hovered over the pasta, which in truth, looked a bit gloopy with its stuck-together strands. He curled a few around his fork, taking a clump of sauce with it, and put it in his mouth.

The poker face was top-notch as he chewed and swallowed.

"This is really good."

"Liar."

Almost defiantly, he added an even bigger coil of pasta and sauce to his fork. "Got any more?"

"You haven't finished that lot!"

He sniffed. Kept eating. The only hint that he might not be

enjoying it as much as he claimed was his addition of a hefty dose of grated Parm.

Cheddar was circuiting under the table. He had taken a liking to Banks, probably because he ignored him, and cats were contrary like that.

Georgia sipped her wine and took a bite of the pasta. Too much flour had turned it glue-like, and the sauce was far too sweet. She'd added sugar to counteract the overabundance of oregano after she practically tipped half a jar of the dried herb in. Yet Banks was tucking it away like a starving man. Maybe he had no taste buds. Maybe he was hungry after his workout.

Maybe he was just being kind to his pitiable wife.

She took another bite, taking her cue from him to add grated Parmesan to give it more—or some—flavor. A gulp of wine, and she tried to determine if the silence was awkward or companionable.

How did they get here? Was an abundance of alcohol necessary to bring out the selves that appealed to the other? Only they hadn't drunk that much. She was near to sober by the time they made it down the aisle.

She was barely halfway through her meal, and he was already finished, wine in hand, sitting back in the chair and watching her.

"Thanks for cooking. I'll do it next time when I'm home from this trip."

Five days, he'd said. It would give her time to settle, though she wondered how she would ever be at ease around him.

"This is weird, isn't it?"

He eyed her over the rim of the glass. "A bit."

"Why do you think that is?"

"We don't know each other all that well and this situation is contrived. Neither of us wants this for the usual reasons on which you base a marriage." He paused, then added, "In a nutshell."

"It would help if I knew your reasons." And might make her more comfortable with her own.

"You asked for a favor. I'm giving it to you."

"But why? You were so certain when I showed up in the bar that this wasn't what you wanted."

He looked at his wine, and a faint blush tinged his cheekbones. "I was still angry with you because I thought we should have talked before we signed the papers back in February. Seeing you again brought it all back. I wasn't in the right headspace to be receptive to your request."

"But you thought about it and now you're okay with it. Purely because I asked?"

"Don't you usually get what you want?"

Yes, but not what I need. A variation of Mick Jagger's whine echoed in her woolly brain.

"Not always."

He tilted his head. "How about this? Once the word was out that we were married, everyone had an opinion. Too many cocktails, too few brain cells, a night of regret. I don't enjoy looking stupid. I figure I can do this for a while and save face."

That's what she had hoped when she saw the news in the *Chicago Tattler*, though she had no idea how it got there. *This will change his mind.* Yet she couldn't imagine Banks caring what anyone thought.

Before she could question him further, he stood and cleared the plates, letting her know that the conversation about this matter was at an end. She hopped up to help.

"I've got it. You cooked."

Standing on the other side of the dishwasher, she sipped her wine while surreptitiously watching his thick forearms as he rinsed and loaded. Incredibly underrated, forearms. The left one had been wrapped around her when she woke that morning in Vegas, and for the briefest second, the security she felt had been amazing. Then panic barreled in.

He finally broke the silence.

"I've been trying to figure out what happened that night. How we got here."

You and me both. "Any conclusions?"

"We connected on some level."

"Sex," she murmured.

Had she said that aloud? Oh, those forearms were a menace! The house was not nearly big enough for *that* dynamic.

So the moment she'd seen him in that bar, sex was her first thought. That instant shot of desire had thrummed through her as she watched this bear of a man, dressed like a woodsman, chatting with his mom and fighting off horny brides. But no way would a normal person think that getting married was the logical next step to sleeping with a guy.

Especially when sleeping was all they did.

"We were attracted to each other," he said.

"We were." A statement of fact, no more, no less.

"Every marriage usually starts with that."

She put her wine glass down on the counter. "But every attraction doesn't usually end in a marriage."

"No. That middle section is tricky."

"Very."

He put a dish detergent tablet in the slot and closed the door. The cycle started with a whoosh.

He leaned against the counter. "You fell asleep in my arms."

She was speechless. That level of intimacy was harder to discuss than sex.

"That night after we got married," he continued. "We ended up in my room and—"

"Nothing happened," she said on a breathy gasp.

"Well, we didn't fuck, if that's what you mean. Not because I didn't want to. We were both wrecked and—" He paused, biting back whatever he'd planned to say. "But it's not exactly accurate to say 'nothing happened,' Peaches. We're here, married, and pretending to the world that this was the plan all along. I'd say something happened, wouldn't you?"

Her pulse spiked. *Peaches?*

He was right. Something happened. That night, she was fearless, initially because of alcohol but then because of ... *him*. Banks had made her feel like the Georgia who takes what she needs, who deserves to be central, not the daughter who recedes into the background because there's no room for her in the front row with her ill sister.

But that Georgia wasn't real. And if Banks knew the real version—the selfish, impulsive, trouble-making version—he wouldn't be so enamored of their supposed connection.

"Something happened," Georgia said, her voice shaky. "A mistake. But we're going to make lemonade from these lemons, and both get something into the bargain."

Where was the Georgia who had jumped at the chance to be with this man?

She was too busy walking out of the kitchen.

12

Georgia parked her Mini outside the ranch house in Skokie and turned off the ignition. She usually liked to take a moment to access the best version of herself before she met with her clients: cheery, but not too over the top; understanding without condescension; kind and ready to take the cues from the family. It was a balancing act, but she'd been walking this tightrope for most of her life.

Today, however, she was feeling out of sorts. This morning, she'd risen earlier than her usual 10 a.m. to find the house empty and a post-it on the fridge from Banks.

See you Saturday.

Five days without him. She'd planned to cook breakfast, to make up for the not-so-stellar dinner last night and her hasty kitchen exit, but he was already gone. She should be glad of the breathing room. She wouldn't have to be on her best behavior, trying to impress a man who excelled at throwing her off her game with his pin-point observations and strip-her-soul looks.

Something happened.

Yes, a huge mess that she needed to fix.

The door to the ranch house opened and Debbie Draven, a pretty brunette in her early forties, stepped outside with a wave. With a wave back, Georgia popped the trunk, climbed out of her car and grabbed the shopping bag, gussied up with ribbons and crepe paper. What must she look like, showing up in her designer duds in a cute seafoam green Mini?

A trust fund chick with a guilty conscience, that's what.

"Hi, Debbie," she said, moving in for the hug. "How are you?"

"Hanging in there. You look gorgeous, but then brides always have a glow, don't they?"

Georgia sighed. "Wouldn't have taken you for a gossip rag reader."

"Are you kidding? You married a Rebel. That's a big deal around here."

Why couldn't she have chosen an anonymous hunk to marry?

Because there's nothing anonymous about Dylan Bankowski.

She threw out the stock lines. "We've been trying to keep it hush hush, so we could settle in."

Debbie led her inside. "Dad's gonna love hearing all about it. We kept you a slice of birthday cake."

"I'm sorry I missed the party."

"Not a bother. We know you have other people to see."

She did. The charity she volunteered for, Cherish the Days, usually had three or four birthday clients for her each week. Her job was to show up with a gift and chat with the recipient, for whom that birthday would likely be their last. Some of them had family, others had no one but hospice care staff. While the charity informed her when one of the people she spent time with had passed on, there wasn't usually any ongoing relationship.

Until Jim Dixon.

A year ago, she showed up with an Ella Fitzgerald CD, a bottle of Glenlivet, and a smile. She'd chatted with Jim, his daughter Debbie, and her husband Mick, and they'd hit it off. There was no expectation of seeing them again—this was the point of her visit after all, to deliver a gift on a final birthday— but Jim had taken his pancreatic cancer diagnosis of eight months and borrowed several more from the gods. At first, she stopped in once a month, but as it became clear that every day was closer to his last, she increased the visit frequency to weekly.

Mick stood in the kitchen, ready with a cup of coffee and a slice of cake. Normally Georgia wouldn't indulge in a slice so huge, and especially not before lunch, but evidently the family had been waiting for her to arrive.

"This is gigantic! I can't eat this alone."

"Oh, just a couple of bites." Debbie added a huge dollop of whipped cream. "Take it in and chat to Dad."

"Will do." Picking up her plate, she took a sip of coffee and headed into the parlor, as Debbie called it. It used to be the room they kept for visitors, but since Jim had come out of the hospital, it had been configured as his bedroom. His weak smile did little to disguise his pain, his sunken features even more pronounced than they had been a week ago.

"Hey, gorgeous." She set the cake down on a sideboard and leaned in to kiss his cheek, its skin as thin as the crepe paper in the gift bag. "Happy birthday."

"You've been a busy girl," he said with a slight cough.

"Let's do the gifts first before we get into all that." Why did everyone want to talk about Banks? She smiled at Debbie, who had followed her in. "You want to help open your dad's gift?"

"Of course. Let's see what we have." Debbie pulled on the

ribbons then withdrew a bottle of Dom Perignon, four flutes, and a—God forgive her—Rebels ball cap. A couple of weeks ago, she had seen the team calendar propped on Jim's dresser beside his military medals and a hockey puck, signed with some illegible signature. (A quick flip through, but no Banks, unfortunately.) As Jim was a fan, she had popped into a sports memorabilia store and bought the hat. Only as she took it out did she realize she could have asked Banks to sign it, but that would have raised questions she wasn't ready to answer.

"Oh, that's fun," Debbie said, holding the cap up. "Perfect for the birthday boy." She placed it gently on his head and smiled.

"And champagne," Mick said. "Very fancy."

"I thought we could have a little something with the cake. Another year, Jim. It's a great reason to celebrate."

"It is!" Debbie sniffed and shared a glance with her husband. "Opening that up without taking an eye out is your job."

Mick wisely elected to uncork the bottle in the kitchen, the loud pop making them all chuckle, even Jim. Debbie set the flutes on the dresser and Mick poured, at which point Debbie worried that the flutes should have been rinsed first. Everyone assured her they were fine.

"Happy birthday, Jim." Georgia helped him hold his glass, clink it with hers and his daughter's, then raise it to his lips. "I know you'd prefer a glass of whiskey, but I couldn't give you the same gift two years in a row."

"Nothing wrong with some variety." He patted her hand and handed the half-empty glass to her, which she set on the nightstand. "You've got some 'splaining to do, Georgia."

"Dad, it's none of our business." Though the sly look Debbie sent Georgia's way said she would love to know the details.

"I have no secrets!" Georgia sipped her champagne and scooped some cake onto her fork. Banks's version of their origin story was as good as any. "I'm not sure I mentioned it, but Dex O'Malley is my neighbor."

"You certainly did not mention it!" Debbie was agog. "You hear that, Dad? She lives next door to that randy so-and-so, Dex O'Malley. A revolving door, I'll bet."

"Not anymore. He's found a lovely girl to settle down with." Tara had texted her the details. Dex had emerged from his court case this morning with a tap on the wrist and a reunion with Ashley before the boys headed to Dallas for a game. "That's how I know Banks. Dylan."

"You're a dark horse, that's for sure," Jim said through dry lips. The cap hung loosely on his head, which had shrunken with the ravages of his illness. Why hadn't she gotten it signed? It was the least she could have done. "All this time, I could've been asking about the Rebels."

"But then we wouldn't have time to listen to Ella and Billy and Count Basie, would we?"

Debbie gave her a look, making it clear she'd much prefer some Rebels gossip. "Was it romantic?"

"What?"

"The wedding!"

"Oh, that. It was Vegas. Glam, quick, unexpected." Not romantic, except for what he called her.

Peaches.

She squeaked.

"You okay?"

"Fine! Absolutely fine. So tell me about the birthday party? Who showed?" As Debbie filled her in on Jim's party, Georgia's mind strayed to that night.

Peaches. That's what you are.

He'd called her that last night—and *that* night. What did

he mean by that? Since then, he'd mostly called her princess, a way to demean her, assess her uselessness. Put her in her place.

As Debbie launched into a recap of Jim's party, Georgia decided that maybe not remembering that night clearly was its own sort of blessing.

13

BANKS

Forgot to tell you the alarm code.

PEACHES

For the house?

BANKS

Going to call you. Pick up.

THE PHONE RANG four times before she answered.

"Hello?"

"Three-two-three-nine."

"That's it? Why didn't you just text it?"

Sighing, he leaned back against the headboard in his Dallas hotel room and adjusted the ice pack on his shoulder. "Because I don't want it written down. You need to memorize it."

"Okay, three-three-three-nine."

"Three-*two*-three-nine. It's Gretzky's point total."

"Who?"

Give me strength. "Wayne Gretkzy, the Great One? The GOAT?"

"A goat?"

"Greatest of All Time. The GOAT. He's a hockey player."

"Oh, good for him. Let me grab a pen."

"Don't write it down. If you forget, you can just look up 'Wayne Gretzky points total'."

"Hmm. So if I've inputted the wrong digits, I shouldn't panic while the alarm counts down my failure but should instead take the time to do a Google search for Gray Wetzky's hockey stats. Gotcha."

He growled.

She laughed, and *zing*, there it was. The ice had started working its magic, but with the debut of that sexy laugh, he'd need another cold pack for his dick.

"Repeat the number back to me."

"I'll look it up later. How's your trip? How's Dex?"

Why the fuck was she asking about him? "We have a game tomorrow night and O'Malley's acting like we've already won the Cup."

"I heard from Tara that he got off with a plea deal *and* made up with Ashley. He must be so happy."

Yeah, insufferably so. He'd also latched onto Banks at a time when Banks did not need the trouble. His shoulder still hurt, and it was easier to hide his pain when he didn't have to talk to anyone or do more than grunt during a conversation. It was bad enough he was rooming with chatty Tate Kazminksi, one of the Rebels D-men. A total gossip hound, he had a million questions about Georgia, all of which were met with Banks's brand of chat-withering silence.

Now he was alone, having cried off going out with the guys because he needed to rest up and focus ahead of the game tomorrow. He also had some financial stuff to do, analyzing the last quarter returns for his brokerage accounts. Better he do it instead of handing it off to some finance bro who would get an easy commission for following Banks's very specific instructions.

"As long as O'Malley's good mood transfers to the ice, then he can be as happy as he wants."

"Aw, what a friend you are!"

Sarcasm noted. "The guy fucked up, then got a woman to make it all better by saying kind things about him to a judge."

"Someone sounds jealous."

"Nope. Just continually amazed at how some guys work the system."

"By 'work the system,' do you mean, 'fall in love'?" She chuckled. "Quit being so grumpy and let him have his moment."

So he was a cantankerous old coot. O'Malley's trajectory was on the up: playing well, finding love, getting away with murder. Banks might be a touch envious at how the kid's life was shaping up when his own was in the toilet.

"He keeps talking to me. Asking for advice about how to manage his energy levels in the business end of the season."

Sleep, kale smoothies, and more sleep.

Georgia cooed. "He looks up to you! You have all this experience, so of course he's going to come to you. You've been at this game forever."

Yep. Banks the Dinosaur, heading for extinction.

He was tempted to ask her what she was up to, maybe what she was wearing. This marriage gig should have some perks. But the other night, she'd walked out of the kitchen when he told her that they'd connected in Vegas. That their marriage had to have *some* foundation. She had assured him it was a mistake and drawn her line in the sand.

Guess that answered that. They would be all business from here on out.

"So what's the code?"

She made an exasperated sound. "Good night, Banks."
Good night, Peaches.

BANKS WAS in line at the hotel breakfast buffet when the Rebels captain, Vadim Petrov, cut in.

"I want a waffle." *I vant a vaffle.*

"Have at it, Cap."

Petrov leaned over and used the tongs to pluck three waffles from the stack. Cheeky. "You ready for tonight?"

"As I'll ever be."

The aristocratic Russian gave a somber nod. "How is married life treating you?"

"We're doing this now?"

Petrov looked amused. "Merely an enquiry after your relationship status."

"Not sure why everyone's so interested."

Several "news" outlets had been in touch, looking to do a joint interview with the new couple. Even the Rebels own PR machine wanted to run a feature on them. Worst of all, Georgia's high value status as a media property meant her Greatest Hits were on a comeback tour. Like the time she splish-splashed in Buckingham Fountain. Or did the Polar Plunge in a tutu. Or covered herself in mud at Coachella to protest climate change.

The new attention meant that the sports media, who until now had treated his journeyman career with the distance it deserved, were suddenly interested in him. Did he trade to Chicago to be with his wife? (Like he had a choice.) Was Georgia excited about the playoffs? (She barely knew they existed.) Did he think the Rebels would renew his contract at the end of the season? (Now, that was a question he'd like to know the answer to.) Having spent the last sixteen years under the radar, his privacy-craving self was not enjoying this.

"People like the new and shiny," Petrov said. "It will die down."

"Can't happen soon enough."

He filled up his plate and took a seat at the table, only to be joined by O'Malley a minute later. Barely had he put a piece of bacon in his mouth and the kid was off to the races.

"Mind if I ask a question, dude?"

"Yes."

"You seem to have your shit together."

Banks chewed his bacon and waited.

"You own a house in Nashville, right?"

"Rented out."

O'Malley nodded. "And you probably know all about the league pension plan, like how that works."

He put down his fork. "What's on your mind?"

"I have responsibilities now. Ashley and Willa. And with a bit of luck, more people to look after. Like a new baby when Ash is ready. My mom, too."

O'Malley's mother was an ex-con who had recently re-entered his life. Sounded primo sketch, but then this was O'Malley, the sketchiest player in the league.

"Play for ten years, get a pension. It's pretty simple."

"Yeah, but what if I want to do other things? Like buy a house? Or set up an education whatsit for Willa? I've got a couple of million in my checking account, and I think maybe I could be making it work better for me."

Jesus. "You keep all your money in your checking?"

"Yeah. I tried to open an investment account, but I didn't know which stocks to buy. Like Apple is good, right? And Google?"

"It's Alphabet."

"What is?"

"Google's parent company. You need a financial advisor. You can pay people to help you make these decisions. Who'll do it for you." Not that Banks trusted anyone else. He handled his mom's and Connie's finances. His sisters' as well, because they were always asking him where they should put their money. He had trusts set up for his nieces. He hired someone to do his taxes because you didn't fuck with the IRS.

"Can you recommend someone?"

"If I do, will you shut up so I can eat my breakfast?"

O'Malley grinned. "I might."

If only it were that easy. Next up in the torture cycle was Hudson Grey, who took a seat and sent a significant glance at O'Malley. After several painful seconds of silent yet urgent conversation between them, Grey finally spoke up.

"Heard Georgia moved in with you." At Banks's glare, he added, "Tara said."

The gossip machine was in peak form, oiled by the hair stylist/GM's wife combo of Tara Fitzpatrick.

"And this is your business because?"

O'Malley took the baton. "When she walked into the Net and told you that the divorce didn't take, you seemed pissed about it. From where Grey and I stood, it looked like you were ripping her a new one."

Banks mentally squirmed, not liking how that sounded. That night in the Empty Net, he'd been annoyed. Not because they were still married, but because he'd liked the idea a little too much. Here she was, dangling this carrot of potential in front of his greedy mouth and he was chasing after it like a cartoon donkey.

Banks offered a noncommittal, "It's complicated."

O'Malley's eyes turned shrewd. "So you're giving it a second chance?"

"Yep."

The kid's mouth dropped open, like this was the best news ever. People in love were always advocating for its myriad benefits to the single losers of their acquaintance. "That's fantastic. Georgia's a hard woman to pin down and here you are—"

"What do you mean she's a hard woman to pin down?"

"She's been engaged before."

The rock star from Bison, Keaton something, though "rock" was a complete misnomer and "star" had never been more wrong. They broke up in a public fight at some nightclub. Another top ten Georgia viral moment.

"Your point?"

"That she didn't go through with it before, but she did with you."

Sure, *way* more meaningful. He took a sip of coffee. He hoped she set the alarm, but maybe she didn't care because she was out with friends or at an all-night party, doing Georgia things with Georgia people. He could check her social media, see if she was being mentioned anywhere, but that sounded like weirdo stalker behavior.

Fuck. He needed to focus on his game and that meant not wondering what Georgia was doing or why she had broken engagements littered in her past. It also meant not imagining her pretty mouth and all the places he wanted it on his body.

"Listen, I don't want to hear a word against her. Understood?"

"Are you kidding?" O'Malley grinned. "Georgia's a great girl. So she's not the best neighbor. Those parties were mighty loud ..." At Banks's glare, he changed his tune. "You're protective of her."

"She's my—" He broke off, restarted. "She might have been featured in gossip rags before, but I don't want anyone having a go at her while she's with me." *Or because of me.* "Are people talking?"

"You mean, the guys?" Grey looked around as if expecting to find their teammates in a good ole gossip right this minute. No one was paying them any mind. "They're surprised, that's all."

Don't ask. "Why?"

O'Malley looked skeptical. "You and Georgia do *not* seem like the most obvious couple."

"Like you and the kitten wrangler."

"I suppose from the outside we might seem like a weird pairing. But Ashley is perfect and she's perfect for me. Why, has someone said something?"

Theo Kershaw plunked his ass down beside Grey. "No one's talking about you or your woman, Oh-Em-Gee. You met at the puppy pound. Big whoop. And Hudster here met his guy on an app, like the rest of the world in this millennium. Banks and Georgia, though? Their origin story is a thousand times more interesting."

"The shelter was a good place to meet. Gave us a chance to get to know each other." O'Malley winced. "Not that you don't know Georgia, Banks."

"Good one, Dexter." Kershaw shook his head in disapproval.

But the kid was right. Banks didn't know her. They'd done this whole thing ass backwards. If he'd asked Georgia out on a date, she sure as hell would not have accepted. He was far too old for her, not to mention cynical, broody, and set in his ways.

The media and his teammates might be enamored of this strange pairing for now, but they wouldn't be surprised when it came to its natural and inevitable conclusion.

And neither would Banks.

14

Banks opened the front door and stood stock-still.

No beep from the alarm.

He dropped his gym bag in the foyer and listened.

The house felt different. Alive. Something brushed by his leg and gave a plaintive mewl. As Banks's instincts were completely off lately, he did the wrong thing.

Picked it up.

Amber-green eyes blinked back at him. "Hey, where's your momma?"

He shouldn't be touching him, but the ball of fur looked positively terrified when he tried returning him to the floor. Banks wasn't sneezing yet, and hopefully, he could keep the creature isolated so it wouldn't be an issue. Telling her he was allergic wouldn't go over well. People loved their animals and he needed to keep her happy.

Holding Cheddar at arm's length, he walked into the living room.

Georgia lay sprawled on the sofa, front down. Her laptop was open, frozen on an image of a smiling girl. Like Georgia, but not her.

One of the cashmere blankets that were usually draped over the armrest covered her left side. On her upper half, she wore a green flannel shirt, which looked familiar. But none of that was responsible for his spiking pulse and the tug of desire in his groin.

That honor went to the rounded ass cheek on display, bisected by lacey white fabric, the perfect *welcome home, Banks.* He had no problem imagining his rough hand touching that soft skin, his fingers delving into the cleft where he'd find her tight, hot, and wet.

She moved in her sleep, and startled to be caught perving, he dropped the cat. Its unappreciative screech echoed to the ceiling. Georgia jerked awake.

"What?" She turned over, twisting her body up in the throw, hiding all that silky skin. "Banks?"

"The cat made a noise."

She blinked and rubbed her eyes. "Where is he?"

"Ran off to the kitchen. Why aren't you in bed?"

"What time is it?"

"Five in the morning. I just got in."

She stretched, which pushed her hard nipples against the T-shirt she was wearing beneath the open flannel. It said "Lurie Children's Hospital" inside a big pink heart and looked lived-in and soft against her perky, braless tits.

"You won your games."

"Won one, lost one." Dallas went well, LA not so much, and he'd barely slept a wink on the redeye back.

Her nose twitched. "I didn't want to mention the loss. But the sports people said you guys will likely make the playoffs anyway, so that's good!"

"Yeah, it is. Why didn't you put on the alarm?"

She looked toward the foyer. "I was worried I'd set it off."

"It's not that complicated."

She shrugged. "Cheddar looks after me."

"The badass that ran to the kitchen when I dropped him?"

"You dropped him?"

Because I saw your ass cheek playing peek-a-boo and it was more than my insured-for-millions hands could handle.

"He's fine. Not the most reliable security, though." He took a seat at the end of the sofa beside a pile of white index cards. The top one was titled "Hockey Rules" beneath which was written in a flowery script: *No kicking the puck into the goal,* followed by: *stupid.*

He rubbed his mouth to hide his smile. It was kind of stupid. "How were the last few days here?"

"Quiet. I cooked a little. Nothing major, just eggs and salads." Her blush was lovely yet mystifying. Was she embarrassed about her cooking skills? "And I explored the house."

"Took a while, I'd wager."

She laughed. "Yep. A few days but Cheddar made a great walking companion. You have a lot of suits."

She'd been in his room. He wasn't sure how he felt about that; he certainly didn't need cat hair all over his bed linen. "Worried I'm cutting into your closet space needs?"

"Just surprised you're such a fashionista."

The cat had returned and decided to now crawl over his lap. He kind of liked how warm it felt, like it was an extension of Georgia.

Her warm little pussy. Georgia straddling him with her soft, damp heat ...

Less than thirty seconds in, and he was turning hard while a creature he was allergic to dug its claws into his thigh.

Distraction needed. He nodded at the laptop. "Is that your sister?"

"Yeah, our 21st birthday party. Just reminiscing." She closed the laptop and smiled at him. Kind of fake, though.

"How about some breakfast?" he asked.

"Don't you want to go to bed?"

"Bed?"

She covered her mouth. "Not with me! I'm guessing you must be tired after your trip."

"I can stay up for a bit to eat."

"Sounds good." Another smile, less forced this time. "Could you grab those PJs?"

He passed over a pair of sleep shorts and headed into the kitchen to give her privacy. He was absolutely wrecked, his shoulder was killing him, and he had definitely bruised a couple of ribs in the LA game, but something about seeing Georgia crashed out on the sofa, falling asleep to memories of her dead sister, gave him pause.

He couldn't imagine losing one of his siblings. It was bad enough losing his dad in Iraq when he was sixteen. But a twin, someone with whom you'd shared space in your mother's womb? That had to have crushed her. No wonder she went a bit wild.

Maybe this marriage was a symptom of her grief. If that was the case, he wasn't sure he was the right person to heal her. That kind of trauma didn't get fixed overnight.

She came into the kitchen, the flannel pulled across her chest so he couldn't see those pretty little nipples poking through.

He grabbed a couple of pods and mugs. "I probably should learn how you take your coffee."

"Half a Splenda, splash of skim. You?"

"Black."

"Of course."

But she drank herbal tea in the evening. He'd seen the mug on the coffee table.

He fixed the coffee and doctored it to her liking. She took

eggs, bread, and butter out of the fridge, but he laid a hand on her arm.

"Sit. I've got this."

"But you must be exhausted."

"Still buzzing from the trip."

She bit her lip. "Okay. Like I'm going to say no to a man who cooks." She took her coffee and sat at the table with one knee up to her chest, revealing the soft, smooth-looking skin of the back of her thigh. "So how are your friends taking your marital status?"

"My friends?"

"Your teammates."

He cracked the eggs into a bowl, added salt and pepper. Checking the fridge for milk, he found it full of new supplies —fruit, salads, things in plastic containers. Weird to see her stuff mixing with his. Weird but nice.

"They think it's hilarious. The press are asking dumb questions, too."

"Like what?"

He grabbed the whisk from the utensils jar. "Did I push for the trade to be with you? How do I get along with your parents? What's our favorite nightclub? You know, perfectly normal queries for a hockey player after a game."

That made her smile. "Sorry?"

"Sure you are. What about you? Any teasing from your crew?"

"About what you'd expect, mostly about how drunk I must have been. Though Tara said we can't have been that bad, that the marriage clerk wouldn't issue a license if you're too trashed." She peeked up at him through the veil of her dark blonde lashes. He saw vulnerability there.

Were we that drunk, husband?

No, wife, we were not.

"My friend Oliver thinks I've betrayed our pact."

He paused the egg whisking. "Your pact?"

"Just this joke we have. If we're single at thirty, we should marry each other, so we're not left on the shelf."

Georgia's oldest friend, the guy from the party. He'd have to keep an eye on him.

"Known him a long time, then?" He turned away, not wanting to see any fondness cross her face.

"Since we were kids. Our parents are friends and we kissed once."

"When?" The word was out before he could claw it back.

"In third grade."

Relief warred with desire to wring this guy's scrawny little neck. "And he's been dining off that memory for years, I bet."

That made her laugh. "Sure. Oliver's dating someone, so nothing to worry about there."

"And you're married."

He faced her, needing to see how that affected her. A blush, which was so damn perfect it made his dick twitch.

"I am."

He should *not* enjoy the sound of that.

A few minutes later, he served up scrambled eggs on toast and orange juice.

She blinked at the plates, then met his gaze. "This is lovely, Banks. Thank you."

"You're welcome." It was only breakfast, but he got the impression Georgia didn't allow herself much in the way of simple pleasures, just complicated ones. He was tired enough to drop, but it was worth delaying his bedtime if it meant giving her this one small thing.

After he'd eaten a few mouthfuls, he picked up his coffee

cup and took a sip. "How come you were sleeping on the sofa?"

"I was watching *Suits*." At his blank look, she explained. "It's this show about New York lawyers with Meghan Markle, now Her Royal Highness Meghan. Anyway, it's a comfort watch. Hot suits, competence porn, and sizzling romance. It was Dani's favorite show."

He remained silent, giving her room to open up, which she took after a moment.

"She had this huge crush on the guy who plays Harvey Specter and for her birthday, I got her this giant cardboard cutout that I had to courier to him in LA to get him to sign it. I was hoping he'd come to the party, but he was filming a movie in Hungary."

"Sounds like a cool gift all the same."

Georgia laughed. "Oh, it was. Kind of silly but what do you get the girl who has everything? Money's no object except— well, it can't fix your health. Not Dani's anyway. So silly gifts were the way to go. Mom thought it was ridiculous, but she didn't get it. No one did."

"Not silly if it meant a lot to her."

"True." She finished chewing a mouthful of eggs. "For my gift, she took me to a karaoke bar, which is kind of absurd because I'm an awful singer. She couldn't do as much as me because she got tired so easily, but that was something we could do together. She had a list of things she wanted to do before—" She shook her head. "We just rented the room and sang our hearts out."

"Song?"

"'Juice' by Lizzo! The gift was to me after all." She smiled. "Last night, after a couple of episodes of *Suits*, I dialed up the old home video. Good times."

"How long since she's been gone?"

"A little over two years. It's getting easier, though."

"Is it?"

"That's what they say, right?" She crumpled up her napkin, then straightened it out again.

"Different for everyone. When my dad died, it took a while. It's been twenty years and I still think about him, wish he was here."

"Did he see you play?"

"Not professionally. I was sixteen when he passed, but he knew I was good. That it was my future."

She nodded. "That must be very reassuring. To know what you want."

He hadn't thought of it like that. "It can be, but there's also a certain tunnel vision associated with that kind of career path. My mom always says 'do what you love, love what you do'. I knew I wanted to play hockey, that I loved it, but once my dad died, I also saw it as a way to ensure my family was provided for. That no one would go hungry."

"That's amazing, Banks."

His family were grateful, that was for sure. Securing their future had always felt like the most important goal, and now that he had, he itched for something else. Something for himself.

Typical thoughts for a guy in the twilight of his career. What came next?

Who came next?

He'd assumed he would find a woman who had baby making and cookie baking on her mind. She'd be a hockey fan, a few years younger but still in her child-bearing prime. Maybe an elementary schoolteacher. Someone with similar life goals.

For all his insistence that he and Georgia had forged a connection that night, how much sense did that really make?

The real reason he'd been drawn to her was more likely a pathetic attempt to have her youth and vibrancy rub off on him. Steal some of the glow for his elderly self.

What had she seen in him? He didn't have charm like Kershaw or O'Malley, or good looks like Petrov or the Durands. No doubt she had explained it away to her friends with a tale of another crazy Georgia escapade.

I was absolutely trashed and managed to get myself hitched to this lecherous old dude. You wouldn't believe what I have to suffer to keep in the good books of Mommy and Daddy.

He sought a change of subject. "So what else was on your sister's list?"

"Travel was a big one. We took a trip to the Grand Canyon a couple of months before she died. She wanted to hike it, but she wasn't strong enough, so we did a helicopter tour instead, which was amazing. We took in some of the best views from the South Rim. Have you been?"

"Once when I was a kid. One of the coolest days I had with my dad." He hadn't thought about that in a long time.

"It's funny how these memories sear into our consciousness, isn't it?"

"Life's highlight reel. Even if you don't remember them clearly, the feeling stays with you."

Her eyes brightened. "Right. Like the karaoke, which thankfully I have a record of."

"I'll need to see that."

She shook her head vehemently. "Nope. It's in the Twin Vault. With the sex stuff."

"The sex stuff?"

She blushed. "We shared everything, but there were always things she wouldn't get a chance to do. I was her proxy, in a way." He must have looked baffled. "She couldn't do overly physical things or anything that got her heart beating too fast. So I would go a little wild on her behalf."

He was still hung up on the sex stuff comment. "Like what?"

"Sneak backstage at a concert. That's how I met Keaton at the Bison gig. Crash a wedding—I've done that a couple of times. Stay the night in a museum. Skinny dipping in Lake Michigan. I was cited for that one."

She chuckled softly as a fond memory took hold. "Mom and Dad were so worried Dani would get more sick, but it was what she wanted. Just to be free of all the poking and prodding. She always knew she could go at any minute, so we were determined to make sure she had as much fun as possible. Sometimes we played pranks."

"Oh yeah?"

Her laugh was music. "Switching sugar for salt, changing all the male photos in the house to Bruce Springsteen, rubber scorpion in Dad's coffee mug. The classics."

"You'd better not try that on me."

A mischievous look crossed her lovely features. "But as we got older, we wanted to do more adult things. Like go to bars with fake IDs and borrow the Merc for a little spin, which unfortunately Dani crashed into the pillar at the end of the driveway. I took the blame because Dad would've killed us if he knew Dani was driving without a license. Sometimes, she was too tired, so she'd encourage me to go out and do my own thing, but text her constantly to keep her updated. She couldn't smoke or drink or"—she averted her eyes—"do anything that might be considered dangerous to her health, so I was a bad girl for two. She got to live vicariously through me for a while."

"And what did your parents think of all this rebellion?"

"Rebellion is such an old-fashioned way to describe it. It

was more a sisterly gift." She crumpled up the napkin, smoothed it out again. "And after she was gone, I'd sometimes find myself doing something a little crazy in her memory. This one's for Dani, I'd say, which was really an excuse for bad behavior. When I was arrested for borrowing a horse during Lolla, it was the last straw for my parents. They cut off my allowance and said I had to get my act together. I was so mad at them. I had some savings, so I moved into Castle Apartments and carried on with my life."

Her partying, wild-child life. Only now she needed their money again because being poor, or Georgia's version of it, must suck. "Is that what Vegas was about?"

Her eyes flew wide. "Getting married?"

He nodded. Waited. Wished like hell he hadn't asked because it sounded like he was hurt.

"You think I married you as a 'screw you' to my parents?"

"It crossed my mind."

She hissed in a breath. "That's a pretty dickish thing to say."

It was, and that critique should have been the signal for him to shut the fuck up. He was never good at listening to that inner voice.

"You said yourself you weren't that drunk. But I'm guessing that buyer's remorse kicked in good and hard the next morning."

Marrying a guy like him would make the perfect revenge against the parents who cut her off—or that might have been her first thought until she realized that even *that* went too far for wild child Georgia. Once her parents found out, she figured she had to keep it up because the Goodwins weren't going to put her back on the company payroll if it looked like she was still up to her old tricks.

She stood quickly. "Well, it looks like my first instinct in leaving that hotel room was absolutely correct." After which she left *this* room without a backward glance.

Only as she walked out did he realize why the flannel she wore was so familiar. It was the one he'd given her that night in Vegas. To keep her warm.

After they got married.

Fuck.

15

Georgia turned to Cheddar, who had just curled up on her bed.

"What the hell happened there?"

Banks had asked if that was what Vegas was about. What *they* were about.

Her parents were the last people on her mind when she tripped down that aisle. No, she was thinking purely of herself. Of this one, precious thing that would be for her. Not for Dani. Not in service to the Goodwin family-industrial complex.

For me.

So it was a mistake. As soon as she woke up, her hangover and her trip-hammering heart told her she needed to backspace the hell out of it. She might not have done it for Dani, but grief had certainly factored into it. Two years without her sister, and Georgia was still trying to figure out how to stand on her own. Marrying a stranger was not the way. It wasn't fair on Banks, either, using him like that.

His accusation stung, but there was more to it. Since reconnecting with him, she'd picked up on a vibe. He was angry, not so much about the incomplete annulment, but the cowardly way she handled it. Neither did he approve of her mercenary motivation for staying married. And here he was again, testy about her supposed reasons for marrying him in the first place.

It was as if he ... *liked her*?

She squirmed on the bed. That could not be right. But at the mention of Oliver and their joke wedding pact, his huge shoulders had tensed.

Her heart beat wildly at the thought. *Don't get ahead of yourself. He just wants you to be an adult about it instead of a scaredy cat.*

She wasn't one to let a fight linger. Time to fix this. On her way downstairs, she passed by his bedroom with its open door, just as he exited the en suite bathroom in a towel.

But it wasn't the rippling muscles, broad shoulders, and perfect sprinkling of chest hair that got her attention. Neither was it the taut abs, thick thighs, or the lazy way he pushed his hand through his wet hair.

She would have thought all those things wonderful if her gaze wasn't instantly drawn to the bruise over his ribs.

"Oh my God, what happened to you?"

His eyes flashed, but he remained silent, so she pressed further.

"Did that happen in a game?"

"It's nothing." He rolled his shoulder, like that Henry Cavill move in *Mission Impossible*, which is when she noticed a bump at the top of it and even *more* bruising.

"And your shoulder?"

"It popped out a week back, but it's fine now."

Popped out? That sounded like something that should not happen to shoulders. And a week? That was the night he came to see her at her apartment—and she gave him a measly aspirin. Good job, Georgia!

She rushed in, not caring that she was invading his sanctum. "But it must really hurt."

"Sure, but athletes play hurt all the time. And the older you get the longer it takes to come back from a hit."

"Shouldn't you be on the injured list?" She'd read about that. Injured Reserve they called it, now on one of her flash cards. "Surely they don't expect you to play like this."

Her hand fluttered near his chest, not wanting to touch the bruise but needing to touch *him*. Her hovering fingertips, the ones that had yet to make chestfall, must have annoyed him. He grasped them and held her hand away from his skin.

"I have a few weeks, a couple months maximum left to the season, assuming we do well, and I can't miss it. This kind of thing is something I deal with. We all deal with."

This big, brave dummy. "You haven't told the team medics, have you?"

His thumb was on her wrist, rubbing back and forth. Soothing her when he was the one who needed comfort. "You worried about me?"

"Yes, I am! I need you intact so I can divorce you without guilt and people won't accuse me of abandoning my invalid husband."

Huffing what sounded like a laugh, he pulled her a little closer. "I like that you're worried about me."

"Well, you shouldn't. Because when I worry about people, I am all up in their business."

"And what form does this caretaking take? Gloopy pasta?"

"You said it was good!"

"I was trying to instill confidence in your housewifely duties." He squinted. "Listen, about what I said back there—"

She cut him off. "I've figured out why you got all crotchety."

"Oh yeah?"

Their joined hands were still suspended between them in no-man's land. She pressed back until they touched his chest, careful not to glance against his bruised flesh. God, the heat of him.

"I think you got all irritable, throwing your silly accusations around, because ... you like me."

"I do, huh?" More amusement. *Oh, laugh, Big Guy, laugh away.*

"Yep. You didn't enjoy the notion that I might have gone into our Vegas adventure with an agenda. Just like you were annoyed because I panicked and sent you those annulment papers without any discussion. You're the kind of man who doesn't like to be dismissed, and I haven't done a good job of giving you the attention you crave."

His lips *almost* curved. "I don't crave attention, Georgia. I just thought we could be adults about the divorce, that's all. I shouldn't have said that about your parents. That was below the belt."

"Is there a reason why you went there?"

He sighed and took a moment to consider her question. "We're not the most obvious pair, are we? I'm a good deal older, don't enjoy the limelight, and am at a different place in my life. You're fresh and young and light up every room you're in." He shook his head. "Just stating the facts as I see them."

Her heart was all aflutter. They came from vastly different worlds, that was for sure. But that night, they had created a world purely for them.

"I'm sorry for being a jerk. Forgive me, Georgia."

Look at us being all mature. "I accept your apology, and I apologize if you ever felt unimportant, then or now. I know what that's like. I should have been more respectful, especially about the annulment. It just seemed like another one of my fuckups and I thought the faster I fix it, the less likely someone would find out. It wasn't a judgment on you or what happened. It was all about me. You get that, don't you?"

He stared at her, those gorgeous brown eyes changing to a warm whiskey hue.

"I get it."

The words were spoken gruffly, barely concealing a subtext she didn't quite understand. She would have questioned it, but she'd overstayed her welcome.

She drew back. Released his hand. Hated how it felt to not be wrapped in that heat and safety.

"Is there anything I can do to help?" She gestured at his body, then cringed on realizing how that sounded.

"Might be best if I got some sleep." His deep inhale drew her attention to his chest. Only this time she was focused on the sheer perfection of his physique rather than the darkened skin, badges of his pain.

Funnily enough, he was also caught up in the staring contest.

"That shirt ..." His gaze raked over her. "Is *mine*."

Her Vegas souvenir. She might have worn it a couple of times since, another layer to keep the Chicago winter and grief at bay. It still carried his scent, something like cedar and citrus, though it was fading.

Now the way he was looking at her and how he uttered the word "mine" sent a bolt of lust through her.

"You gave it to me that night because I was cold." She pulled it off one shoulder. "You can have it back."

He shook his head, his gaze skimming her bare shoulder before he dragged it away. "You keep it as long as you need it."

"Thanks," she whispered with a shaky step back.

She didn't dare dip her gaze, so instead she backed out, doing her best *eyes-up-here*, conscious that one look at that barely knotted towel draped over those slim hips would have her drooling.

Or casting a spell to make it drop.

"Sleep well, Banks."

"Later, Georgia."

16

After a decent showing in Dallas and a not so sparkling perfor-mance in LA, the Rebels have to be asking themselves if the addi-tion of veteran center Dylan Bankowski is worth the money. He might be good at taking a team to the playoffs, but he's never been all that reliable in the home stretch. Despite these misgivings, Banks, one of the game's perennial bridesmaids, has played adequately for his new team considering he must be distracted by his abruptly more interesting home life. A young bride who craves so much attention has to be a tough proposition for a player past his prime. Let's hope, for the Rebels' sake, that the new Mrs. Bankowski lets her husband get his rest as the business end of the season wraps up.

— Curtis Deacon, *Chicago Tribune*

BANKS TURNED the heat down on the stove and checked the team's text thread, which could usually be relied upon to conduct a thorough analysis of the hockey media's latest hot take.

KERSHAW

That Deacon fucker. Bast should have laid him out properly when he had a chance.

BABY DURAND

Ignore him. It's just click-bait.

KAZ

Still, Banks, make sure you get plenty of naps over the next few days.

KERSHAW

Hey, let the guy enjoy his honeymoon.

DURAND SENIOR

They got married months ago. The honeymoon has to be over by now. Right, Banks?

O'MALLEY

Is this what we do on the text thread? Trash talk a fellow player?

Banks grunted. *Don't need your defense, kid.*

BOND

O'Malley, Banks is a big boy and your participation in this group text is probationary. Read the room before you try moving the furniture.

That made Banks smile.

BANKS

Are we still on for cards at Hunt's place tomorrow?

THE SWEDE

Someone is trying to change the subject. I'm making kroppkakor right now. I can bring it over for cards.

Sounds like shit, but we'll give it a go.

"What's cooking?"

Georgia appeared at the entrance to the kitchen in those sleep shorts from this morning, the neckline of her sweatshirt slipping to reveal a creamy-skinned shoulder. The one Banks had been dreaming about since she tried to remove his shirt and give it back.

He needed that shoulder covered, preferably with one of his jerseys. His flannel would do in a pinch.

"Tacos. Plenty for two." Cheddar brushed against his leg and Banks dropped a tiny morsel of cooked ground turkey to the floor, where the little guy lapped it up. "Or three. Sorry, should've asked if it's okay to feed him."

"It's fine." Georgia moved closer, bringing her shoulder of temptation. "You make them with turkey?"

"This surprises you?"

"I'd have thought you need to eat tons of high calorie foods to keep up your energy levels."

"I do. But I also have a specific diet to follow that's mostly healthy."

It looked like she was filing that away.

"I don't want to take your taco meat away from you." She made a funny face. "That sounded weird, didn't it?"

He turned away to hide his smile. "Just a touch. And like I said, I'm making plenty for everyone. Even the stupid cat."

"He's not stupid."

On cue the orange-striped dummy bumped into a cupboard door, then jumped back like the door had done it on purpose.

Georgia shook her head. "He's just a little challenged. I thought you didn't like him, yet here you are feeding him."

"He keeps giving me the sad eyes and the meow-meow. Can't ignore it." He turned away, this time not to smile but to sneeze into his elbow.

"Bless you."

"Thanks." Washing his hands, he saw that Georgia had knelt to give the cat a quick pet. The move made her sweatshirt dip and reveal the valley between her breasts. She peered up, catching him in the act.

"You're not getting a cold, are you?"

"Just allergies. Pollen."

After their little dust-up this morning—which was down to him because he was a moody fucker—and that moment in his bedroom when she apologized for how she'd handled the annulment, he'd like to have said it eased any tension between them.

But that would be a bare-faced lie.

On the surface, they were easy as could be, so damn friendly that she could joke about Banks liking her. That's what she thought—ha, ha, very funny—so he needed to go with that.

She had spent the day out of the house, though he'd watched out his window as she placed a couple of gift bags in the trunk of her clown car, then lifted her fancy dress as she climbed into the driver's seat. He'd been living off that flash of gorgeous thigh all day.

"You want to help?"

"Me?"

"The cat's useless so you're on deck."

She swallowed, a nervy little move that made her slender throat bulge. "Where should I start?"

"I was thinking along the lines of taco fixings."

"You mean shred some cheese or something like that?"

She sounded excited at the prospect, like this matched her skillset exactly.

"There's cheddar and mozzarella in the fridge. Usually, I mix them for tacos. You could also cut up some red onion and limes."

"Definitely!" She got busy pulling the raw ingredients out of the fridge while he directed her on the location of a cutting board and the box grater.

"And we could do margaritas! But maybe you don't do alcohol during the season, except on your wedding night, of course." The saucy wench winked at that. *Look at them, joking about their big mistake in Vegas.*

"I can do a margarita. Work on the cheese first."

"Si, señor!" She gave him a jaunty salute.

He continued browning the ground turkey, then added the taco seasoning and some water.

"You okay with cilantro?"

"Love it."

"My sister April is one of those weirdos who thinks it tastes like soap."

"Oh, Dani was like that too. I used to think she was faking it until I read an article about it. They can't help being weird. It's genetic."

He scoffed. "April can. She's weird about everything. Won't let her food touch on the plate. Won't share a bottle. The cilantro thing is definitely on brand for her."

"There's one in every family."

He waited a moment, letting the silence settle. It felt nice working side by side.

"How do you get along with yours?"

He felt her stiffen. Georgia hadn't mentioned her parents much except to say continuing this was needed to impress them. Maybe that said it all. The vibe at that gala was definitely off.

"Oh, not too bad. I'm a bit of a strange duck as far as they're concerned."

"How so?"

"They have certain expectations for me. Contributing to the family, upholding the name. I don't really fit into their plans."

"And what are their plans?"

"Have me become the face of one of their many companies. Or chair of a charity foundation they approve of. Failing that, marry someone in their circle."

Like that Oliver douche. "Well, that last one's off the list."

He was supposed to add *for now* to that, but he didn't have it in him.

"I know it seems kind of frivolous not to be more ... useful."

"I didn't say that."

She smiled. "You didn't have to. It's okay. A life like mine is always going to look suspect to someone who works so hard."

"How do you know I work hard?"

"I looked it up online. Theo Kershaw has a huge Insta following, and he's always talking about his diet and his exercise regimen and all the skating practices. If you're doing half of that, then yeah, you're working your ass off."

At his age, he was working twice as hard as Kershaw. But did she have to look at Superglutes's videos to learn this?

"The playoffs start soon. Assuming we qualify, you can come to a game. If you want."

"Fantastic! Maybe I'll ask Tara if I can sit with her."

"She's married to the GM, so she usually sits in the owner's box." That would be more Georgia's speed. Barely watching the game, surrounded by luxury.

She blinked. "Okay. And that way you can keep your tickets for your family."

Like he wouldn't find one for his wife?

They carried on in silence until he declared the taco filling ready. She whipped up the margaritas in a martini shaker. After heating tortillas, he filled a couple with lettuce, taco meat, tomatoes, onions, cheese, and sour cream. "Hot sauce here, if you need it."

"Definitely. I'm betting those tacos are white-guy mild."

"Maybe try it first."

Ignoring his advice, she added hot sauce to the filling and lifted the entire taco to her mouth. "Let's see what you're made of."

She chewed. Turned red. Reached for her margarita and downed it in one go.

"Easy there."

"This ... is ... hot!"

"I told you to try it first before adding more sauce."

"I thought you were exaggerating! I have a high tolerance, but this is outrageous."

"Just a couple of chopped chilis. Nothing *I* can't handle." He added more hot sauce to prove it, then took a bite. The flavors danced on his tongue, gave a burn, numbed him up, then tripped merrily on their way. "Perfect."

"Is that a challenge?"

"No. That would be childish."

Grabbing the hot sauce, she held it aloft and dabbed a few drops on her taco.

"Not sure that's a good idea," he murmured.

"That's what the second margarita is for." While she took a bite, he poured the drink for her and passed it over. Panting, she downed a huge gulp and grinned like she'd won a prize. "Good. Tacos."

This was the girl he met in Vegas. The fearless woman who saw nothing as an obstacle, not even a grouchy asshole like him.

"Ease up there, princess."

"You think that's funny, don't ya?"

"Just calling it how I see it."

"Privileged, pampered, spoiled."

He blew out a sigh. "You have a trust fund, Georgia. You throw parties for a living. And you asked me not to divorce you so you could keep the cash flowing."

She snatched a quick breath and waved a hand casually. "So you have my number, Big Guy."

He'd hurt her feelings. Yet he couldn't come up with a way to apologize that didn't sound like he was accepting of her life strategy.

They continued eating with Georgia sipping on her margarita. Once she'd finished her second taco, she hopped up with the plate.

"That was great. Thanks for cooking." She took the plate to the sink and started to run the water.

"Georgia, you don't have to do this."

"Why? Because a spoiled princess like me couldn't possibly know how? So tell me, what does this do?" She held up the dish soap. "Or this?" Next, a wave of the scrubbing brush.

"Georgia."

"What? You were only telling the truth as you see it."

"And this would be your turn to tell me the truth as *you* see it."

"Ah, so you need me to justify why I live my life this way." She shook her head, almost pitying. "I don't owe you an explanation for a thing. We both have our reasons for why we're staying married. At least I'm honest about mine. You say you're doing it to save face; only you don't seem like the kind of guy who cares what anyone thinks."

He brought his plate to the sink. "You really care that much about my motives?"

"Nope."

"Liar. You're furious because I won't spill my guts."

She scoffed. "Well, it is like pulling teeth. You weren't like this in Vegas. You were much chattier then."

"Hardly."

"You must have been because there's no way I would have married ... this!"

He moved in closer. "We both know why you married me."

"Please spill."

"Because no one had ever kissed you as good as I did. No one had ever held you as tightly as I did. And no one had ever made you feel like the only girl in my world."

She gasped, the perfect audible cue to the heart beating in his chest.

Why the fuck did I say that?

Why the fuck did I even think *that?*

He was just goading her, trying to get her to admit that there was a reason she said yes. They'd connected that night. Something crazy and magical had happened, and for it to have meant nothing at all ... that just didn't fly with him.

17

THE ONLY GIRL in my world.

Rihanna was onto something. To have a man treat you that way was more than comforting ... it was everything. And to have Banks—close-mouthed, hot-lipped, bear-grunts-are-my-love-language Banks—admit it was a shock that Georgia had no idea what to do with.

Stunned stupid, she turned away to the sink.

"You have a pretty high opinion of those arms and lips, Mister. Powerful enough to make me lose all inhibition and marry you, you say?"

"We weren't drunk. From what I can see you can hold your liquor."

He sounded closer, almost on top of her. If she turned, she'd end up right in his arms. Better not to risk it. They needed to keep the lines clear between them.

Let him call her princess, spoiled, whatever made sense to him.

Let her think one too many drinks had blurred his decision-making to the point a man as closed off as Banks would marry a bona fide mess like Georgia.

She didn't want him to come up with valid reasons to be married. Such as he wanted her so much that he had to have her for his own. Or that he saw something in her that she couldn't quite see in herself. Why else was she throwing out playground taunts of "you like me"? Because the joke carved out space between them, distance she needed so she wouldn't make a mistake.

She'd made so many in her life.

Yet she'd never forget that feeling of waking in that vise of a grip, the scent of him in her lungs, the heat of him warming her through. And here she was within fingertips' reach—she could have all that again. She could take something for her own.

She turned. He was close but not quite as much as she'd expected. Giving her space, perhaps, to make some bad decisions all by herself.

"You think I'm going to admit I wanted this to happen? That this marriage isn't a fluke?"

"Wouldn't expect you to admit a thing, Peaches." He placed an arm at her side, hand on the counter, barely an inch from her waist.

She jumped at the opportunity to deflect. "You called me that before. Why?"

His mouth twitched. "That's what I thought the second I saw you. Princess Peach."

"From the video game?"

He nodded. "Then you said your name was Georgia. And your skin, damn, it felt as soft as the skin of a peach."

His fingertips on her arm as he guided her down the strip ...

"But you usually defer to princess."

"Formal title, your majesty."

He was closer now. She could feel him everywhere and he had yet to touch her.

"All you have to do is tell the truth." His whisper was a seductive cajole.

He'd held her hand, callused against her peach-soft skin, and she'd tripped into that marriage license office, giddy as a schoolgirl.

This is crazy, she'd thought.

Go with your gut, Dani told her.

Her dead sister's fault. Of course.

In the breath-stealing space between them, she placed a hand on his chest. He said no one had ever kissed her so good. Maybe that explained it.

"You really think your mouth made me see God, Banks?"

He smirked. Oh, she would show him angels weeping!

Her hand stroked up, heading for his neck, needing to get a grip because her knees were already starting to falter. Something preternatural in him acknowledged this; his hand curled around her hip and pulled her close. For a moment they stared at each other while realization dawned.

She was too short. He would have to lean down or—

Scoop her up and onto the counter. With a quick pivot, her ass landed softly on the granite, the surface cool to the backs of her thighs but not enough to bank the fires within her.

A sultry gasp escaped her as his palms splayed on her thighs and forced them apart. One hand curled around her bottom and pulled her close. In this position, she looked down on him; he peered up at her.

Still his lips refused to meet hers. Infuriating.

"Worried you can't take me to the stratosphere again?"

A squeeze of her ass cheek was her punishment for that cheeky query, and then he moved in and brushed her lower lip with his mouth.

"I'll take you there, Georgia."

Please. This was what it felt like that night. This was the fizzy sensation she was trying to replicate.

Better this dangerous feeling than none at all.

She sighed into his mouth and finally let go of what was holding her back. No more jokes. No more denials. Just this onslaught of feeling.

Her surrender spurred him on. The kiss turned real. Gone were the tentative nibbles, timid brushes of lips. This was now an exploration of her mouth. She loved how good it felt, the spice of him, the scent of male flooding her nostrils.

His hand curled around her jaw, held her in place to be plundered. His beard scratched, heightened every sense. The kiss was better for it.

He pulled away, his lips wet and a touch puffy, and she wanted to dive back in and suck, on the lower lip particularly. She was panting and barely holding on.

"Is that why we married?" she finally managed.

"I think it's part of it."

He still held her, one hand at her neck, the other curved over her ass. That hand flexed, checking for fit. *Absolutely perfect*, she wanted to say.

"That's quite the superpower you have there, Big Guy. One kiss and 'here comes the bride'."

"It was your idea."

Her mouth fell open. "What?"

"We had just got done watching the Bellagio fountain—"

"Before or after the club?"

"After. You on that dance floor ... well, let's just say it did things to me."

"Lowered your inhibitions?"

His eyes glowed. "Something like that. We went for a walk, and you were excited about the fountain, some opera song."

"'Time to Say Goodbye,'" she said, the memory taking a clearer shape as it broke the surface. "Sarah Brightman and Andrea Bocelli."

"Right. And when it ended, you said, 'I don't want to say goodbye.'"

"I did?"

But she remembered. Every word.

His nod was solemn. "And I said, 'let's not. Let's keep going.'"

"Which I took as an invitation to get hitched?"

He considered that for a moment. "More like, neither of us wanted the night to be over. I think we were looking for a way to keep that feeling alive. Sometimes those feelings are your best guide."

Into hell. "We went to that bar, the small one behind the Palms."

Another nod. "And we had another drink and by the end of it, I think we knew. Neither of us wanted to return to ... before."

Before. For Georgia, that meant alone in a crowd, missing Dani all the time. For Banks, it meant ... she had no idea.

Because he wouldn't tell her. She had no idea what he was getting out of this.

"So we thought the very deliberate action of going to the marriage license place and finding someone to marry us was the next logical step? Instead of sex?"

She pushed back and slid off the counter, though he didn't let her do that alone. Not that she needed his help, but his hands held her steady at the waist as he guided her down. For a moment she enjoyed the fluttery sensation of being in the clouds, suspended inside some dream state where people fell in love and got married and it mattered.

Her feet hit the floor and reality rose up to meet her like a two by four.

"I know you want to think that this wasn't an accident, Banks. That a man as solid and sensible and straight-shooting as you wouldn't be stupid enough to hitch your star to someone you had just met. But that night, I was in a strange place. It had been two years since—since Dani died."

He sucked in a breath. "Georgia."

"And I think I went a little crazy. I wanted something for myself. Something to ease the pain." She placed a hand on his chest. "So you're right. It wasn't an accident because of too much alcohol or Nevada's ridiculously easy access to marriage licenses and wedding celebrants, though that didn't help. I was not in the right headspace to make such a big decision." At his parted lips, she held up her hand to stop him. "I know you weren't happy with how I handled the paperwork—both times. I'm sorry I was a coward. We should have discussed it, but it doesn't change the fundamentals. Neither of us fought for this. I set the annulment in motion, and you accepted it. This was a mistake, and once we've both allowed sufficient time to pass, we can get back to our separate lives."

For the second time that day, she walked out of the kitchen.

18

THEY QUALIFIED FOR THE PLAYOFFS.

Even better they qualified at home. They could begin the celebrations early without having to worry about being hungover on the plane ride back to Chicago.

O'Malley sidled up to Banks at the bar in the Empty Net, a big, stupid smile on his face.

"What gives?"

"We made it, man! The playoffs."

"You've made the playoffs before. We did it two years ago in Nashville."

"Yeah, but it's different this time." Meaning, Dex was different this time. He was in love and apparently, that made the air smell sweeter, food taste better, and the standard qualification for a knock-out contest where half the teams made par feel like he'd already won the Cup.

"How are your girls?" As well as a new girlfriend, O'Malley had landed a stepdad-in-all-but-name gig to Ashley's butterfly-obsessed daughter.

"Awesome. Ashley should be stopping by soon and Willa just sent me this photo." He showed his screen with a sweet photo of a kid wearing O'Malley's jersey and a huge grin that made Banks's teeth ache.

"Nice." He meant it, though he didn't especially enjoy that twinge in his chest. Banks didn't want O'Malley's life. He had plenty of people reaching out to wish him well—family, friends, former teammates. He wasn't alone.

O'Malley looked like he wanted to say something. Banks remained silent, hoping that was enough of a damper to the kid's efforts at bonding. Alas, no such luck.

"Where's Georgia?"

At home, not thinking about the kiss I laid on her.

Pity it was all Banks could think about. That was the problem with having a woman like Georgia in his life. She didn't make that life easier, and that's what he needed for the next two weeks and hopefully six weeks after that.

"We're not joined at the hip."

In truth, he'd been avoiding her, which should have been easy. The house was big, and she spent a lot of time out of it. His leaving early and coming home late, except for the odd check-in during the day, was working gangbusters to maintain the distance he needed for his game and his sanity.

Except there were whispers of her presence everywhere. Her stuff in the fridge, her scent in the foyer, and those damn affirmations on the mirrors. *I believe in myself* and *I am capable* and the most telling one of all: *I learn from my mistakes.*

Each day this week, he had come across a different message of encouragement on the fridge door, aimed at him, he supposed. *You can do this!* or *Today's Your Day!* or *Pressure is a Privilege!* (Sure thing, Billie Jean King.) If all he had to do was recite a bunch of dumb mantras, he'd have won the fucking Cup by now.

O'Malley tapped a finger on the bar. "Maybe you should

call her and ask her to join us? If anyone knows how to celebrate, it's Georgia."

True, the party girl would really dig this. Her husband?
Not so much. The last thing he needed was to watch his wife
whooping it up with this lot.

Banks stared him down and O'Malley dropped his gaze,
except he wasn't looking away because Banks intimidated him
but because Ashley had just walked in.

"Better hop to it, Dexter. Your owner's here."

O'Malley laughed. "Wearing the badge with pride,
brother. Later." Off he went, like a Golden Retriever looking
for a nice and vigorous pet down. Before he reached her and
no doubt greeted his woman with a kiss, Banks turned away.

He sure as hell did not need to be reminded of what he
didn't have, not when he was too hung up on what was in his
shaky possession.

A wife in name only.

A marriage with no benefits.

A partner for a financial arrangement.

Hers.

The playoffs started in three days, and Banks planned to
spend every one of them in the gym or on the ice—and
nowhere near his hot, far-too-young-for-him wife.

BANKS WAS TALKING TO A WOMAN.

It was early—okay, so it was after nine in the morning,
which was early for Georgia—and a female voice carried
through the house. Georgia crept down the stairs, skulking
her way toward the kitchen.

He stood against the island, coffee cup in hand, wearing
shorts (oh, Mama!) and a tee that shaped his pectorals to

perfection. The T-shirt said: *I walk on water. What's your superpower?*

Love!

"So what's she like? The old ball and chain?"

The voice came from his iPad, propped up on a stand. Georgia held back, curious about how Banks would describe her to someone else.

"Chatty. Blonde. Cute. Not your type."

"As if you know what my type is."

"Yeah, I do. Big-muscled volleyball players."

A dramatic sigh ensued. "I fucked *one* volleyball player ten years ago. Now I'm all about the nurturing woman, like my Amy."

"Where is your better half? I'd much rather talk to her."

"She's taking Scarlet to school, then chilling at a coffee shop because we drive her mad."

Someone else laughed. "That's what Jason says about me. He's soundproofing the man cave as we speak. But enough about that. We want to meet her!"

"You're coming to Chicago soon enough."

"And we can't wait." Yet another voice rang out.

These must be his sisters.

Georgia hadn't seen much of Banks over the last few days. He'd spent most of his time at practice or the gym, and then played a game last night that qualified the team for the playoffs. She'd written "CONGRATS!" on the magnetized notepad on the fridge and sent him a text with an iconic GIF of Julia Roberts fist-pumping in *Pretty Woman.*

He'd responded with a very succinct, and to her mind unnecessarily terse, "TY."

This shift in their dynamic was her fault. A few nights ago, they'd been making progress with tacos and talking, but then came The Kiss. A kiss so good that she had to ruin it with a reminder of reality. Georgia couldn't enjoy the fantasy on offer, Banks's amazing mouth and ass-clenching hand. No, she had to get into the weeds of the absurdity of their decision-making when it came to their marriage.

Banks hadn't liked that, probably because who wanted to be reminded of a rash decision?

Oh, you thought there was a good reason for this sham of a marriage? Think again, Big Guy. Tequila and fountains and grief, oh my!

Feeling like a creeper, she took a step forward, enough to tease a creak from the hardwood floor and make her presence known. Banks looked up and she waited for his disappointment or annoyance, especially after how they'd parted previously.

Neither came. Or maybe he was getting better at hiding his feelings around her.

"Morning."

"Hi!" She sounded squeaky. "I didn't mean to interrupt."

"No, it's perfect timing. Come meet the coven."

The coven? A wave of high-pitched protests sounded as Georgia moved in closer. The screen was split with three curious faces shining out at her.

"Don't mind him! Coven! I mean, really, D." The woman who spoke first was dark-haired with pixie features. "I'm April."

She recalled her Bankowski flash cards. *April: oldest sister, 33, married to Carlos, daughter Jenny, 3. Doesn't like cilantro. Weird about food touching on her plate.*

"Hi, I'm Georgia. I'm sorry we haven't spoken until now."

"It's all my brother's fault. Unfortunately, we told him how much we wanted to say hello, which means he tortures us by hiding you away." This came out in a rush from another dark-haired woman, this one with a strong chin and determined eyes, just like Banks.

"That's Sandy," he said. "She's the worst."

"I am!" Sandy confirmed, which set them off laughing.

Sandy: middle sister, 31, married to Amy, daughter Scarlet, 6.

"And I'm Kelly, the baby of the bunch," the third woman piped in. She had lovely auburn hair and dark eyes like her sisters and brother. *Kelly: youngest sister, 29, married to Jason, twin daughters, Lottie and Lila, 4.* "But I think you must be younger than me, Georgia."

"I'm twenty-four. Almost twenty-five." She slid a quick glance at Banks, who was watching her intently.

"She's the new baby," Sandy said. "Bro, you are such a cradle snatcher."

"Yep, that's me," he said, which should have been amusing but, judging by Banks's face, was not. He didn't like references to their age difference.

April chimed in. "I'm going to get Mom and Gran. They can't miss this."

"Nope." Banks held up a hand. "Let's keep it tight for today and not overwhelm Georgia."

"Spoilsport." Kelly made a face, and everyone but Banks laughed.

"Georgia, you're even more beautiful in person than online," Sandy said, "and you are *so* gorgeous in all the pics we've seen. You looked amazing in your wedding photo."

She did? She'd checked her phone's camera roll, and nothing existed from that night.

"Oh, that's so kind of you. This is me, straight out of bed pre-makeup. Bit of a mess."

"Nonsense," Kelly said. "I would kill for that skin."

"Cast a spell, witch," Banks said laconically.

"You hear how he talks to us?" Sandy pointed. "You're scaring Georgia away."

"It'll take more than some light witchcraft to frighten this woman. She ate my tacos."

Exclamations of incredulity met this statement.

"They were so good!" Georgia laughed and sent an amused glance toward Banks. "I like 'em spicy. The hotter the better."

Everyone was laughing, except Banks, who never seemed to find her amusing at all.

"Wait until he starts making you curries," April said. "They'll blow your top off."

Like that kiss. No way did Georgia want to look horny in front of Banks's family. Quickly, she changed the subject.

"So you're coming to Chicago to watch your brother play?"

"Oh, yeah." Sandy raised her hands. "The first two playoff games at home. Best to get in there now in case they get swept."

Cries of "don't jinx it!" and "Sandy!" went up while Sandy defended herself vociferously. They were all so raucous and fun, quite unlike their stoic brother.

"And Mom and Gran will be there, too. Gran's *so* excited to meet the woman that finally hooked her favorite grandchild."

Georgia chuckled. "Aw, he's the favorite? I can't wait to hear all the stories about him."

"Oh, we have so many!" Kelly leaned in and cupped her mouth. "There was one time he snuck a girl into his room and—"

"Kel." Just one word from Banks was enough.

"Scarred for life, I was!" She winked at the camera. "We'll talk later. With wine."

Georgia gave an exaggerated wink right back. "Gotcha!"

"Alright, time to wrap up this love fest." Banks sketched a brief hand wave and ended the call by touching the screen.

"They're lovely."

"Don't be fooled. They're very likely on another call talking about you." She must have looked horrified because Banks stepped in quickly, his hand on her hip. "Don't fret. They'll have nothing but good things to say about you because what else is there?"

"How about that time I lured you down the aisle? Or how I'm clearly after your big hockey salary? What about the fact I've taken one of the game's most eligible bachelors off the market? I see what they're saying about me on social media. The other day, some chick was ranting about me on TikTok."

"TikTok? Who gives a fuck about a bunch of strangers online?"

"I do! They said I'm not a true hockey wife because I don't know anything about the game. I'm not even worthy of being called a puck bunny."

He smirked. So he *did* find her amusing.

She thumped him lightly on his chest, making sure to stay away from known bruises. Though, judging by the balls-to-the-boards way Banks played, he had probably accumulated more. She'd watched the game last night with a Wikipedia article on her phone and a stack of flash cards as she tried to parse the rules. Offside? Icing? No clue.

"It's not funny."

"Kind of is. And what do you care what my sisters think?"

"Because it's your family. And they'll talk to your mom and gran and tell them things."

"Like how you love my spicy tacos." He added an expressive scoot upward of his eyebrows.

"Banks!" She couldn't help her laugh. "All that innuendo made me sound like a thirsty bitch."

"I'm feeding you. Of course you're going to be hot for your husband."

Husband. "Cooking *is* very attractive in a man."

He was closer now, looking down on her with a searing focus on her eyes, then her lips. Her tongue darted out to wet her lips. Her throat was dry, her hunger for this man making her desperate for more of those drugging kisses.

But this had the capacity to become very complicated. She had drawn her line, and now they needed to move on. She redirected her thoughts to non-sexy ones. "Are you looking forward to their visit?"

"They're very annoying, but they're family."

She nodded, remembering how they joshed and joked on the call a few moments ago. The love was plain to see.

"Hey." He brushed a thumb over her cheek.

A rebel tear had escaped. *Awesome work, Georgia. From sexy to sad in a heartbeat.*

"I'm fine."

"Georgia." He pulled her close, placing his other hand on her hip. "What's going on?"

"I just like seeing you all together. It reminds me of happier times with Dani. I'd forgotten how much we laughed, and seeing you with your sisters brought it back."

"I'm sorry."

"Oh, please, don't be." She swiped at her eye. "Never apologize for being happy. It's important to recognize these moments when you're in them."

He nodded, waiting for her to get a grip. His hands on her were changing her mood from sad to something-not-so-sad, so she took a step back with a sucked in breath.

"I was worried you weren't talking to me," she said. "Because of how we ended our conversation the other night."

"You do have a habit of exiting the kitchen dramatically and leaving me with the clean-up. Don't think I haven't noticed."

"So I'm given to dramatic flourishes."

"And the housework suffers. Coffee?"

"Please."

He poured her a cup and fixed it the way she liked it.

"Thanks. Oh, wait a second. What was that about a wedding photo? Sandy mentioned it."

"You don't have a copy?"

"I never got one."

"The celebrant texted me a link. I thought he did the same for you."

She shook her head. He opened his phone and found the photo, rather quickly, she thought.

Banks was in his green flannel shirt but wouldn't be for long because he gave it to her right after. She wore her pink Milla cocktail dress with a strapless bodice and applique organza skirt and of course, Manolos. As good a wedding day outfit as any. But it was their pose that struck her dead. Banks slightly turned to her, his mouth touching the top of her head, his arm circling her waist. His beard was lighter than what he had now, which made it easier to spot the curve to his lips, his tell that he had a secret.

Her. She was the secret and Banks liked it.

"It'd be nice to have a copy," she said, peeking up to find him studying her. "My friends keep asking for visual proof."

"I'll text it to you." He took a sip of his coffee. "So, about the playoffs. The first game is the day after tomorrow. I have a ticket set aside for you."

She had planned to talk to Tara about getting a seat in the box. "You do?"

"Of course. You're my wife."

Heat ascended her cheeks. Anytime he used that word—or the *H* word—her pussy started to throb and her whole body sparked with desire. "Well, yes. I am."

"If you don't want to go—"

"It's not that. I assumed you'd need all the tickets for your family. And I'm worried about not knowing how the game works and embarrassing you. I won't understand when you're doing well. Or badly."

"You could never embarrass me. And you'll understand. The crowd has a pulse."

"A pulse?"

He nodded and placed a fist to his chest. "A heartbeat." He gently banged against his left pec, like he was knocking at a door. *Th-thump. Th-thump.*

Her heart rate picked up, beating in rhythm with that fist.

"I've been watching YouTube videos to learn the rules. But if all I need to do is commune with the crowd to figure it out, maybe I don't need it?"

"So you'll come to the game?"

"I suppose it would look suspicious if I didn't go." *Giving him an out.*

"It would." Before disappointment could take over, he added, "But I'd like you to be there anyway."

It sounded like he meant it, like her presence mattered.

"I'd love to be there."

"Good."

19

It was far too early in the morning for that kind of thing, but he preferred it, so she usually went along with it. After all, he was her oldest friend. (Something she said a lot to excuse his behavior.)

"G, where have you been?"

He looked handsome, though it was ten in the morning, and he must have just woken up. Oliver never got up before 9:30, if he could help it.

"Oh, here and there."

"Playing the good little wifey, huh? I went by your place. Doorman was super cagey about your whereabouts."

"I moved in with Dyl—Banks. It seemed the best thing in the circumstances."

He frowned. "Did he *make* you move in with him?"

"God, no. We both agreed that keeping the fiction required certain things that are expected of married couples. Like living in the same house ..." *And kissing.* Damn Oli and his FaceTime demands, which required her to school her expression to a neutral she was incapable of feeling. "Married people are supposed to want to spend time together."

"My parents would disagree." He sniffed. "How about we meet up for a boozy lunch?"

"I wish I could, but I have some things going on."

"You never have time for me anymore. Skye and Paris were saying so as well. The gang's falling apart."

She sighed at his amateur dramatics. "It'll only be for a short time." Banks had said that getting through the playoffs was imperative, as if that was the deadline for their marriage. "There's a bigger spotlight on us at this time because of the playoffs, which start tomorrow, but once that's done, we'll be out of the glare."

"Well, I guess you must be enjoying the attention. Classic Georgia. People seem to go mad for these weird hookups, don't they?"

The gossip rags certainly loved playing up their differences—background, size, age, outlook. The hard-working professional athlete at the tail-end of his career slumming it with the party girl who sat around on her tush all day. But did her friends have to be so dismissive? After all, she and Banks had once thought this was worth a shot, and while she insisted it was a mistake, she didn't enjoy everyone else agreeing with her.

Oli was still talking. "You could always throw a party at—where are you living now?"

"Winnetka. It's really nice here."

She had taken a walk along the beach this morning, loving the serenity of this pocket of peace so close to the city. Though she would not have minded a big, muscled hockey player by her side. The thought of a party in this calm space did not sit well.

"When can we visit?"

She jerked back to the conversation, wondering why her body was reacting so negatively to Oli's suggestion. He was her friend. They all were, yet she'd felt a distance from them for months now.

She had an incoming call from Carol Vesney, her boss at Cherish the Days. *Saved.*

"Hey, that's my other line. I'll check in later."

"You'd better!"

She answered the other call. "Hey, Carol!"

"Hello, Georgia." Carol was a grump who was unappreciative of Georgia's cheer levels. "You left a message saying you needed to talk."

"I did! So I wanted to ask about getting some home help for one of our clients."

"Home help?"

"Yes, Jim Dixon's family isn't getting the assistance they need from social services, and I wondered if—"

"Dixon?" Georgia heard the clack-clack of a keyboard. "That's one of our clients from last year."

"Yes, and he's still with us. But his family is stretched to the limit and—"

"You mean you went to see him again?"

"I pop in on occasion. They're a lovely family and I'd like to figure out more ways we can help beyond a birthday gift. I feel as though we're letting the caregivers down."

"Georgia," Carol said, her voice strained. "We're here for the person who won't be around much longer. Our resources can't stretch to helping the families. That's what the city and county's social services are for."

"But they're not getting the help. Debbie is run off her feet and she'd like to go back to work."

Carol sighed. "And we don't have the budget to do that.

Now I have you down for a birthday visit with Melinda Cartwright tomorrow. Are you still on for that?"

"Yes, of course." Banks's family would be arriving from Wisconsin around noon, and she planned to spend the morning getting the house ready. But she would make time for a birthday gift drop-off.

The doorbell rang.

"Thanks, Carol." *For being singularly unhelpful.*

She rang off, annoyed that the charity had such tunnel vision when it came to helping people. Debbie had to give up her job a couple of years ago to become her father's full-time caregiver. Her husband Mick did his best but had a chronic back injury that didn't allow him to help much or do any of the heavy lifting. Debbie was on the hook for all of it.

The door chime went again and was soon followed by an impatient thump. Cheddar ran for the laundry room, his typical hide-out when things got noisy.

Another chime sounded as she approached.

"Okay, okay, hold your horses!" She pulled open the door and looked down. The woman was shorter than Georgia, which was saying something, given Georgia's diminutive stature. Eighty if she was a day, she had a shock of white hair, dancing brown eyes, and a curve to her lips that said she was trouble.

"Georgia!"

"Guilty."

"Kochanie!" She moved in and wrapped herself around Georgia's waist with a tight hug. "You're just as gorgeous as they said!"

"I am?" The words had hardly escaped her mouth when realization dawned. "Are you—"

"Connie Bankowski, Dylan's grandmother. Yours, too!"

Another woman, about mid-fifties with dark and softly

waved hair, was opening the trunk of an SUV. She removed at least six suitcases.

"Mama, let her breathe!" The woman came up and pulled the old lady back. "Sorry, you'd swear she never gets out. Hi, I'm Trish, Dylan's mom."

"I'm Georgia, but I'm guessing you know that. We thought you weren't arriving until tomorrow."

Connie chuckled. "The girls are coming up tomorrow, but we figured we'd scout ahead. See if maybe you have any good news for me." She added a pointed look at Georgia's stomach.

"Mama!" Trish shook her head.

She thought ... "No, I-I'm not. Not yet!" Good Lord, they'd have to do the deed first. "Oh, so sorry to leave you standing on the doorstep. Come in, come in!"

"She could be expecting," Connie was saying. "They got married almost three months ago. And no one waits until marriage to have sex anymore. She could be five months along for all we know."

Georgia could only laugh at the logic. Trish was struggling with the luggage, so Georgia stepped in and started dragging.

"Bowling balls," Connie said with a wink. "Gotta keep my arm loose for the league."

"I'm not sure where Ba—we were planning to put you."

"Probably as far away from the lovebirds as possible," Connie said.

From the love—oh. They'd expect Banks and Georgia to be in their own room. Together. With one bed.

She'd known that was a likelihood, but she had assumed they'd discuss it first.

What's to discuss? You're married and should be lying beside your husband for long, sleepless nights ...

"Let's worry about the room assignments later." Georgia

cupped Connie's elbow and guided her toward the living room. "You guys must be tired. What time did you start traveling?" The Bankowskis lived in Apple Falls, Wisconsin, just outside of Green Bay.

"Just after 6:30. Best way to beat the traffic." Trish screwed up her mouth. "Did we wake you? We probably should have warned you."

"Oh, no, it's fine. How about tea or coffee?"

Connie sank into the corner of the large sectional while Trish arranged cushions around her. "Coffee would be great. Need a hand?" Trish asked.

"Not at all!" In the kitchen, Georgia shot off a text to Banks.

> Surprise! Your mom and grandmother are here.

The phone rang immediately.

"Hotel Banks, how can I direct your call?"

"Are you kidding?"

"Why would I kid about that?"

His growl went to places that were unfortunately very receptive. "Are they okay?"

"Of course they are. They have six suitcases and look like they're planning to stay a month."

More growling. *Yum.* "Could you hold the fort until I get there? Morning skate's about to start, though it's optional and I could probably skip it."

"Don't change your plans. In case you haven't heard, I can be very charming. Not that it's ever worked on you."

Manly grunt.

"Excuse me?"

"Married you, didn't I?"

Her lips tugged up in a smile. "*My* charm's to blame?"

"Certainly wasn't mine."

Was he ... flirting with her? "Yep, you're as charmless as they come, Big Guy."

And she was flirting right back. *Enough of that, ya hussy.*

"What are they doing now?"

"Settling in. I said we'd give them rooms later, mostly because I didn't want them seeing that we're not"—she lowered her voice to a whisper—"in the same one."

"Okay, we can figure that out. They won't question why your clothes aren't in mine. You need a lot of space for your collection."

She chuckled. "Right, *my* collection. Because there's plenty of room with the fifty million suits in your closet."

"I like to have choices."

"I've never seen so many men's clothes. I can see why you leased this place. You needed storage for your habit."

"If looking good is a habit, then it's one I'm not gonna break."

"It's okay. You're vain. It can't be helped."

His laugh was low and rumbly and went straight to her core. "You object to me looking fine?"

Not for a second. "I object to you spending that much time in a relationship with one person. Yourself."

Another Banks laugh warmed her through. "You'd better get back and get our story straight."

Our story. She'd do well to remember that was all it was: a fairy tale.

"Okay. I'll hold back the hordes until you swoop in to save me."

Another grunt, and he rang off.

Trish put her head around the door, which meant that she probably overheard some or all of that. "Need a hand?"

"As I haven't gotten very far, probably yes." She held up her phone. "Thought I'd better warn him."

Trish smiled, her eyes whiskey warm, just like her son's. "You two iron out your plan of attack?"

Alarm streaked through her. Just how much did Trish know? She wished Banks had been more up front about who was part of the inner circle.

"Now, why ever would you think we'd need that?"

"Oh, no reason, except you were a bit of a surprise. My son is not the most impulsive person. He's always been the rock of the family."

"Since your husband died."

Trish nodded and moved to grab mugs from the cupboard. "It was a lot to put on him. Made him so determined to succeed, so he could provide for us all. He's always been so unselfish and ..." She paused, clearly trying to think of a way to phrase this without offending her new daughter-in-law. "This is kind of out of character."

"But not out of character for me. I'm guessing you've done some research."

Trish looked embarrassed, but not enough to hold off on the interrogation. "Did you really drive a golf cart into a swimming pool?"

"That's old news. But ... yes." Dani's voice echoed in her ear. *Do it, G. All the way.*

"It's really none of my business."

Georgia bit her lip. "Of course you're going to be worried about your son. Here he is, stable as they come, and married to a wild child with a history of getting into trouble. I'd be worried, too. But you can be assured that's behind me."

Now I just ensnare innocent hockey players and force them to stay married for my own selfish, fucked up reasons.

Trish waved a hand that said she was drawing a line under it. "I'm sorry. You shouldn't have to suffer intrusive questions from your dreaded mother-in-law."

"I get it, truly I do. He's your baby and you want to protect him."

Brow in a rumple, Trish seemed to think a moment before pulling Georgia into a hug as warm as it was surprising.

"Georgia, I get that this is awkward considering how fast it happened and that we haven't had a chance to meet. Connie's thrilled. She's always worried about Dylan—the golden child, y'know?" She winked at that, which made Georgia relax a little. "So we're going to do anything we can to make sure she's not disappointed."

Georgia tensed up again, which Trish sensed immediately.

"No, that came out wrong! Not that you would ever disappoint us. Just that, we all know this isn't the real deal. All of us except Connie."

"You do?"

"Yes. So we're all going to act like this is perfectly normal, which I'm sure it is." She scrunched up her mouth. "Is it?"

"Not in the slightest."

Trish barked out a laugh. "Got it. Well, you only need to pretend you're crazy about my son in front of his grandmother. The rest of us are all in on it. Wink, wink. A little less pressure, right?"

"Appreciate it." Tightness thickened her throat. So Banks wasn't able to maintain the lie for his mom and sisters. No one bought them as a couple except the little old lady who probably had poor eyesight.

He'd said he wanted to save face, but evidently that didn't extend to fooling his family. She supposed she should be glad he had this great, open relationship with them. She was rather envious, to be honest.

Trish took a long hard look at her. "My son knows how to pick 'em, that's for sure."

Georgia had no clue if that was a good or bad thing. Regardless, she felt as though Trish understood her.

Which made one of them.

20

THE SOUND of laughter echoed in the hallway as he opened the door. He shouldn't have worried—after all, his family were top quality. They would treat Georgia with respect because she belonged to Banks.

Okay, *belonged* wasn't the right word. She was *connected* to Banks. Legally.

He preferred his instinctual take on it.

He had planned to sit Georgia down tonight and give her the lay of the land. Essentially, he was setting her up for a clash with a gaggle of highly opinionated women who would go to the ends of the earth to protect him. They were usually able to spot trouble of the female variety a mile off and could size up any woman in his orbit in seconds.

One of their strategies was plying their victim with alcohol.

"Day drinking's begun, I see."

His mom jumped to her feet, a half-full martini glass in hand, which meant she could manage that and the tight hug for her son with no damage to either.

"My boy! My married, full-of-secrets boy!" Post-hug, she

rubbed his arm, squinted, and gave him a hammy wink. "You got yourself a wife without telling me? And then kept it a secret for two months? And you think the fact she's gorgeous and knows how to make a French martini is going to win me over?"

Laying it on a bit thick, Mom.

"We wanted to settle in first."

"Right. And how's that going?"

He cast a quick glance at Georgia, who had skipped the adult beverage in favor of raspberry tea. She offered an almost imperceptible eyebrow raise and a sly grin that immediately relaxed him.

"It's ... going."

His mother narrowed her eyes, looking for a chink in his armor. Was he in control here or was he laboring under the delusion that his wife might like him? Banks had made a mistake with a woman before. Thought it was the real thing and learned quickly that not everyone is as enamored of a big-muscled guy with the personality of Sequoia. That money and fame and talent can only get you so far.

So when his mom took that deep-dive into the depths of his soul, he tried to put her at ease as he held her gaze, beat for beat.

Finally, she let him off the hook. "Georgia's been keeping us entertained."

"Oh yeah?" He wouldn't mind hearing this, but first he needed to hug his grandmother. Stuffed into the cushions of the giant sectional, she was trying to get up. Both Banks and Georgia jumped to her aid. The little sprite that was his wife got there a second before him, but instead of helping his gran up, she placed a hand on her shoulder.

"Stay right there, Connie. Let your grandson come to you."

She looked up and smiled at him, while he sank into the spot beside his grandmother.

"Babcia," he murmured as he put his arms around her frail body. "I can't believe you're here."

"Where else would I be? You think I'm missing this series?"

"I know you wouldn't miss it, but this visit is sooner than I expected."

"It's what she wanted," his mom said. Connie was her mother-in-law, but from the moment she married his dad, they were as good as mom and daughter. Mom came from money and her own parents disowned her when she hitched her wagon to an Army private. The two women were alike in temperament, neither of them willing to back down.

He set his grandmother back to look at her. She'd lost weight, though his mom was always trying to make her eat more. He'd do what he could while she was here. Other than that, she looked spry for a woman of eighty-three.

"How are you?"

"Just fine. Don't you be worrying about me. You have games to win."

"I can do both."

You wouldn't believe how much my focus is fragmented—did you hear I have a hot young wife who's completely upended my life?—yet I'm still here, winning games and taking names.

"Well, you shouldn't have to worry. We're here to spend time with Georgia and induct her into the family."

He met Georgia's gaze over his grandmother's head. She should be afraid—he wouldn't have blamed her if she was—but that wasn't fear he was seeing. More like glee.

"You ready to be inducted?" he asked her.

"Are there jackets?"

Mom's eyes lit up, and he pointed at her. "No." A couple of his teammates had granny fan clubs who went nuts at the games, complete with specially designed merch. "No jackets. Just be normal. If that's possible."

His mom and Georgia shared a playful look that should have put the fear of God into him, but instead gave him a little thrill. They liked each other.

"While we figure out which photo of Banks to use on the jackets," Georgia said, "I can top everyone up."

His mom jumped to her feet. "I'll do it. Dylan, could you get your gran's room ready?" In other words, a nap was in her future.

"Will do." He kissed Gran on the forehead. "Relax while I figure out the guest room situation." When he stood, Georgia did as well, and the sight of them side by side sent his grandmother into a frenzy.

"Hold that pose! I need a pic to send to the girls. Trish, do the honors."

A slender arm snaked around his waist and she—meaning his soft, supple, sexy wife—leaned in, laying her head on his pec.

"Gotta give your public what they want, Big Guy."

On hearing that nickname, his mother's eyes practically popped out of her head.

"Take the damn photo."

She did, though she took an age with it, to the point that Banks's body was not his own. He was on the verge of losing control and throwing his woman caveman-style down on the hearth rug and nailing her until she screamed his name.

He'd already mauled her a couple of nights ago, and as for what happened in Vegas … He assumed that was part of the reason for running out of the hotel room instead of sticking around to discuss what had happened. She'd awoken trap-wrapped in his aging bulk and had quickly figured out her escape route.

"Absolutely perfect!" Mom was grinning, and he wondered what she really thought of all this. She knew it was just for his gran, so why was she acting so weird?

He pulled away, a little too fast. Georgia wasn't quite ready, and she stumbled back into his arms.

"Sorry," she murmured, sounding embarrassed. That was the last thing he wanted.

"Stay here." He didn't want her hauling luggage.

"No, I want to make sure everyone gets settled in right." She moved ahead of him and grabbed the largest suitcase in the foyer. Then dropped it.

"Jesus, what's in here? A dead body?"

"Shoes, I'm guessing. Mom likes to have her boot collection wherever she goes." He took the case along with two others. "You grab that smaller one—that's Gran's."

He followed her upstairs, careful to keep his eyes north of her shoulder blades. But that didn't help because she'd put her hair up into a messy bun, and small tendrils of hair were stuck to her neck.

Thoughts invaded, wicked ones about placing his nose along the curve of her neck. His lips. Maybe even his tongue. He bet she tasted sweet with a touch of salt because that would be Georgia. A mass of contradictions.

"You okay?"

He jerked to attention to find her looking at him curiously with those blue lights. Could she not see how much her wispy, rebellious hair was affecting him?

"Sorry about before," he muttered with a glance downstairs.

"About what?"

"My gran demanding photographic evidence to share with the rest of them. Making us—"

"Get physical?" The corner of her mouth hooked up. "But

you dropped me like I burned! We'll have to figure out how to handle those kinds of interactions if we're to keep the fiction alive." She brought his gran's case into the room where she'd been sleeping. "Now I think maybe your gran should go in here after I change the sheets. The lake views are especially lovely, and it gets a lot of sun in the morning."

He knew that. It was why he'd chosen this room for Georgia.

"I'll move my undies into yours." She took a quick look over her shoulder. "Maybe now before Connie gets nosy. I'll leave my clothes as if this is my closet space."

Quickly she grabbed stuff from drawers and threw it into an empty case while he stood at the door, gawping and trying to parse her words about how he'd dropped her like she burned. Anxious to distract himself, he focused on her quick movements and the things she was packing away. Frilly bits. Lacy and silky scraps of material that would barely cover her curves and would not hold up under scrutiny or his ravenous grasp.

Shuttering the suitcase, she looked up and frowned as if to ask, *why are you here again, perv?*

I can't stay away from you.

She pulled the suitcase by him and headed to his room where she popped it on the bed and unzipped again.

"Now for your mom, maybe put her in the blue room? It's got that extra closet space, and she could lay out her boots in those cute little cubbies."

Good, back to the task at hand. After lugging and stashing the remaining cases, he sought out Georgia, who was unpacking in his room.

Their room.

He closed the door behind him. "Could I have a word?"

She looked up, her eyes wide and curious.

"About what happened downstairs, you've got it all wrong."

"I do?"

He inhaled a breath. "I separated from you quickly because I didn't want you to think I was taking advantage."

"Advantage? How would I think a fake hug was taking advantage?"

Did he have to spell it out? "Because it didn't feel fake. It felt ... good. And that's not what you signed on for."

She took a couple of steps toward him, then placed a hand on his chest. "What did I sign on for? Is it about Connie?"

"Yes." *Liar, liar, cup on fire.* The hand on his chest started to make tight, comforting circles.

"Is she ill?"

"No, nothing more than typical old age. But she worries she could go at any minute, and she won't have seen me with a wife and a family of my own."

"I see." She reached up to his jaw and cupped it. "Making your grandmother happy is a great reason to do this. I'm guessing she's harbored the dream for you for a while."

She really should leave off, but now she was stroking his jaw with her thumb—and he was the fool letting her.

"She's always wanted to see me settled, like my sisters."

"An old lady's wish. Beats my mercenary motives, for sure."

This wasn't a competition for self-sacrifice. As if living with Georgia, even with all the pretense, was a hardship. Sure, it was "hard" in a different way, but not unpleasurable in the slightest.

"We both have our reasons, and one isn't better than the other."

"Hmm." She wanted to disagree. "I had a chat with Trish. She mentioned that she and your sisters are in on the caper, so that's good."

"They're hard to fool. But my gran sees what she wants to see."

Maybe we all do. With Georgia standing close, stroking his jaw, the situation was feeling more real with each successive heartbeat. And with her next question, he felt himself sinking deeper.

"So you dropped me like a hot coal because it felt good. What about it felt good, Banks?"

Jesus, her hands, her touch, the way she smelled, how tiny and precious she was standing next to him, before him, in his arms ... he could make lists for days.

"All of it."

Her breath hitched. "Then you'll have no problems faking it."

Faking it. Excellent. He needed the reminder. Her hand was still on his jaw, showing tenderness because of his ailing gran. Not for any other reason that his starry-eyed imagination might conjure.

He cupped her hand, because she seemed loathe to leave his jaw be, and while he had no objections, he didn't want her to feel obligated out of some sort of pity. But now her hand was clasped in his and something occurred to him, something that had been bothering him since the moment she moved in.

"This isn't right."

She looked startled and pulled her hand away.

He held on. Rubbed a thumb over the fourth finger. "You're not wearing my ring."

Color tagged her cheeks. "I left it behind in the hotel room. It didn't seem fair to hold onto it." She peered up at him, almost shy. "Do you still have it?"

He nodded, and not letting go, guided her to the dresser. He pulled open the top drawer and removed the small box beneath his underwear. That night, she'd chosen it from a selection at the chapel and he vaguely recalled some discussion about choosing what was effectively a traditional engagement ring over a wedding band. He hadn't cared. She could have whatever the fuck she wanted as long as she wore it forever.

Less than six hours later, it was on the nightstand, and Cinderella was gone.

Making a big deal of opening it and slipping it onto her finger would assign this too much significance. He put the box on the dresser and pushed it a couple of inches toward her.

No hesitation, she flipped the lid and sucked in a breath.

"I wasn't sure if I imagined it."

A pale pink solitaire, all the more beautiful for its rarity. Pricey for a quickie Vegas wedding, but it was her choice. *He* was her choice.

Until he wasn't.

"Could you put it on?"

Could he ...?

"Because you're holding my hand and ..."

Right. He still had her hand clasped in his, limiting her mobility. Hauling air into his lungs, he let go of her long enough to pull the ring out of its snug, velvet bed. It caught a shard of sunlight, though maybe that was the reflection of her bright, shining eyes.

She offered her hand. "I feel like we should say something."

"Repeat our vows?" He slipped the ring onto her finger, slowly, wanting the moment to last. *With this ring, I thee wed. I promise to cherish, defend, and fight for you ...* He looked into her eyes and said with his gaze what he couldn't with his voice.

"What about yours?"

He extracted the platinum band from the drawer. It would

have been easier to just put it on, get it done, but he wanted her to do it.

He would examine the why of that later.

She took it from him and slid it onto his finger. "With this ring, I promise ... to cheer like hell at my husband's hockey match."

"Game."

"And not embarrass him with my lack of hockey knowledge."

He laughed, relieved she'd pricked the balloon of tension. At least one of them was thinking straight.

21

CONNIE WENT for a nap because a three-hour drive and a morning martini will do that. That left Georgia with Trish while Banks was busy making lunch.

"I probably should see if he needs help."

Trish patted Georgia's arm. "My son is well trained. I want to hear all about you. So you grew up in Chicago?"

"Yeah, not too far from here. Lake Forest. It's a suburb a few miles north."

"Brothers? Sisters?"

"A twin sister, Dani. She died a couple of years ago. She had a heart condition; she'd had it since she was a child."

Trish's eyes filled with tears. "Oh, honey. I'm so sorry. That's awful, for you and your parents."

"It was. We were so close and well, life hasn't been the same without her." She sucked in a breath. "But you know what it's like. When you lost Dylan's father in Iraq."

Trish sighed. "I do. It was the saddest time of my life. Thankfully I had Connie and the kids to get me through. As for Dylan, he made it his mission to ensure we were taken care of. I had Jonah's pension, of course, but it never stretches far enough, not with four kids and a mother-in-law."

"Gotta keep Connie in martinis."

Trish chuckled. "Exactly! That woman will never say no to a cocktail. As for Dylan ... he was only sixteen when his father passed and while he was good at hockey, you just never know if it'll be enough. Those first couple of years until he got his scholarship were touch and go. There was so much competition, but he stepped up and made sure he had a contract, though he did get a finance degree as a backup. Always good with numbers, that boy. Takes care of everyone's accounts. Then the first thing he does is pay off the house!"

"Wow!"

"Yep. I had a second mortgage on it and had fallen behind—oh, that money came in so useful. But that's Dylan. Always puts us first."

Georgia saw that, and knowing Banks's true motivation for marrying her, it made her admire him all the more. He was a family man, and these lovely people were his priority. As it should be. Georgia would never be Banks's number one, which was fine. She was used to being the background artist in a family dynamic.

But that ring exchange in the bedroom? A foolish romantic might read a whole ton into that.

"Lunch is up," he called out.

Georgia expected it to be in the kitchen where they'd eaten before, but Banks had set the dining room table with colorful plates, a jug of water, a bottle of Sauv Blanc in an ice bucket, no less, and a platter of sandwiches. A vase of fresh-cut flowers sat in the center. He must have bought them on his way home from practice.

"Oh, this is lovely," Georgia said. "Fancy presentation of sandwiches. I like."

Trish kissed her son on the cheek. "You shouldn't have gone to so much trouble, but I'm glad to see you haven't forgotten how to treat the women in your life."

Banks blushed at his mom's words, but Georgia didn't have time to enjoy it because a screech pierced the air.

"What. Is. That?" Trish pointed at Cheddar, who had finally deigned to join them.

"That's Cheddar."

"A cat?"

Kind of a weird reaction. "That's right."

"But you're allergic!" This was addressed to her son.

"It's not a big deal, Mom."

Georgia snapped her gaze to Banks. "You are? Why didn't you say?"

"Because it's not important. I took an antihistamine. No trouble."

She flew to him, unable to resist cradling his jaw, if only to ensure he would meet her eyes with his big, fat, lying gaze.

"You said it was allergies. I can't believe you—oh God, you had him in your lap the other day!"

"He likes me."

Who wouldn't? Yet, here she was, a terrible wife forcing her husband to engage with a creature that could harm his health.

"Come on, Cheddar." She scooped him up.

"Georgia, it's okay," Banks called out, but she ignored him. Lies, the whole lot of it.

She took Cheddar into the laundry room where she'd set up his litter box. "Sorry, little guy. This is only temporary until I figure out what's best." Should she really be surprised that Banks had kept up this fiction? After all, everything happening here was completely bogus. The marriage, the ring, the whole lot of it.

She heard a snick behind her, the door closing. She turned to find Banks, looking agitated. (Though, the only difference from non-agitated Banks was a thinning of his sensual lips.)

He exhaled roughly. "I didn't tell you because I suspected you'd react like this."

"Like what?"

"Think of *this* as one more obstacle."

An obstacle to what? She hated the idea of him in any sort of discomfort, which was weird because he was constantly getting smashed up on the ice. But that was by choice.

"I just don't want to see you suffering. That's not fair on you. Your home is supposed to be your haven from the craziness of this world and the game and the playoffs. It's already bad enough I'm here upsetting your routine. Now you're sneezing constantly."

He stepped in quickly and cupped the back of her head. There was a lot of that today—her with him, him with her, and she was completely on board with it. The warmth of his hand cradling the back of her neck was divine.

"Never said upsetting my routine was a bad thing."

"It's in the phrase itself. 'Upsetting'."

"Sometimes people need that change to kickstart them into the next phase."

She placed a hand on his chest. For balance, for comfort, to feel all that vitality beneath her fingertips.

"Explain."

"Well, I'm not sure if you've figured this out yet, but I am considerably older than you."

"Yeah. The cradle snatcher references from family, friends, and foe have not been lost on me."

He let out a little puff of air. "So, my career is coming to an end, which means it's time to think of what comes next. For the last twenty-five years, I've lived and breathed a specific routine. Diet, training, sleep. A regimen that keeps me at the top. There hasn't been time for a life, to be honest. I thought there was but ..." His voice faded out.

Something about a woman, she suspected.

"But ..."

"I couldn't juggle this life and what was needed to make it all work. But now, this—what's happening here—has brought what I've been missing into focus. How I need to make some changes to figure out what comes next."

"And my presence here is helpful?" She placed verbal quotes around that last word.

"Not in the slightest." He grinned. "But your presence here has made me realize that I need to learn to ... adapt. To let someone else in."

Was he saying what she thought he was saying? Before she could get ahead of herself, he spoke again.

"Not that you're *the someone*. I know that's not what you signed on for. More that you're helping me realize that compromise is the essence of relationships. With my teammates. The people in my life. Even a creature that makes me sneeze."

"You know what else is the essence of relationships? *Com-mun-i-ca-tion*." She finger-tapped each syllable against his hard chest. Oh my, that felt good, though his dismissal of her as "the someone" dampened the pleasure slightly. "You should have told me about your allergy, and we could have figured out a plan together."

He inhaled deep and there it was, that lovely skitter of sensation she felt at watching this stoic man think. The way he was looking at her right now was doing major things to her libido.

"I didn't want you to get second thoughts. About us."

They were an *us*? "You thought I'd bail if you told me?

Haven't you heard? I need this marriage to look real. But you know what else I need? For my husband to talk to me about his health."

He placed a hand over her finger, trapped it against his chest. "Cheddar deserves a home, too."

So sweet. "And he'll have one. This place is large enough that we can carve out a space for him so he's not contaminating where you live. For God's sake, Banks, you need to be in top form for the playoffs!"

But she wouldn't forget how he'd let Cheddar jump on him with no complaint. Her enduring, stoic, magnanimous husband.

They were close now and she could feel her heels lifting, her calves stretching, her lips moving closer to his.

Voices trickled through the bated-breath silence, the female murmurs of their guests. Connie must be awake.

She drew back. Banks blinked.

"We should eat lunch," she said.

"Yeah, but something else. I need to know if ..."

"If what?"

"It's okay to touch you. Show you affection that's a bit more natural than a photo pose. In front of Gran."

"Oh." She bit her lip. "Can you give me examples?"

"Just touching your back perhaps. Or a light pat on—"

"My ass?"

"Funny how you go there."

Funny how you don't. "I just assumed that would be how a big lug like you would treat his woman. Possessive ass grabs."

Manifesting seemed to be as good a strategy as any.

"I was thinking more along the lines of a gentle touch of my fingertips to your spine."

Not nearly enough. "You're very touchy-feely with your

mom and gran. I assumed you'd be like that with your girl-friend. Or wife."

"I would be." *If this were real* was the unspoken coda. "But I'm aware that this is awkward for you."

"I'd be fine with you touching me." She moved in closer, pressed her hand to his chest. "How would you feel if I touched you? Like this?"

She moved her hand over his pectorals, down his torso, then quickly around his hip until ... damn. She cupped that very fine ass.

She drew away quickly. "If that's too much ..."

"I can handle it."

A challenge? She placed her hand back on his ass and squeezed, filling her palm with one perfect Banks bun. No slouch, he moved his hand around and coasted it over the rise of her ass. Then down.

"How's that?"

As test squeezing went, it was perfect. Her body inched closer and stretched up—whether it was a move on her part or his hand pulling her flush, she wasn't sure. It didn't matter. Her breasts were now smashed against his chest, their hips were touching, and she desperately wanted his fingers to work their way into the snug recess between her thighs.

It was unlikely they'd be feeling each other up to this degree in front of his family, but it was good to know the limits. For science.

"Hungry?" he murmured, his gaze dipping to her lips.

"Starving."

"Dylan, we're going to start without you!" Trish's voice broke the spell.

He pulled his hand away, she returned the favor, and they took a step back.

Then exhaled as one.
He found his voice first. "Let's eat."

22

HIS MOM and Connie called it an early night, and though it was close to ten, he was feeling like maybe he should do that, too. He had cooked dinner while Georgia kept everyone entertained with stories about the exploits that got her Page Six attention. Like the time she set off a fire alarm in a church. Or when she "borrowed" a police horse during Lollapalooza.

His sisters would be here tomorrow, so he had less than twenty-four hours to re-frame his game face for them. He was a master of passivity, but his sisters knew him a little too well. They'd see how he was around Georgia and would recognize that he might be pretending to fake it for his gran's sake, but that his body language with his wife screamed his attraction to her.

They were both in the kitchen now, tidying up in that domestic shorthand of established couples. Dishes stowed, leftovers stored, and countertops wiped.

"Thanks for today, for being so cool with Mom and Gran. I know it's not easy to be on show like that."

"Are you kidding? Plenty of stories to mine for your entertainment, sir." She gave a mock bow.

"You don't have to entertain us. This is your life we're talking about."

"It's okay, Big Guy." She rubbed her hands together. "Next hurdle—sleeping together!"

"Hurdle?" This was going to be awkward/difficult/excruciating for her?

She folded her arms, cocked her hip. "You need to get some rest for the game tomorrow. I don't want to interfere with that. I can sleep on the floor if that's easier."

"The bed is big enough. Go on ahead. I'll be there in a few."

Let her have time to brush her teeth. Cleanse her face. Change into one of those wispy camisole things and get under the covers.

He futzed about, making sure everything was tidy, though nothing really needed doing. Stalling for time, he headed to the laundry room. The slight tang of the cat litter tickled his nostrils, and he looked down at Cheddar, who took a couple of steps toward him.

He hunkered down and because he was a sucker, he rubbed a hand over his arching back. "Sorry about this, dummy. If it were up to me, you'd have the run of the place."

A plaintive mewl was his response. Banks closed the door and headed to the first-floor restroom to wash his hands and take a good look at himself in the mirror.

That kiss meant nothing. All these light touches in front of his gran? Nothing. When Georgia groped his ass in the laundry room? Nothing. The ring ... He turned his own band, marveling at how strange it didn't feel on his finger. Like it belonged there.

He had to stay focused on his game, and not just the one on the ice. So what if he had to sleep in the same bed as his wife? It was king-sized, and while he usually took up most of it, not tonight.

Tonight, he would hover on the edge at risk of falling off, anything to ensure he did not touch Georgia.

SHE WAS SITTING up under the covers, e-reader propped on her knees, the soft light of the bedside lamp suffusing her creamy skin with a lovely glow. A couple of thin silky straps bisected her perfectly-rounded shoulders. He looked away quickly.

"Everything okay?" she asked.

"Sure. Why wouldn't it be?"

"Just wondering what took you so long. Did you need to check all the doors and windows?"

"Doesn't hurt to do a walk-through."

A slight smirk. "So I chose this side. But if you have a preference—"

"No preference." His gaze slid to the bedside table on the opposite side, taking note of the couple of millimeters the drawer was extended.

"I saw you had condoms, so I assumed that was your side."

He nodded, feeling his color rising. "Fine. Just going to ..." He gestured to the bathroom then headed there quickly and shut the door.

Fuck. He should have thought of that. Not that condoms were embarrassing, but it meant now he was thinking about sex. (*Sure, blame the condoms.*) Maybe *she* was thinking about sex or the fact that he had protection, which they could use if—

Nope. They were just there, little coils of rubber that would get no use for a while.

He had agreed to play out this charade for months, at least

until Georgia's parents put her back on the payroll. All that time, he'd have to be celibate because he was married.

Since Vegas, he hadn't been interested in any other woman. Even when he thought he was divorced, he'd kept it in his pants. He'd known she didn't want to give him the time of day, had figured out how to eighty-six him from her life within a week of marriage, yet he'd still placed her on some sort of pedestal. A woman worthy of his fidelity.

His psyche knew he was taken.

Mighty fucked up, that. He had signed the annulment papers—which weren't worth the tree pulp they were printed on, apparently—and had still craved a woman who clearly didn't want him. At least, not until she had a monetary reason.

This was good. *Remember why she's here. Remember she doesn't want you that way.*

A couple of minutes later, he was out of the bathroom after splashing his face with cold water to wake himself the fuck up.

She'd turned out the lamp on her side; now only the pale glow of her e-reader cast about the room. At least he could undress in the shadows, which he did down to his boxer briefs. He pulled back the covers, slid under them, and steeled his body for the night ahead.

MERE INCHES SEPARATED THEM. All she had to do was stretch her arm and she could touch him.

This bed had looked huge when she came into the room earlier and quickly undressed. But now, with her giant of a husband in it, it had taken on a smaller footprint. No bigger than a postage stamp, really.

He'd stood at the side as he stripped, giving her that perfect vista of taut muscle and chest hair. She couldn't help sneaking a peek while he unpeeled his sweater off over his head. Then he'd stood at the edge of the bed, his back to her, like he was waiting for something.

She couldn't decide if it was better for him to be outside, showcasing the body of a bruised and battered warrior, or under the covers, a few, tempting inches away from her. An impossible choice.

She'd made it clear she already snooped and found the condoms. They had protection. Yay! A different type of protection might be more optimal, a forcefield or hex that would keep her on this side of the bed and ensure her hands did not wander. Because they wanted to. They wanted to explore those broad shoulders and apply her lips to steely flesh and solid warmth.

But she had to resist those thoughts, and one way to do that was to talk.

"Tell me about Connie."

"Connie?"

She turned over to face him, just about able to make out his face in the half-dark. "You're so close. Closer than I think a lot of people are to their grandparents." How else to explain why he was maintaining this fakery?

"You're not close to yours?"

"They're not around anymore and my memory of them is kind of dim."

"She had breast cancer fourteen years ago. Beat it like a boss."

"Knew she was a tough cookie. What else?"

She felt him relax. "She protested during the sixties. Burned her bra in the seventies. Probably did a ton of coke in the eighties."

"Really?"

"Maybe? What I'm trying to say is that she's always been a woman of her time. Nothing fazes her."

She inched closer. "It sounds like she's led a very full life."

"Yet for some reason she claims she won't be happy if she doesn't see us all paired off."

"So, that's why you came back to me with your offer?"

He hesitated, likely trying to think of some way to phrase it that wouldn't give offense. She let him off the hook.

"Hey, we both have our reasons. It's okay. And like I said, yours is far more noble than mine."

"Georgia—"

"I promise to do whatever I can to make her wishes come true." After all, she did it for complete strangers on their birthday. Why not her husband's grandmother? Why not bring a tiny speck of joy to this lovely family?

He shifted to face her. "The things I said before about you being—"

"Mercenary?"

"In a word. That wasn't fair. We all have ways of surviving. I don't know you well enough to assume your ways are more preferable to mine."

Perhaps her performance had pleased him. *You did good, Georgia! Here are a few morsels of kindness as your reward.*

"It's okay. You can only draw conclusions on the information you're given."

He snorted.

"It's true!"

"So what you're saying is that either I'm terrible at reading a situation or you're amazing at fooling the world about what you're really like."

She opened her mouth. Closed it quickly. She had no good response for that.

He leaned over, close enough that she could feel his breath hot against her cheek. "Which is it? Banks the dummy or Georgia the faker?"

"Neither of those options are very flattering."

"No," he murmured, his voice soft and low. "Tell me what I need to hear."

"That you're a dummy?"

He chuckled. "Sounds about right. But I think both can be true at once. You're hiding things from me."

Of course she was. If he had any clue of how much she was enjoying this incredibly awkward conversation, he'd think she was crazy. Just talking to him like this, closer than she'd ever felt with anyone since Dani, was more than she deserved.

Especially after how she had trapped him, all because she'd been looking for a way to soothe her pain.

"So what secrets are you keeping, Peaches?" He was still close, and the whisper in the words made him seem even closer.

"I'm an open book."

"Liar."

She sat up. "Hey! You can't say that."

"Can and did. Do you really need your trust fund badly enough that you'd stay married to a stranger?"

"I told you I did."

A scoffing noise. "Yeah, you did."

She saw what was happening here. He had a noble reason and he wanted to think she had one, too. He didn't like thinking so poorly of his wife, probably because it reflected badly on him and his judgment of character.

She could give him something. A little piece of herself for being such a good sport.

She lay back down. "All those stories I told at dinner—well, my parents are disappointed with me. I don't ever manage to live up to their expectations, and when I found out we were still married, I thought that maybe they might look at me differently."

He turned to her, leaning on his elbow. "You thought the label 'wife' would make them see you as all grown up?"

"Separate, independent." She hauled in a shaky breath. "I need the money to create my own charity, something that isn't an extension of my parents' business interests or what they think is appropriate."

That shut him up.

"I know, just looking for another way to put off working for a living," she joked.

Say something, please.

Finally he spoke. "What kind of charity?"

"I'm not sure yet. I'm currently researching options, meeting with Chicagoland foundations, looking for gaps in the philanthropic space." She wasn't ready to share just how hands-on she was in her research. Meeting the people who needed help was her favorite part. "My family would prefer I do something to honor Dani, and while that would be great—"

"You want something of your own."

Relief that he understood washed over her.

"But you need seed money to make it happen and that's where your parents come in?"

She nodded. "I need to show them that I'm not the wild child they think I am. That I can run a business and not just be the face of it. What we did in Vegas was reckless and not exactly the behavior of a budding foundation CEO. I'm sorry all this has happened and that the timing sucks and—"

He pressed a thumb to her lips. "Peaches, it's okay. You didn't act alone. I've got your back and we're gonna make sure this works out."

His thumb dipped to her lower lip, the action pressing enough to part them. The urge to flick her tongue over that pillowy-pad of flesh was overwhelming. He was staring at her mouth, and that craving inside her was building, building, and *please, Banks, kiss me again.*

Her silent plea went unheard.

He pulled back, and if it took him a little longer to remove his thumb from her lip, then that was purely in the realm of her imagination.

"We should sleep," he muttered gruffly.

She swallowed back her emotion and nodded yes, but he was already turning away, giving her his strong, unyielding back. Mr. Stoic in all things.

24

Banks knew something was wrong because it felt so right.

That's how low his thinking had sunk. Up was down. Black was white. Nothing made sense anymore.

Morning had finally come, not that he'd slept much. But he managed a couple of fitful hours after the last time he checked his phone, about 4 a.m.

Now she was wrapped around him, her tiny, fuckable body finding countless ways to creep into any space available. One slender arm around his torso. A dainty hand gripping his shoulder. Her knee slotted between his thighs.

She'd buried her face into his neck, her lips a dick-raising suction against his throat.

And the heat? The covers were half off, so he should be freezing, but not with Georgia giving off nuclear levels of thermal energy.

He managed to shift his head slightly, just so he could dip his gaze down his body. As suspected, he was standing to attention, his dick tenting his briefs, daring him to move and find delicious friction.

Using the hand not trapped by the temptation in his bed,

he pulled the cover up and over his erection. Not that it solved anything but at least it wouldn't look so bad.

Sure, because appearances were what mattered right now.

He did a check-in with the rest of his body. His pulse was running a sprint, his skin burned with sensation, but apart from his irrepressible cock, his biggest problem was her shoulder.

It was right there within a whisper of his lips. All he had to do was turn his head and brush his mouth over her skin. He could play it off as an accident. As if her shoulder had pushed its way into his mouth and that sweet patch of flesh was his for a brief second.

But he didn't have permission to do that. As things stood, he didn't have permission to even be *thinking* about doing it.

He needed to get out of here. A cold shower, a double shot of espresso, ten hours in the gym. This was not the way to prepare for Game 1 of the series.

He shifted an inch. Then another. But that was a mistake because it got her body's attention. Her knee bent further and came perilously close to—*fuck*, it brushed his dick and made him jerk. (Not the jerk he'd have preferred, but a body spasm that rocked the bed.)

Her eyes fluttered open, and she took far too long, but not long enough, to realize where she was.

"Oh—oh, hi!"

"Morning," he gruffed out.

Any second now she'd move away, taking all that heat and softness away from him. Any second now, he'd groan because of what he couldn't have, which was for the best. Because if she stayed in this position, pretzeled around his body, he might not be responsible.

She didn't move. It was like she was frozen in place, terrified.

"Sorry, I didn't mean—" he said at the same time she uttered, "No, it's okay."

She stayed still, as if knowing a millimeter either direction would detonate the bomb of desire in the bed.

She turned her head slightly, seemed to burrow in even more. *Fuck.*

"This is what it was like before." Her voice was tiny, almost timid.

"Before?"

"The morning after."

That before.

He swallowed. "I don't remember. You were gone when I woke up."

"I know."

Silence, but also not. Volumes were spoken, as they said.

"Why did you leave?"

He already knew the answer. She'd awoken in the arms— he assumed—of a stranger, a man with muscles that could crush her. Who was far too old for her. Of course she was going to bolt.

"I was scared."

Well, that confirmed it. Still, he couldn't resist probing for more evidence against him.

"Of me?"

"No. Of me."

She still lay against his neck, so he moved to get a better look at her.

"Georgia, what does that mean?"

"Look what we'd done. What *I* had done. This crazy thing. And I figured that it was just one more example of Georgia screwing up and pulling another innocent into her web."

"Innocent old me, you mean?"

Her eyebrows slammed together. "How else do you explain

what happened, Banks? I have a reputation, mostly well-earned, of making trouble. And usually that's only harmful to me. But here I am, dragging you into my nonsense, and I thought it would be best to get out of there."

"Instead of sticking around to fix it?"

She blew out a breath. "I never said this self-awareness came with good problem-solving skills."

That made him chuckle. He thought about last night, how she admitted she wanted to start her own charity, separate from her parents' sphere of influence. Something for her.

None of this meant that Georgia had wanted more from their mistaken marriage. After all, she'd put it down to grief over Dani. But he felt like he understood her a little bit better than before.

Plus there was the added bonus: she was still in his arms.

Yep, he'd adjusted his free hand to slide over and curl around her back. Now it rested, palm-down on her lower spine, just a skosh above the rise of her sweet little ass. No harm, no foul.

"No more apologies, okay? We're making it work for … reasons."

"Hmm. Reasons." She gave a raspy chuckle and that sound —God—it did things to him. Not just to his dick. "Is this great act working?"

His grandmother liked Georgia. His mom, too. That was all that mattered.

"Well enough."

She squirmed a fraction, and it reminded him of how close she was. How exquisite it felt to be on the edge like this. In the last few moments, his hand on her back had started to move in tight, soothing circles. *To comfort her*, he said. *To put her at ease.*

Now he coasted it down her back, grazed the top of her ass, and came back again.

She didn't pull away. If anything, she moved infinitesimally closer, enough to have him make an embarrassing sound of what could only be termed as pleasure.

"What?" she whispered. "Did I hurt you?"

"As if you could."

She made the same move, testing his limits. Always testing, this girl. He swallowed back a groan, determined she would get nothing from him. This was madness enough already.

"This is nice," she murmured, a whisper of breath against his chest.

He made an indeterminate sound.

"Did you sleep okay?"

"Eventually." Shit.

She raised her head, met his tired gaze head on. "You couldn't sleep? Because I'm here?"

Yes. No. "I'm not used to sharing a bed."

"At all? You mean ... you're a virgin?"

He smiled. "No, but it's been a while since I've slept in the same bed with someone. Not since ..." That night in Vegas. "I was engaged."

"This Stacy chick. I read about her online." She tapped his chest with her fingers. "What happened between you two?"

"We broke up. It happens."

"Yes, but why?"

"We didn't have much in common. Once the initial attraction faded there wasn't much to bind us together." It was too easy to say it was about what he could give her: money, fame, a life of luxury that really appealed to her. She wanted those things, but she figured out quickly that she could get them elsewhere. That he wasn't the kind of man to make her happy.

"You broke up with her?"

He barked a laugh. "That's kind of you, Georgia, but no. I knew something was wrong, but I didn't have the self-respect to end it." He wouldn't make that mistake again. Once this thing with Georgia was finished, he would ensure the separation was clean with no strings remaining to connect them.

"Sometimes we know something doesn't feel right but we want to believe so much. That our instincts can't be so off."

He turned his head to her. Is that what she thought … about them?

"What do you want to believe in?"

"That maybe I'll get it right one day. That I won't keep making the same mistakes."

Yet *this* felt right. Holding her, inhaling lungfuls of that sweet floral scent in her hair, this quiet talking before the rest of the house came awake.

Even his painful dick felt right.

But maybe that was because he *should* ache around her. Georgia was a woman worth yearning for.

"You're not quite the disaster you think you are, you know that?"

She hummed, the sound reverberating against his chest, and Christ, he loved the feeling. This closeness.

"I'm poisoning you with my food and my cat, disturbing your sleep patterns, and whining about my life." She peeked up at him. "You're not denying any of this."

"It's all true."

"Banks!" She pushed up on her elbow, sending her camisole off her shoulder and his dick into a tailspin. "You're supposed to soothe me. Tell me that I've done none of those things."

"Told you I was poor husband material."

"Awful." But she grinned, and his heart went *ka-boom*. Her

leg was still draped over his, her knee so close—and there it was again. That brush against his cock. He shifted and she noticed.

"Oh God, I'm sorry." She lifted the cover and peeked. "Is that my fault?"

"You're not to blame for everything, despite your preference for martyrdom."

"Hey!" She picked up her pillow and thumped him with it.

He quickly returned the favor, and soon Georgia was grappling with him to try to steal *his* pillow (after she'd lost control of hers and it landed on the floor on his side of the bed). The struggle ended with Banks holding her upper arms to keep her at length. His shoulder ached but nothing compared to his dick.

"Weakling."

"I am not!"

"Puny as a petal."

"How dare—"

She rolled over on top of him, smashing her breasts into his chest as she vainly tried for his pillow again. Angling for leverage, she straddled his hips while he lay back and refused to budge, his head keeping the pillow trapped.

"I've got you now," she panted.

That she did. She leaned over, one hand on his uninjured shoulder, the other splayed on one pec, and pushed as if that somehow signaled victory. Shifting an inch, her ass nudged his erection, the heat of her fabric-covered pussy over his abs an erotic furnace.

She squirmed, and there it was: a reveal of pleasure across her pretty features.

"I'm at your mercy," he said.

"You are." Her words were soft, accompanying another slight shift of her body, an ever so subtle grind.

"Take it."

She swallowed. "What?"

Your pleasure. "Your revenge."

Her fingers curled around his good shoulder, digging in. "For what?"

"Underestimating you. Calling you weak."

"You might not like it."

He had a feeling he would. He had a feeling he'd like any form Georgia's revenge took. "So what if I don't? This is for you."

She moved back another inch, another glance of his erection, the effect obvious. The fabric of her panties felt hot and damp against his skin.

Her lips parted but nothing emerged. She seemed frozen, unsure how to proceed.

"Tell me what you need," he whispered, and when she still appeared hesitant, he added, "Or show me."

That seemed to work better for her. Verbal wasn't in her wheelhouse right now, but she could take his hand and—

Place it over the front of her panties.

"You don't have to get too wordy, but I need one thing. A yes."

"Yes," she said immediately.

"And you'll tell me if you don't want anything. If I do a single thing you don't like."

"Yes."

Reaching up, she placed a hand on the headboard and her body a few inches off his abs. He slipped his hand underneath, in between her thighs, and cupped her.

Christ, she was as warm as the sun right there.

He rubbed along the fabric, getting her used to how his hand felt. Tracing a finger along the lacy edge inside one thigh, he pulled at the elastic and snuck inside. Just a touch. Then out again.

She squirmed. "Tease."

Again, he traced the edge, only this time he stretched the strip of cotton back to reveal soft, wet flesh.

She moaned, which had him practically hissing with pleasure. With a seeking index finger, he rubbed along her slit, then took his other hand and pulled her panties aside for better access. Still not enough.

"Take 'em off." His voice sounded gruff, bossy.

She adjusted enough so he could roll her panties off, then hold her steady while she pulled them down one leg, then the other. Positioning her back over him, he palmed the soft thatch of blonde curls before delving between her folds with one thumb. Her entire body shivered at the intrusion.

Taking two fingers, he stroked through her soft, sensitive flesh, relishing all the wetness he found there.

"Fuck, you feel good."

She sawed her body over his fingers, evidently desperate for more friction. "Oh please, oh God, yes. Please." She was so wet, so hot. So perfect with her pouty bottom lip being dragged by her teeth and her hard nipples poking through the camisole. He had no idea where to look: her body undulating over him, her gorgeous lips parted in ecstasy, her sweet little pussy just begging for his cock.

That bad boy was dying to get in on the action. But this was Georgia's show—his perfect, sensual peach of a wife. How fucking lucky was he?

But she's not your wife. She's here because of some fucked up quid pro quo, not because she wants you.

Yet her body wanted this. Her hot little ass wanted it. Those nipples and her dripping pussy needed it, and while he couldn't take what he wanted, he was happy to give her the best his fingers could provide.

He circled her clit, spreading moisture, and there it was again—that shiver of pleasure, followed by Georgia's raspy moan. She hitched back and forth, her movements agitated to the point that she rubbed against his erection. His cock was so damn hard, and that was the last straw—or would be if he didn't switch her position.

He had a choice: get her on her back, finish her off with his fingers, or pull her over his mouth and get a taste that might keep him going for a while.

His body made the call for him. Shifting down, pulling her forward, spreading her to give his mouth the best possible access. For a moment, he hesitated, wondering if he was about to cross a line, go to a place from which there was no return.

"Dylan." His raspy name on her lips was the push he needed. One hand on her sweet ass, the other on her inner thigh, and then heaven. Soft, heated flesh on his tongue, the tang of her like nothing he'd ever tasted. He held her still as he licked inside her, savoring each sweet drop that dripped down his throat. She started to shake. He speared harder with his tongue, then continued in long, languorous licks of her pussy.

She shook more. Moaned his name. Tried to get more friction, but he knew what she needed. His mouth eating her out like the best treat. He licked her little clit, sucked on it, alternating between licking and sucking and tongue-fucking until she came with clenched thighs and something like a squeak.

Of course, his wife's orgasm sounds would be different than any other woman's.

Immediately she lifted her body to give him air while she rested her arms on the headboard.

He squeezed her ass. "You okay?"

"No."

His heart sank. Had he gone too far? Should he have sought further consent to put his tongue inside her like that?

"Georgia, I'm sorry."

She pulled her leg over and settled at his shoulder with her legs tucked under her body. "For what? Giving me the best orgasm of my life?"

His heart soared. "Maybe?"

"Banks, I'm only mad because I've been missing out all these years. I had no idea it could be that good."

He'd surprised her. Well, of course. No one who knew him would think he had those kinds of skills.

Her face was flushed, her pupils dilated, and her lips—Christ, he wanted to kiss her so badly. She was staring at him, and with the way her chin dipped, he thought that maybe she felt the same way.

She traced a hand over his chest, careful to avoid his bruises. "Thanks."

"Any time."

Her gaze moved down his body to where his dick was saluting the royalty in the room. His wife. He'd just been intimate with his wife.

And it was nowhere near enough. It wasn't just an ache to be satisfied, his cock inside her, the crushing desire for release —it was more. It was a need for connection. For purpose.

This woman was feeling like his reason for ... he didn't know yet.

Tentatively, he reached for her, knuckles first, a brush against her naked hip.

She didn't object. She moved her hand down to cup his cock, still encased in his briefs.

"Hi," she whispered.

"He says hi back."

A lovely laugh erupted from her as she palmed him with more pressure. "You'll have to translate for me."

A knock sounded on the door, making Georgia jump and unfortunately drop her hand from his dick.

"Breakfast is up, lovebirds!" His mother's voice crashed the party. "And we need to get ready for your sisters."

"Your sisters." Georgia's eyes reflected terror. "And the game! Oh my God, you have so much to do today and here I am, interfering with your prep again."

Squeezing one out would work perfectly for his prep, but it looked like that was no longer an option because Georgia was busily scouring the bed for her panties. Far too quickly, she found them, and had them on before he could spend any significant time enjoying the sight of her gorgeous, round ass.

"Okay if I use the bathroom first?"

"Su—" But she was already gone.

He took a gander at his aching dick and sighed. Looked like he'd be heading into the series, frustrated as ever.

25

Georgia tapped her fingers on the table at the coffee shop and sent another longing look toward the door. What had she been thinking?

Sending out an SOS on the first day of the playoffs was probably one of her worst ideas. Of course everyone would be busy. She checked her phone again, expecting to see an incoming message from Tara, telling her that she couldn't join a frivolous bitch like Georgia for coffee after all.

"Watch you don't burn a hole in that phone."

Georgia looked up to find a grinning Tara, looking as glamorous as ever, pushing a stroller with her daughter, Esme. Behind her was a tall, striking woman with familiar cheekbones.

"Oh, hi, you're here!"

"Of course! I don't think you guys have met—this is my bestie, Mia Wallace. I know you wanted me all to yourself, but given your request, she is really the best person to help here. I'll get the coffees in. Another for you, G?"

"No, I'm fine."

Leaving Esme in her stroller playing with a cuddly giraffe, Tara waltzed off.

Mia took a seat opposite Georgia. "We've met before."

"We have. Outside the Empty Net a couple of weeks ago."

"You were on the verge of something, I think."

That was perceptive. "It's kind of complicated."

Mia held up her hand. "I won't pry, and if you'd rather I left so you can chat with Tara, then I'll take my coffee to go."

"Not at all. If Tara thinks you should be here, then that's fine by me."

Esme held up her giraffe, her grin toothy and bright. "Mama!"

"She'll be back in a second, sweetheart." Georgia turned to Mia with a grimace. "I know zero about babies."

"Neither do I, but this one is her mother's daughter. A real attention-seeker." Mia's lips twitched. "So, Banks, huh?"

Georgia could feel a blush coming on, the mere mention of his name taking her back to the morning's delights. His mouth on her, sucking, licking, kissing ...

Mia chuckled. "I see."

"Do you know him?"

"Not well. He and my husband are teammates, so we've crossed paths. He's got a great line drive, amazing vision from the center half."

"You're married to Cal Foreman, right?" He occupied one of her flash cards, but she hadn't done any research on his wife beyond her name.

"Yep, one of the first line right wingers. He's not having quite as good a season as Banks, plus-minus not up to scratch, but all that can change in the playoffs."

"Wallace, you have to take it slow." Tara sat down with two coffees and an assortment of pastries. She pulled a sippy cup out of her Givenchy slouchy hobo and gave it to Esme, then pushed a scone toward Georgia. "Mia is an Olympic gold medal-winning hockey player and plays for the Athenas, the women's pro-hockey franchise in Chicago."

"Oh, wow!" Georgia was seriously impressed. "I didn't understand much of what you said, though, which is why I called on Tara for help. I'm starting to realize that it's not a good day to do it. Both of you must be so busy."

"Doing what? Supporting our men?" Tara winked at Mia, who devolved into laughter.

"Uh, no." Mia broke off a corner of one of the scones. "The guys do not need us messing up their prep, not today of all days."

Exactly what she'd been doing for the last week, and then this morning, when she tempted Banks into touching and tasting and licking—oh God! She covered her face in her hands.

Tara pulled at her wrist gently. "Hey, what's wrong? We'll get you up to speed. You'll arrive at that game, knowing all the ins and outs of hockey."

"That's not it. Well, I need to know that, but all I can think of is how disruptive my presence is for Banks. Between Cheddar making him sneeze, practically poisoning him with my cooking, not to mention the sleeping situation ... is it any wonder he was dying to get out of the house this morning?"

Tara and Mia exchanged concerned glances.

"The sleeping situation?" Tara asked.

"We're—well—putting on a bit of a performance for his grandmother."

Mia's mouth dropped open. "Come again?"

"God, no!" Georgia huffed out a wispy laugh. "I mean, our marriage. We should be divorced by now, but there was a paperwork issue and Banks asked that we stay hitched because his grandmother wants to see him happy."

Ten minutes later, she'd filled them in, though she left out the morning's more intimate details, along with her own reasoning for staying in the marriage. Both women stared at her for an embarrassingly long time.

"I know this is kind of out there."

"Not at all," Tara said. "You're looking at the woman who was paid to fake date a hockey player, then fell for the team's general manager after she had insulted him several times with the label, 'geriatric'."

"And if crazy inciting incidents are your jam," Mia said, "how about the one where a certain player was called out online for being a jerk, then the person who slandered him proceeded to demand he dispense all his masculine wisdom *and* help her seduce another guy?" She thumbed at herself to indicate she was the person. "And he happened to be her brother's best friend!"

"Not to mention my ex," Tara piped up with a laugh.

Georgia inhaled a calming breath. "So I'm joining an exclusive club, it seems."

"Sure, the club of rocky and ridiculous relationship starts." Tara grinned. "And that's just us two. Everyone on the team has a story to tell. An accidental marriage in Vegas coupled with some fakery for the rellies and the media? That's pretty tame, G. You're going to have to do better than that." Esme giggled, and Tara poked her gently in the belly. "Isn't she, Ezzie?"

Mia laughed. "Like send him divorce papers right before Game 7 of the Cup Finals."

"Or tell him you're pregnant. With triplets!"

Mia pointed at Tara. "Right before Game 7 with a big sign against the plexi."

Georgia had to laugh at that one. She could get through this. Just a few more weeks, with Banks practicing or playing or traveling for most of it. By then, hopefully, her parents would have released her funds.

"Luckily this is a purely business arrangement. There will eventually be divorce papers, but I won't be milking the drama and doing it during an important game. And neither will I be announcing my triplet pregnancy to the world, at least not before I tell my husband."

Even saying *my husband* aloud was just part of the crazy scheme. She could enjoy the skitter of pleasure down her spine, a perk of this kooky caper.

"A business arrangement?" Mia shot a quick look at Tara. "Sorry, but we've heard that one a million times, too. Ask Kennedy and Reid. Or Violet and Bren. Something about the forced proximity and only one bed ... that's going to blow that business arrangement out of the water."

"No, it's not!" Georgia pointed a finger at Mia. "Neither of us is interested in anything for the long-term. This is just to help each other out." Realizing that she'd revealed more than she intended—this was all supposed to be a favor to Banks after all—she rushed on. "But I need to keep up my cover and give the middle finger to those TikTok bitches, which means I need to know how the game works before I sit with his family in his seats and make a fool of myself."

She took out a new set of index cards and a pen and placed them on the table.

"Okay, okay," Tara said with a raised hand. "Mia, babe, you're up."

~

"OH MY GOD, these seats are amazing!"

April, the oldest of Banks's sisters, wended her way along the seat row with her mouth agape.

Sandra ("call me Sandy!") poked her in the rear. "Move it along, rubbernecker. At this rate, the game'll be over before we sit down."

"Can I not enjoy the moment? Georgia, you have to sit in the middle so we can all have access."

"No problem."

She'd tried to dress "sporty," which for Georgia meant the team's colors—a dark blue dress with a tulip skirt, though navy wasn't really her best color, along with white trimmings of a Kate Spade purse, belt, and shoes. (Stella McCartney wedge trainers to give her a boost.) But then everyone insisted she wear a Banks jersey, so here she was swimming in Sandy's spare, wearing dark-washed denim and a pair of Trish's Tecovas cowgirl boots, trying not to overtly enjoy the fact she had BANKOWSKI in large letters across her back.

"You okay, Connie?" Georgia leaned over and squeezed the old lady's hand.

"I will be as soon as I have a drink inside me. Where's the martini boy?"

"Oh, martini boy?" Trish called out, which set everyone off, especially as the "martini boy" who arrived was sixty if he was a day. He only stocked beers, however, which Georgia knew from her research was the drink of choice at the Big Game. "Five of your finest, please."

"That'll be $65."

For five beers? Daylight robbery.

"Let me buy this round." Given Georgia's dislike of beer, she'd be nursing this one to the end.

"Not at all." Trish already had the cash out. She paid and started passing just-poured beers down the row.

Once everyone was beered up and settled, Georgia looked around. She spotted Mia a couple of rows back with Ashley,

Dex's girlfriend, and her lovely daughter, Willa. Raising her beer, she got a thumbs up from Mia in return.

"Better seats than me, Bankowski?" Mia called out. "So much for player seniority!"

Georgia laughed. And Bankowski? She hadn't given *that* any thought at all. This wasn't a real marriage, so she wouldn't be changing her name, but the idea of leaving "Goodwin" behind held a lot more appeal than expected.

Sandy looked over her shoulder. "That's Mia Wallace. Do you know her?"

"A little. We had coffee today, actually. She's so nice."

"Killer player," April said. "And her husband is so fit. You must know them all, Georgia."

"Not terribly well."

"Right." Sandy winked at her. "Because you and Dylan were keeping it all under wraps for a while. He probably wouldn't let you out of the house."

"Or bedroom," April added.

"Girls, don't be crass," Trish said.

"Sorry, Mom!" Both of them said in unison with a conspiratorial snigger in Georgia's direction.

That was the story they'd been going with for Connie's sake, only Banks's sisters were supposed to be in on the scheme. Why then were they acting as though this marriage was real?

April and Sandy had arrived mid-afternoon. After a quick pizza delivery dinner/Q&A at the house, they'd checked in with the rest of the family in Apple Falls. Kelly, Banks's youngest sister, and her husband, Jason, and their adorable twins were on the call along with Sandy's wife, Amy, and their daughter, Scarlet, and April's husband, Carlos, and their little girl, Jenny. (Thank God for her flash cards.) Busy with school and spring activities, they'd all stayed home, but they would be watching with a ton of other Bankowski relatives at Kelly's house later and had plans to come to Chicago if the team made it to the later rounds.

After the call, the Chicago contingent had bundled into a couple of Ubers to head to the arena (not stadium, as Georgia had learned from Mia this morning).

Georgia was used to surrounding herself with people—it was her go-to strategy to keep her grief on a simmer instead of a boil—but she was usually able to keep everyone focused on the party, the fun, what so-and-so was wearing. Rarely was she the center of attention except in the most superficial way. Georgia and her amazing taste in clothes. Georgia and her rock star boyfriend. Georgia and her latest escapade.

But now she was part of something that felt *authentic*, for want of a better word, and while it wasn't real, it was nice to pretend.

"I'm guessing you guys have seen your brother play tons of times."

April waved both hands. "A zillion. But the playoffs are where it's at."

"Yeah, even this first round is exciting." Georgia had read up on the playoffs structure as well as Banks's history in them. He'd never won the Cup, though he'd come close a couple of times in the last fifteen years. "Must be heartbreaking for him to not have won the big one. And for you guys, too."

Sandy looked a touch emotional as she checked to see that Connie and Trish were distracted, chatting with a woman and her teenage daughter behind them. "To be honest, it's toughest for Mom and Gran. He's got a few years left in him, but he'd love nothing more than to win it for Gran this year. It's kind of weird that he'd mess with his routine like this."

April shot a glare at her sister. "Quit it," then to Georgia, "Don't mind her. She's filter-free sometimes."

"No, it's okay. I understand why this would seem an odd choice."

Sandy shook her head. "Not you. I mean, you're amazing. But hockey players are creatures of habit. And our brother has always been a slave to his regimen. To see him go a little, well, *mad* is kind of out there."

April cut in. "What's weirder is that he kept it on the down low for so long."

"Probably because we hate everyone he dates." Sandy grinned. "But the ones he marries ... that's another story."

"Thank God for that," Georgia said, keeping her tone light. "But he did think we were finished. The paperwork said otherwise."

"Yeah, but he usually tells us stuff, even his supposed mistakes. Still, I'm not surprised he was quiet about you. We were not kind to Stacy."

Stacy again.

"She was such a bitch." April was definitive. "And we *knew* her! We don't know you, but if you made it down the aisle with our boy, you've got to be an improvement."

Trish leaned over. "You okay, Georgia? Not letting these two browbeat you into revealing all your marital secrets?"

"They're just protective of their brother. It's sweet."

Trish raised an eyebrow. "These girls are a lot of things, but sweet is not one of them."

"Mom!" Sandy winked at Georgia. "We need to see if she can handle the Bankowski Babes in all their glory. Membership is pending."

"Only pending?" Georgia asked. "What do I need to do to make the grade?"

"Don't fuck up our brother."

"Sandy!" April leaned over to thump her sister, which had

Sandy reaching behind Georgia to pull on April's ear, who then started complaining that Sandy was the problem.

Georgia really missed her sister.

Connie let out a piercing whistle that brought everyone to attention. "Quit your tomfoolery! The boys are here."

The lights dimmed and the announcer launched into introductions. It was all very Vegas, which appealed to Georgia given her history with Banks. First the players of the opposing team, the Boston Cougars, came on, then the home-town boys. When Banks's name was called, the Bankowski Babes went wild—and Georgia was right there with them.

After all, she was being judged for membership.

26

BANKS WAS TIRED.

He'd barely slept. Waking up to find his wife wrapped around him was both excruciatingly torturous and absolutely amazing at the same time. Which made no sense. How could he be enjoying this drama that had taken over his life when he was the least drama-free person on the planet?

It was hard to say which gave him more pleasure: the easy roll into the morning conversing with Georgia or the fact she'd let him taste her. And not just chaste kisses, but his tongue inside her, his lips drenched with her come, his—

"Banks, you're up," Coach called out.

Clearing the boards, he skated into position, on the same line as O'Malley and Petrov. He won the face-off—his 67% winning percentage still stood—and they were off. Two minutes later, he was back on the bench with a shot on goal and the satisfaction of having acquitted himself decently on his first shift.

Every playoff series, his family came to as many games as they could. He took comfort in their presence, but he didn't feel a need to check on them every thirty seconds. Tonight should be no different, except all he could think of was Georgia.

Was she excited to be here?

Did she understand what was going on?

Why the hell was she all he could see, her platinum crown a beacon in the wave of blue-and-white, a lighthouse calling him in? (Though lighthouses were supposed to keep ships *away* from rocky shores, not draw them closer to oblivion.)

Even if he couldn't have picked her out, it wouldn't have mattered. The Jumbotron was determined to show her at every opportunity, which is how he knew she was wearing his Rebels jersey. That his wife had his name on her back, a proxy for his claim on her, turned him on in a big way. He should not be going there, but once the idea took root, it was *all* he could think of.

And what it would be like to peel that jersey off her later.

"Banks!" He looked up. Coach had that exasperated look on his face that indicated he'd been screaming his head off for longer than he felt necessary.

Focus, man. Get it together.

The first period ended, scoreless, and Banks skated off with O'Malley by his side.

"Georgia's here, huh?" Kind of shifty with it.

"Yep."

"First time at a hockey game?"

"No idea."

"Still keeping your cards close to your chest, then."

He accepted skate guards from an assistant. "Just don't have a whole lot to say."

"Is that a dig at me because I can't shut up about Ash?"

"Sure. Now how about you zip it and let me focus during the break?"

O'Malley just grinned. Like Kershaw, another chatty

fucker, he was impossible to offend. Since he'd pulled his head out of his ass and found true love, he thought he was a cut above the rest of the singletons on the team.

But you're not single. You are husband to a queen, and well and truly fucked.

With the start of the second period, he resolved to apply every ounce of concentration to Game Freakin' 1. His job was hockey player, not husband, and he needed to put all thoughts of his hot wife aside and set about scoring.

On his first shift in, he won the face-off, natch, and passed to O'Malley. Back to center, a flick to Petrov, who sent it around the back of the net where O'Malley was waiting. After a few more seconds of do-si-do, Banks spotted an opening. The Boston tender was a couple of inches off his line and McMillan, their D-man, had moved too far left. Petrov was waiting for the setup, but Banks could already visualize the throughline. The second the puck left his stick he knew it was destined for the back of the net.

The buzzer went off and finally, the Rebels were on the scoreboard.

McMillan was pissed, enough to whack at the puck and send it flying toward the plexi. Only it missed and went over the glass into the crowd, a result that became obvious when a groan went up in response.

But there was more. Shouting, sort of high-pitched, and the realization that the puck hadn't merely *landed* in the crowd.

It had hit someone.

The officials weren't restarting the game and that was usually down to one reason: a spectator needed a medic. Banks paid more attention now, especially as the puck had landed close to the players' comp section. His first thought was Connie, but he immediately spotted her, looking uninjured, thank God. His mom was beside her, moving, then standing. She was fine, too.

Please let no one he knew be hurt. Not that he'd wish it on anyone else, but—shit, there was no way to make that palatable. Someone else stood and he recognized April from the back. Skating closer, he sought her out, willing her to turn to him. When she didn't, he moved along the row.

Georgia was supposed to be sitting next to her, but Sandy was blocking his view. Get the fuck out of the way!

Out of the corner of his eye, he watched with an increasing sense of panic as medics made their way to the section. April turned around and met his gaze squarely, mouthing the words he did not want to hear.

It's Georgia.

Georgia was hurt.

The medics were in there now, and people were stepping aside into the aisle to make room, which gave him his first unobstructed view. Her hand was at her forehead and the unmistakable, oily hue of blood was staining her fingers.

Someone nudged him from behind. O'Malley. "Is that Georgia?"

Keep her name out of your mouth.

The medics would take her somewhere and get her checked out.

Bleeding. Maybe blinded.

She was standing. That had to be a good sign. And then the crowd groaned again because Georgia had lost her footing, or perhaps fainted, and she was half-carried out of the row and into the aisle. The usual hockey stick taps from the players accompanied her exit, with the crowd clapping to encourage a quick recovery.

Back to hockey, people!

Fuck that. With a desperate pivot, he skated back to the boards and hopped over.

Coach eyed him. "Shift's not over, Banks."

"Is for me."

Coach looked flummoxed.

"That's his wife who got hurt, Coach." O'Malley was at his shoulder to explain.

Coach opened his mouth, whether to give or deny permission, Banks had no idea. He was already heading to the tunnel.

Georgia did not consider herself accident-prone. Sure, she'd landed in hot water plenty of times but that was usually engineered by her own hands.

And then she met Dylan Bankowski.

Within hours of knowing him, she was married.

Within days of knowing him, she should have been divorced.

Within months of knowing him, she was embedded in this drawing room farce, playacting at husband and wife.

Now she was holding a lump of gauze to her forehead, surrounded by several people who were probably *very* concerned about litigation.

"I'm so sorry about this," she said to April. "You should go back to your seats."

April barked out a nervy laugh. "Like we could leave you alone!"

"Dylan would kill us if we did," Sandy added, which didn't make Georgia feel better.

She had been cheering Banks's goal like everyone else and had just stood when she felt like she'd been shot. Instinctively she'd touched her stinging forehead, only to find wetness. With her hand covered in blood, she sank to her seat, and then all hell broke loose.

Georgia, is it your eye? Did it break your nose? Why aren't you speaking, crying, howling?

Shocked into silence, she'd spent the next minute protecting her eyes from the dripping blood. There were so many people, and she could barely breathe with all the attention. By the time the medics arrived, the adrenaline was starting to wear off and dizziness was setting in.

"Where are Connie and Trish?"

"We told them to stay put so as not to overwhelm you," Sandy said. "We're keeping them updated. Or we would, *if we could get some medical assistance!*"

On cue, someone entered with an authoritative air and now proceeded to examine her more closely.

"Georgia, is it?"

"That's right."

"I'm Dr. Morgan. You've got a nasty cut there. If you were a player, I'd stitch you up, but it might leave a scar."

"I can live with a scar. I'm more worried about internal damage." *And how to get blood out of this Kate Spade.*

He smiled. "The fact you can string a sentence together bodes well. Any dizziness? Blurred vision? Nausea?"

She shook her head, though that didn't feel so good. "A slight headache."

"Understandable."

Outside the room, a commotion was brewing.

"Where is she?"

That sounded like Banks! He was supposed to be out on the ice, for God's sake.

"I need to see my wife."

Without dropping his gaze, the doc called out. "She's here."

A wild-eyed Banks plowed his way through the crowd. Shouldering the doctor out of the way—kind of rudely, she thought—he cupped her face with both hands and searched her face.

"You okay?"

"I-I think so. The dizziness has passed—"

"You're dizzy?" He snapped his stormy gaze to the doctor. "Why isn't she getting a scan? She has a concussion."

"Possibly," the doctor said amiably. "We were just about to send her to the hospital. She'll need stitches."

"Is the game ... stopped?" Is that what they did when a spectator was injured? She blinked at Banks, not understanding how he was here. He looked like he was about to explode.

"No, it's started up again," he gritted out.

She placed both hands on his chest, but it was all padding and not much Banks. Seeing him in his hockey gear up close was doing strange, wonderful things to her, though that might have been the brain injury. "And you're here?"

"Where else would I be?"

She pushed but it was like trying to move a statue. "No, no, no. You need to get back out there."

"They already have my goal. And as I can't rely on my family to keep you out of trouble, I'm going to have to do it myself." He turned to the doctor. "Now where's that ambulance?"

27

IT WAS ALMOST two in the morning by the time they made it home. The lights were on in the foyer, but all was quiet. Over the course of multiple calls, Banks had insisted to his family that they needn't stay up, and Georgia was glad they heeded his advice. She really didn't want to talk to anyone after spending the last four hours being prodded, scanned, and interrogated.

She felt stupid. Intellectually she knew that it was purely bad luck that she was seated there, and the puck came hurtling her way. But she couldn't help feeling that this was one more mark in the column of things that Georgia did to make a bad situation worse. Banks had missed the rest of the game because he insisted on accompanying her to the hospital and sticking by her side through every test. The radiologist had to threaten to call security so Banks would remain outside the imaging facility. (Threats to his sperm count didn't work.)

He'd held her hand in the ambulance. He'd held her hand as they waited to be seen, only letting go to fill out the paperwork (he had to ask for things like her social security number and her date of birth, but he gave his insurance information because "we're married"). He'd held her hand as the ER doctor examined her and Banks insisted that a plastic surgeon be called in to do the stitch job.

There would be a small scar, the specialist had said. Banks held her hand through that as well, as if worried she was going to break down in tears at this insult to her classically beautiful forehead. The potential for scarring didn't bother her, but she liked that he held her hand all the same.

She'd take another puck to the head if it meant he held her like this forever.

The CT scan said there was no bleeding on the brain and that everything looked fine. She was allowed to sleep, but if her headache persisted or other symptoms like nausea or vomiting occurred, she should return to the doctor.

Only when they left the taxi that took them to Banks's front door did he release her hand.

"How are you feeling?"

"Tired, but punchy."

"I could punch someone. Fucking McMillan."

"Was that the player who—"

"Lost his shit because we scored."

Thankfully, the team had gone on to win, 3-1. Georgia would never have forgiven herself if Banks's absence had resulted in a loss on top of everything else.

"Next time, I'll duck."

He rubbed his mouth. "I'd understand if there wasn't a next time. You've done your duty."

"Are you kidding? I barely got a chance to show off my skills."

"Your skills?"

She walked into the kitchen and picked up the electric kettle, only to have Banks take it from her, set it down, then set *her* down on one of the kitchen island stools.

He filled the kettle and flicked the power switch. "The raspberry one?"

"No, lemon ginger."

He nodded. "What was that about your skills?"

"I learned all about hockey today. The rules, the playoffs, the stats." *What a big deal you are.* "And I was just about to drop some knowledge when that puck dropped me instead."

Through his beard she could discern the Banks smirk. "Drop it on me."

Suddenly every single factoid she had learned vanished from her brain (puck to the head, remember?). Probably for the best. How silly would it be to tell *him* the rules?

Maybe something about his career instead.

"You won the Hart Memorial award ten years ago. The Art Ross one, too."

"That was the year before."

"For scoring the most points."

He tore open the packet for the tea bag and put it in the mug. "Awards are a thing of the past for me now."

"Why?"

He shrugged his broad shoulders. "Hockey's a young man's game. I've got a couple more years left in me, but I won't be scaling those heights again."

His chances at the Cup were running out, yet another reason for her to be mad at herself. She was distracting him at this most important time.

The water finished its boil and Banks filled the mug. Placing it on the counter, he took a seat beside her. "Are you hungry?"

She shook her head, resigned defeat overwhelming her.

"I'm sorry about what happened at the game. That was so important to you, and you were playing so well, scoring a goal, and then I go and screw it up. Again. All night you've been nothing but kind and—"

He kissed her.

Not soft, not hard, just perfect. Maybe to shut her up?

Definitely to shut her up.

He had heard the panic in her voice, and he knew this was what she needed. It was like she could breathe again.

His lips tugged at hers, parting them, taking control. She felt the press of his hands to her waist and the subtle dig of his fingers into her flesh, like he was molding her to a calmer state. Before the kiss went too deep, he pulled back.

"This isn't your fault. It could have happened to anyone, and I'm so fucking relieved it didn't blind you or break your nose or give you a brain injury. You could have blacked out and woken up forgetting we were married."

She blinked. "And that would be a bad thing?"

"A terrible thing."

He wanted her to remember they were married. To remember *them*.

"But you missed the rest of the game."

"You think that was important to me?"

She placed a fist against his chest. "Yes! It was Game 1 of the playoffs. At home. In front of your family. And you scored a goal. After a season where your face-time percentage is the highest in the league."

"It's face-offs, but I like your spin on it." He raised an eyebrow. "Someone's been doing her homework."

"I told you! I have all the freakin' knowledge."

That made him laugh, a deep rumble that she'd take to her grave as her favorite sound in the world. All the more precious for its rarity.

His gaze dipped to her mouth again, then down over her blood-stained Rebels jersey. His demeanor turned grave again.

"I'm okay, Dylan."

He blew out a breath, a hot puff of air that tickled her lips. She wanted him to kiss her again, to peel off this jersey, the one with his name. To move those hot, rough hands over her skin.

He curled a hand around her neck and used his thumb to hold her still while he looked her over. "My wife took a puck to the head. If I wasn't so worried I'd be pretty proud."

That thrill through her body when he said "my wife" was a dangerous, dangerous thing.

"I've got the scar to prove it."

"A keepsake for when this is over."

Her heart dropped to the floor tile. Of course he had the end in sight, as he should. He'd want his no-drama life back.

His family would be leaving soon, and Banks would probably want to start the process of separation. He wouldn't need to have Georgia on site any longer. Sure he might pretend for Connie, but the mental severance would begin. It would be better for his game, for his life, for his sanity.

But what about *her* life? *Her* sanity? She wanted something to remember, something to hold onto. This scar wouldn't be enough.

His hand stayed where it was, his thumb tracing a gentle line over her cheekbone and jawline.

"Come on, Champ, let's check in on Cheddar then get you to bed."

She turned back to her herbal tea, seeking the calm his callused hands couldn't give her. Wishing like hell she was brave enough to ask for what she really needed.

～

By the time he came out of the bathroom, Georgia was under the covers, curled up like a cat. Seeing her lying there, vulnerable and quiet, almost had him shaking again.

He'd thought he lost her.

Overstating it, maybe, but a puck to the head was not trivial. There could have been brain damage, and even now there might be lasting effects. All because he asked her to sit in his section.

Insisted. Not for his family, not to save face. Because he wanted people to know his wife was there, rooting for him. He wanted to show her off.

What a selfish fuck he was.

Head injury care protocol had moved on in the last few years. No longer was there an expectation to wake the patient every couple of hours to make sure they hadn't slipped into a coma. These days, uninterrupted rest was preferred. Not that he'd get any. But he was fine with watching Georgia breathe, ensuring that it was steady, even, unlabored. The tiny bandage strips over her cut were as wispy as she was.

Stripping to his briefs, he slipped under the covers, turned out the light, and lay on his back staring at the ceiling.

She placed an arm around his torso and snuggled into his good shoulder. "Go to sleep, Big Guy."

Like this? Not likely.

He should not have kissed her in the kitchen. He'd only wanted to calm her down. She was so worried she'd upset his routine, his game, his life—and while it was true, he couldn't let her feel like that. She needed to know she wasn't a burden. She could never be.

She didn't think he should have left the game. That she wasn't worth leaving the game for. He got the impression Georgia was not used to being the center of attention. Strange, considering her upbringing and her many appearances in the media, but she'd taken a backseat to her sister for much of her life. He'd read up on it, curious about the psychological impact of being the healthy sibling of an unwell child. They even had a name for it: glass child syndrome. Overlooked, ignored, with expectations that the well sibling remain on an even keel and not rock the boat.

Tonight, she'd been anxious that no one make a fuss. Didn't even want him to contact her parents.

Georgia needed someone to take care of her, not that she'd ever admit it. He wasn't even sure why *he* was admitting it. Probably guilt over what happened.

Her soft breathing against his neck should have soothed instead of inflamed. But then that was Georgia. What should have been comfort was closer to torture. She moved her head, and he moved his, so he could brush his lips against her forehead. He remained like that, contorted like an ogre, holding onto his princess for dear life.

"You're tense," she whispered.

"You should be sleeping."

"I can't. My heart is racing." She took his hand and placed it against her breast. "See?"

The heat and life beneath his fingertips traveled an electric current down his arm and onward. His belly. His cock.

That fucker twitched, loving the closeness. The sheer, sexy potential.

His hand flexed against her chest, and his fingers itched to cup and curve her gorgeous tit. Just as he was about to pull away, she covered his hand with hers and placed it where it needed to be.

"Georgia—"

"Please." The tone in her voice was desperate. "Touch me, Dylan."

His fingers tingled, his hand flexing to shape that mound

of heated flesh through her camisole. Gently he massaged his thumb over the pebbled nipple. He turned to her, seeking better access, and caught her eyes striped by lights from the partially open blind. They shone bright, her lips parted and wet from the flick of her tongue.

Jesus, she was beautiful.

He needed to feel her skin, all the gorgeous heat of it. Pulling at the hem of her top, he pushed it up over her breasts. His hand found purchase again, this time without the barrier of her top, and he took a moment to explore. Her tits were small but perfectly formed, gorgeous swells in his palm.

His mouth watered with desire. Just a quick taste because he might not have the stamina for anything longer. His cock was thickening, desperate for attention.

Meanwhile these pretty tits needed his mouth on them now. Tongue first, the flat against a nipple. Her breathy gasp became a whimper when he plumped her flesh and took it between his lips. He sucked on her tit, then kissed a path between them before applying his efforts to the other one.

His dick started to leak. *Not gonna last.*

Mouth full and busy, he coasted his hand down her stomach over the round of her belly until he reached—

Shocked, he withdrew his fingers. *No panties.*

The darkness made it seem like a secret, one that would vanish in the night shadows along with their fake marriage. He didn't want fake.

He wanted real.

He leaned over to turn on the lamp and pulled back the covers.

His beautiful wife lay before him, her camisole pushed up above her breasts, which were tinged pink from where he'd suckled them. Otherwise, she was completely naked, wild-eyed, and panting.

"Where are your panties, Peaches?"

"The laundry basket." She licked her lips, sucked in a breath. "If what you're really asking is why am I naked, I'm hoping that's obvious."

It was becoming so. His wife needed a little TLC.

"Are we sure this isn't you in a weakened state after suffering a brain injury?"

"Someone else will have a brain injury if he doesn't satisfy his wife's conjugal rights."

For all that sass, she still looked vulnerable. Like asking for what she wanted was a big deal. She was worried that he might not want to reciprocate.

While he was worried that she was still recovering from a puck to the head and once he started, he'd drill her into the mattress.

"We'll take it slow." He pulled at her bunched-up top, gently eased it over her head and dropped it on the floor. Another heated stare down her lovely nakedness was soon followed by his rough hand over her tits, her stomach, and around to her sweet ass for a squeeze.

She inhaled sharply and arched her back a touch. Her fingertips touched his cheek, then moved over his bruised shoulder, the bump from the separation.

"Still hurts?" she asked.

"Can only feel you."

Curling a hand around his bearded jaw, she pulled him closer and touched her lips to his. The barest brush, and it set him on fire. "Can you feel this?"

She was asking about more than the physical.

"Can feel you everywhere, Georgia."

The kiss started softly but that didn't last long. Lust slammed through him, and that promise to take it slow vanished with the next stuttering heartbeat.

I want this woman so bad.

Too bad.

He drew back, trying to rein in these deeper feelings and transmute them into base desire. That was all this was. A dry spell, a warm woman in his bed, the adrenaline from seeing her hurt.

She chased his mouth, and that notion that she wasn't playing hard to get, that she needed this as much as he did crashed through him.

Let go. Enjoy this gift because it'll be gone soon.

He kissed her deeper, going all in with his gorgeous wife.

28

This kiss felt different.

It *all* felt different. More intense, more focused, just more.

This morning—was that only this morning?—he'd tasted her with his head between her thighs, and it had been wonderful. So hot.

But now, face to face, drinking each other in, she wouldn't let him get away with pleasing her and denying himself. This time, it would be for them both.

So when he moved his hand down her stomach, seeking the hot, wet flesh that ached for him, she followed suit. Her hand mapped each muscle from his shoulder to his chest to his abs to the one that was hard and thick against her thigh.

Wrapping her hand around him, she marveled at his girth. Her husband was big all over and she couldn't wait to feel him stretching and filling her. Until then, she'd drive him a little bit crazy.

"Tell me how you like it," she whispered as he swiped a finger through her damp folds. On her breathy gasp, she tightened her grip on his cock and got a very satisfying groan in return.

"More, baby. Don't be afraid of roughing me up a little."

Oh God, the way his voice thrummed through her, like he was rubbing it all over her skin, was so delicious. She parted her legs, letting them fall open to give him better access, and he took it. Two fingers now, rubbing and swirling through all that wetness. With each stroke, ribbons of pleasure eddied through her.

She rubbed her nose against his and he took it for the invitation it was: another deep, tongue-tangling kiss. She bowed her back, seeking more of that lovely friction. His mouth, his fingers, that mat of chest hair against her nipples.

His cock pulsed in her hands. She stroked again, harder, just how he liked it. She wanted to know everything he liked, not just this one, tiny—or big—thing. She wanted to know her husband.

"Is this good?" She cupped his cock and moved her palm up and down, squeezing at the base then again at the head.

His lips parted. "So good." One thick, callused finger glanced her clit and she almost exploded. Her body rose again, crashing into his.

"Dylan—oh God, yes. Yes."

More kisses, his fingers inside her now, getting her ready. Her hand was coated with his pre-come and she couldn't take her eyes off him. His panting sped up, as did hers, and a coil of tightness built in her core. She tensed as sensation rocked through her, that sweet flood of pressure finding an outlet.

Riding his fingers, she arched again, seeking his mouth, loving it with her own. He continued to rub, gentler now but no less inflaming. Then his hand was gone, taking over where hers had stopped, back on his cock.

He watched her carefully as he stroked, and it took a moment for her to realize what was happening.

"You don't want to be inside me?"

He closed his eyes, halted his stroke, and opened them again.

"You got hit with a fucking puck tonight."

"Right. And now I want to be hit with your fucking cock."

He squinted and she shook her head, laughing softly. "Sorry, that came out weird."

"Kind of."

"But the sentiment is the same. Don't treat me like a fragile doll. I can handle you, Banks."

To prove she meant business, she pushed his hand away and took over the job of pleasing him. *Her* job. A wife's duty, but one she was happy to fulfill.

"Georgia," he gutted out. "Not sure I can be inside you and not want to roar like a rutting beast."

He was worried about his family in the rooms beyond. Maybe about his shoulder injury, too, though he'd never admit it.

"We can be quiet. Just slip inside me and lose yourself." When he still hesitated, she moaned, "please."

He leaned back and yanked at the drawer, extracted a condom, tore it open. She released him long enough for him to suit up, then stroked the gorgeous length of him and guided him to her entrance.

"You sure?"

She loved that he was checking in. That he still had the brain cells to do it.

She planned to leave him with none by the end of this.

"Yes. Fuck me, Banks."

He was big and she was tight, and as he inched his way in, she tried to relax enough to take him fully. Holding his face, she pressed her lips to his, ready to take his groans and keep them inside her.

"Jesus, Peaches, you—fuck, you feel good."

She threw her leg over his hip and pulled him into her. Slowly he rocked, in and out, finding a rhythm that filled the hollow ache and turned everything soft and golden. And all the time, his eyes never left hers, those deep brown pools of desire.

He gripped her ass and plumped it, holding her tight and still while he moved inside her. Each thrust found new nerves, new ways to stoke the flames. She didn't expect to come. This was for him, but the sensation was building again, and suddenly it was for *them*. He moaned, so she kissed him, her rutting beast.

He withdrew a couple of inches, and they instinctively looked down to where their bodies connected. The sight of him, huge, slick with her, as he plunged made her pussy contract.

"Georgia!"

Too loud, but God, she loved her name on his lips. This was what it felt like to be important to someone, a moment distilled when she was at the center of another person's universe, and he hers.

"Shush," she hummed against his lips.

But he was too far gone. His strokes became quicker, more fervent, and his moans increased in volume. This man wanted the world to know his pleasure, and she was so caught up in it. The throbs in her core peaked, her pleasure tipped over, and she clamped down on his cock as a loud sob escaped her.

He met her orgasm with a juddering thrust and a groan loud enough to wake the entire house.

Lying still, she luxuriated in the weight of him, the solid comfort he brought. Seeming to shake himself back to reality, he propped himself up and stared at her.

"We good?"

"We are *so* good," she whispered back before a raspy laugh

erupted from her mouth. She clapped a hand over it and murmured, "sorry!"

"For what?"

"I was trying to be quiet and even keep you quiet so we wouldn't wake anyone, but damn, you're a noisy boy."

He chuckled. "That's what you do to me. Don't want to be quiet around you." He turned serious. "How's the head?"

"Didn't get any."

He grunted. "You did this morning, you greedy girl. And I meant your actual head."

"Could be worse. I could have *not* just had an amazing orgasm."

"Or two."

That set her off laughing again. He kissed her, probably to keep her quiet, but soon it was more than a kiss. It was everything.

He stopped on a sigh. "Gotta take care of business." Slowly he withdrew from her, as if worried he might hurt her. He headed to the bathroom, and she lay there quietly, pondering on what just happened. She wasn't fool enough to think it meant more than a tension release or him feeling sorry for her after what happened at the game. She would enjoy it for what it was: a lovely connection with a wonderful man.

He returned and climbed into bed. For a second, she thought he would stay on his side, but then he reached for her and pulled her close.

"You need your sleep." A tender kiss to her temple made her smile.

She'd rather stay awake, listen to his breathing, to all that life. But it turned out he was right: she did need it, and soon tiredness overtook her as she sank deeper into his embrace.

29

APRIL STOOD AT THE COUNTER, a whisk in one hand, the pancake mix box in the other. She looked up at Banks as he entered the kitchen.

"Is Georgia okay? What time did you guys get in last night?"

"She is. And almost two." He made himself a cup of coffee. "She's sleeping. Nasty cut and a bruise starting to show. But she'll be okay."

His sister shook her head. "I thought it took her eye out. I've never been so scared in my life. All I could think was: this poor girl. Quickly followed by: Dylan is going to kill me."

He hid his smile behind his cup. "You got the order of operations right."

"And she didn't even cry. I think she was just stunned. Literally." She measured some of the mix into the bowl. "Fucking McMillan."

"Yep," he affirmed.

"I don't think I've ever seen you so ..."

"Pissed."

"Smitten."

He put his cup down. "Smitten? What the fuck does that mean?"

"Infatuated, taken, affected, afflicted—"

"Are you reading from a thesaurus?" She had her phone on the counter, so it wouldn't have surprised him. "Afflicted makes it sound like I've come down with some sort of disease."

"Love is a disease, isn't it?"

Before he could respond, Sandy walked in. "Are we talking about Dylan's OTT reaction to not being able to get to his wife quickly enough?"

April grinned. "We are."

He picked up his coffee. "How is it OTT that I need to see the woman I married after she was injured? I'd be the same if it happened to one of you."

"'The woman I married'?" Sandy tilted her head and added in a deep voice that was supposed to be an impression of him, he gathered. "'*Where's my wife?*' You sounded like one of those beasts in the romances I read. The guys who turn into werewolves and have to find their mate or die trying."

"Which is kind of strange because we assumed you were just doing this for Gran." April quirked a very annoying eyebrow.

His coffee cup halted midway to his mouth. "I am."

"Right," April said. "But then what?" She shared a look with Sandy. "We understand, honestly. You did something crazy in Vegas. Something out of character, and instead of getting divorced, you decided to work through it because you're a good guy. For Gran. For Georgia. But maybe for yourself?"

He didn't respond. Someone might say he was curious to hear them out.

That someone was *not* him.

Sandy lowered her voice. "We encouraged you to do this

for Gran. And we wanted to meet her because we're messy like that. But we're wondering why Georgia agreed to it."

"She has her reasons." He didn't want people to know she was in it for the money, to stop her parents from cutting her off completely. That made her look mercenary and him look like a fool.

"Well, whatever they are, she's in it now." April dropped butter in the pan and it started to sizzle.

"Meaning?"

April made a face. "Dylan, you're sweet on her. Maybe more than that because as much as you love Gran, and as much as you're willing to follow the advice of your wise and wonderful sisters, I don't think you'd act quite so obsessed unless you were maybe—"

"Totally fucking obsessed," Sandy finished.

"I'm not obsessed. I just ..." He trailed off, unable to explain it.

"Exactly." Sandy patted him on the arm. "We love to see it. Especially the caveman invasion of the exam room to find your wife."

"She was hurt." Was it not common decency to barge in and demand to see the person who was injured during the game to which you invited her?

His sisters stared at him until April finally said, "Is this marriage real?"

"I have a certificate that says so."

"Sure, D." Sandy smirked at April. "A certificate."

He opened his mouth to protest, but Georgia had just walked in, and she looked so damn pretty and fucked out, he lost the power of speech. His sisters started fussing over her, making sure she was settled, getting her coffee, enquiring about her pancake preferences. Then it started all over again when his mom came out with Gran. Throughout this malarkey, Georgia accepted their attention patiently while sending impish looks his way.

He did the smile-behind-his-cup thing again, and she rolled in her lips because his wife knew all. Last night was their secret, and while it shouldn't be a surprise that he and Georgia had fucked, it felt like something for them, and them alone.

His phone buzzed with a text from an unknown number.

> Is your wife okay?

> BANKS
> Who wants to know?

> UNKNOWN
> This is McMillan. Fuck, I'm sorry.

Banks inhaled deeply, thinking about all the things he'd like to say. At the same time, he recognized that striking a puck in anger during the playoffs was not unheard of. Rarely did it end so badly, but his wife was fine. Better than fine, and last night he'd taken care of her.

In *all* the ways.

> BANKS
> She's okay.

And then because he didn't want to let him off too lightly, he added:

> See you on the ice tomorrow.

Hockey players had ways to sort out their differences.

> UNKNOWN
> ...

Sure. Tell her I'm sorry.

You will be.

"REALLY, I'm perfectly fine. I only wish I could go with you."

Trish frowned. "We can't leave you."

Georgia held up her phone with the text thread from Skye. "See? My bestie is coming over. You guys have tickets to *Wicked!* You should *not* be missing that. I've already seen it twice."

The Bankowski Babes looked torn. All morning, they had been so attentive, along with Banks before he headed into Rebels HQ for practice, and Georgia had squirmed at being the center of such focus. Dani used to call it "The Eye of Goodwin" when their parents were laser-focused on her, whether it was her temperature, her breathing, or her constantly monitored heartbeat. Whenever her parents said good morning, they'd respond with "Under his eye" and dissolve into giggles.

People looked at Georgia, but no one actually saw her. Which was why it was very easy to fob the crowd off with protestations about how fine she was. She'd been doing it for years.

"Text me at intermission. And if you don't hear from me, shoot an SOS to your brother."

April pointed her finger. "You know he'll kill us if anything happens to you."

"Again," Sandy said.

Connie added, "When he should be saving that aggression for McMillan and Boston tomorrow night."

"Nothing will happen. The doctors gave me the all-clear

and you know Banks is just being overprotective. Go enjoy your show!"

Thirty minutes later, they were out the door and Georgia had sent a message to Skye telling her she would see her in a couple of hours, which gave her time for her real errand: to go see Jim.

"How is he today?"

Debbie stared at her, clearly amazed that Georgia was here at all. "You got hit by a puck! We saw it on TV. Are you okay?"

Georgia touched her wound. "It was a bit of a shock, but I'm fine. Hard head, you know?"

"Dad's going to love hearing all about it. And your husband scored before he left the rink. I assume he raced to be at your side."

Georgia could feel her cheeks heating. "I would have much preferred he stayed on the ice. He was on a roll."

"Thankfully they won. And you're so lucky that puck didn't land an inch lower." Debbie took her by the arm and led her inside. A woman Georgia didn't recognize walked by with a lunch tray and headed into Jim's room.

"Who's that?" Though she had her suspicions.

"You know how I said I was trying to get home help? Well, this new charity sent someone over. I've applied to so many that I didn't even remember this one."

"That's great news." After the usual charitable sources had tapped out, Georgia arranged something anonymously with an agency. She wasn't sure how long she could continue to pay for this, but if it gave Debbie a break, then that was all that mattered.

"So I have a favor to ask," Debbie said.

"Anything."

Debbie brought her upstairs to a room, where several outfits lay in a messy heap on the bed.

"I have a job interview tomorrow. I know I might not have this help for long, but between that and Mick, I'm hoping I can get back on the market."

"Oh, that's exciting. What's it for?"

"A receptionist at a law firm downtown. But it's been a while since I've been, well, anywhere, and all my clothes are kind of out of date. I thought maybe I could match this"—she picked up a brown skirt with pleats and a peach blouse with anchors all over it—"with this. What do you think?"

"I'm sorry, Debs, but that's just hideous."

The poor woman groaned. "I know."

"Now what kind of place is this? Not all law firms are fuddy duddy where everyone has to wear suits."

"The partners are kind of hot, actually." She showed Georgia the firm's website, where the evidence affirmed that they were indeed hot.

"Kind of younger. Divorce lawyers. Smartly dressed." She didn't add that these guys were wearing four-thousand-dollar suits. Not that their receptionist would be expected to match that, but Debbie was going to have to do better.

After a quick perusal of the paltry offerings in the woman's closet, Georgia made an executive decision.

"Can you get away for an hour or so?"

THREE HOURS LATER, Georgia got in her car, waved at Debbie, and set off for home. The aspiring receptionist was now in possession of a couple of business-casual blazers, a tweed pencil skirt, a belted A-line skirt, three silk shells in jewel tones, and a pretty azure blue blouse. Three years ago, Georgia had interned at an advertising agency, a gig purely to please her parents who had wondered what to do with her after she graduated college. To prepare, she'd bought a few classic pieces that weren't really her style, and now they had a new owner.

"I can't take these." Debbie had run her hand over the tweed skirt, then snatched it back like she'd been caught guiltily enjoying the fabric. "I can borrow them, but that's it."

"Sure," Georgia lied, knowing they were going to a much more deserving home. "Now how about shoes?"

Turned out they were roughly the same size in skirts but not footwear, so they went shopping. *This is just as fun for me as it is for you*, she'd insisted as they scanned the shoe section of Nordstrom's. Not a lie in the slightest.

"When's the last time you bought clothes or something for yourself?"

"It's hard to find the time." Debbie didn't add "money" but Georgia heard it all the same.

When a family member was ill, it tended to take over the lives of everyone in their orbit. Not a criticism of the sick person, just an observation. With Dani as her family's focus, Georgia had sometimes marveled at how much energy was expended in service to one individual.

And Georgia's family had the wealth and resources to make Dani's life as comfortable as possible and ensure that Georgia wasn't completely forgotten. She had horse-riding and ballet lessons, spa treatments and birthday parties, overseas trips and beautiful gifts. With a steady stream of nannies and drivers, there was always someone to eat dinner with, pick her up from school, even attend recitals and plays when her parents had to take Dani in for check-ups or be at her bedside after a procedure.

But for someone like Debbie, who spent all her time caregiving and rarely had help, when did she get a shot at me-time?

"I'm not sure this is a good idea," Debbie said after she'd checked the underside of the fiftieth pair of shoes. "It's one thing to borrow clothes, but for you to buy shoes …"

"If you were able to squeeze into mine, I would have happily handed off a pair. But you don't have to get anything expensive. These ones are only"—she held up a pair of Franco Sarto's pumps—"$120." Realizing that sounded rather elitist, she moved on to the more sensible, and likely cheaper, options. "These very ugly Naturalizers are $65 on sale, but I will never forgive you if you buy them."

Debbie laughed. "I'm sure we can find something that doesn't stop you from talking to me."

As Georgia watched the sales assistant fussing over Debbie and bringing her low-heeled, office-appropriate shoes to try on, her phone buzzed.

THE HUBS

Where are you?

GEORGIA

Just running an errand.

THE HUBS

You're supposed to be home resting.

Home. She'd never get used to that, which was good because that warm, syrupy glow in her chest was almost as dangerous as hearing Banks call her "wife."

GEORGIA

I'll be there soon!

THE HUBS

Don't make me come looking for you.

Oh, she shouldn't like this feeling, having someone worry

about you for all the right reasons. She shouldn't but she did. Her parents weren't to blame for putting Dani first, but Georgia couldn't deny the hurt their neglect had caused. Having Banks fuss over her was nice. She should take a puck to the head more often.

Everyone needed that kind of TLC, but with limited resources, we tended to focus on the ones who needed it most. An illness created all sorts of collateral damage to a family. It wasn't just that people had to give up jobs or never got the chance to have date nights with their husbands or go shopping for sensible shoes.

Her brain was ticking over, the seed of an idea seeking out the sun.

Her phone rang, and she steeled herself for another call from Banks, who had left three messages already before the texting began. It was her mom.

"Hello?"

"Darling, are you okay?" Her mother sounded a touch frantic. "Caroline Wilkins said you were hit by an ice hockey ball last night. I only just heard."

"I'm fine, honestly. It wasn't a big deal. Just bad luck."

Her mother offered a tentative, "Was it ... Dylan?"

She laughed. Wouldn't the press have loved that? "No, Mom. Another player. Purely an accident."

"Well, accident or not, I expect it'll still get negative media attention. One of those viral things."

Georgia stiffened. Did her mother think she had attracted that puck with her magnetic, partying personality?

She took a quick look at Debbie, who was trying on some loafers with—*ugh*—tassels. She shook her head to signify stern disapproval and returned to her mother. "It'll die down soon enough."

"I hope so. I'm not sure that's the image we want to cultivate for the new foundation. You've been doing so well since news of your marriage got out. Much more like the Georgia of old! Now, did you get the meeting request from Emily? We need to get the media release out soon."

Damn. "I did, but things are kind of busy right now. Banks's family is in town, the playoffs are taking all our focus, and ..." *I have an idea for something different. Something special.*

Her mom cut in. "If you can't make the meeting, we'll reschedule. Again. We also have to discuss the wedding reception. Can you send Emily a list of invitees for Dylan's side? And shoot her some dates for dinner." She muttered something to someone else, probably poor, overworked Emily. "Darling, I have to go."

"Okay, Mom—"

The line had already gone dead.

Debbie held up a pair of classic, but incredibly boring Calvin Klein slingbacks. "Will these do?"

"Do you like them?"

"Yes."

"Then that's all that matters."

As she pulled up alongside Banks's SUV, the front door opened, and the man himself appeared with Cheddar in his arms, looking stormy. (Both Banks and her cat.)

She had barely opened the car door and he was launching into a critique. "You're supposed to be resting, not gallivanting around town. You shouldn't even be driving."

"I'm here now!" The Nordstrom shopping bag on the back seat would stay exactly where it was. Like she could resist a Marc Jacobs dress on sale.

She took Cheddar from him and gave him a rub. "Has Daddy been taking care of you when he should be leaving you the hell alone?"

"He's not bothering me." Followed by a sneeze.

Men. "Let's take you back to the west wing," she said to Cheddar. When she opened the laundry room, she got the shock of her life.

"What happened here?"

A new cat bed sat in the corner, along with three scratching posts, cushions placed on shelves at different heights, and new toys dotted about the room.

She looked at Banks, who shrugged.

"If he's stuck in the laundry room, we may as well make it more comfortable for him."

Banks getting sweet on Cheddar was not on her bingo card.

She placed her kitty down and watched as he lapped at his water, which was now dispensed into one of those pet fountains that started the water flowing when Cheddar approached. Fancy.

Leaving him to his new playground, she returned to the kitchen. She picked up the kettle and started to fill it, only for Banks to do a dispossession move that wouldn't have looked out of place on a rink: take it out of her hand, push her gently to a seat at the counter, and take over.

With her internal organs turning squishy, she watched as he went through the motions of making her tea.

"Did anyone give you a hard time about missing the rest of the game?"

He scowled. "Why would they?"

"Because you abandoned your teammates."

"With good reason."

"I just don't want you to get into trouble. Because of me."

He squinted at her. "Placing my wife above the needs of a game? They get it. They're all loved up, so they know exactly what it's like."

Loved up? Was he comparing himself to his teammates?

Before she could question that, he pulled open the cupboard. "Lemon ginger?"

"Perfect Peach."

"That she is," he murmured. He set up the mug and turned, his arms threaded across his substantial chest. "Don't think I haven't noticed you changing the subject. You told my family you'd rest up and a friend was coming over."

"How do you know that?"

"Because I called them the minute I got home after I'd left you *several* messages. They texted back during the intermission."

"Right. They had tickets to a matinee so they shouldn't be expected to change their plans because of me."

His expression was one of "why the fuck not"?

"I decided to postpone Skye's visit. It's not a big deal. I'm sorry I wasn't more honest. But if I was, you would've made one of your sisters stick with me and it's their vacation. They have tickets to *Wicked*!"

"I assume that's a big deal."

"It is."

Still scowling, he made her tea and a cup for himself. She took the mug he offered, letting it warm her hands while she waited for it to steep. That's when she noticed a basket on the back counter, its clear plastic showcasing shortbread cookies, Lady Earl Grey tea, and several oranges.

"Where did that come from?"

"Harper Chase, the Rebels' CEO. It's called the don't-sue-us package."

"You are *so* cynical." She read the card: *Hope you're feeling better! Welcome to the Rebels family! xoxo Harper Chase-DuPre.*

The Rebels family. Wasn't that lovely? Feeling a touch emotional, she turned away to reread it, then set it down on the counter.

"They seem like a nice bunch of people." Tara, Mia, Ashley, and even Dex had all reached out to check on her.

"They're alright."

"Must be strange to have to start over with a new team. Just up sticks and re-jig your life."

"It is. But it's what we sign up for. And this will be my last team."

"How's your shoulder?"

"I was just about to ice it." On the counter was a pack, sitting on a dishtowel.

"Is that what Dr. Morgan advised?"

"Pretty much." He sipped his tea, looked kind of cagey.

"You still haven't told them, have you?"

"I know how to handle it."

He was exasperating. "So you're a medical professional now?"

After a brief pause, he responded. "About three years ago, I suffered a similar injury. Back then, the docs recommended I get surgery, but it would have put me out for six months, maybe longer. Instead, I rehabbed it and figured out a way, but it's left it weaker, more prone to re-injury."

"And now time is running out." While she was here, sucking up all his focus.

"I was brought onto this team for one reason: to qualify them for the playoffs and make a serious Cup run. I just need to hold on for six more weeks."

"Then what are you doing drinking tea you don't like and petting a cat you're allergic to?" She stood and grabbed the ice pack. "Come on, let's take care of this."

PEELING off his shirt hurt but seeing Georgia kneeling beside him, the ice pack in her hand, sent a rush of dopamine to his brain. A sexy nurse rush? No ... more like a-woman-taking-care-of-her-man rush. The boost wasn't enough to dull the pain completely, but he wouldn't want that. He needed a reminder that this wasn't a dream.

"So, like this?" She placed the pack over his shoulder and held it there.

"Yeah, like that. Now you scoot that sweet peach of an ass down and lie beside me."

Sure, just put it out there.

"You don't want to be alone?"

"We finally have the house to ourselves. I'm not wasting another minute."

Too much? Probably. But she didn't run screaming, so he took it as a win.

She lay her cheek against the pillow and ran her fingertips over his bicep. Just lying like this beside her, in this peaceful way, was amazing. Kind of like the night they married, only she slipped through his fingers the next morning.

"Where did you go this afternoon?"

"I had to help a friend get ready for an interview. She needed an outfit, so we had a rummage through Georgia's Closet."

"I was worried about you."

"No need."

"Because?"

She seemed surprised to be called on it. "I've always managed."

Because her parents were so focused on her sister. This girl —this woman—had learned emotional independence at an early age. She was used to hiding how she felt, all in deference to Dani and her parents' needs.

"I'm not trying to be a helicopter husband. I'm just concerned for you, that's all."

"Helicopter husband. I like that." She grinned. "Keep rotating around me, Big Guy."

As long as he was able.

"Did you tell your parents about what happened?"

"My mom heard and called me. Get this: she thought you might have done it!"

"I hope you told her it was an accident."

She sighed. "I did. She's worried about any negative publicity, how that might affect the foundation she wants to set up for Dani."

Strange angle to take. He suspected Georgia downplayed her injury, but all the same, her parents should be worried about her, not the optics.

"That reminds me." He turned to the nightstand. "I printed off some stuff for you."

She took the sheaf of papers from him and scanned the top page. "This is information on how to set up a charity in Illinois."

"Yeah, I'm guessing you have people who can do that for you and sure, your family are the experts." The longer he spoke, the stupider it sounded. She came from a clan of noted philanthropists. "But there are still some things you'll want to do to get off on the right foot."

Her gaze was focused on the documents. "Like registering it and all that?"

"That, but because you're the person in charge, you want to be sure you choose the right people as your directors. People who can contribute and aren't just there for the credit. And you'll need a business plan, a registered agent, and experienced staff."

She looked up, her eyes troubled. "You don't think I can do it?"

"Peaches, I think you can do anything. I didn't print this off to show you how hard it is. I just wanted to give you a roadmap. I'm on your side."

"It-it seems like a lot." Her voice trembled.

"And you can do it. Just open up another pack of flash cards, attack it like you do everything else, and if you have questions about the financial stuff, I can help."

She bit her lip. "Trish said you're really good with numbers."

"I do alright."

That reminded him: he needed to do that financial planner research for O'Malley. Though really, it would be easier if he looked over the kid's accounts himself.

"Thanks, Dylan." She snuggled in close and wrapped her arm around his torso, and he closed his eyes, safe in the knowledge his wife was where she was supposed to be.

31

"Now, Georgia, I don't like the idea of leaving you alone." Trish pulled one of Connie's suitcases out to her car, while Banks managed the others. "Dylan, surely you can bring her with you on the trip to Boston."

Before Banks could comment, Georgia jumped in. They'd had this discussion all morning, a back and forth over whether it was okay to leave Georgia alone in Chicago while life and hockey went on without her. As it stood, the Rebels were headed to Beantown with a two-love lead in the series.

"He needs to bond with his teammates. And I will be perfectly fine with Cheddar." She gave Connie a hug, then Trish, April, and Sandy. "Have a good trip back and send me a text when you're home."

Connie grinned. "You should come with us to Apple Falls. Plenty of room. We can introduce you to the neighbors."

"Babcia, Georgia needs a break from us." Trish held onto the hug with Georgia a little longer.

She couldn't disagree, but if she had to spend time with any family, it would be this one.

Trish raised her hand. "Oh, I think I've forgotten my phone charger. Georgia, could you help me find it?"

Georgia sent a sideways look Banks's way. He gave her a knowing eye roll right back.

"Subtle, Mom."

"What? I need that charger."

She marched back into the house with Georgia following and made a show of looking for it under a seat cushion while Georgia waited for her to get to the point. After about ten seconds, she pulled her daughter-in-law to sit down.

"So, can I say something without you taking it the wrong way?"

Georgia tensed. "Go for it."

"If you divorce my son, I will never forgive you."

"Excuse me?"

"You make him happy."

"I-I don't know about that. Things are kind of up in the air right now and—"

Trish took her hand. "Are they? Or are they just settling down after the initial shock? Georgia, my son is not a risk taker or an impetuous man. He barely drinks."

"Which probably explains his low alcohol tolerance."

Trish's expression was all pity. "Deny all you want. I know what I see here, and I hope you two give this thing a real go of it."

She would *not* like what Georgia had planned as soon as they left. Best to keep that to herself.

"Mom, we have to go," April called out.

"Coming!" Trish stood, dragging Georgia upright before giving her a tight hug. "If you need anything, and I mean anything, text, call, video, whatever. Okay?"

Tears threatened. This was likely the last time she would see them.

"Okay!" Smile wide, eyes bright. *You're fine, Georgia. You're always fine.*

Back outside, more hugs were dispensed in all the people combinations and finally, everyone was on their way. Georgia turned to Banks as the cars turned onto Sheridan.

"How are you doing?"

He blew out a breath. "I'll see them again soon."

"I know. But it's okay to be upset that they're gone."

He nodded, her stoic man unable to verbalize, so she wrapped herself around the one person she'd missed during the hug fest. Even better, he let her, sinking into her like she was weighty enough to handle it. But then she always was the dependable one in the Goodwin family, the girl who could manage her own emotions so as not to steal focus from the people who needed attention. Like Dani.

Guilt pinched at her. Dani wasn't to blame for Georgia not getting a little more Mom and Dad time. And she'd sure made up for those neglected years, hadn't she?

She pulled back, realizing that she was using him to make herself feel better when he was the one who needed comfort. Just like that night in Vegas when she told him she didn't want to say goodbye and reeled him in for a trip to the altar.

"You have to get ready for your trip." Desperate to shift gears, she moved away and headed for the door. "And I probably should ..."

He followed her inside. "You probably should what?"

"Pack up."

His eyebrows crashed together. "Why the fuck would you want to do that?"

"Because your family is gone and I'm sure you'd like to get back to some sense of normal. When you come back, I'll be out of your flow, and you can focus on what's important."

She had planned to be gone by the time he returned and

not tell him before he left. But neither did she want to be sneaky about it.

"What about your parents?"

"We can worry about that later. It's not as if they're going to come visit. I thought that once we'd done this, for Connie and your family, you might be ready to ... move on."

He closed the gap between them quickly and held her face with both hands. "Do you want to leave?"

Never. "It's what you need. For your game."

"Georgia." Her name on his lips was almost beseeching. "What I need right now is for my wife to tell me the truth."

It wasn't fair of him to use the *W* word, not when she was feeling sad.

"What do you need?"

Suddenly, this wasn't about the bargain they'd struck. She didn't want to keep lying to him—or to herself.

"I need ... you."

He released a pent-up breath, its warm puff a signal of intent against her lips. Which he claimed roughly, possessively. Her response was frenzied, a recognition by her body that they were finally alone—properly—and this couldn't wait.

The kiss didn't stop, not even as he lifted her onto a table in the foyer. Not even as her house keys fell to the floor with a clattering sound. Not even as she wrapped her legs around his waist and his hands grasped her ass, pulling her flush with his erection.

"You need me," he panted. "And I need you. So fucking bad, Georgia."

She didn't doubt his sincerity. But he was also in a weird place, already missing his family, worried about his body holding up. She could do that for him, be the placeholder, while taking a little something for herself.

No more second-guessing. She curled a hand inside his sweatpants and pulled them down, freeing his thick cock. Wrapping a hand around it, she stroked roughly, just how he liked it. His groan was loud, echoing in the entryway and all the way to her pussy.

"Please, Dylan. Need—"

He was already one step ahead of her. Leggings down, a hand shoved between her thighs. Two fingers stroked and drew her moan. His other hand pulled at her bottoms, forcing them down until she had to let go of him and finish the job of removing them.

With one hand on his cock, the other under her ass, he plunged inside her with a deep all-consuming thrust. He held her close for the longest moment, the most perfect moment, his mouth close to hers as he murmured her name. *Georgia.* Not any of the nicknames, just "Georgia." His eyes were closed like the sight of her might be too painfully sweet to bear. She reached for his jaw and held him close as her body adjusted to his size. To everything Banks.

She squeezed one perfect butt cheek. He withdrew a few inches, then sank inside her again.

"Ohhh!"

His eyes snapped open, and in their depths, she saw desire and compassion and all the things she loved about this man. Her heart was beating like a hammer, just like the lyrics of that old Metric song, "Help, I'm Alive."

She was. Finally. Banks had brought her back from a deep, dead place, but with new life came old fears.

He paused his thrusts, held her face. "Hey, it's okay." He swiped at a tear. "I'm here, okay? Not going anywhere."

But you are. Eventually you'll leave, just like Dani.

He waited, though it must have been killing him, and she squeezed her inner muscles to let him know she was back from the hole she'd dropped into for a moment. Blanking her mind, she let the numbing sensation of pleasure take over, let her heart soar, and take this moment for herself. He wasn't far behind with a roar that didn't need muffling now that they were alone.

Only when he pulled out did she realize they'd not used a condom.

He looked down between their still throbbing bodies, then back up. "Fuck."

"I'm sorry."

He frowned. "Why are you sorry? This is on me, I practically mauled you."

She laughed. "I was all in on the mauling, Big Guy. And I'm on birth control. As for the rest ..."

"Full physical when I joined the team in February and no one but you since. I think we're good."

Her lust-fogged brain tried to parse what he'd said. *February ... no one but you ... we're good.*

Had he abstained because of her? Surely not. After all, they had believed they were divorced.

"Going raw like that, Georgia ... it was really fucking hot."

"It was." Something about no barriers. Skin to skin ...

Another look between them landed on his come pooling on the table. They really should move and clean up but neither of them seemed ready to go anywhere. Banks's cock was ... oh God, thickening before her eyes.

"You like the mess, don't you?" Strange, considering how regimented he liked his life to be. Could Banks be adapting to the untidier aspects of Tornado Georgia barreling into his life?

"I'm guessing you don't. We can get you cleaned—"

He broke off as his lips parted in shock.

She had shocked herself. But here she was, her fingers rubbing Banks's cooling come on her exposed pussy. She wasn't an exhibitionist. She'd never done anything like this for any guy.

But this was for her, too.

A dark flush came over Banks's cheeks as his gaze locked on her hand, swirling, stroking.

"Georgia." His voice was strained through gravel. "You are so sexy."

She needed him to see more, to see right into the heart of her. Lifting one leg, she placed her foot on the table, widening her thighs and showing him everything.

His erection climbed to full mast once more. That was hockey player resilience for you.

"Touch yourself." The demand from her lips didn't sound like her. She felt strong, emboldened, powerful as she continued erotic, circular strokes over her swollen folds.

He took himself in hand again and pulled lazily on his perfect cock.

"You like my come on you?" The words were harsh, labored. "You like my mark?"

As sexy as it was to rub herself with her husband's sperm, just hearing how this affected him raised it to another level.

My mark.

She nodded, rubbed harder. It should have taken forever after she'd orgasmed only a few minutes ago, but with Banks everything was heightened. She was close to coming again.

"Show me your pretty tits, wife."

Oh my Banks. Lust-dazed, she peeled off her T-shirt and yanked down her bralette. He continued jerking off, his strokes getting choppier, the head of his cock becoming redder, as raw as the feelings coursing through her. Taking her hands, still covered with his release, she squeezed her right breast, then the other. Pushed them together for her husband.

"Come on me, Dylan."

Another rough jerk and he sprayed silky ropes of come across her chest. Then he fell on her, all wet and sloppy kisses, so deep she wondered how she'd ever find her way back to the shallows. They spent a few minutes, coming down from the high as the kisses turned softer and more tender.

"You have to go," she finally said. "The plane's waiting."

"Let 'em wait. My wife needs me."

Scooping her up like she weighed nothing, he marched them to the bathroom.

32

Banks put his bag down inside the hotel room at the Hyatt Regency in Boston and stared at the goober on the bed closest to the window.

O'Malley grinned. "I switched with Kaz. He wanted to be closer to the elevator. For emergencies."

"In emergencies, you're not supposed to use the elevator."

"Tell it to Kaz. So I figured you'd want the bed nearest to the bathroom, what with your aging prostate and all."

"Generous." He unzipped his hold-all and took out his underwear, aiming to pop it in the closet's drawer. He jerked in surprise—fuck.

"Jesus! Is that ... a snake?" O'Malley sat up, visibly recoiled, and was now peering at Banks's hands.

"A fake snake."

"Didn't think it was real." He twitched his nose. "A good luck charm or something?"

"Or something." He put it back in his bag and moved the whole lot to the closet. He'd unpack later. Right now, he wanted to find a quiet spot and call Georgia. Make sure she was okay.

"You need the john?"

O'Malley smirked, like that joke about his aging prostate had finally landed. Banks stepped into the bathroom, knowing it wouldn't give him the privacy he needed.

He shot off a text.

> Did you think I'd screech like a little girl?

PEACHES

> Say you did. Just for me.

BANKS

> Not a chance. O'Malley let out a yelp, though.

He'd arrived fifteen minutes late to the bus for the airport, and then spent the entire trip trying not to think about how his wife had commanded him to come all over her sweet little tits.

For a brief, crazy moment, he had considered telling the medical team about his injury. Calling it quits so he could stay home and look after Georgia.

April was right. He was obsessed, and it was affecting his focus. Like a complete sap, he needed to hear her voice. Maybe a quick chat, just to put his mind at ease.

He hit the call button and was much too gratified when she picked up on the first ring.

"So you're sharing a room with Dex? Those huge salaries and you have to bunk up with another adult?"

"It's for team building. And to make sure everyone obeys curfew."

She gasped. "You mean your roomie would rat you out if you play at Cinderella?"

"Depends. But you don't want them holding anything over

you. The org knows what they're doing with the room assignments."

"Sounds like they think you can be a good friend to Dex."

"Actually, O'Malley pulled a roommate switch."

"He wants your mentorship. I told you!"

Hardly. Just because he'd been in this business longer than this kid was alive didn't mean he had any useful advice. He'd never won the Cup. Had a solid but uneventful career. He had kept his head down and invested well because this gig could end at any moment, though the thought of giving it up killed him.

He sucked in a breath, wondering how the next stage would play out. Kids maybe. Yard work. Buy a share in a restaurant or a bar. Try to keep useful.

No matter how hard he tried he couldn't see Georgia in that future movie playing in his mind. Sure she was a woman of leisure, but why the hell would a life with a past-his-prime ex-athlete interest her? Just as he was thinking about settling, she'd be looking for her next fix. Another party. A more exciting boyfriend.

Not him.

Yet here he was, obsessing, barely able to think straight. Time to get a grip.

"I've got to go. Heading for dinner."

"Okay. Be nice to Dex!"

"Oh wow! You have done well for yourself, girl!"

Skye dropped her Hermes bag on the foyer table, the one where Banks had fucked her—was that only three days ago?—and twirled around.

"Not bad, G. Not bad." Skye was acting as if luxury was

unusual for Georgia, but she probably meant this was a hundred times better than her old place in Castle Apartments. She held up a bottle of Dom. "Got any glasses for these?"

Georgia had been sorely neglecting her friends since she moved in with Banks, and while she had an invite to Mia Wallace's house for the Chicago-Boston Game 4 with the other WAGs—the poor guys had lost Game 3—she thought it would be nice to have a watch party with the girls and Oliver. A way to integrate her worlds, which seemed necessary after Banks had told her to tell the truth and take what she wanted.

What if she wanted ... her husband?

Paris and Skye walked into the kitchen while Oliver lingered behind. He looked around, made a face, and frowned at her.

"If I thought all you needed was a better crib, I would have offered to have you move in with me."

Ah, ruffled feathers needed smoothing. "That wasn't why I moved in. It needs to look good for my parents."

But now it's looking good for me ...

"Hmm." He moved in closer. "Is that the only reason?"

"What else would there be?"

Oliver huffed out a dark laugh. "Yeah, Georgia and the jock. That'd be something." He touched a finger under her chin. "And you can't even go to a game without getting hurt."

"Banks felt awful about it. Like it was his fault."

"Well, it is! This world, G ..." He booped her nose. "It's not for you."

Now whose feathers were ruffled? Georgia mentally squirmed, not enjoying her friend's snap judgment or condescension. But maybe he was right. Gorgeous lakeside mansions aside, she and Banks came from vastly different worlds.

"Guess you're not interested in watching my husband play hockey, then."

Oliver didn't like the mention of the H word, either of them. He'd always been possessive when she dated someone, and this whole situation clearly bothered him.

"That's why we're here, isn't it?"

A carefully curated collection of snacks from Trader Joe's Game Night section was laid out on the coffee table: mini quiches, jalapeno and cream cheese wontons, garlic and asiago cheese dip, and three types of popcorn. With one eye and ear on the game, Georgia caught up with her friends. Paris was dating a DJ—her third in as many months—while Skye had landed a PR assistant job in her dad's company and lost it a day later. ("They expected me to show up at 8:30 in the freakin' a.m. and now Mom's furious with me.") In the same breath, she complained of her poor financials, the connection completely lost on her. That Hermes purse was this season, and Georgia suspected she'd be asked to float her friend before the night was through.

The fissure between them had expanded to a gorge. She wanted to think it was because she was here, married, suddenly in a different stage of her life—or on the cusp of it. But it had been happening for longer than that. Since Dani had died.

She had credited pulling away from her friends to grief, but losing her sister had changed her more fundamentally. Put her on a different path, though the destination was still a mystery.

"How's Savannah doing?" she asked Oliver.

"We broke up."

"Oh, I'm sorry."

He shrugged. "It was just casual."

She felt his eyes on her, especially when her focus turned

to the game. Watching Banks play with such skill and effort gave her a thrill she had a tough time hiding. That was her husband on the ice! He had held her hand when she was hurt. Made her tea to soothe her. Come inside her.

Her body heated at the memory, and she grasped a glass of iced water to cool down. The game continued along with her friends' chatter, and ninety minutes later it was over. The Rebels lost which meant the series was back on even standing at 2-2.

She sent a text to Banks:

> Sorry, Big Guy.

He didn't answer, probably because he was getting ready to come home. She wanted to call him, hear his voice, and let him know she was in his corner. She would always be here for him.

More than anything, she wanted her friends to leave. The shallow gossip and catty commentary no longer appealed to her. Over the next forty minutes, she stretched and yawned, praying it would be contagious.

The doorbell chimed. She looked at her friends. "Kind of late for someone to be stopping by."

Skye laughed. "Listen to the old married woman! That'll be Callie and Fortnum."

"And JoJo and his boy." Paris held her phone aloft and headed to the door. "It's been ages since we had a Georgia party, girl."

A party? Before she could object, Paris opened the door and a steady stream of people started to trickle in.

33

No one would leave.

Georgia could turn off the music or kill the lights or go to each person individually and tell them the party was over, but the people pleaser in her hated the idea of being a buzzkill. Mere weeks ago, she was a party queen. Now she was wishing everyone would scoot so she could clean up and ready the place for Banks's arrival in the morning.

As it stood, she had spent the last four and a half hours following people around, telling them to use a coaster or take their smoke out to the patio or not pick up Cheddar who didn't like anyone touching him except for Banks. After a while, she placed him in the laundry room and locked it behind her.

Which made her think that she should lock the rest of the rooms. Knowing her friends and acquaintances as she did, open bedrooms were like catnip. She bounded up the stairs, stepping over a couple mid-make out, and did a circuit. None of the rooms featured anyone banging, thank God, so she happily cut off those avenues with locked doors then went to Banks's bedroom for a breather. Their bedroom.

The steady thump of music sounded distant but not distant enough. Time to shut this down, even if it made her a party pooper. Goodness, she was a married woman.

She opened the door. Oliver stood on the other side, his fist raised pre-knock.

"Hey!"

"Could I have a word?"

"Sure. But make it quick because I'm about to call time on this gathering."

He gentled her backward and shut the door behind him. "I'm worried about you, G."

"You are? Why?"

He rubbed his chin, which had the beginnings of some blond jaw scruff, but nothing near as glorious as her husband's beard.

"This marriage. This whole situation. It's not right." He reached for her cheek and cupped it. "If you need money or a way out of this drama, let me help."

Alarm streaked through her. Oliver had always been clingy, but not to this extent.

She curled out of his grasp. "What's going on, Oli? Are you feeling down about Sav?"

His eyes flashed. "No, Georgia. This isn't about Savannah. I'm your oldest friend. I was there for you through everything, when Dani died, when your parents cut you off. I've been waiting for you to realize that I'm your guy, the one who will save you. From yourself, really, because that's clearly what you need. You owe me."

About halfway through that speech, she felt sorry for him. She'd always suspected a puppy dog crush from his end, but she had assumed it was resolved years ago. By the time his rant ended, anger was on the rise.

"Owe you what exactly?"

He shook his head. "That's not what I meant. I'm a nice guy, your best guy. We had a pact and you ruined it by marrying this brainless jock who is so not your type."

So everyone kept telling her. Her husband was no dummy, and while he might not be her type, he was something better. He was her man, and she wouldn't hear a word against him.

"We're going to forget this ever happened and put it firmly in the camp of bad-decisions-courtesy-of-alcohol." She wouldn't push for an apology, not when she just wanted everyone to leave.

"You'd know all about bad drunken decisions. It's why you made this mistake."

Okay, enough. "That's where you're wrong, Oliver. Sure I'd had a couple of drinks, but you know my tolerance is sky-high. I wasn't drunk when I married Banks. I knew exactly what I was doing, and if I had a chance to repeat 'my mistake,' I'd do it in a heartbeat."

She went to walk by him. He placed a hand on her arm and pulled her back.

And kissed her.

THE PLANE RIDE home was nowhere near as exuberant as the one out. Boston had come to play and now the series headed back to Chicago. Banks had been praying to get it done in four or five, but now they had to go to at least six. And that was just the first round.

His shoulder felt worse, and he needed to ice it. Not exactly doable when surrounded by a fitfully sleeping team and support staff. A couple of painkillers down the hatch, and he tried his best to get comfortable, playing on repeat the image of Georgia's tight, lithe body splayed on that foyer table while she rubbed his come into her pussy.

His wife was something else—and he needed to see her.

It was after three by the time he arrived to find his driveway filled with cars, some parked haphazardly. The house lights blazed into the sky like a nightclub advertisement.

Someone was throwing a party, and the number one suspect was his wife. Disappointment chilled him.

She was young and vibrant, and he'd never forbidden her to host her friends. This was her home for as long as she needed it. But he didn't like parties—and he especially didn't like parties in his house when he wasn't there.

The garage was blocked by a car. Irritation made him itchy. He parked in a small space on the grassy verge of the driveway, then headed into his house. Not as busy as he expected, probably because the size of the great room made it look more spread out than the last party Georgia hosted. A couple of people nodded at him as he walked through. He ignored them, his wife his singular focus.

A girl about Georgia's age—and damn, he had never felt older—grabbed his arm.

"You're Banks!" She cast an excited look about the room. "Hey everyone, it's—"

He cut her off. "Where's Georgia?"

"Around here somewhere. I think I saw her heading upstairs." Her eyes glittered, a mix of inebriation and mischief.

He was tall enough to make a quick scan of the room. No sign of a blonde sprite, so he took the stairs two at a time. It was quieter up here and the doors were locked when he checked, so that was something.

He was about ten feet out from his bedroom when the

door opened and Georgia emerged, looking flushed. A hand followed and grasped her arm.

"Georgia, let's talk about this." It was her friend. Oliver.

Rage reared up in him. *"Get your hands off her."*

Georgia's gaze snapped to Banks's. She was upset, but not with him. Within a nanosecond, that spark in her eyes had turned to something closer to relief.

He closed the distance between them faster than any move he'd made on the ice last night. She pulled away from Oliver's grip.

"What did you do to her?" His move toward the asshole who had just laid hands on his wife was blocked by five feet and change of gale-force blonde.

That petite hand on his chest was supposed to pacify. Instead, it agitated him even more.

"What happened?"

"It's okay, Big Guy. I've got this."

Got what? He shot a glare over her head at Oliver, all while his pulse rate ratcheted higher and higher. This guy had taken advantage of his wife's hospitality and Banks would love nothing more than to tear the silver spoon from his aristocratic mouth.

Georgia's hand rubbed circles on his pec. *Calm down. It's okay.*

Banks placed a possessive hand on her hip, then moved it around to the rise of her ass, where he let it linger. This fucker needed to recognize what he could never, ever have, in this lifetime or the next.

"Party's over, asshole."

Oliver blinked and turned an ugly shade of red. Walking by, he tried to look at Georgia, but she wasn't having it. She kept her focus on Banks until her friend reached the stairs and descended. He was tempted to help him along, the over-the-rail route.

"You want to tell me what's going on?"

"Just a misunderstanding." She still looked upset. "I'm sorry about all this. I invited a couple of people over to watch your game and word got out about an after-party. I've been trying to shut it down for hours."

"They don't look like hockey fans."

She sighed, probably relieved that he wasn't making a fuss. "No, they're not. I'm so glad to see you, but I didn't want it to be in a crowd. I don't want this." She waved in the general direction of the party.

"Let me handle it."

Easy enough to do once Banks had cut the music and glared at people long enough for them to get the message. Years in the hotel bar trenches chaperoning his teammates had prepared him well for quick sobriety testing and the summoning of taxis for anyone who didn't pass muster. Not enjoying the idea that any of the revelers might be a danger to themselves or others, he called the local cops to ask them to keep an eye out for anyone he might have missed.

If Oliver got pulled over, he wouldn't be sorry.

Alone at last, they surveyed the post-party rubble. Georgia started picking up bottles, but he took them from her and set them down.

"Tomorrow."

She inhaled a breath. "None of this appeals to me anymore."

She might be saying that to put him at ease. He wouldn't expect her to change her personality to make him feel better.

"What happened with Oliver?"

"He was under the misapprehension that I owed him for his friendship." She frowned. "That I owed him ... *me*."

The fucking nerve. In his house! He should have hit him.

"I handled it, Banks." She splayed her fingers over his chest again, and this time it worked better to placate him. His heart steadied.

"How's your shoulder?"

"A little sore. Not that it would stop me."

She peered at him from beneath hooded eyes. "From playing?"

"From this." He palmed her ass and cleaved her to his body and all the parts that ached. The motion lifted her a couple of inches off the ground, bringing her lips close to his. If she wanted this, she'd have to close the gap herself.

She did.

Fuck. Her mouth, the feel of her lips on his ... the heat of her tits against his chest ... the curve of her ass in his palm ... it was all too much, sensory overload that did a perfect job of numbing the ache in his shoulder and sending all that blood and adrenaline to his groin. He kissed her like a starving man, and she took it, every nip, suck, and sloppy kiss he had to give her.

He charged up the stairs with this perfect woman in his arms. Once in the bedroom, he kicked the door shut. Cheddar was probably locked away, but old habits. He needed a cocoon, a space no one else could enter. This was their time.

With a quick pivot, he lay her on the bed, then peeled off his sweatshirt and threw it on the floor. He placed a hand on the waistband of his sweats. Georgia sat up and covered his hand with hers.

"Let me."

He removed his hand, though really, he wanted to strip quickly. To lie over her, skin to skin. But if this was what she wanted, he'd obey every command she gave.

Tentatively she pulled his sweats down a couple of inches,

then moved soft fingertips over one side of his V-cut. Then the other. Almost reverent.

Another few inches south with the sweats, and his cock showed up, ready for a shift.

"Oh, there you are, gorgeous." Wrapping one soft hand around him, she stroked gently. He pulsed in her hand and let out a moan.

"Hold on. Back in a sec." She hopped up quickly and left the room. What the fuck?

Twenty seconds later, she was back, the shadows unable to steal her light. In her hand was an ice pack.

"I got this ready before the game. I had a feeling you might need it."

Jesus, this girl. "Yeah, I do."

Smiling, she placed it over his shoulder. He pressed down on it with his right hand.

"Fuck!"

She dropped the hand that had returned to his dick. "Sorry! I forgot they were cold."

A rough laugh escaped him. "Just surprised me."

You're constantly doing that.

She rubbed her hands together. "Might be better if you hold while I ..." She licked the crown of his cock, and he forgot all about her cold hands and his aching shoulder and the two games they'd just lost. All he could focus on was Georgia's pink lips and cat's tongue and what she was about to do to him.

With his free hand he pumped his dick while she placed both hands on either side of his body.

"You gonna suck me, Peaches?"

"I might lick you first. All over." She applied her tongue to the underside of his cock, flat against the pulsing vein, then worked it over from base to tip. Pearls of pre-come leaked from the slit and his good little kitty lapped it up before taking his cock head and sucking it into the wet warmth of her luscious mouth.

He lay back, reveling in the glory of his gorgeous wife sucking him off, taking him inside her sweet mouth, inch by hard inch. Watching her pleasure him was the hottest thing he'd ever experienced.

The pressure was building, his balls filling and needing release. Any second now …

"Gonna come, baby."

She didn't pull off. Just kept that perfect suction, her lovely mouth giving it her all, until he exploded and unloaded down her throat.

So good. So tired. But she needed him …

He pulled her up to lay by his side and yanked at her yoga pants. His hand between her thighs was like coming home.

"Banks, your shoulder."

"Fuck my shoulder. My wife needs to come." She was already so wet and on the edge of going off. He could tell from those needy little sounds, the way her body curled around his hand. He could tell from the way her eyes hazed over with desire yet still managed to lock onto his and give him everything he needed.

This connection. This moment.

This is why I have no regrets.

Her body tensed and the feel of her muscles tightening around his fingers got him half-hard again. She came with a cry and collapsed against his side.

He didn't remember the rest as exhaustion finally claimed him.

34

"Darling, this is Georgia." Tara winked at Georgia and grinned at the handsome man at her side. "But then you probably know that. Or your legal team does. Georgia, this is my husband, Hale."

Hale Fitzpatrick, or Fitz as he was better known, shook her hand. "Georgia, it's great to meet you at last. I sure hope you're feeling better." He had a Southern accent, super sexy.

"Oh, I'm fine."

"And thanks for accepting our invite to watch the game in the box."

"Thanks for letting me hang with you guys."

Tara took her by the arm. "Something good should come out of *the Incident*, as they're calling it around here. Come sit with me and let's chat." She raised an eyebrow at her husband. "Don't worry, I'll deny, deny, deny!"

With an amiable eye roll, Fitz turned to someone who had just handed him a phone, a very boss move.

Tara chuckled. "They get so worried when I speak my truth."

They sat in a couple of seats near the glass, a lovely, safe way to watch the game. But something about it was a touch sanitized. Georgia had enjoyed being in the crowd, feeling the pulse of the fans. An executive box should be more her speed —luxury, distance, away from the hoi polloi—but apparently, she was becoming a woman of the people.

"Champagne?"

"Just ginger ale, thanks." Someone scurried off to get drinks, though the box's bar was barely three feet away.

Tara took her hand. "How are you? Really?"

"Absolutely fine. Everyone's being so attentive you'd swear I intercepted that puck on purpose."

Tara narrowed her eyes. "There I was thinking you're enjoying being back in the news."

"I don't want to be in the news because of something so silly." Or for any reason. She was starting to realize that she'd never enjoyed the attention all that much. "Banks is watching me like a hawk. All his focus is on me when it should be on the playoffs."

Tara squeezed her hand. "You'd be surprised how many of these athletes can walk and chew gum, or in your case, play hockey and be good husbands."

But he's not my husband. Though he is a good one.

"I don't want him to worry about me. Not at such an important time."

"Then it's a good thing you have lots of people who care about you and can take some of the load off Banks's all-hockey-all-the-time brain."

Georgia laughed. "You're really nice, you know that? Even if your assignment is to stop me from calling in the lawyers."

"It's much more than that. I'm here to continue your hockey education. Oh, hold on a sec." Up popped a photo of Esme, blonde and cherub faced, with a smudge of tomato sauce on her chin. What a cutie. "The nanny likes to send me a few pics before she puts her down."

"Sure, blame the nanny."

Tara's husband seemed to instinctually know pictures of his daughter were doing the rounds. "That's my girl." He handed the phone off to his wife, adding a passionate kiss that had Georgia blushing.

"Still in your honeymoon phase, I see," Georgia said, once Fitz had walked away.

"Hale's never been unafraid to show his feelings. I'm the reserved one. What's your dynamic with Banks?"

Did they have one? She could feel her cheeks heating. The last few days had been perfect, just the two of them cuddling, cooking, and christening all the furniture. But it wasn't all orgasms, all the time. They also found time to talk, mostly about his career dreams and her charity hopes, though they were still indistinct and unformed.

Tara's green eyes went wide. "Ah, so things have developed."

"Sort of. It's just … stress relief."

"Keeping your man in tip-top shape for the playoffs?"

"Exactly."

Tara smiled. "The franchise salutes you."

Georgia rolled her eyes and tried not to let the "your man" moniker get her any more excited than she already was. This was Game 5, which was all the excitement she needed.

THE REBELS WON, which put them 3-2 ahead in the series, with Banks contributing one goal and one assist. The atmosphere in the arena and the box was electric, the celebration so loud she barely heard the buzz of her phone. Outside the owner's box, she found a relatively quiet spot and checked the message from her mother.

MOM

Come for dinner this weekend. Bring Dylan.

She had already explained that Banks had a big assignment at work. Couching it in corporate speak was the best way to communicate that.

GEORGIA

He'll be out of town for a game, but maybe next week?

MOM

Just let us know. We need to talk about Dani's Heart.

Georgia touched her throat. Before she could query that, another message came in.

MOM

That's what we're calling the new foundation. Stephen has the papers drawn up, waiting for your signature.

GEORGIA

We should discuss it first.

MOM

Of course! You've been very quiet lately. Dylan must be a good influence!

Right, because Georgia couldn't get there by herself.

She also had messages from her friends. Oliver had sent her a text of apology, then left several voicemails when she didn't respond. Skye and Paris had picked sides, likely because Oliver had spun it in a way that made him look like the victim. They hadn't appreciated how Banks had cut the party short.

"Georgia!"

She looked up into the smiling face of Mia Wallace. "Hey!"

Mia bent over to hug her. Damn, this girl was as tall as a Wookie. "We won!"

"Yes, we did!"

Mia threw an arm around her shoulder. "Let's go see our boys."

Five minutes later, they found themselves outside the locker room.

"Are you sure it's okay to go in? Aren't they getting dressed?" Georgia didn't like the idea of anyone being able to see a half-naked or better Banks. That should be her privilege alone.

"This is the one they use for press. You won't see anything interesting, except your husband being tongue-tied with the reporters."

"Really?"

"He's on press duty for this game, but he never gives them anything. You wouldn't believe how much they've been trying to poke him since they found out he's married."

"Then maybe I shouldn't be here?"

"Not at all. Come on."

Mia pushed open the door and walked in, taking up a spot behind a few people who looked like they might be team organization staff. Georgia recognized a couple of them from her time in the exam room after the puck hit.

Mia waved at her husband, Cal Foreman, who was talking to the press and stopped to give her a big grin. No sign of Banks.

She turned and walked right into the wall that was her husband. "Oh, hi."

"Hello there." Sexy lip twitch.

"Great game."

"Thanks."

She leaned in close. "Listen, I'm sorry for showing up unannounced like this. I thought it was the regular locker room."

"Disappointed you didn't get to see me naked?"

She waggled her eyebrows lasciviously. "Crushed."

That earned her a humorous bark, which simultaneously had a magnetic effect on the reporters. *Dylan Bankowski in shock laughter eruption.* Suddenly they were surrounded.

"Banks, you had a good game tonight," one of the media wags offered. "Married life must suit you."

Banks sniffed. "Is there a question in there?"

She tried to shuffle back a few steps, give him the space he needed to do his job, but she didn't get far. Someone blocked her from behind and soon several microphones were shoved in her face.

"Georgia, how's the injury?"

"Georgia, are you proud of your husband's play tonight?"

"Georgia, we haven't seen you at the clubs lately. Is marriage cramping your style?"

She stared at the questioner of that last one. That didn't sound like a legitimate query for a sports reporter.

Claustrophobia was setting in. Before she could freak out, a strong arm wrapped around her shoulder as Banks pulled her into the shelter of his body.

"How about giving my wife some space?"

"Georgia, you spent the game in the owner's box. Are you worried about another puck to the head?"

What a stupid question. She sent a sidelong glance at Banks, who obviously agreed.

"I think that's enough," he said, drawing her away.

"No, it's fine." She turned to the reporter who asked that last question. "I'm no statistics expert, but I'm guessing the probability of getting hit twice by a puck at a hockey game is probably in the region of a gazillion to one. However, neither am I the kind of girl who's willing to tempt fate. For now, I'm happy to watch from a glass-enclosed, puck-proof box with easy access to top-shelf alcohol."

The press corps laughed, and another journalist jumped in.

"So, were you a hockey fan before your marriage, Georgia?"

"Can't say I was. But I'm learning. Still not sure about the offside rule, but I've figured out most of the penalties. And I think the Cougars' Nilsson should have been penalized for holding in that third period."

A couple of the reporters nodded, likely placating the dumb blonde with the sports opinions. She snuck another look at Banks, worried she'd gone too far, and found him gazing at her indulgently.

"You heard it from my wife. The ref shit the bed on that one." He squeezed her tighter. "Now, I think we have some celebrating to do."

Taking her by the hand, he escorted her out into the corridor, through a back entrance that led to an underground car park.

"I messed up, didn't I? Back there with the press?" This man loved his life on the down low. Her presence in it had brought unwanted attention, and she hated to make him uncomfortable.

"Nope. You were perfect."

"Banks, I sounded like an idiot."

He opened the passenger door and helped her up into the seat. She didn't need it, but she loved when he was a gentleman.

And when he wasn't.

He put on her seatbelt and brushed his lips over hers. "You were charming and made me look like a genius for marrying you."

"Well, as long as *you* look good." She curled a hand around his jaw and ran her thumb over his bottom lip. How strange that touching another person brought such comfort.

"I love watching you play."

"I love knowing you're watching me."

They stared, neither of them willing to break away. She wanted to say more, but it already felt like too much. That whiskey-warm gaze heated her through.

"Are we heading to the Empty Net?"

"Not tonight." His eyes glowed with the desire. Oh boy. It looked like they'd be celebrating the win in their own way.

35

"Something's wrong with Banks." Kershaw pulled the pot of dollar bills toward him and rolled his shoulders against the seat back in the plane's lounge. "That's the third hand in a row he's lost."

"Nothing's wrong."

Foreman patted his arm, all condescension. "It's okay. Happens to the best of us."

"Dick problems?" Kershaw asked.

"Losing at cards," Banks said with a scowl.

"Wrong on both counts. Falling in love." Foreman dealt the next hand but hovered over the last couple of cards. "You've been off your card game since news of your nuptials got out."

O'Malley chuckled. "It's true. No more poker face."

Banks glared at the kid, but it had no impact. No one took him seriously anymore.

They were flying out to Boston for Game 6. With luck, they would clinch it on the road and would have a few days rest before Round 2.

Back to cards. With his ability to hide his pain, he should be better at this. He resolved to school his expression on the next hand. Two queens and a ten. He discarded a couple of cards and picked up two more. Nothing good, but he could bluff with the best of them.

Sixty seconds later, he was beaten with a pair of nines by O'Malley of all people. The guy couldn't bluff his way out of a paper bag but now he suddenly had game?

"See, no good." Kershaw smirked. "Long may Banks enjoy his lovely wife, so we all have a chance at winning at poker. How's Mrs. B, by the way?"

"Fine. No lasting effects of the injury."

"Except she's still married to you," Kaz said, barely looking up from his phone.

"What the fuck does that mean?"

His teammate exchanged a quick look with Foreman, who rolled his eyes.

"Just doesn't seem like your type."

Kershaw winced and muttered, "Kaz, shut it."

"Why, because she's far too good for me?" He knew what they all thought. *Hot, young, sexy Georgia.*

Foreman pointed. "That's standard around here. All our wives are out of our league."

Kaz gave a sour look. He'd gone through a messy divorce a couple of years back, and by all accounts, was still smarting over it.

"She took that puck like a champ, though," Gunnar Bond said.

"My wife is braver than most of you."

"True." Foreman started the deal. "Who can forget Baby Durand's screams when Piper took him out last fall?" The unfortunate clash between Bast Durand and Coach Calhoun's daughter in a Rowdy Rebel costume had fueled the Internet for weeks.

"Hey, dickheads!" Durand Junior called out from the

seating area. "I sprained my fucking wrist. After it had just healed from being broken almost a year before."

"Still cried more than Georgia," Bond said. "Like a French-Canadian baby."

The next few minutes were spent detailing past player injuries and the decibel levels of the resulting screams. After Foreman won the next hand, Kershaw changed the subject.

"So my brother says I should be investing in Crypto."

"Jason or Sean?" Bond asked.

"Sean. He's the computer genius."

Foreman narrowed his eyes. "Isn't he fifteen?"

"Sixteen," Kershaw clarified, "but the kids know all about that tech stuff. He's making out like a bandit with GameStop stocks."

"Jesus H.," Banks muttered. "First, you have to be over eighteen to trade stocks. Second, you're getting financial advice from a kid whose balls have barely dropped?"

Kershaw pointed. "I heard you majored in finance at Wisconsin. Maybe you could look at my portfolio? I never know if my guy is trying to rook me."

"Index funds," O'Malley said as he peeked at his cards. "That's what Banks advises. And a 529 fund for education. You got one of those for your kids?"

Kershaw frowned. "Maybe? My dad asked me to invest in a restaurant as well."

"Do not invest in a restaurant. Do not go into business with a family member." Banks blew out a breath. "You could suffer a career-ending injury next week, so you need to get your ducks in a row now, especially with your growing family." Kershaw had survived a brain aneurysm a few years back and he was still fucking around with his money? Banks looked around the table with its mix of veterans and rookies. All of them were eyeing him with interest. "If you're not already working with a financial advisor with real qualifications and no curfew, then let me know. I'll recommend someone."

"Or take a look at it himself." O'Malley grinned at him. "That's what he did for mine."

Just a couple of hours spent poring over financial statements and coming up with a few obvious recs. He'd kind of enjoyed it, but then he'd always liked working with numbers.

Foreman nodded. "Excellent. Banks is going to make us all rich. Let's play poker."

THE DOOR OPENED, revealing Tara holding a very tired-looking toddler.

"Yay, it's Auntie Georgia."

Georgia laughed. "I'm an auntie, now?"

"Everyone's an auntie. That way, I always have an army of babysitters to call on in an emergency." She ushered her inside. "Come on, the game's about to start."

This would be the first time Georgia had met the rest of the WAGs. She already knew Mia and Tara, but everyone else was new, and she was extremely nervous.

"Say hi to Georgia, Ezzie." Little Esme burrowed into her mom's neck while Georgia waved at her.

"Aw, she's shy."

"It's past her bedtime but she said she wanted to see all the pretty ladies. Didn't you, sweetie?" Tara gestured toward the back of the house. "Go on in and meet everyone. I'm going to put this one down."

Without Tara's bubbly chatter as her shield, Georgia took tentative steps toward the gathering. Within a few feet, she found herself in a great room with a buffet of snacks, a help-yourself-bar, and at least eight women gathered in various convo-combinations. Mia spotted her and came bounding over, then wrapped Georgia in a hug.

"Hey everyone, come meet Georgia and her wicked scar."

Georgia's wicked scar made for a great icebreaker. Everyone wanted a recounting of the event, how much it hurt, and what kind of compensation she expected (a joke, but maybe not?). She was the first WAG that anyone could recall getting hit during a game, and that gave her some sort of cachet.

In Tara's absence, Mia made the introductions.

"So this is Elle—she's married to Theo Kershaw and they have two adorable littles, Hatch and Adeline."

"Oh, I love his Insta. He's so funny." And sexy, though she didn't add that. Instead, she tried to imagine Banks on social media and came up blank.

"And this is Casey. She works in the front office and is married to Erik Jorgenson, the Rebels goalie."

Georgia went for handshakes but got cheek kisses instead. "Great to meet you both."

"Likewise," Casey said. "I hope you enjoyed the tea hamper Harper sent."

"I did! Was that you?"

Casey grinned. "It was. We talked to your husband, and he told us you were a big tea drinker. And that you love oranges. Harper is dying for you to come in and have tea with her one afternoon. She has a new Wedgewood set she wants to try out."

Banks told people she liked tea? And oranges?

Oh, she got it now. Their origin story, the one he told her parents. He'd chased an orange that dropped from her shopping bag. That was unaccountably cute.

She jerked herself back to the conversation and specifically Casey's invitation to tea with Harper. "I'd love that."

On it went. Sadie was married to forward Gunnar Bond and was a famous dress designer. Georgia had one of her dresses, which she was glad she didn't wear tonight because that would have been a little too much. Jordan was married to center, Levi Hunt, currently injured and being "an absolute bear" about it, per his wife. She was a hockey reporter with a well-known podcast that Georgia had listened to during her research. Such a smart lady. Piper, daughter of the Rebels head coach, was dating Bast Durand and was a student finishing up her master's in education. A very pregnant Kennedy was married to Bast's brother Reid. She ran the concierge business that managed errands and dog-walking for high-end clients, many of whom were the Rebels.

"You do our grocery shopping!"

Kennedy chuckled. "Well, not me personally but one of my minions."

"I used to be a minion." Tara had just walked in. "Great way to make friends with hockey players and snoop in their medicine cabinets."

"And *that* is why Tara didn't last long in the personal assistant-slash-concierge business." Casey's comment produced chuckles from everyone.

These women had history together, a special connection because of their husbands' jobs. If Georgia wanted to be a good hockey wife, then she could learn so much from them.

IT TOOK BARELY a moment for Georgia to feel at ease.

The Rebels WAGs didn't think the Bankowskis' origin story so strange. As Tara and Mia had already hinted, these couples all had stranger than fiction beginnings. Met your man after he texted his dead wife and you got her recycled number? That happened! Got knocked up by a cinnamon roll defenseman in the early hours of Christmas morning? You'd better believe it! How about becoming a live-in dog nanny for the puppy you jointly saved from Lake Michigan with a grouchy right winger? Why not!

A drunken marriage in Vegas was positively tame by comparison. Laughing about it in present company relaxed Georgia and, once the game started, gave her confidence to ask silly questions like why one kind of penalty got two minutes in the box, and another got five. Or what constituted offside (she still didn't get it). Or why the game was just so darn physical.

It seemed like all kind of contact was allowed short of bashing another player over the head with a stick—and Georgia suspected some officials might turn a blind eye to *that* if it happened. Neither did she understand why the shifts were so short. Just as a line started to build some momentum, they were replaced by a different set of players. "Fresh legs are competitive legs," explained Mia. Basically, sprinting for 45-60 seconds was super fatiguing, and an opponent's switch to a new line would give them an advantage if the team kept the same players on the ice.

Mostly, Georgia watched her husband, marveling at his determination and skill, and cringing whenever he took a hit. Every opposing player seemed to know the exact location of his bruises. How to press on them. How to hurt him.

So when Boston won, sending the series to a Game 7 back in Chicago, all Georgia could think of was how much more Dylan had to endure. The relentless pounding on his body. He would barely get a break before the next game.

Most everyone left to relieve babysitters and check in with their husbands and boyfriends. Mia and Georgia remained behind to help Tara clean up, and when Mia stepped outside to take a call from her husband, Georgia wondered if she should be calling Banks.

"Thanks so much for including me tonight," Georgia said to Tara. "I learned so much."

"You're always welcome. And you can text me anytime, y'know."

"Do you mind if I ask you something now?"

Tara picked up a couple of wine glasses and put them on the counter near the sink. "Shoot."

"Do all the guys play through their injuries?"

"It depends. I mean, if something is broken then knocking back painkillers is probably only going to get you so far. But if it's a light sprain or bruised ribs or something like that, then yeah, lots of them do that. Especially the older guys."

"Why the older guys?"

Tara shrugged. "The younger ones came up with a different attitude. More open to talking about their feelings, their needs, their injuries. The older generation of players prefer to get on with it, plus they have fewer years left. Every second counts so they're more likely to play hurt. Why, is Banks hurt right now?"

Before she could answer, Mia walked in. "Tara, you cannot blab about injuries to Fitz."

Tara pressed a hand to her chest. "I wouldn't!"

Oh. Georgia hadn't thought about that.

Mia rolled her eyes. "If she thinks one of the guys is over-doing it, she'll say something."

"Only to the player when they're in my salon chair, which is as sacrosanct as the confessional. I will not be telling anyone in the Rebels front office anything." She glared at Mia who shook her head.

Mia turned to Georgia. "Listen, hockey players are the most resilient of all pro-athletes. They play hurt. They exist on diets of pasta, kale smoothies, and Toradol. They push through the pain. Banks knows his own body, and frankly, he's in the twilight of his career. This year or next are probably his last shots at the Cup, so he's going to push through."

That was what Georgia was afraid of. After her years with Dani, she hated to see someone else she cared about suffer. But Mia was right: Banks had been doing this for years. He knew his pain tolerance.

Georgia feared she didn't know her own.

36

———

DEBBIE LOOKED around the box and clamped a hand over her mouth.

"Oh my. This is ..." She turned to Georgia, tears in her eyes. "Too much. I can't believe you've done this for us."

A petite blonde in a gorgeous Natori sheath dress approached them. "Mrs. Draven? I'm Harper Chase-DuPre. We have a prime spot for your father over here near the window."

Debbie blinked and took Harper's outstretched hand. The woman was a legend in the NHL, this city, and the world of women kicking ass. "Oh, it's so nice to meet you. Thanks so much for organizing this and for a Game 7, no less!"

"Well, you can thank Tara and Georgia." She leaned over Jim and curled her small hand around his frail one. "Welcome, Mr. Dixon, I hear you're a big fan."

He peered up at her with rheumy eyes. "The day you won the Cup, and your husband lifted you on that ice was the third best day of my life. After my wedding day and my Debbie screaming her way into the world."

"One of my best days, too." Harper smiled. "Let's hope we have more of them ahead of us."

Debbie gripped her dad's shoulder. "You old softie."

One of the box assistants led the way to a dedicated spot by the window. The Rebels boss lingered behind with Georgia. "Sorry we haven't met officially yet. I hope you've recovered from the accident."

"Oh, I'm fine." She touched her forehead and the healing scar. "Thanks for the lovely gift basket."

Harper waved it off, her gaze following Jim and his family as they were settled near the window. "This is a kind thing you've done. How do you know them?"

"I met them through Cherish the Days."

"Is that part of your parents' foundation? I'm a big fan of the work they do."

Georgia smiled, and instead of answering directly, said, "I'm sorry Tara couldn't make it."

"Yeah, her little one is sickly with a cold." Harper regarded her with a full, pointed appraisal. "I'm glad you came tonight. I like to meet with new people in the org."

"The org?"

"You're married to one of my players. That makes you part of the org."

"You really needn't carve out time for me." Worried that came off as ungenerous, she added quickly, "I'm sure you must be very busy."

"I am, but I always have time to ensure the people who mean the most to my boys feel welcome." She pressed her hand against Georgia's arm. "Call Casey and let's get tea on the schedule."

Georgia could only nod. *The people who mean the most to my boys.* Apparently, she was included in that sacred group.

~

BANKS GRABBED his gym bag and walked out of the dressing room.

The Rebels had finally put it away in overtime and now they were on to Round 2. Everyone was heading to the Empty Net to celebrate, but a few of the guys had been asked to say hi to some fans post-game. He shot off a message to Georgia, telling her to come to the bar. It was time he showed his wife off properly.

She had spent the game in the owners' box, so he was surprised to see her in the visitors' reception room, a coffee cup in her hand (peppermint tea, he guessed), chatting away to a dark-haired woman in jeans and a Rebels jersey and an older man in a wheelchair.

Spotting him, she waved him over. "Congratulations, Big Guy!"

He'd just won a Game 7, and his gorgeous wife was on hand to greet him. Did it get better than this?

It could.

He kissed her because he wanted to, and no one was on hand to tell him this wasn't real.

"Thanks, Peaches," he murmured against her mouth after he'd kissed the stuffing out of her. Her pupils were dilated, and she looked fairly stunned.

She blinked and shook herself. "Dylan, this is Debbie."

He nodded at the woman standing beside Georgia, who was wide-eyed after his performance—and not the one on the ice.

"It's so amazing to meet you. We didn't want to take advantage, but when Georgia invited us, we jumped at the chance."

"Of course I'm going to use my connections for good." Georgia squeezed Banks's hand. "Dylan, I want you to meet someone. This is Jim Dixon, Debbie's dad. He's a big fan of the Rebels, and of you."

Banks met the sharp gaze of the wheelchair-bound man, clearly sick with something that would soon kill him.

"Mr. Dixon, you've come on a good night."

"Certainly have. You played a barnburner out there, son."

Georgia inched closer to him. "Banks, Jim was in the Army and did three tours of Iraq."

"We're grateful for your service, sir."

Jim nodded, then started coughing. "No need to 'sir' me. I hear your dad served as well."

"He did. Second Battalion, First Infantry out of Fort Washington."

Jim nodded thoughtfully. "They had a bad go of it. Your dad see you play?"

"Not professionally. But he saw me during my junior years. He was a pretty good player himself."

Jim's daughter jumped in. "So's Dad. He taught us all to play. Made us hockey mad as well."

Banks smiled at her. "If you're going to be mad about anything, hockey is probably the best thing."

He took one look at Georgia and immediately revised that in his head. *Georgia was the best thing.*

After a few minutes, Jim started to flag. Georgia shared a look with Debbie and within seconds, she was on her phone, texting.

"The car will pick you guys up at the west entrance." She hugged Debbie and her husband. "I'm so glad you could make it."

Debbie's eyes were shiny. "This was amazing. Thank you, Georgia. For everything."

Georgia leaned over and whispered something in Jim's ear that had him chuckling. Then she kissed his cheek, exchanged goodbyes, and watched as they headed out. A few people remained, fans brought in by various charities. Part of Banks's job was to glad-hand, but it wasn't Georgia's. Regardless, she stuck around asking everyone how they'd enjoyed the game and impressing all with her cheer and charm.

Finally, after one too many ogles of his wife by supposed fans, he'd had enough. "I need a word with you."

She looked alarmed as he grasped her hand and pulled her into the corridor, then around a corner where he pinned her against the wall.

"How do you know those people?"

"Jim and Debbie?"

"Yeah."

She blushed. He knew it.

"You've been helping them somehow."

"Nothing much. Just a few visits, small gifts, that kind of thing." He continued to stare until the moment she relaxed and let go. "I work with an organization that brings birthday gifts to people who are dying."

To say he was stunned was an understatement. "Georgia, that's amazing."

"I don't know about that. There are a lot of organizations that help with bucket lists and last wishes. Take someone to a ball game or Disneyland, but I wanted to do something more understated and personal."

He trapped her hand between them. "How often do you do this?"

"Two or three times a week. I show up with a card and something small. Sometimes they have family. A lot of times they don't. It's usually a one-and-done deal, but Jim ..." She smiled through teary eyes. "He's still here after a year, Dylan. He probably won't last long. You saw how fragile he is. But working with him and Debbie—sure it's not even work."

"What you're doing is a good thing."

Another watery smile. "Getting to know them has given me an idea for what I want to do. A charity for wishes, but for the caregivers. They suffer almost as much as the loved ones in their care. Their lives are so taken up by this dreadful thing that's happening—the slow dying of someone they love."

Like Dani. His heart keened, amazed at how this tiny woman could house such a big heart.

She went on. "There are caregiver support groups, but they're mostly focused on the patient, the person at the center. I want to do something practical for the people on the edges. The ones who are forgotten in all this."

Georgia had been forgotten, and she wanted to make sure it didn't happen to other families.

"You've been working hands-on with these people who need it, and your parents don't even know, do they?"

She looked embarrassed. "They want me to do something that they can control. That's all about Dani. I want to honor Dani, too, but I also want to—"

"Carve your own path."

She nodded.

"Why the fuck wouldn't you tell me any of this?"

"I did. I told you I wanted to create my own charity."

"Yeah, but you didn't tell me you do *this*." He waved back behind him toward the reception room where his wife just made a dying man's wish come true.

"I didn't want to ..." She trailed off.

"Toot your own horn? Look like you were self-serving? Show me your beautiful heart?"

She peeked up at him with the gaze of a puckish sprite. "Now you know."

But there was so much more. "I want to learn you, Georgia."

Her eyes flashed, all that blue turning to gaslight. She remained silent, so he leaned in close, his lips close to hers.

"I want to learn everything about you. Not just Georgia, the flash-card version."

Her lips trembled. "What if you don't like what you find?"

"What if I like it even more?"

She snatched a quick breath. "No one can be completely known. People need secrets for self-preservation."

He understood that. His secrets—injuries, dreams, deep, dark desires—were the things that kept him focused on his goals. The Cup. Ending his career on a high.

But he had other secrets. Wishes for something of his own, a family that belonged to him instead of the other way around. A woman at the center of his world.

Georgia was not that woman. She couldn't be. Yet she'd thrown herself into the role of wife with gusto.

The role. An acting gig. But every second with her helped him separate it out. Showed him a different Georgia. A woman who wanted to step out of the long shadow of her sister.

Step into the light. Maybe with him.

"Self-preservation is important, but so's letting go of some of the burdens that come with that weight. Because it's heavy, Georgia, keeping it all in."

She stroked gentle fingers through his beard. "And how are you doing, Big Guy?"

His wife understood him so well.

"My shoulder's aching. But you touch me, and I feel ..." He let it go, the tension in his gut that kept everything coiled tight. "You take my mind off it. Off all of it."

He had just won Game 7 of Round 1 and lived to fight another day. Even better, he had this beautiful woman in his bed, his home. His life.

The coven was right. Consider him obsessed.

"Look at us. *Com-mun-i-cat-ing.*" She dragged the word out, making him laugh.

"Like we're married or something." The thought of hitting a bar no longer appealed. He would much rather celebrate between Georgia's lovely thighs. "Well, wife, let's go home and communicate."

GEORGIA WAS SITTING at the vanity, trying to decide if demure drop diamond earrings went better with her scar than platinum hoops, when Banks appeared at the door to the room they'd labeled "Georgia's Closet, Part II."

She'd returned late from one of her birthday party gigs and Banks had been in the shower. Tempted to join him, she decided that would be better left until later. She would need the stress relief after a visit with her parents, and she suspected Banks would, too.

Tonight, her knockout husband wore a burgundy shirt, open to one button, with black dress pants. She doubted her mother would approve of that beard, but his wife thought he was on fire.

She opened her mouth to say hi to his reflection in the mirror, but bit off a greeting at the sight of him approaching. More like stalking.

Heart beating like a hammer ...

Every damn time.

He halted behind her, still staring, still consuming her with his gaze. With a gentle sweep, he moved her hair aside, leaving her neck exposed. Then he inhaled at the sensitive spot where her neck met her shoulder like her scent was the oxygen he needed to breathe.

She shivered with pleasure. Words dried in her throat.

His lips brushed her earlobe, inducing another delicious shiver. He applied a kiss just under her ear, then another to the curve of her neck. Her nipples hardened. Dampness pooled between her thighs. Reaching up, she hooked a hand around his neck, and her touch fanned the flames. His kisses became more ardent, desperate to cover more ground.

She let out a whimper. He sucked on her lobe, then gave it a small nip that set her whole body ablaze.

They were going to be late.

She didn't care.

Her phone vibrated. She ignored it. Banks's mouth was all she could think of, all she could feel.

Her phone buzzed again, and he raised his head.

"Your mom," he said with a kiss that felt final to her neck.

Gah!

MOM

Darling, Rosetta wants to know if you're still vegetarian. She could probably whip up some pasta primavera at the last minute.

She closed her eyes.

"Still?" Banks asked.

"Never. I experimented for a week in eighth grade before I remembered I couldn't live without pepperoni pizza." Her mother had a memory like a steel trap, which she chose to use selectively. "Just a dig about my lack of commitment to any course of action."

He screwed up his mouth, ready to defend her.

She cut him off. "We should get going."

"Yep."

"GEORGIA, YOU HAVE A SCAR!"

"I told you I got hit by a puck."

Her mother blinked. "Yes, but I had no idea it was so … obvious."

Her father leaned in for a closer look then turned to her mother. "We should get Stephen to assess the legal options."

"Dad, it was an accident and not a big deal." As moguls, her parents lived their lives on the litigious edge. Lawyering up was usually the first option.

A warm weight wrapped around her hand. Banks had curled his fingers in hers, and the knowledge that he was here at her side gave her strength.

Her mother wrinkled her nose. "Dylan, does this kind of thing happen often?"

"No, Penny, it's pretty rare, but then so is Georgia."

There went her pulse again. She slid a look at Banks to find him smiling at her. She would think it all part of the act if Banks hadn't held her hand on the car ride over or all the way up the elevator. If he hadn't turned to her before they knocked on the door to her parents' penthouse and said, "We've got this, Peaches." If he hadn't given her a kiss so sweet her knees were still knocking when Rosetta opened the door.

She would never have considered herself rare enough to deserve the undivided attention of a man like Dylan Bankowski. But in this world they'd created, she was at the center, and she wished more than anything it could stay that way.

THE GOODWINS LIVED in a penthouse in the John Hancock Center on Michigan Avenue, which, given Banks's own wealth, he really couldn't fault them for. (Though he wanted to.) It was filled with expensive art and uncomfortable furniture and looked like it was used for a few weeks a year.

One thing stood out: Dani was not forgotten. Photographs of her covered sideboards, mantels, and walls. There were pictures of Georgia as well, but mostly in official-looking family portraits or with her sister. Scanning the offerings, he found one of her solo, on a horse. Not more than fifteen, he'd guess, she had the imperious look of someone who had been born into wealth and privilege and expected everyone else to bow down before her.

Curious that this would be the photo they kept on public display.

Dinner was served in the dining room with large picture windows overlooking Lake Shore Drive.

"We hope you like Cornish game hen, Dylan," Penny said. "Georgia said you're not a fussy eater."

"He can't be, not with how often I've tried to poison him."

Her father raised an eyebrow. "You mean you've cooked, GiGi? Meals?"

"Yes, Dad. If you can call it cooking."

Banks chuckled. "She's better than she lets on. It's nice to see her trying."

Penny narrowed her eyes at him. "Your job ... pays quite well, doesn't it?"

"Mom. Rude."

"Well enough," he said, seeing where they were going. These people had a housekeeper and a personal chef. "But I like to cook, and I prefer the privacy. Also, better to keep my money for retirement."

Marcus coughed. "Quite a short career span in your profession."

"True. A couple more years in me, then I'll settle. Start a family."

He'd like to say that had come out of nowhere, but he couldn't. It had been on his mind for a while, the next phase, and though he and Georgia hadn't talked about it—hell, they hadn't talked about anything future-focused—the thought of her in his life on a more permanent basis had taken hold.

He took a quick look at a blushing Georgia and prayed he hadn't gone too far.

"A family?" Penny shifted to look at Georgia, as if the notion had only just occurred to her. "That's ..." She blinked at her husband, who was remaining quiet. "Marvelous. Jenny at the *Tattler* will love that."

So, he was going with the flow here, making small talk with his fake wife's parents about their future imaginary grandbabies, but a part of him was digging it. More than digging it. Craving it.

Georgia as mother to his kids. But she wouldn't have to do it alone because he'd be retired in a couple of years and ready and willing to be a good co-parent.

Something Georgia's mom had said niggled, though. "The *Tattler*? The society magazine?"

"Oh, just a little joke. We're on great terms with the editor over there. They loved getting the marriage news straight from the horse's mouth."

"Mom!" Georgia groaned. "Are you saying you spilled the beans about my marriage to the *Tattler*?"

Her mother looked baffled. "Darling, it wasn't exactly a secret. Once you told us, I wanted it handled properly, and the *Chicago Tattler* is where all the society news is revealed."

Georgia looked embarrassed. She mouthed, "sorry" at

him, and he tried to puzzle out why. Because she told her parents?

Because she told her parents.

They were the reason word about their marriage was made public.

Penny had moved on. "Darling, I'm thrilled to see you more ... settled. You've had us worried." She turned to Banks. "She's become quite wild."

"Nothing wrong with a bit of wild, Penny."

"Well, she's all yours now!"

Georgia gave one of her patented fake smiles. She must have spent her childhood perfecting them.

"You make it sound like my wife's a problem to be managed. I assure you, she's not."

Georgia's father stared at him for a second. "We could always rely on Georgia to never cause a fuss when she was younger. We had so many pressures with Dani being ill, and Georgia made it easy for us to be there for the daughter that needed us most. But then—"

"Dad, Dylan doesn't need to hear this."

Marcus held up a hand, cutting his daughter off. *Dick move, man.* "Like all teens, she started to act out. And Georgia's teen years seem to have lasted longer than most."

A quick look at Mrs. G tagged her in. "That's why we think Dani's charity would be the perfect thing for you to fill your time. Your husband"—at that, Mama Goodwin's expression took on the strain of incredulity—"is a busy man with his sports. Dylan, tell her she can't be sitting around at home."

Anger flared, but instead of showing it, he reached for the comfort of Georgia's hand. "As far as I'm concerned, my wife can do whatever the hell she wants."

Penny winced. "Is that typical of the other wives of your teammates? Doing whatever they want?"

"There's no standard template for how a hockey wife or husband has to behave or fill their time. Some of them have jobs, own businesses, stay home with children. Some of them like learning to cook or the rules of hockey. There's space for all kinds of journeys here."

Georgia squeezed his hand, and he risked a glance at her. She was smiling at him, her eyes shiny enough to make his heart contract.

"Darling, aren't you lucky to have such support?" Penny managed to make "support" sound like a four-letter word.

"Absolutely blessed," Georgia murmured, like she meant it.

Which was good because he would have her back through hellfire if she needed him.

Mrs. G wasn't finished. "And with all that support, you'd still have time for Dani. You wouldn't have to do any of the operational work, just liaise with the appointed head on the optics. Tell her, Marcus."

"If she doesn't want to do it, we can't force her." Marcus patted his wife's arm and sent her a quelling look. Clearly, Georgia's intransigence was a much-discussed topic. Why wouldn't she tell them about her plans? Her dreams?

He caught her gaze. *Tell them, Peaches.*

She looked away, and the moment passed.

"Now, Dylan, we'd love to hear more about you," Penny said. "When did you start playing ice hockey?"

38

BANKS WAS broody as they headed down the elevator to the parking garage. He still held her hand, but there was a tension there since they'd left her parents' penthouse.

"You okay?"

"Nope."

She swallowed hard. Banks never admitted when he was unhappy. Or happy, for that matter.

"I'm sorry about how nosy they were. All those questions about your salary."

"That's not it." He turned to her, his usually golden-brown eyes as dark as night.

"Is it because they blabbed to the *Chicago Tattler* about our marriage? I didn't mean to tell them. I thought they already knew and it just came out—"

"Don't care about that. What I do care about is how they treat you. How critical they are of your choices."

"Oh, they don't mean anything by it."

He snorted. "They have more than one daughter."

Her chest tightened. So he'd noticed. Georgia had never questioned how her parents' homes were shrines to Dani.

Dwelling on it would manifest as resentment, and if she started resenting her parents, then the next step was resenting Dani. She refused to go down that road.

"They miss her. We all do."

"And you're still here. Full of life and with a heart so big it can barely be contained. Why won't you tell them about what you want to do with the charity?"

They reached the parking level and the elevator doors opened.

"I need to be careful how I propose it. They have expectations—"

"So you keep lying about how you feel. What you want. What you need."

She stepped out of the elevator and turned back to him.

"I'm not a liar."

He scoffed. "Yeah, you are. You've been lying your entire life, telling your parents and anyone who asked that you're fine. The healthy one. The reliable daughter. All their focus was on Dani, so you did your best to fade into the background and not give them any trouble."

"Hardly! I made trouble."

He waved a hand between them. "Later. When you realized Dani didn't have long and you wanted to make her happy with pranks and scandal and acting out. Even then, you were doing it for your sister."

"You don't know a thing about it."

Eyes welling, she started a march toward the car, then stopped and threw her hands up because she couldn't remember where it was.

She turned as he reached her. "I married you, didn't I? How is that 'for my sister'?"

"Y'know, I think that's the first thing you did without Dani being at the forefront of your mind. You wanted something for yourself."

She was breathing heavily. "It was a—"

"Mistake. Yeah, you've said." He closed the gap, backing her up against the nearest car, his solidity the perfect salve. "Sometimes mistakes are a cry for attention. Sometimes they're a way for us to learn. About ourselves."

He cupped her cheek and ran his thumb over her lower lip.

"Every time you say you're fine and you're not, you might think it's a harmless lie. You're keeping a lid on all those feelings, containing it so you won't be a bother. But it's not harmless. It's not good to keep it in. You don't have to do that with me. Our marriage is a safe space. It's all about communication."

She sniffed. "That's my line."

"I'm co-opting it."

"I don't know where to start."

He rubbed along her cheek. "Tell me what you want to tell them."

"If we're going to do any kind of role-playing, I'd rather it was sexy."

"It can get sexy later. For now, I need you to stop being passive and start telling the truth."

"Passive? Is that what you think?"

"Sure." He shrugged in an infuriatingly casual manner that pissed her off. That was intended to. "You've let them railroad you forever because it's easier. Don't rock the boat, be the good girl, keep life on an even keel. But once Dani died, all that pressure, pain, and grief that built up needed an outlet. You went a bit wild, acted out all that hurt, not just because of Dani, but because of how you've been second to your parents forever. Now you're falling back on those old patterns. People-pleaser, all's fine, nothing to see here when really you should be thinking about how to be your own person. How to do that without Dani."

Her next breath was labored, and she turned her head away.

"Georgia." He lay his forehead to hers, which meant he had to bend to meet her at her level. Lately, this beautiful man had been doing that in all the ways. "I'll support you no matter what. You want to head up this foundation in your sister's name, then do that. You want to create something new, make your own way in this world, I'll be right behind you. But be honest with yourself about what you want."

A tear fell, and he brushed it away.

"I hate seeing you upset, but sometimes you need to go there to let it out. Start anew. Now tell me what's in here." He touched her forehead with his finger.

"I don't want to head up Dani's charity," and then softer, "which makes me a terrible person."

"No, it doesn't. You want to have an identity of your own and there's nothing wrong with that. You've been volunteering your time, but for some reason, you'd rather your parents thought you were lying around, eating bon bons."

"If it's not how they do things, then it's not the right way."

"Screw that. You do it your way. Find your joy."

This is my joy. You are it for me. She placed her hands on his chest. "You had my back in there."

"Fuck yeah. They're not easy, but ..."

"But?"

"Some of this is on you. You need to tell them how you're feeling. How you've always felt. No more 'I'm fine' when you're not."

She reached for his hand and kissed his fingertips. "I could say the same for you, Mr. I'm-pretending-not-to-be-hurt."

"I'm not pretending. You know all about it."

She did. He trusted her with this precious intel. "So we can't say we're fine anymore when we're not," she murmured. "Honesty in all things."

Most things. Inside her heart was thundering. She couldn't tell him everything, that she'd fallen in the worst way.

That she was head over Manolos in love with her husband.

HONESTY IN ALL THINGS.

She was the only one he wanted to share with about his problems.

Except for the fact that she was his biggest one.

"The thing is, *I* can say it. Meaning I can say my wife is fine because she so fucking is." His hand coasted down the front of her dress in between her gorgeous tits, claiming. Possessing. Inclining his head, he kissed her, sucking on those luscious lips, taking all that sweetness for himself.

She responded in kind, her mouth wet and greedy. She needed him. His wife needed him.

And fuck, he needed her right back.

But not here. He would take her home, even though his cock was an iron spike and he had serious doubts he would make it without coming in his pants.

Taking her hand, he led her around the pillar where the SUV was parked. Just another few steps to the safety of tinted windows, but his wife had other ideas.

"Dylan." She pulled at his belt buckle.

"Baby, not here. I have to protect you."

She paid him no heed. Zipper down, her small hand inside grasping him tight. His groan echoed in the cavernous space.

"I can't wait," she murmured. "Need you now."

The best option was to lift her against the pillar, and while his shoulder would bitch, he would happily suffer to feel her perfect pussy wrapped around him. Or maybe lay her on the hood of his car and eat her out until she came, clamping her lovely thighs around his ears.

But she was already asserting her need and carving her own path, just as he'd advised a moment ago. Panties down, then kicked away. The little white scrap of lace lay at the back of the wheel, like a fancy society invitation.

Stunned, he watched as his wife turned from him, placed both hands on the hood of the SUV, and bent over. Looking over her shoulder, she smiled.

"I'm so wet for you, Dylan."

Oh, fuck.

More slowly than he would have thought possible given his erection situation, he hitched up the skirt of her dress and groaned at the sight of her peach-perfect ass. Taking those sweet cheeks in hand, he palmed and squeezed, yielding a sexy little shiver.

"Let's see if you've been telling the truth."

She was.

Absolutely soaked between her legs.

Another gush greeted his hand as he stroked her slit.

Leaning over, he whispered in her ear. "Spread 'em, Georgia. Lemme see that pretty pink pussy."

That earned him a sultry whimper and extra access as she moved her feet further apart.

"Good girl."

"Please. Inside me. Need it. Need you."

He released his cock, which was already weeping and desperate to get in the game. Pulling her hips forward, he nudged against her opening, bathed the head in her wetness, and plunged home.

The notion that she might be begging him to fuck her, to do this reckless act in the parking garage of her parents' condo building, glanced across his brain for a second. Was he another crazy stepping stone in her rebellion or was this the real deal?

Because as he withdrew and thrust again, he recognized that this felt as real as it could get. For once, he didn't mind the flood of feeling. He let it wash over him as every stroke yielded a moan from her and a corresponding groan from him. The two of them in sync.

On he went, making her his.

Losing his mind while losing his heart.

39

GEORGIA KEPT one eye on the browning turkey and the other on Banks, who was sitting at the kitchen counter reading and wearing ... glasses. How had this man found new ways to ramp up the hotness levels? The Georgia of four months ago would not have paid the slightest attention to a guy with specs.

"So what do you think?"

He didn't even look up. "Not finished yet. How's that turkey coming along?"

"I think it's ready for the taco seasoning."

"Just half the packet with a little water. Don't overdo it."

She followed the instructions and gave the mixture a stir. Then she returned her nervous gaze to her husband—who had just placed the documents down and, *boo-hoo*, removed his glasses.

"Well?"

"It's great, Georgia. Clear, precise, to the point."

"But?"

He rubbed his beard. "You have the start-up funding, but nothing about how you're going to raise money going forward. It needs to be self-sustaining."

"My trust fund will make up most of the seed money and I'm hoping my parents will contribute as well." The trust was at least five million and she planned to sign over most of it to the charity.

"Sure, but you'll need an investment prospectus for the funds, a way to ensure they continue to compound interest and the fund stays healthy. And you need to have a plan to solicit donors to keep the coffers full."

"I'm worried people won't think it's as worthy as other causes. That it's kind of frivolous to think of the caregivers instead of the people who are truly suffering. If I keep the funding source to my trust, I won't have to worry about it."

He slid off the bar stool and reached behind her to turn off the pan. Then he lifted her like she weighed nothing and popped her on the counter.

"Dylan, your shoulder!"

He pressed his fingers to her waist and held her steady, while she parted her thighs and invited him in. So natural. "I want you to listen to me, Peaches, and listen good."

She snatched a shaky breath. "Okay. Listening."

"Why do you want to start this charity?"

"I told you. I see a need."

"Give me the spiel."

Okay. "Caregivers need a break. They need therapy. They need ways to get back into the job market after being out of it for a while. Hell, they need a mani-pedi every now and then." She shook her head. *Too frivolous. Too Georgia.*

But Banks was soaking her in, his eyes full of encouragement for her to find some inner recess of strength.

"The current social services network is focused on the needs of the patient, the person at the center of this web of suffering. My charity will address the needs of the people who support that person, whose lives are consumed with loving that person, often to the extent that they lose all sense of themselves. Supporting them in small but meaningful ways will demonstrate that they are not forgotten. That their contributions and sacrifice are honored."

Banks remained silent. Was he expecting more?

A smile peeked through his playoff beard.

"See? You can sell this to anyone. It's worthy because you make it so, by your commitment and passion to this cause. You're putting your money where your mouth is, you have a compelling backstory because of Dani, and you have the connections to make this happen. Agreed?"

She nodded.

"I think we should add a section on future fundraising sources, and you should bring a PR person onto the staff, someone who can help us with the messaging."

We. Us. "Okay."

She had once thought that if she ever fell in love, it would feel like floating on a cloud, tingles in every extremity, and happy sighing for eternity. None of the books mentioned this sense of security, this recognition that another person had your best interests at heart and was fully invested in the person you were trying to become.

This was the definition of love.

She touched her forehead to his. "Can you hold my hand through every funding pitch?"

"You won't need me, Georgia. You're so much stronger than you know."

She was starting to realize that. But having Banks in her corner was the bonus she hadn't known she needed.

You're jinxing it.

Probably. But in the last few days, she had felt closer to Banks than ever. His support in the face of her parents had emboldened her, so much so that she seduced him in the parking garage of their building. Maybe that was one more crazy Georgia stunt—or maybe it was a sign she was throwing off the shackles of her past and taking what was rightfully hers.

Her future. One which she hoped included Banks.

A sorry mewling sound rose up from the ground.

"Cheddar! You're supposed to be in your room."

Banks grunted. "Let him be. He's suffered enough."

"You'll be suffering if you let him have the run of the house."

She pushed back at his chest, and he gentled her to the ground. Only this time, reality didn't set in. Her heart remained in the clouds playing with cupids and arrows and harps.

Cheddar snaked around Banks's ankles as he returned to the stove and turned the heat back on under the skillet. *Hold on, now.* She hip-checked Banks out of the way.

"I'm making lunch, Big Guy. You can start shredding cheese."

He looked on approvingly. "Bosshole wife? I like it."

So did she.

40

AHEAD OF MORNING SKATE, Banks placed his gym bag in his cubby and unzipped his jacket. He'd knocked back a couple of extra painkillers while sitting in the car, feeling like he was doing something wrong. He wasn't. He suspected every other guy here was performing their own little self-med-ritual, faking it 'till they made it in the player parking lot.

O'Malley walked into the locker room, all swagger, and bumped against Banks's bad shoulder. "Our old team, dude."

They would fly out tomorrow afternoon for Game 1 of the second round against Nashville. It was a surprise they'd squeaked into the playoffs, to be honest, as they had offloaded Banks precisely because they thought they wouldn't. There were always mixed feelings when you went up against former teammates, but for now Banks was erring on the side of "fuck those guys."

"They won't know what hit 'em."

O'Malley chuckled, then after a furtive look over his shoulder, took out his phone with its lock screen of Ashley and Willa and opened it to a website. "What do you think of this one?"

A house in Riverbrook, a nice faux Tudor priced just under a million five.

"What do you want me to think of it?"

The kid's eyes turned dreamy. "I'm gonna buy it for Ash and Sparkle. That's what I call Willa."

Cute. "Before you sign a contract?"

He moved closer. "I got the offer yesterday. I'm meeting the brass and my agent after morning skate to sign on the dotted line. Can't believe it's happening, to be honest."

"Since you got your shit together, you've played great. Congrats on the contract. It's thoroughly deserved."

O'Malley blinked like he couldn't believe the words out of Banks's mouth. He couldn't quite believe them himself, but he meant it. The kid was a great player when his head was in the right space.

On the subject of contracts, Banks's agent was currently in negotiations for an extension, one more year at least to see out his career. He'd contributed a shit ton to this franchise in the last four months, and frankly, he wanted to stay here. In this city. On this team.

With this woman.

He'd even looked into selling his house in Nashville and putting an offer on the one in Winnetka.

"Thanks, man," O'Malley said in response to Banks's compliment. "That means a lot."

Because it was getting a bit soppy in here, Banks followed with, "You'd better keep it up. Justify the millions they're spending on you."

O'Malley grinned. "I will. But the house? Is it too much?"

"I wouldn't recommend springing it on your woman without running it by her first. It might seem like this big romantic gesture but there are other considerations, too. School districts, work commutes, who pays for what." He held up a hand. "Yeah, yeah, you've got millions in your checking account—"

"Not anymore. This genius I know showed me how to open a brokerage account and invest in index funds."

Banks had opened it for him, then spent an hour walking him through dollar-cost averaging and automatic investing. Hard to know if it stuck, but it was a start.

"Right. My point is that you and Ashley are a team now. Don't go making a unilateral decision that affects her life and the life of her daughter. Communication is what you need, ya feel me?"

Like him and Georgia. It felt like they were in a good place, telling each other the deep stuff and working through it together. He had never expected to be in this position. In love, and with his wife, no less. Maybe he had more to offer than tips on injury prevention and where to invest your hard-earned cash.

O'Malley still looked misty-eyed. "I just want to take care of them, y'know?"

Banks could feel a smile tugging at his lips.

"Maybe slow your roll and involve your partner. She'll assume it's a great signifier of your maturity and God knows, you need all the proof you can get."

"I think you just insulted me, but I'm gonna give you a pass because you generally know what you're talking about. *And* you seem different."

"Yeah?"

"Happier. Marriage suits you."

Love, man, the fucking worst.

But he was grinning as he thought it, so much so he had to turn away from O'Malley to hide it.

Owen, one of the trainers, came into the locker room. "Banks, the doc wants to see you in Exam 1."

His defensive hackles rose. "What about?"

Bond and O'Malley stared at him, which was appropriate because that was a stupid question. You didn't clap back to a request for a meetup with the medics. You just did as you were told.

Owen shrugged, obviously not used to being probed on a perfectly normal ask.

Calm down. "Be right there."

Once Owen left, Banks smoothed his expression to neutral to hide his pain. The meds had yet to kick in and for a second there, he'd been riding the high of Georgia.

"You okay?" Foreman asked.

"Fine," he bit out, then put as much pep as possible into his stride. One foot in front of the other. Easy peasy.

In the exam room, the doc was standing with Coach, and Banks's heart plummeted. No one ever wanted to see this specific combination of people. "You needed a word?"

"How you feelin', Banks?" Coach sounded gruff, but that was par for the course.

"Good. A few aches, no more than usual."

Dr. Morgan patted the exam table. "Hop up there and take off your shirt."

Okay, Houston, we have a problem.

"Sure." He used the shirt peel-off to hide any telltale signals of pain. By the time he was shirtless, his face was back to passive.

There was no missing his bruised shoulder. Not as bad as a couple of weeks ago, but still noticeable.

"You've had a shoulder separation before? Couple of years back?" The doc placed his hand on the AC joint, but didn't press, thankfully.

"Yeah, touch of rheumatism since, but nothing I can't handle."

"How many painkillers are you taking?"

"A couple of extra strength Ibuprofen, two or three times a day." In Nashville, no one questioned what a player did to make sure he could play in the final rounds. Mollycoddling grown men who knew their own bodies was not done.

"And this recent shoulder separation? When did that happen?"

Not tripping me up that easily. "It didn't. It was just a hard check to the boards in the first game against Boston."

"Fuck, Banks!" Coach barked. "That was almost three weeks ago."

"And it feels better."

"And what about this bruising here?" Dr. Morgan gestured to Banks's ribs.

"No big deal." *Keep it breezy.*

With an eye on the door, he willed this meeting to be over. If this was a World War 2 movie, he'd be looking for his chance to spring off the table and leg it out of the POW compound. In the ongoing silence, Banks tried to put positive thoughts out there.

It's going to be just fine.

I'm going to get away with this.

For fuck's sake, everything is going right in my life. Let me have this.

But that bitch of a universe was on a smoke break. Without warning, the doc pressed a hand to his AC and Banks couldn't hide his pained response.

"Let's get an X-ray and see where we stand."

Georgia put the broom against the wall and set to folding up the tarps. The patio was looking good after she'd wiped down the weather-resistant furniture and added a couple of Treviso lanterns and planters from Restoration Hardware. She had a rug on order and a plan to hit Pottery Barn later for some throw cushions. So it was Banks's place and a lease at that, but she wanted to make it nice for his family who would be returning for the Round 2 home games.

She cast her gaze over the patio, with its sweeping view to the beach and Lake Michigan. When Banks's family returned, would this feel different? Would they abandon the charade and accept that this marriage was real? She had no doubt they had work to do, but once the playoffs were over, there would be time for *them*. They could figure out if this blazing attraction had the potential for more.

The glass door to the patio opened and Banks appeared.

"You're home!" Her smile faded at seeing his expression and her first instinct was *Connie*.

Her second was to open her arms. He fell into them, hugging her like she was his lifeline, the reason for everything.

"What happened?"

"I'm on IR." He drew back. "Injured Reserve."

"Oh, I'm so sorry. That must be awful." He didn't respond, so she filled the silence. "But it's also brave. To admit you're not quite at a hundred percent. I'm proud of you. Tara said you guys are always so tough and will never fess up to an injury."

He stiffened, and his expression turned dark. "I didn't fess up. They knew already. When did you talk to Tara?"

"About a week ago."

"And you discussed my injury?"

"I might have mentioned it." Best to be honest. "Okay, I did mention it."

He released her, rubbed a hand across his mouth. "Why would you do that? She's married to the general manager."

"We were talking about how stoic you all are. I worried that you were overdoing it."

"So you blab to another wife? Anything I tell you is between us, Georgia. How hard is that to understand?"

"Even when it's at risk to your health?"

That wasn't what he wanted to hear. "It's two more weeks, maybe a month. That's all I needed, just time to get through this so I can finally get what I've wanted for years. Years, Georgia!"

"And you're going to be in pain that whole time. Maybe hurt yourself to the point where you won't be able to have a decent quality of life once you retire."

"Who cares about that? I'd have the Cup and a ring. I'd have achieved what I set out to do."

She found it hard to believe that Tara would take what she'd heard and run that up the chain. But Georgia probably should have kept her mouth closed.

"I wanted to know if it was normal. And if the team thinks it's serious enough that they can't just spit and slap a bandage on it, then that says it all. You're not fit to play."

Digging her heels in just made him angrier. "This was none of your business."

"Why? Because I'm your fake wife? Is it not enough that I care about you and want only the best for you?"

"That's not—fuck, Georgia, that's not the point."

"Then what *is* the point?"

"I had a shot in these playoffs and now I don't."

The defeat in his voice made her recalibrate her response. He needed comfort not argument. "You have next year."

He balled his hands at his hips. "If they bother renewing my contract. And even if by some miracle they do, now I'm on their radar. They'll be watching me like a hawk. The slightest twinge and I'll be on IR."

For a man as dependent on his physicality as Banks—as any professional athlete—that had to be crushing. He had said he had a couple of years left, maximum. With this latest blow, he might not make it back on the ice at all.

She tried to see the bright side. "But retirement was bound to happen eventually. Only the other night at dinner with my parents you were talking about settling down." Maybe even starting a family. She added weakly, "So it starts a little sooner."

He was strong enough to come out of this. To find meaning in a life after hockey.

Only right this minute, he didn't agree. His expression was incredulous. Nothing she said was right.

"Are you fucking kidding me? I am not ready for that. I have things I want to achieve. This is my career, Georgia, and I sure as shit do not need some party girl who knows nothing about hockey telling me how to run it."

She flinched. Of course he wouldn't see this as any kind of blessing in disguise, not when the disguise was atrophy in the suburbs with your flighty mistake of a wife.

"I shouldn't have said anything to the girls. I didn't think—"

"Exactly. You didn't think. I live a very private life, Georgia, but since I met you, it's been anything but. Media attention and everyone up in my business. Your parents announcing our marriage to the world. Why the hell did you even tell them?"

"It-it was an accident." Another blinding moment of self-sabotage, except this one might have been deliberate. A part of her had wanted them to know about Banks. About this one perfect stroke of intent that was all for her.

"Or another way to get your parents' attention."

No, a way to get yours.

Moments ago, she was imagining a happy ending—the

playoffs, his family, this man relying on her as his rock, just as she relied on him as hers. Even if he could forgive her mistake, he wouldn't want her around, reminding him of it. Of his failure at the last hurdle.

He certainly wouldn't want attention-seeking Georgia, who trapped him into this fake marriage because she couldn't keep her mouth shut.

"I'm sorry," she said. *For dragging you into my poor little rich girl drama. For caring about your health.*

For falling hopelessly in love with you.

For a moment it looked like he regretted his tone. He took a step toward her, but she held up a hand. The damage was done.

"No, I get it. This is your career." She bent to pick up the broom and stood quickly. "I'll give you some space."

"Georgia—" But she'd already retreated inside.

41

A LIFE AFTER HOCKEY? With her? Because if that was what she was hinting at here, that was crazy. Her life was just beginning while his was stumbling towards an ignominious conclusion. This beautiful young thing should not be thinking of binding herself to a man heading downhill fast.

Through the patio sliding door, he peered into the living room for a sign that she hadn't gone far. Nothing. She was giving the wounded beast space, which was probably for the best. If he spent another second in her presence, he might say worse.

This year had felt like his last shot. He was doing it for his gran, for his mom, for his sisters. For his dad. And now this.

He understood Georgia's concern, but he knew his body better than anyone. To have her second-guess that was infuriating. If she couldn't fathom this fundamental thing, then she didn't know him at all.

He had no idea how long he spent on the patio, staring blindly out toward the lake. Only this morning he was thinking he'd like to take Georgia for a walk along the beach after lunch, her petite hand in his big mitt. Then back to the house for a cuddle and more because it would be days without her while he worked toward his future in the next round of the playoffs.

Their future.

Now, that had all shifted sideways, like the sand before him. Worse, it had vanished into nothing because he was a man with no future. No career, no plan, and a wife in name only.

He was going to lose her.

Though in truth, he'd never had her. He had a marriage certificate, a ring, and a woman who needed someone to have her back against her parents. Georgia was stronger than she looked, and now that she'd worked out how to stand up for herself, what good was he to her?

He was barely able to hold her without wincing in pain. Big, strong man? *Sure.*

A text came in from O'Malley.

Petrov just told us. That sucks, dude.

Yeah, dude, it did.

He ignored it, but he couldn't ignore the call from his captain a couple of minutes later.

"Yep?"

Vadim Petrov blew out a resigned sigh. "You're home?"

"Instead of in some bar trying to forget the last couple of hours, you mean?"

"The thought crossed my mind."

"I'm home."

Petrov huffed out a laugh. "This is better. Let your woman soothe you."

He had no response to that, so he moved on. "Timing sucks, but you'll be stronger without me."

"You don't believe that but sure, whatever. This is your time to rest and reset."

"Don't need it."

His captain scoffed. "Your face has been contorted in pain after every practice. After every game. Did you think we hadn't noticed how you left every celebration or commiseration early to go ice your shoulder?"

Shit. "You knew this?"

"I am your captain. I know everything. You were doing what you had to do, but I didn't tell the tales. I learned that lesson years ago with my wife. One of the trainers figured it out and it got you on their radar."

Not Georgia.

The straight-talking Russian went on. "Listen, Banks, I have come back from surgery. It can be done."

Petrov had been skating on a supposedly bum knee for years, but it had struck him at a young enough age for him to recover. Even if Banks went for the surgery, it would be a six-month rehab, maybe longer because he was older and not as resilient. Effectively a death sentence to his time in the NHL.

"Time's running out."

"Maybe. But if we win the Cup this year, you'll still get a ring."

It wasn't the same. It would feel like he was getting it by default. And if they didn't win—if he wasn't there to push them all the way, which was why he'd been brought on in the first place—how would that play out? He wasn't sure he had another year in him.

"Thanks for checking in. Watch out for Hamilton. He's a sneaky fucker on the breakaway."

"Will do. Call me if you need to talk." He rang off.

Instead of wallowing, he should talk to Georgia. Apologize for lashing out.

Two minutes later, he was forced to conclude that he had fucked up, not just his career, but his marriage.

His flannel shirt, the one she wore to bed when he was out of town, lay neatly folded on the kitchen counter with a post-it note on top of it.

Sorry. I'll pick up my stuff later.

Her stuff? It was a stupid argument, his broody asshole self taking center stage. Surely they were strong enough to overcome that.

Only this wasn't a real marriage. Never had been. There was no foundation here on which to build.

Georgia might have nothing to be sorry about, but it didn't change the facts. His career was over. Her life, the independence she sought after the loss of her sister, was just beginning. Twelve years was a big gap when two people were at vastly different stages of their lives.

He picked up the shirt, intending to inhale any scent she might have left on it into his lungs. But he didn't get that far.

A clinking sound echoed in the suddenly too-big space.

Her diamond ring lay on the tiled floor—and that's when he knew it was truly over.

42

———

WHY DID some of the saddest days have to be the sunniest?

Georgia placed her sunglasses in her tote and took a seat a few rows back from Jim's family. Though this wasn't the church they used for Dani's service, it smelled the same. Incense, perfume, and tears.

Jim had passed away a few days ago, a day after the Rebels won the first game away in Nashville, but before they lost the second. "Going out on a win," Debbie had said, though she was crushed he wouldn't get a chance to see them lift the Cup again.

There had been no sign of Banks on the game broadcasts in Nashville, though she knew he'd traveled with them. (The house was empty when she stopped by to pack up her clothes and Cheddar's gear, for which the coward in her was grateful.) After Tara had assured Georgia that she didn't tattle to her husband, she had told her that when a player was injured, they didn't even sit on the bench or behind it. Instead they spent the game in the press box, which sounded awful. With all that media attention, how was a player supposed to move on? How could he grieve?

Because Georgia had no doubt that was what Dylan was doing now. Mourning his season and his career.

Debbie turned, then left her seat to come see her.

"What are you doing back here?" Before Georgia could offer an excuse, she touched her arm. "Come sit with the family."

"I don't want to intrude."

"Nonsense. Dad would have wanted you there. We want you there."

Georgia took her seat with the VIPs, kissed the cheeks of a couple of family members, and listened while Debbie filled her in on who was who. Her gaze arced over the flowers that practically covered the altar.

"There's one shaped like a hockey stick."

Debbie smiled. "From the Rebels. Nice of them, wasn't it?"

"Very." At Debbie's raised eyebrow, Georgia quickly added, "And nothing to do with me."

"Probably your husband. He called last week to ask if Jim wanted to attend the first home game of the series against Nashville. I told him he wouldn't make it. It was so kind of him to think of us, though."

Kind, but unsurprising. Her big guy had a big heart.

Debbie didn't pry about why Banks wasn't with her today, though the Rebels were playing at home tonight, and he was in town.

"Maybe you should take him up on the offer anyway. Jim would want you to go."

She chuckled. "Probably, but I'm sure Banks has given them away to someone else. Everyone will want those tickets."

"I'll ask him."

Debbie fussed a little but didn't protest too much. She wanted to attend the game.

"Everyone is so generous. A new charity gave me this suit

along with a personal shopper experience at Ann Taylor. Even had a car pick me up."

"Oh, that sounds nice."

"Yeah, there are caregiver support organizations, but they're more geared towards home help or mental support. They usually consider anything like this as a luxury. Too extra."

"These things are important, too. And that suit looks good on you. Very sharp. You could wear it at your new job."

Debbie took her hand. "I'm so glad you came."

Georgia wished she had her sunglasses on because her eyes felt a touch watery. "So am I."

After the service, Debbie invited her back to the house for a celebration of Jim's life. Once seated in her Mini, she sent a text to Banks:

> I have a favor to ask. It's for Debbie Draven, Jim Dixon's daughter.

Three dots appeared, then vanished. Her phone rang.

"Hello?"

"Are you okay?"

"Fine."

"Liar."

She swiped at a tear. He thought he knew her so well.

"How's Jim's family doing?"

"It's a tough day. They got your flowers."

"The org never forgets a true fan."

She knew it was him, but she didn't push it. "Debbie said you offered playoff tickets to Jim last week. Would you still have them? I think she'd like to attend, but she won't ask."

"Of course. I'll have the ticketing office call her to confirm."

She smiled. "That's good of you. I thought you might have set them aside for your family."

"I told them to stay home. If I'm not playing, there's not much point."

He sounded so down that her heart broke for him. "I'm sorry you're missing the series. How are you holding up?"

"Oh, fine."

"Now who's the liar?"

His chuckle was knowing, and she thanked the gods that, at least they had this, a little spark that might one day morph into friendship.

"Any chance you'd let me apologize?" He sounded gruff, but contrite.

"You're allowed to have a bad day."

"Georgia, that does not mean I get to use you as my punch bag. That wasn't fair."

No, it wasn't. But she'd forgiven him before she walked out the door.

"We're good, Dylan. Honestly."

"Good enough to meet up and talk?"

She bit her lip. She'd love nothing more than to see him again, be his support through this tough time. It was a role she was used to. Caregiver, people-pleaser, background artist.

But that didn't have to be her function. While she never considered herself second best when it came to her marriage with Banks, neither did she want to use him as a crutch while she figured out next steps. He deserved better than that.

"I don't think it's such a good idea. We always said it was time-limited."

"What will your parents think?"

She sighed. "They'll be disappointed. But I need to stand on my own two feet, tell them what I want. Who I want to be, separate from Dani. You helped me see that and I'm so grateful. You helped me much more than I helped you—"

"Peaches, that's not true. You were always there for me, the person I could talk to about anything. That's it, isn't it? I've been a selfish asshole, making it all about me."

"No, you haven't. But you were right when you said I don't know anything about hockey, about your world." Flash cards would only get her so far. "We're in different places, you and I."

He sounded so resigned when he said, "I hear you."

He had always been a great listener. She'd miss him terribly, but this would be best for him. He could settle with someone who could give him exactly what he needed, be there for him through this next phase.

On a deep pull of air into her lungs, she reached for the words that she suspected would kill her.

"Banks, I think we should get a divorce."

43

JENNY, his three-year-old niece, took a flying leap off the back of the sofa and landed right on Banks's chest. His shoulder twinged but held up. A good sign? Maybe. But thirty pounds of little girl was a lot different than two hundred pounds of asshole hockey player.

April scooped her up. "Leave your uncle alone. He's old and wizened."

"Hey!"

"A wizard?" Jenny asked hopefully.

"No, more like a crone," April said.

His sister returned his scowl with one of her own, which he liked to think was about 10% less scary than the day before, which was about 5% less than the day before that. Since he'd arrived home in Apple Falls, they'd given him the mostly silent treatment, all pissed at him because of Georgia. Even his gran. So much for Dylan the Golden Child. Everyone was on his case except his mom, who understood that he was in no frame of mind to rehab a marriage when he could barely rehab his body.

He went looking for her now and found her in the kitchen with Sandy, reading a recipe on her iPad. It reminded him of Georgia, learning to cook, and made him pissy all over again.

"Need any help?"

"Sure! Want to peel carrots?"

Sandy muttered, "Better if we do it. Pretend it's a bag of hockey player dicks."

His mom sighed. "How about you go to the store and get some ice cream for the apple pie?"

"But we've got plenty—"

"I want the Madagascar vanilla bean one."

His sister rolled her eyes. "Sure, Mom."

Once she was gone, he picked up the vegetable scraper and ran a carrot under cold water in the sink. Then he got busy. If only he could scrape away the last four months. Figure out how he could have handled it all better—his shoulder, his game, his marriage.

"Is Gran okay?"

"She's napping."

"I never intended to disappoint her."

She nodded. "I know. You don't have it in you to hurt anyone, Dylan."

Except Georgia. He'd taken it out on her, and while she was nice enough to forgive him, she didn't see a future for them. He took comfort in the fact she had yet to send over the annulment papers. For now, he was still her husband.

He'd come home a couple of days ago after the Rebels were knocked out of the second round against Nashville in a Game 7 heartbreaker. (The irony that if he'd stayed with his old team, he might still be playing wasn't lost on him.) He wasn't obliged to travel with the Rebels or sit through any of the games, but these were his ice brothers, and he wanted to be there. He'd like to think he could have made a difference if he'd been on that ice, but the boys had skated their hearts out. He couldn't fault their performance. Like hasty Vegas marriages, sometimes these things don't work out.

"You want to talk about Georgia?"

He looked up at his mom, whose face was all concern.

"What's there to talk about? We're in different places in our lives. She's young, just finding her feet, and I'm—not."

"You don't think you can meet in the middle?"

"Not when I'm feeling this sorry for myself."

She laughed at his self-awareness. At least he had that going for him.

He finished with the carrots and placed them on a paper towel to dry. A quick mix with olive oil, salt, and rosemary, and he arranged them on a roasting pan.

"Have a seat."

"*Mom*." He sounded like a whiny teen, but he did as he was told.

"So you missed the rest of the playoffs because you were injured. Want to tell me what Georgia thought of that?"

"She thought I shouldn't be playing hurt. I blamed her because I thought she was the reason the org found out. She wasn't, I apologized for being an asshole, but it opened up this chasm between us." He sighed. "She spent a long time taking care of her sister, then taking a background role in her own life. I don't want her to ever feel she's not important, and while I'm in this funk, I'm not sure I can be what she needs. I love her too much."

His mom's eyes had turned suspiciously shiny. "That sounds very selfless, but maybe you should tell her all that."

And expect her to soothe him through his foul moods as the clock ticked down on his career? Be a drag on all that joy?

He needed to stay away and let her fully blossom into the beautiful person he knew her to be.

"This is for the best, Mom."

His phone vibrated in his pocket, and he took it out, quick enough for his mother to notice and for his heart to drop on seeing it wasn't from Georgia.

BABY DURAND

You okay?

All the guys had checked in regularly, somehow managing to find time amidst their own disappointment.

BANKS

Back in Apple Falls, peeling carrots.

BABY DURAND

Is that code for something?

BANKS

Nope. What's up?

BABY DURAND

I heard you're the man to figure out
investment stuff for the team.

A couple of the guys had sent their financials to him, looking for advice. Probably a way to make him feel useful.

BANKS

I just know what works for me.

BABY DURAND

But you have a finance degree, right? My
dad's been looking after my accounts for
years but he's Canadian.

> **BANKS**
>
> So? They have banks and brokerages in Canada.

BABY DURAND

Yeah, but I earn my money in the US, so I figure I should have someone on this side of the border advising me.

> **BANKS**
>
> I'm not qualified to give advice. You need a CFP.

BABY DURAND

Just give me the Rebels Finance Advice package.

Three orthos had already told him he'd be better off with PT for his shoulder instead of a risky surgery, so he had appointments set up at a local clinic. If the Rebels liked what they saw after a couple of months, they were open to extending his contract for a year. Running numbers and poring over brokerage accounts would be as good a way as any to fill the rest of his time. Better than moping about the demise of his marriage and the fact he was a dead man walking in the league.

> **BANKS**
>
> Sure, I can take a look.

BABY DURAND

Sweet! Reid wants in as well. We'll email you our latest statements.

> **BANKS**
>
> Don't email them! I'll send you a secure link where you can upload them.

These kids didn't have a clue.

He ran a quick search on his phone: *Certified Financial Planner qualification.* If he was going to be answering more of these kinds of questions, he may as well investigate how to do it officially.

44

Four months later
September

BANKS LEFT Fitz's office and nodded at Casey, the front office assistant.

"Congrats, Dylan. Great to have you on board for next season."

"Thanks." He had signed a contract extension after the medical report came back, assuring the brass he had life in him yet. After four months of PT, his shoulder felt good, and so did he. Physically.

"Do you have a few moments? Coach asked if you would stop by his office before you head out."

"Sure, I can do that."

A few minutes later, he was outside Coach's office, but no one was home. Crossed wires, perhaps?

"Hey, Banks! You're back." O'Malley stuck his head out of the player lounge. "Got a sec?"

All summer, he'd monitored the team's group chat, hovering on the edges like a creeper. It was the usual crap:

bad-mouthing the team that won the Cup that year, invites to bar meetups and cookouts for whoever was in the city, the usual flurry of pet and kid pics, and recipes (Grey was the only one who thought this was a good use of the thread).

He'd enjoyed it, though. It was nice to keep his hand in even if it felt like life was passing him by.

"Sure, what's up?"

The kid gestured for him to come into the lounge, where he was greeted by the entire team with a cake as big as a face-off circle.

"Congratulations, Banks!" O'Malley looked thrilled that his ambush had worked out spectacularly. "As soon as we heard you were signing today, we got busy."

His teammates rushed forward, clapping him on the back (probably testing his shoulder, the fuckers) and letting him know in their own way that he was still part of the team, even though he'd failed at the final hurdle in May.

"You missed O'Malley's big cookout yesterday," Kershaw said around a mouthful of cake.

"Don't you mean *your* big cookout?" Foreman asked. "You spent the whole afternoon defending that grill like it was your zone."

"He's a baby! He needs to learn from his grill meister elders." Kershaw gave Banks a crafty look. "You still married, Banks?"

"For now. It's working its way through the system."

The annulment papers were sitting on his kitchen counter, the same place they'd landed after the courier dropped them off two weeks ago. After not hearing from her for several months, he'd harbored the slightest hope that she might be having second thoughts.

But no. All he had to do was sign and send them on. Delaney had said there should be no problems; he had a guy on deck in Nevada who would shepherd it through the system on the grounds of intoxication (lie) and want of understanding (more lies). The marriage would be null and void from the date they'd tied the knot, like it never happened.

But it had happened, and while Banks didn't think that was the kind of thing that should be erased from existence, he had to honor Georgia's wishes.

"Heard Georgia set up a charity." Petrov thumbed a dob of icing from the corner of his mouth. "She is always in the news these days, galas and the like. Harper went to one of them."

"She wore one of Sadie's dresses at that last one." Bond's wife was a dress designer, and Banks knew exactly which dress Georgia had worn. Another pink number, it had a full skirt, like a ballet tutu of feathers, and now it was listed on Sadie's site, simply titled "the Georgia."

Baby Durand put a slice of cake on a plate. "She wasn't with anyone, though, was she?"

Jorgenson shook his head. "No, she's probably not going to start dating until the divorce goes through officially."

Banks slammed his plate down. "I'd appreciate it if you stop gossiping about my wife like a gaggle of hens."

"Your wife?" Kershaw chuckled. "From what I heard it was all a 'big mistake'."

Banks offered a soul-killing glare. He knew what they were doing, trying to goad him into fucking *emoting*.

"Not a mistake," he bit out. Big or otherwise. "Just something that happened."

"Now she's a free agent," O'Malley said, running with Kershaw's inanity. "With her hockey know-how, I'm guessing her next husband will be a player. She's got a taste for it now. Maybe one of our rookies?"

Kershaw shook his head. "Georgia's got too much class to

date a player on her ex's team. I reckon she'll go for someone on the Hawks instead."

Rage reared up. "Kershaw, if you don't shut your mouth, I'm gonna take that cake slice and put an end to your genetic line."

His teammate looked unimpressed. "All this feeling, man, and you're *still* going through with the divorce."

"It's an annulment. Like it never happened."

O'Malley blew out a breath. "But you just said it did happen. And you're still wearing your wedding ring."

Damn thing wouldn't come off. Too much salty food this summer.

The kid looked serious. "You probably don't want to hear it—"

"Correct."

"But you looked like you were really happy together. Or about as happy as a guy with your brand of resting prick face *can* look."

"We were." He couldn't keep it in any longer. "I fucked up."

The Bromance Heavens opened their floodgates. Suddenly, everyone was pummeling him with questions.

What happened?

Were you an asshole? (Or more than usual.)

Why are you going through with it?

"She's got her whole life in front of her. She doesn't need me dragging her down." They had one argument and she left, which said it all. The foundation of their marriage was flimsy, no stronger than his fucked-up shoulder. He'd tried to talk to her on the day of Jim Dixon's funeral, but she'd obviously decided she was better off without him.

"She said that?" Foreman asked.

"She would never. She's too nice."

"So, this is *your* sparkling conclusion?" Kershaw laughed,

kind of evil-sounding. "Let me guess. You had just been nixed from the playoffs, and you were feeling like the world was ending, so you decided to blow up all the good things in your life to have a matching set."

Dex patted his arm, which, given Banks's mood, was a bold move. "But look at you now. New contract, rehabbed shoulder, and another shot at that ring. You're ready to fight for your career, for a chance at the Cup, but not for her?"

Banks stared at Dumb and Dumber, not quite believing that these two were suddenly the Rebels sages—and even more of a shocker, were making sense?

Neither of us fought for this. That was what she'd said about the first annulment.

"I need to go."

"Aw, he's getting it now." Kershaw pointed. "Go take care of business, but fair warning: if you leave, don't expect any of this cake to be left when you get back."

Georgia checked the bulletin board and moved a card from the right side to the left.

"You know there's computer software that can handle this kind of thing. Like Airtable." Debbie handed off a peppermint tea and stood beside her. When she set up Georgia's Godmothers in this Riverbrook office a little over two months ago, she had brought Debbie on board to manage the applications and administration of funds for the new charity.

"You know I'm old school." She loved seeing the wishes on clean white cards, each one brimming with the potential to make a difference. "This family is asking for car repairs. Maybe we should just buy them a new car?"

"That would go way over the cap." As well as being an

office manager and administration goddess, Debbie was also Georgia's sounding board and let's be fair, dream-crusher. She didn't mean to be such a downer, but they had to be realistic about how much they could dedicate to each wish, usually a thousand dollars. Debbie had no problem reining Georgia in.

"Let's offer them the full amount for the repairs."

Debbie nodded. "We have more applications for fairy godmothers, so I've blocked out tomorrow morning for volunteer interviews. And your mother called asking if you could do lunch on Thursday."

"She wants to make sure their money is being used wisely."

Her friend raised an eyebrow. "Or maybe she just wants lunch with her daughter."

Anything was possible, she supposed. Since she'd set up Georgia's Godmothers, her parents had become more involved in her life, in a positive way. She'd finally told them the truth about her marriage, its beginning and end, and they had been more understanding than she expected. Of course, they assumed that what started as a mistake was best acknowledged as such, though her mom thought Dylan was very nice for "someone who plays a game for a living."

She'd spent the last four months working on herself. Therapy to deal with losing Dani and the effects of her upbringing. Talking with her parents to let them know how their attitudes hurt and stunted her growth. Setting up her new foundation and ensuring that caregivers were rewarded and supported.

Mostly she'd worked on getting over Banks.

If only the man could be easily dismissed, assigned to a forgotten corner of her mind. But she saw him everywhere: a bottle of hot sauce, a cup of tea, even stupid oranges all had the capacity to remind her of what she'd loved and lost.

She had been so busy with the foundation that it took her months to get around to initiating the annulment again. (It was her story and she was sticking with it.) Two weeks after sending them on, and he still hadn't returned the signed papers.

Back to the board, to her new purpose. This was what she was meant to do. This would help her through.

An hour later, she had the cards arranged to her liking. The godmothers assigned to each case would work with the families to distribute the grant funds, set up appointments, and ensure the needs of the caregivers were met.

She sipped on her tea, though it had gone cold. Time to take a break.

The door to her office opened and Debbie put her head in. "Do you have a minute? We have someone here who wants to make a donation."

"Of course! Send them in."

Debbie looked excited—a little too excited, to be honest—and Georgia soon learned why.

In walked Banks.

"Dylan!"

He wore dark denim, a gray Henley that shaped his muscled chest perfectly, and a Rebels zip-up. The full beard was gone, but a very appealing scruff remained.

Closing the door behind him, he raised his whiskey-hued gaze to her. "Hey, Peaches."

Her heart went pitter-patter.

He dragged his eyes away and fixed them on the wall of cards. "You did it."

"I did." He would never know how much his support had meant to her. She was here because he had been in her corner from the start. She missed him so much, but the low wasn't worth the high.

"You look good." His gaze raked over her, and there it was: this man saw her like no other.

"Thank you." *So do you. So good.* "How've you been?"

"Okay."

"And your shoulder?"

"Pretty good. PT throughout the summer, and it's feeling as strong as ever."

What a relief. "Tara said you got your contract extension. Congrats."

"Yeah, another year, another shot."

She was so happy for him. He didn't have that championship ring yet, but he was still in with a fighting chance. No one deserved it more.

"I also finished coursework to become a Certified Financial Planner. Figured I should start thinking of the next phase."

"Oh, Dylan, that's wonderful. So many of your fellow athletes could use a service like that." She shook her head, marveling at how silly she sounded. Of course he knew that.

He nodded. "You're probably wondering why I'm here."

"Debbie said you wanted to make a donation."

He pulled out an envelope from inside his jacket, one she instantly recognized.

The annulment papers.

He also had a check, which he passed off to her. She covered her mouth in shock because even a woman with a once healthy trust fund could appreciate a sum like this: two hundred and fifty thousand dollars.

"Dylan, this is too much."

"I'm good for it, Peaches." He put the envelope down on her desk. "But I'm not good for this."

"You mean—"

"I'm contesting the annulment."

Her knees buckled and she leaned against the desk. "Why?"

"Thought we should talk first, face to face."

"But you agreed."

He walked over to the window and sat on the sill. The noon-day sun caught his dark hair and cheekbones, giving him an angelic glow.

"We didn't discuss it last time, and it turned out kind of messy."

He was right. But it wouldn't change a thing. "What did you want to talk about?"

"That night in Vegas."

"Oh."

He gave a curt nod. "You told me once that you were in a bad place when we first met. Still grieving Dani, looking for a way to ease the pain. I was the salve, or we were. Together. Only neither of us fought to stay married and that convinced you this wasn't supposed to be. Do you remember that?"

She nodded slowly.

"Except I think we did fight, just in a more subtle way. We made choices, not always the best choices, but choices all the same. Ones that pushed us together."

"I don't know—"

"You told your parents we got married."

She blinked. "What's that got to do with anything?"

"You said it was an accident, letting the cat out of the bag. How's Cheddar, by the way?"

"Still fighting his own shadow. I assumed my parents knew and I let it slip out."

He stared at her, those deep brown eyes seeing all. "Is it possible that you told your parents because a part of you wanted to grab the horns of this wild thing you'd done and see if you could stay on?"

The lump of emotion in her throat was growing. "You think I leaked the news ... on purpose?"

"Maybe. Subconsciously. Perhaps, to kickstart life into this thing we both thought was dead. Sure you wanted to convince your parents that you were stable and trustworthy, but to stay married to a stranger when you were convinced it was a mistake? That's like me pretending I wanted to stay married to please my grandmother."

She gasped. "Pretending? But that's what you—you— what's happening here?"

He straightened and took a few steps toward her. Just the sight of him standing tall and strong made her heart flutter dangerously.

I'm over you. I'm over you.

"We both needed permission to give this a shot, Peaches. So we invented reasons. My grandmother, your parents. And they were semi-decent reasons, ones that kept us in each other's orbit where neither of us had to tell the whole truth. We could say we were doing each other a favor, nothing more. But the real reason was that something happened that night. Something magical and real and undeniable. I fell for you hard, and I think you fell right back."

I'm over you. I'm over—

He kept going like he was heading for the blue zone.

Relentless. Unyielding. Banks.

"Then we panicked, only not at the same time because God forbid we be in sync about anything. First, you did when you tried to get it annulled a few days after we married. Then it was my turn when I thought this could never work because you're young and fresh and so goddamn perfect. The idea of you taking that sickness and in health vow and sticking with a broken-down loser like me made me mad. I've been mad all summer. I was ready to sign those papers. Give you your freedom."

"And now?"

His smile was a little sad. "I'm still ready because I would never tie you down if you need to fly free. That's why I'm here. To talk to you, face to face. To see if you're still lying your peach-perfect ass off. I need you to tell me you don't care about me."

"I-I can't do that. And I never thought you were a broken-down loser," she whispered. "You're the bravest, toughest, most amazing man I know."

He inched closer. "And you're the kindest, strongest, most vibrant woman I've ever met. I was never prouder than when you were my wife. Baby, you took a puck to the head and didn't even cry."

If he didn't stop talking, she would make up for that. Tears thickened her throat, and she wanted to speak, tell him to *stop, stop, stop*.

But she couldn't.

And he didn't.

"Am I right here, Georgia? Did something happen in Vegas?"

I'm not over you. I'll never be over you.

She nodded.

"Tell me."

"I found something of my own. Someone who saw me." She wailed, "Then I second-guessed everything! When the annulment didn't take, I saw a second chance to grab what I truly wanted, even if I couldn't admit it aloud. I could have kept quiet, but you're right. A part of me wanted my parents to know I'd taken this step." She pressed a hand to her chest, as if that could keep her heart inside.

Impossible, as it turned out.

"*For me.* But once we were together, faking it or pretending to—God, I don't know—all the doubts came flooding back. I'd tricked you into this caper, and you were being so kind to go through with it."

He smiled. "Not kind. Completely selfish. I wanted you so badly. This fine, beautiful woman who was so full of life and joy. I saw my chance to make it happen, first in Vegas and then again, here, when you walked into the Empty Net and blew up my world. But damn, I fought it hard. No way could you truly want this guy with one foot in retirement, one foot in this half-life. And when I ended up riding the pine in the middle of the playoffs, it messed with my head. Made me feel like I couldn't take care of you, be the man you need. I took it out on you and that was wrong. It had nothing to do with what you told Tara, but even if it was, it wouldn't have mattered. You were worried about me. You had a right to be worried about me, because that's what people who care for each other do."

"It's okay. I understand." She placed a hand on his chest, where it belonged. "But to think that somehow you were diminished because of your injury, that I wouldn't see you as strong enough to be my rock, to be my everything is crazy. I'm so mad at you for even going there."

His hands slipped to her waist. "Mad enough to *not* give me a divorce?"

"It's an annulment. And I'd have to think about it."

He jack-knifed to the floor.

She gasped. Then gasped again when he pulled out a ring box.

It was already open, her pink solitaire winking back at her. No other would do.

"Are you sober?" she whispered.

"Drunk as a lord on Georgia Bankowski."

She swiped at a tear. *Georgia Bankowski.* She didn't like that much.

She *loved* it.

"Oh, Dylan."

"I love you, Peaches. I love your strength, your optimism, your cheer, how you pulled me out of my funk in Vegas and gave me something to hope for. To strive for. A future after hockey."

She covered her mouth. "With me?"

"No one else I'd rather spend it with. Now, I know I'm older and things are just kicking off for you—"

She fell to her knees, meeting him where he knelt, and placed two fingers on his lips.

"I don't care that you're older. I don't care that it seems like we're in different places because when we're together, it feels like the same place. The kitchen with you making me tea. The sofa with you explaining hockey. Our bed with you doing very naughty things."

He grasped her fingers, pulled them from his lips, and kissed the tips. "They're not naughty when they're done to your gorgeous peach of a wife."

"They're the naughtiest of all!" She placed her hands on his chest and absorbed all the strength that gave her. Her rock. Her man. "I love what you do to me in bed. What you do to me everywhere. Because what you do is see me. You've always put me at the center of your world. I love you for that, Dylan. For every heartbeat and happy thought and shining moment. I love you so much."

His eyes grew misty, and a smile teased his lips.

"Where does that leave us?"

Where, indeed? "You called me Georgia Bankowski."

"I did."

"That's where it leaves us." She held out her hand.

On a harsh pull of breath, he wasted no time extracting the ring and placed it at the fingertip of her wedding ring finger. That's when she noticed he still wore his.

"You didn't take yours off?"

"A part of me refused to believe it was over." He slipped the diamond ring on, down to the first knuckle. "With this ring, I thee wed. I promise to love, cherish, and do naughty things to you as often as possible. I promise to try everything you cook, walk with you on the beach, and take care of your cat. Most important, I promise to make sure you never for one second regret a single moment of that night in Vegas."

He pushed the ring all the way onto her finger.

Her breath caught, and those tears finally made good on their threat.

"Peaches." He wiped them away. "You okay?"

"Yes! Happy tears, I promise. And speaking of vows ..." She held his face, this lovely, lived-in face of her husband, and leaned close. "With this kiss, I thee wed. I promise to cheer you when you're down and support you in everything. I promise to listen to your advice when I might be about to do something impulsive, like put too much hot sauce on my tacos, or marry a stranger in Vegas. I promise to love you as much as I want to be loved, which is a lot because I'm very selfish when it comes to you, Dylan Bankowski."

She kissed him to seal her promise. He took that kiss and triple-downed on it for intensity.

"You've made me a very happy man, wife."

She smiled through joyful tears. "I'm officially a Bankowski Babe! I can't wait to tell your family. And make jackets!"

He raised an eyebrow. "No jackets."

"T-shirts?" She gave her sauciest grin, which stretched

wider as her husband relented. This man was a bit of a pushover where his wife was concerned.

"Maybe. As for telling my family, that can wait. Can you leave early?"

"I'm the boss, I can do anything."

"Good. Because right now, I'd like to take Babe Prime to bed and start fulfilling all the vows I just made."

Which he did.

Three wonderful times.

EPILOGUE

Seven months later
April

It's more than a door.

Though Georgia had visited the Empty Net several times over the last seven months—she would never feel in the know enough to call it *the Net*—it still gave her a thrill to pull that big oak door open and walk on through.

Like stepping into her future.

Tonight was a good night to be a Rebels fan. The team had made the playoffs, the bar was heaving, and a still height-challenged Georgia could barely make out anyone she knew. That blond crown in the distance might have been Erik Jorgenson, the Rebels goalie, or maybe a different Viking hockey player altogether.

She should have met Banks in the dressing room right after the game, but she had been called away by a Georgia's Godmothers emergency. One of their clients was on a date night with her husband when some miscommunication snafu had resulted in their reservation being canceled. No other restaurant would do because this was the one they'd gotten engaged in twenty three years ago—wow!—so Georgia made a personal call to the chef-owner, Tony DeLuca. When he didn't answer because he was in the middle of service, she had paid a visit to DeLuca's in Wicker Park herself. The couple were soon seated at a chef's table in the kitchen, and all was well again. It might have seemed trivial—*boo hoo, they couldn't eat in a fancy restaurant*—but not to Georgia. These were the moments that mattered.

So, she was late to the celebration. But she hoped she would add to it with news of her own.

She arced her gaze again over the crowd, and that's when it happened, just like that first night. Parting the crowd like the Red Sea, her husband moved toward her like she was the mission. He scooped her up and kissed her deep and she thought, *how lucky am I?*

"Everything good?" he asked when he let her up for air. "You fix it?"

"I did."

"Course you did."

"You won."

"Course I did." He grinned. "So glad you're here. Last year when we qualified, I was miserable."

"You were?"

"Yeah, I'd just kissed you in the kitchen and you weren't quite ready to fall for my charms. Bonus: O'Malley was rubbing it in with his uber-successful love life."

She sighed. "We were such dummies."

"A lot of stupid choices needed before the light bulb goes off."

What about stupid *non*-choices? Would he be okay with her news? Or would he think of it as another distraction when he needed his focus more than ever? While his shoulder was still holding its own, there was only so long he could stay at this peak level.

"Could we go somewhere private for a sec?"

His face fell. "What's going on?"

"Nothing! Just need to run something by you." Doubts assailed her. She changed tack. "You know something? It can wait."

But her husband knew better. He was already moving toward the rear of the bar, half-carrying her, her feet hardly touching the ground. "Comin' through!" Of course they all made room, because that's what you did when a man like Banks forged a path through any and all obstacle. That's what he'd done with her.

"Georgia!" Tara tried to give her a hug, but Banks had her all wrapped up.

"Hi! Just got here."

"Perfect timing. We just opened the champagne." Tara took a quick look at Banks, then her. "Everything okay?"

"Fine, fine!"

Banks got the attention of the bar's owner. "Tina, okay if we use the office?"

She waved them through with an eye roll. The Rebels players were known for taking liberties with the staff spaces at this bar, so this was par for the course. "Sure, mi casa and all that."

"Georgia, you made it!" Ashley kissed her on the cheek, then Mia tried to get in on the action.

"I just need a sec and then I'll be—"

Banks had been waiting semi-patiently during the greetings of the WAG squad, then decided patience was overrated and removed her mid-sentence.

Once in the office, he took a seat in a large swivel chair,

pulled her into his lap, and got her settled. "What's up, Peaches?"

Here goes. "So, this is probably the worst timing but ... I'm pregnant."

No expression change. Still her gloriously glowering Banks.

"Uh, say something?"

"Should've known."

"What? Why?"

He grimaced. "Baby, you've stopped drinking coffee—"

"It made me sick. Or sicker."

"And your tits are fuller. Don't get me wrong, I love your sweet little beauties, but ..." He cupped her left one softly. (He claimed it was his favorite.) "These are giving me all sorts of ideas."

She snatched a breath. "That's the problem. The ideas that suck up your focus while you worry about me. This is going to be like last year when I moved in right before the playoffs with my poisonous cat and dubious cooking and then I got hit by that puck and—"

He kissed her, his usual tactic to calm her down. It worked. Sort of.

"Peaches, why would this be a problem? Unless you don't want it?"

She blew out a breath. "I-I do. More than anything. I just thought we'd plan for it after you retire. When things are more settled."

"When have Dylan and Georgia Bankowski ever 'planned' anything? I'd say this is very much in keeping with how we roll." He smiled, giving her all the sun she needed to warm her through and chase away the doubts. "Never thought you could make me happier than the night I married you or the day you told me you wanted to keep my name. But here we are."

She blinked. "You're pleased?"

"Baby, I'm fucking ecstatic." But because this was Banks, he wasn't whooping or hollering or going overboard. He was just being his stoic, solid, enduring self. This was the man who would be the father of her child—of all her children—and she had enough drama for the two of them.

"I'm pregnant," she whispered, the reality and dream colliding to produce the perfect sensation of peace and joy.

"You are." The grin broke free at last. "We're having a baby."

They stared, drinking each other and the moment in. Finally, he said, "The families are gonna be stoked."

"About that. Can we keep it to ourselves for now? I took a test, but I still need to see a doctor. I'm pretty sure it happened six weeks ago, though."

He squinted, thought on that for a second. "The morning after the New York game?"

"Yeah, I have a feeling that was it. You were extra, uh, spurty. Nothing was going to stop your powerful boys."

Color flushed his cheeks, and his nostrils flared. "I came twice, Peaches, because that's what my gorgeous wife does to me." He tilted his head. "How you feelin'?"

"Okay. Relieved. I know I've been here since but standing outside that door had me thinking about the first time I came into this bar. How my life was about to change, but I had no idea, really, of just how much. And here we are again."

"More life changing." He nuzzled his nose against hers. "Thank you, Georgia."

"For what?"

"Bringing color into my life. Giving me another reason to strive for glory outside of the game. But mostly, for being my compass and always guiding me home."

She sniffed. "Baby hormones."

His eyes took on a suspicious shine. "Me, too."

He kissed her again, and the fear vanished in the warmth of that kiss. Because she had this man, fighting for her. For them. Lucky? No, blessed—and happy to count each of her blessings every single day.

BONUS EPILOGUE

"Are you finished yet?"

"Nope," came a small voice.

Similarly small hands continued tugging and shaping his hair into ... well, he wasn't sure yet. He'd need to look in a mirror and he suspected he would be unimpressed with what he saw.

"Just one more, Daddy."

"One more what?"

"One more pretty bow," Hallie said.

Her twin, Gracie looked up from the book she was reading and giggled.

"What's so funny?"

"Oh, Daddy." She shook her head like he hadn't a clue—often a valid assumption when it came to his kids. "Hallie wants to be a hair artist like Aunt Tara."

"Is she any good?"

Gracie gave another sad head shake. "You look funny."

Not in a good way, he reckoned. Gracie was the more straight-talking of his girls. Hallie was the dreamer.

"Can I look?"

Hallie had a mirror at the ready—she was a hair artist in the making like her Aunt Tara, after all—and she passed it to him now. His hair was hedgehog style, tied in multiple pink bows, but more concerning was the eyeshadow and lipstick.

"When did you do that?"

"You were taking a nap!" Hallie jumped off the sofa and took a closer look at her handiwork. "Mommy said I could."

"Hallie Constance Bankowski, I did not say you could do that." Georgia appeared at the door to the den, where he had indeed been trying to nap, and gave her eldest four-year old— by five whole minutes—a mini glare. Which, coming from his wife, was on the more indulgent side. "I said you could say hi to him, but only if he was awake."

"I said hi," Hallie said. "With my lipstick."

"It's Mommy's lipstick." Gracie was a bit of a stickler, but that was okay because everyone was already possessed of these incontrovertible facts.

He caught the eye of his wife of, damn, almost six years now, and smiled. "How'd I look, Peaches?"

"It's a good color on you, Big Guy."

"Prefer when it's transferred the more traditional way." With an eyebrow waggle, he patted the seat beside him, the one Hallie had vacated so she could pack up her beauty supplies. "Sit a spell."

"Uh, the suitcases won't pack themselves. Have you forgotten we're heading to Apple Falls for the holidays? And on the busiest traffic day of the year?"

"Road trip!" Hallie shouted, and Gracie soon joined in, running around like the demon four-year-olds they were.

"Shush, now," Banks said softly, gesturing to the monitor. "You'll wake the baby."

Hallie put her finger to her lips. "Shush now," she said to her sister, though she was the one who'd started it.

His eight-month-old daughter, Iris, was currently sleeping safe and sound upstairs in Connie's room, as they called it. It was where his gran had stayed several times until she slipped away just after the twins were born.

I got to see my grandson win that championship ring, nab a gorgeous wife, and give me two more great-grandbabies! My maker better be ready for me because I sure as hell am ready for him.

Speaking of championship rings, Gracie had picked up Banks's from the cabinet where he displayed his hardware and was examining it closely, something she liked to do on the regular. The details fascinated her: the hockey stick and cutlass crossed in the center, the year of the championship and Chicago Rebels emblazoned on one side, his name on the other (Banks, not Bankowski). He preferred the shorter version for the ring because it stood out more. Longer names tended to look squashed, case in point, poor Jorgenson, whose name was practically illegible on his ring (his second, but no one was counting).

That contract extension with the Rebels had worked out well. The next season, everything clicked. He was almost glad the guys hadn't done it the previous year without him—this way, he could truly say he'd been there to the end. He couldn't even begrudge O'Malley scoring the winning goal in Game 7's overtime. The kid was now a father of three, a complete pushover when it came to his kids, and had just signed a four-year contract with the Rebels. Thankfully Ashley was on hand as the brains of the operation.

He patted the sofa seat again, and felt that familiar thrill when his gorgeous wife sat beside him. Last month, she had turned twenty-nine—which made him, at forty one, far too old for her—and still looked as fresh-faced and vibrant as the day he met her in that dive bar in Vegas. The scar on her forehead had faded; now it was no more than a silver thread with a great backstory.

Since his retirement four years ago, he'd become the more hands-on parent so his wife could expand her foundation into other cities. Georgia's Godmothers was now in St. Louis, Milwaukee, and Madison, and was about to open a branch in Indianapolis. He hated when she was away for work, but hey, turnabout was fair play. His wife was a powerhouse CEO in every way, including how she ran him and their kids.

"Wanna kiss?" He puckered his lipstick-stained lips as he slid a sneaky arm around her.

She cupped his jaw, stroked through his beard, and leaned in close. "I already know that color looks good on me."

"Lemme see for myself, wife." He laid one on her, relishing the fireworks that sparked in his blood. Every time. He sent up a quick prayer that the day he tired of kissing this woman would never come.

"Hmm," he murmured, looking her over. "I think it looks better on me."

She thumped his arm lightly, then caught the eye of Gracie, who was holding his championship ring. "What's up, Gracie-Lou?"

"Daddy never wears his ring."

"I've got this other one that means more to me."

A frowning Gracie did a quick comparison of the blinged-out championship ring and the plain platinum band on his wedding finger. She wasn't buying it.

"This one's prettier."

"I dunno," Banks said, holding up his hand. "This one has a better story."

"Better than winning the Cup?" Hailey's contribution.

"Well, you see, I got this one because I won a prize bigger than the Cup." He added, "your mom" because literal worked better for his girls right now.

"Mom was bigger than the Cup?" Gracie looked confused.

"Actually, she was a tiny thing. Still is." He turned to his wife who was watching him with those ocean-blue pools he adored. "But the day I met her, I fell for her so hard, that the only way I could get up off the floor was to walk down the aisle and put a ring on her finger."

"Mommy's ring!" Hailey moved in and grabbed her mom's hand, where her pink solitaire still took pride of place. "This is pretty, too. But not as good as the cocky ring."

Sometimes she said "cocky" instead of "hockey," a slip-up that Georgia enjoyed immensely. *(Just think if she dropped the "y"?)*

Gracie climbed up onto the sofa on his other side. "Mommy, did you fall on the ground for Daddy, too?"

"Oh, yeah. I fell like a fool, for sure. The first thing I noticed was his voice. He had the nicest voice when he talked to his mom, Gram Trish, and I knew there was something special about him. Every girl in that b—uh, room wanted him."

"But you were the winner," Hailey said definitively. "Like a princess."

"I was the winner." She smiled, her lipstick smudged, her eyes as bright as those Vegas lights almost six years ago. He still found it hard to believe she had chosen him. "Go put the ring back in its spot, honey. Then come upstairs and tell me which dresses you want to bring to Apple Falls."

"I don't want to wear a dress," Gracie said. "I want to wear ice-skating clothes."

Both girls liked to skate, but Gracie had taken to hockey

like Cheddar to a climbing post. Between her and his nieces, he expected he'd be squiring a girl squad of budding hockey players to the Apple Falls rink several times over the next week.

"You can bring those, too. But you have to wear a dress for Christmas Day dinner."

With some grumbling, the girls headed upstairs to finish packing while Banks veered off in another direction. First the bathroom to wash his face, then Connie's room, where he found Cheddar curled up at the end of the bassinet. They'd formed a bro-alliance over the years. Surrounded by all these females, the guys had to stick together.

"Hey, buddy, you okay?"

Cheddar yawned, then returned to his important sentry duty.

Iris was stirring, not quite in this world yet, but it wouldn't be long. He picked her up, knowing that the body heat of her daddy would help the transition to wakefulness. He had a couple of things to check on for his clients before the holidays started proper, but for now, he let the peace draw him in as he stood before the window and looked out over Lake Michigan.

He had thought retirement would be hard, and while he missed the camaraderie of his former team, he also recognized that his post-NHL life was as good as it got. Three gorgeous girls, an extended family that still drove him around the bend, a second career he enjoyed, his health, and financial security for everyone he loved.

But mostly, he had Georgia. If someone had told him his quickie Vegas wedding would have resulted in the love of a lifetime, he'd have scoffed and told them they were fools.

His little one shifted and her big blue eyes fluttered open. Sensing that she was in good hands, she gave him a smile.

With each passing day, she looked more and more like Georgia. His baby peach.

"Hey, Big Guy," a soft voice sounded behind him. His wife placed a soothing hand on his back. "She okay?"

"Yeah." He turned and smiled at the woman who made everything golden. "We both are."

ACKNOWLEDGMENTS

Thank you to my editor, Kristi Yanta - you are amazing! Thanks also to proofreader Julia Griffis for your perfect attention to detail.

To my classic cover designer Michele Catalano Creative, thanks for another great Rebels cover, and to the team at Qamber Designs, my gratitude knows no bounds for the beautiful illustrated covers you've created for this series.

Thank you, Jimmie, for all your support these last couple of years as we adjusted to life on the road. Onward to the next adventure!

ABOUT THE AUTHOR

Originally from Ireland, *USA Today* bestselling author Kate Meader cut her romance reader teeth on Maeve Binchy and Jilly Cooper novels, with some Harlequins thrown in for variety. Give her tales about brooding mill owners, oversexed equestrians, and men who can rock an apron, a fire hose, or a hockey stick, and she's there. Now traveling the world with her soulmate, she writes sexy contemporary, sports, and LGBTQ+ romance featuring strong heroes and amazing women and men who can match their guys quip for quip.

ALSO BY KATE MEADER

Rookie Rebels

GOOD GUY

INSTACRUSH

MAN DOWN

FOREPLAYER

DEAR ROOMIE

REBEL YULE

JOCK WANTED

SUPERSTAR

WILD RIDE

HOCKEY WIFE

Chicago Rebels

IN SKATES TROUBLE

IRRESISTIBLE YOU

SO OVER YOU

UNDONE BY YOU

HOOKED ON YOU

WRAPPED UP IN YOU

Hot in Chicago Rookies

COMING IN HOT

UP IN SMOKE

DOWN IN FLAMES

HOT TO THE TOUCH

Laws of Attraction
DOWN WITH LOVE
ILLEGALLY YOURS
THEN CAME YOU

Hot in Chicago
REKINDLE THE FLAME
FLIRTING WITH FIRE
MELTING POINT
PLAYING WITH FIRE
SPARKING THE FIRE
FOREVER IN FIRE

Tall, Dark, and Texan
EVEN THE SCORE
TAKING THE SCORE
ONE WEEK TO SCORE

Hot in the Kitchen
FEEL THE HEAT
ALL FIRED UP
HOT AND BOTHERED

For updates, giveaways, and new release information,
sign up for Kate's newsletter at katemeader.com.